www.lostranchbooks.com

My Heart Lies Here

a novel

Blessings & Joy,
Laurie Marr Wasmund

Laurie Marr Wasmund

My Heart Lies Here is a work of fiction. Apart from the well-known actual people, events, and locales that figure in the narrative, all names, characters, places, and incidents are the products of the author's imagination or are used fictitiously. Any resemblance to current events or locales, or to living persons, is entirely coincidental.

Copyright © 2012 by Laurie Marr Wasmund

All rights reserved.

Cover design and map by Joanne McLain

Cover photograph of Delagua Arroyo in Ludlow, Colorado by Laurie Marr Wasmund

Published in the United States by lost ranch books
www.lostranchbooks.com
ISBN 978-0-9859675-0-5

For Bill

The Crossroads of the Kingdom of Coal

PART I
BERWIND, COLORADO

My heart's in the Highlands, my heart is not here;
My heart's in the Highlands a-chasing the deer;
Chasing the wild deer, and following the roe,
My heart's in the Highlands wherever I go.
                                    Robert Burns

In peace, Love tunes the shepherd's reed;
In war, he mounts the warrior's steed;
In halls, in gay attire is seen;
In hamlets, dances on the green.
Loves rules the court, the camp, the grove,
And men below and saints above;
For love is heaven, and heaven is love.
                                    Sir Walter Scott

Chapter 1

My father spread his homesickness like a disease.

Oh, Scotland, he said, as the wind whipped dust through bone-dry air. It was rainy, damp and fogged, the clouds lying flat on the ground, so thick, you could taste them.

Sitting on his lap, I cuddled against his chest. "What's a cloud taste like?"

His arms wrapped around me, my fortress. "The sea. The salt of it, the wet of it. Ah, don't you recall, Kirstie?"

My own memories were darker. Clouds hanging over gray waves. The boat to America, with its shadowed wooden alleyways and rolling slosh. My mother holding a bucket for me—one that had been used by others—or for Elspeth.

Alex, so much older, knew it all.

"And the birds at the cliffs," he said. "With their nests and eggs all along the rocks. The boys would chase them away and shoot at them when they flew. When they dropped, it was straight into the sea."

Like my mother, I shuddered. Like Elspeth. We can't keep bodies on board, the captain of the ship had said. The sickness will spread. And so, wrapped in tarpaulins, the sailors had cast the dead overboard to make their graves in the ocean.

"Those birds were only taking care of their babies," I said. "They shouldn't be shot."

"So they were," Dad soothed. "So they were, Kirstie my Kind Heart."

Oh, Scotland, oh, it was green, the land blossoming with ferns and forest, not parched and dead like this godforsaken spot of gray twisted sagebrush and cholla. The soil lay black and wet on the hills and didn't blow like red death in the wind. And other things, too—songbirds, trout, moss, heather, oh, the heather.

We were seated beside a sandstone boulder, high on the mesa. The last rays of the sun lingered in the west, too weak to creep over the bluff. We were left within half-light.

"This is a pitiful entertainment," Dad said. "We're cheated even of sunset in these deep canyons."

"It shouldn't be long now before the Northern Lights," I offered, hoping to please him.

"In Scotland, we had own our house," he lamented. "Floors and walls of stone, clean spring water pumped right into the house, and great, burning fireplaces. The flames kept out the cold, they did. We pushed grass and dirt into the chinks every summer to seal the walls."

"I think I remember," I said, wishing that I did.

"Aye, I remember it all," Alex boasted.

Dad pointed toward the northern sky. "Look there."

The sky was brilliantly alight with the Northern Lights—our Northern Lights. Orange, red, and yellow, they flashed on the underbellies of the clouds, whisked through the darkness, then disappeared, quick as they had come. Moments later, they split the dark of night again.

"In Scotland, you'd see blue and green, too," Dad said. "Just crackling away. One of these days, Kirstie, I'll take you home to see it."

I curled closer to him, trying to hide how afraid I was. I feared the long, cinder-choked trip by train across the brown, empty stretches of America, and the noise and confusion of the great ports, and most of all, that deep, deep ocean that had swallowed my mother and sister.

What would keep it from taking me as well?

So I worked hard to imagine that I could see and hear and smell Scotland, but the wind blew across our broad, flat mesa, cutting up from the canyon, and the stars were brittle and distant in the dry, black sky. Not one of us mentioned that we could not see the Northern Lights from Colorado. No, we gazed at the sky as if the lights were a promise that was already realized, and not just reflections of the flames from the coke ovens over in Hastings Canyon, which flared up and gave the men who stoked them a peek into hell.

Dad read to us on Sunday mornings, his only day off from the mine. His brogue thickened when he recited the names of villages or the heroes and fair maids of Scotland, and his eyes grew moist. Alex and I sat at his feet, eager listeners, our hearts and heads enchanted by verses of Sir Walter Scott or Robert Burns, our dreams of the intrigues of the Highlands, and the mystery of the lochs, and the thrill of battle.

"*At Bannockburn the English lay,—The Scots they were na far away,*" my father read. "*Scots, wha hae wi' Wallace bled—Scots, wham Bruce has aften led—*"

Lying on the floor, Alex sketched, decorating sheet after sheet of old cardboard with muscled horses and strong warriors in full battle, flanked by flags bearing the crests of the Scottish clans. I played with my china dolls, their tiny arms and legs looped together with metal eyelets, their eyes painted brilliant blue and their lips pure red. Each one was Jean, or bonnie Mary, or Flora.

Holding the little green cloth book, Dad turned the fragile pages with hands that were swollen into tough mitts, his palms callused by plying a pick and shovel for twelve hours a day.

"We're related to royalty," he told us, his bur finely primed. "Right down through the bloodlines, from Mary Queen of Scots, the bravest queen of all. You know that, don't you, Kirstie?"

"Sure, I do."

"You're as good as a Scottish princess, brave and strong and true."

I did a clumsy curtsey, and he laughed in a sad way that sounded half like longing, half like a cough. I wanted only to please him. He had come to Berwind by mistake, a man who had no will to go forward, who wanted nothing more than to undo what was done. Left with two young children—I was three and Alex ten—he could still taste the deaths of his wife and middle child like the salt spray of the ocean.

For a while, he had floundered in Chicago, trying to earn enough for passage home. On New Year's Day of 1900, he met John McCormick, an Irishman bound for Colorado.

"Out west," McCormick told him. "There's so many foreigners in the mines, you see, that a man who speaks good English and proves himself a steady hand is a prize."

"I can do that," my father said.

"No drinkin', you know, and no layin' off work to sober—"

"Not a single drop touches my lips."

"Church of Scotland, then? Aye, Gordon, you'll do all right."

John McCormick was right. In Berwind, a man with white skin and knowledge of English was a rare sight. He was wrong, too. Shoulder to shoulder in the mines with the Italians and Czechs and Mexicans and even a few Japanese, no man was a prize.

Berwind Canyon lay side by side with its twin, Delagua, between walls that rose like stony spines into wide, flat mesas. In the canyons, spring run-off twisted along the green bottoms and pinkish sandstone jutted forward into crags and cliffs. On the rugged slopes, sandy ravines splintered away into gullies and draws.

Oh, what was hidden in those canyons—tipples, portals, depots, burning hills of slag, hundreds of mules, thousands of men with faces blackened by coal dust, two-room houses stacked one atop the other, graves filled with babies dead at birth, with children dead of scarlet fever, with picture brides from the Old Country who died of grief, with men, men, men overcome by gas, or lost in collapses, or coughing themselves to death.

Berwind itself—like Hastings, Delagua, Tabasco and others—was the property of John D. Rockefeller. All over, signs proclaimed it. His name hung over us like the smoke from the slag heap. Tunnels, tipple, depot, company store, school, meeting hall, stables, latrines, houses. Rails, mules, ore cars, cables, winches, smokestacks, engines. Every fence, or wall, or box, every book, or Bible, or newspaper: PROPERTY OF JOHN D. ROCKEFELLER, COLORADO FUEL & IRON.

The *Camp and Plant* magazine that Colorado Fuel & Iron published from its offices in New York showed photos of model coal camps, places with wide, clean streets and happy children eagerly learning the alphabet. But no photo showed the bitter wind through the cardboard walls of our house in Berwind, or the typhoid that rose with the snowmelt and flowed in the currents of the creek that ran below the footbridges and next to the privies. No article featured the prices at the Colorado Supply Company, which were double those in Trinidad or Walsenburg or any other liberty town, or the scrip doled out to the miners each payday in place of American currency.

Yet every day, trains arrived in Berwind crowded with men dressed in brand new American pants and coats who'd pushed a broken-down plow in some starved European country until their backs bent like saplings. At the mine offices, they adopted American names—Joe, Pete, Charlie, Mike—and buried the Old World in the blandness of their new names. They came to Berwind for change, for happier circumstance, only to find themselves betrayed by opportunity and trapped in the coal canyons—one way in, no way out.

Oh, Scotland, my father mourned.

Dad kept us in tight form. We learned the finest table manners, the politest replies to our elders, the most gracious expressions of thanks. It just came naturally that we would be the smartest children in the Berwind School.

Alex was a wizard at all things scientific, the teacher told Dad. Mr. Rhine wanted Alex to attend the high school in Trinidad once he graduated eighth grade. Alex would have to live with a family there, eighteen miles to the south, and pay for his room and board and all his school costs.

"So you will," Dad said and began working extra shifts. "If we were home, you'd go to university in Edinburgh, if you'd a mind to."

Alex collected rocks, eggshells, leaves, bones—anything that could be picked up and carried home. He stowed his treasures under his bed in cigar boxes. He did not play with other children, and he didn't seem to care that he was one of the few boys of his age in the schoolhouse. He let me follow him as long as I didn't act all "girlish and ghoulish," as he called it.

Together, we scrambled up the mesa, the fingers of piñon scrub snagging the hem of my skirt and the legs of his trousers. Alex vaulted over boulders and shimmied up half-walls of rock. He carried no weight on him, for every inch was muscle or bone. His hair rolled in waves of rust-red, with more brown in it than mine, but just as heavy and thick. His eyes were green, flecked with a soft brown that sometimes made them hazel, and his skin, like mine, seared bright red in the sun, which left it stippled with freckles.

When I slipped on a sandy ledge and scraped my arms, Alex came back for me. My grazed elbows bled in short, narrow strips.

"Why are you so clumsy?" he demanded.

"My shoes are too slick. They're too old."

"Ah, no, you're just clumsy as hell."

"No, my shoes are slick as hell."

We giggled then, the word "hell" so forbidden, and the two of us so bold to say it. Dad's objection to our language would have been one of propriety. He had abandoned all faith in God as my mother's and sister's bodies dropped into the ocean. Anyway, there was no Presbyterian church in Berwind—only a Methodist circuit rider who appeared now and then, stupefied by travel through the rugged canyons of coal country.

"The miners call it soft rock because they can drill through it so easily," Alex told me, dabbing at my cuts with his handkerchief. "But look out, the edges are sharp."

He spoke of the salmon-pink Trinidad sandstone. Rough to the touch, it shattered like crockery when broken. When I licked it, it shone the color of dried blood.

I started, "Sharp—"

And we both finished, "As hell!"

"This is what Dad tunnels through every day to get the coal," Alex said. "The coal's in layers between the sandstone. It's been pressed for millions of years by all those tons of rock, all that weight."

"No wonder he's always so tired," I said. At night, he had barely enough strength to lift his fork or saucer his tea.

"Aye, mining's a hard life. I'm glad I'm never to have it."

"What will you do, Alex?"

"Maybe I'll be a natural scientist," he said. "Finding out how things work."

I would not be left behind. If Alex was to be a natural scientist, what would stop me from becoming one, too? So I started studying plants. I gathered wildflowers by the handfuls in the spring and pocketed seeds to plant in a scratched-out patch at the foot of the steps of our house. My favorite was sage. It grew everywhere in Berwind—on the mesas, on the paths, against the walls of our houses. Silvery-green clumps spidered across the ground, and silver feathers waved in the wind, or clung to tough, ugly brush.

Rolled in my fingers, the sage released a spicy, warm scent. Picked as a bouquet, it freshened the stale smell of our house.

Soon, I began to cut and dry the leaves. I cooked with it, tucked sachets of it into my drawers, and even sewed some of it into a little pillow that I slept with under my chin.

And that is when I started to dream. I dreamed of my mother, rising out of an ocean turned to Trinidad sandstone, blood-red sharp-edged rock that heaved like waves. I dreamed of the heather of Scotland, with prickles and tough, withered skins like the cholla. I wanted to be

Kirstie of the Scottish Highlands, my father's lassie, yet my dreams could never escape Berwind Canyon. They pressed down, as if a cap had been laid over the sky from mesa to mesa, trapping my imagination and forcing it to earth, until I forgot what I dreamed of home, or which place was my home.

During the fall of Alex's last year at Berwind School, our father came down with the sickness, coughing so hard as he journeyed from the tipple to home that he had to bend double. He kept working, reporting for his shift day after day, and quieting his wheezing by stuffing a rag in his mouth. Every morning I fixed him a dose of sage and honey tea. He went on this way for a good month, past the new year of 1905, until the day when he walked in the door after work and fell in a heap on the bare wooden planks of the floor. His breathing was as labored as the bellows of a mighty furnace, and his face had turned brick red.

Alex ran his hand over Dad's brow and neck. "We have to get him undressed."

We dragged him to his cot and tugged at his soaking coat, boots and pants. Dad was not a tall man, but he was broad across the shoulders and back, and heavy with muscle through the thighs. As we stripped him down to his long johns, he muttered, "Cold."

"I'll get more blankets," I said.

"No," Alex said. "Do we have any bacon? Raw bacon?"

"I think so. Why?"

"Get it and put it against his feet." He pulled the covers from Dad's feet. "It'll draw out the fever. Quick, now!"

I did as Alex wanted, laying slabs of bacon against the soles of Dad's feet and wrapping them tight with cheesecloth. Soon, the fat in the bacon melted, and the cheesecloth stained with grease. But Dad's forehead cooled, and he began to doze despite his ragged breathing.

"How did you know to do that?" I asked Alex.

"Mrs. McCormick told me," he admitted, adding mournfully, "She told me this day was coming."

Day turned to night and night to day again, but our lamps stayed lit and our fire stoked. Under Alex's direction, I brewed broth and spooned it into his mouth. I chopped onions until my hair and skin reeked of them. Cooking them until they were half-tender, I wrapped them in a poultice of cheesecloth. After Alex swabbed Dad's chest with camphor, I laid the poultice on top of it.

Dad coughed up cup after cup of greenish phlegm. I wiped his lips, while Alex wrapped his arms around him and hugged his ribs whenever he coughed. "You have to promise, son," he wheezed. "Promise me you'll take Kirstie home. Promise me—"

"Dad," I pleaded. "Don't try to talk."

"Promise—"

"I will," Alex said. "Aye, Dad, I will."

By morning, only Dad's heart still worked. His fingers and toes were bluish, his breath came in spasms, and his arms and legs were stiff. Alex set buckets of sizzling coals near the bed, and even called for the company doctor, who never came. I laid my head against Dad's hand and recited every line of Scott or Burns I could recall. Dad himself had not read to us in ages, too tired to sort out the small words on the page. So I became his voice: *And I will love thee still, my dear, Till a' the seas gang dry.*

"Kirstie," he murmured. "So beautiful, so like your mother. How I wish I could take you home—"

There was no settlement from Colorado Fuel & Iron after he was dead, because he had not died in the mines. Only because of them.

Without Dad, the air hung in our house without moving, and the silence wrapped around us in the night. John and Edith McCormick offered to take us in to live with them, but Alex refused. He sat with his face in his hands at our dining table. "I've got to take you home. I promised Dad I would. Oh, Kirstie—"

Kirstie, the girl of the Scottish Highlands. Kirstie, the girl of the lochs. Running through the heather, dancing in the mist of the morn. Kirstie, so bonny and fair in her ribbons and ringlets. Kirstie, the pride of her father's eye.

"Kirstie was Dad's name for me," I said. "I'm Christian now."

Alex wept. "You're grown up," he said. "We both are, we have to be."

For him, grown up meant that he went to work in the mine. He burned his drawings and threw out his collections, along with his dreams of being a natural scientist. On his first day, he donned our father's hard hat, which had hung on a peg inside the door. Already his shoulders sagged, as if he had spent a lifetime digging coal.

I went back to school to complete my third grade year. The school in Berwind—its windows blackened by smoke and soot—stood on the opposite side of the creek from the houses, beyond the main road through the canyon and the railroad tracks and the company store. It housed all eight grades in one room. The youngest students sat in neat rows to the teacher's right and progressed across the room with the years. By the sixth grade, there were so few students left—and those mostly girls—that one row sufficed for sixth, seventh and eighth grades.

Most of the boys went into the sorting house at the mine after third grade, but a few of the more gifted or lucky stayed. The Ruddy boys—all five of them—came back to school year after year. The oldest, Jake, was a squat bully who sat in the secondary grade row every autumn until he towered over nearly everyone else. When he was six, he had plunged off a swing into a nearby culm heap and landed on the lid from a tin can. It gave him a squinty left eye—a hair closer and it would have been lost—and a red tangle of scar.

Jake was known for his pranks. He delighted in planting spiders in girls' desks or pouring water onto the chairs to make it look like someone had wet himself. Once, he had captured a family of blind, newborn mice. Spreading them across his palm, he showed them to the girls, then clapped his other hand down on them, smashing them.

His brother Russell looked as if someone had shaved a sliver from Jake and made a second boy. He and Jake shared the same golden brown hair and brittle, blue eyes, but Russell was thin and pale, a handkerchief clutched in the fist that his brother would use as a bludgeon.

He suffered from sickness every winter, once running a fever so high his mother took to screaming from the door of the cabin until the doctor arrived to give both Russell and Mrs. Ruddy a paregoric. He spent recess huddling next to the wood stove and drinking boiled water from the pot his mother brought to him. Russell, she was sure, would manage Berwind someday, he was so smart and capable.

The Ruddy boys and I sat near the front of the classroom, along with golden-haired Ethel May Farrington, whose father ranched in the canyon, and Mary McCormick and a few others. We were all white, with light eyes and quick English tongues. Ethel May could even claim to have been born in America. Behind us were the Poles and Germans and Swedes.

And then came a sea of dark faces.

Italian, Mexican, Croatian, Slav. Mr. Rhine called them the "unteachables." No English, no correct understanding of American customs, no proper Christianity, only papist rot, and sometimes no shoes. With the exception of a few, like the Pavlovski brothers, who were brilliant in math, they stayed in the same grade until they finally disappeared into the mines or from Berwind Canyon all together.

That year, a Greek had come to our classroom. He was probably ten or so, old enough to work in the sorting house, and as tall as Jake Ruddy, though not as fleshy. He wore a clean white shirt every day against skin that the sun could never redden. Theo Sky sat at the very back of the room, behind the first graders, who sent terrified glimpses over their shoulders at his glowering form. Everyone, even Mr. Rhine, called him by his full name, as if "Theo Sky" were one word, like thunderhead or snowmelt.

Ethel May sniffed at him in disdain. "Greeks marry their own sisters."

He was a true unteachable, for he never even made a pretense of copying down the lessons. He simply sprawled at his desk, with an elbow hooked over the back of his chair, while the rest of us sat with erect spines, shoulders painfully arched backward and our hands tented in perfect prayer. Asking him, humiliating him, and shouting had no effect on him. Even Mr. Rhine's steel-edged ruler did not shake him.

Soon, he started to slide from the first grade row, inching his desk across the room, wedging himself behind the second grade row, and then the third, and then the fourth. He finally settled into a pocket of warm air near the woodstove, without ever having learned a thing.

We could hardly ignore such a solid body, such an unyielding force, in the classroom, so Mr. Rhine found a use for Theo Sky. Odd jobs fell to the teacher, and by then, Mr. Rhine smelled of fermented jelly and had to be told the date each morning. He had no objection to letting Theo Sky feed the wood stove, or dump the quick lime in the privy, or stuff the cracks in the walls with old newspapers.

And so, Theo Sky became our handyman.

One day, he was puttying the loose and leaking windows near my seat as the class did math problems. Mr. Rhine had assigned the equation: 532 divided by 22.

We scratched at our slates, doing tedious long division. I raised my hand, and Mr. Rhine called on me. "What is the answer, Christian?"

Standing, I said, "28 with a remainder of 16."

Mr. Rhine frowned at the answer book in his hand, and in the silence, I heard Theo Sky snort. Almost immediately after, Mr. Rhine pronounced, "That is incorrect. Take your seat and check your work. Ethel May, tell us the answer."

As Ethel May sang out the correct answer, I figured the equation again and discovered I had carelessly brought a 1 down when I subtracted 44 from 532. I shrank into my work, humiliated, angry at myself, but mostly, dismayed by Theo Sky's derision. Surely he could not have figured the equation in his head. No one could do long division that quickly in his head. Surely he was mocking me simply because he thought I was too prim or too skinny and homely—as the other boys did—or too pleased with my own intelligence, as almost everyone did.

But after that day, I began to take notice of him and of the other Greeks in Berwind. They were a mysterious lot, with their black hair and olive skin. In the company store, they doffed their caps and greeted the women with polite nods. They scooted out of the aisles and opened the doors with gallant, gracious gestures. Yet Alex's friend, Rory Capstan, talked of how they stank from eating goat and how they crowded into the bathing house and so fouled the water with their Greek slime that no one else could use it. The Greeks, Rory said, were worse than the rest of the dagos and wops and chinks put together.

None of them was married or had a family. It was rumored that they were soldiers from the Bulgarian Wars. As mere boys, they had traipsed through the Balkans chopping off the ears and noses and hands and any other fleshy parts of the enemy Turks, and pouring lye in their eyes and mouths. If they were feeling merciful, Ethel May said, they would just mangle and strangle you.

And what they did to the women—

Ethel May told me that the Greeks flocked to a house a half-mile up the canyon from the coal camp. The ladies who lived there sunned themselves in the windows dressed only in camisoles and bloomers. She had seen the Greek men leaving there, talking their strange tongue, and tightening their belts while the ladies leaned out the windows and waved. After all, she had to walk by that house every morning on her way to school, and her mother had made her promise to walk fast and never lift her eyes from the ground.

Which made Ethel May capable of describing every single lady.

"One of them has hair the color of yours," she told me. "As red as a new penny. Ma says that color hair comes from the devil's bottle." She eyed me, then asked with the scathing contempt of her mother, "You don't dye your hair, do you, Christian?"

"I'm Scottish," I snapped, as if that explained it all. Ethel May stuck out her tongue, and I turned away, hiding tears. It wasn't Ethel May who upset me, but my own ignorance. Here I was—the smartest student in the school—and I had no idea why the women sat in full view in their underthings or the Greeks laughed as they buckled their belts. And what was wrong with the color of my hair?

Soon, I realized that someone was watching me as I sat at the front of the classroom. My shoulders and back would grow itchy and sore, and a patch of heat would creep up my neck and into my jaws, flushing my cheeks with crimson. I tried to ignore the sensation, but my heart tightened with shame and excitement and fear and defiance every time I felt it. At last, it grew unbearable, and I had to know. Turning toward the back of the room, I met Theo Sky's eyes.

They were not black, like his countrymen's eyes, but greenish-gray. He seemed nothing like a mangler and strangler or his own sister's bridegroom to me, but more like a curious boy. Like Alex, before he went to the mines.

He watched me hour after hour, day after day. He could see me plainly from where he sat in the fourth grade row. Distracted from my lessons, I wondered why. What did he want? Did he think my hair unnatural, as Ethel May and her mother did? I thought maybe he was jealous of me, because I was Mr. Rhine's pet, and he was nothing but a strong ox. Maybe he thought he would learn something from watching me, so he would not always be so hopeless and Greek.

So I straightened my spine and pushed back my shoulders. If he wanted to look, let him. When I felt that burn in my shoulder, I worked all the harder. An extra flourish to my penmanship, perfect columns for addition and subtraction problems, and the correct answers to Mr. Rhine's questions, pertly delivered. I even adopted my father's bur when reciting poetry, lilting away at "O Captain, My Captain" or Longfellow. When Mr. Rhine plucked at the piano during chorus, I sang out in a thin, wobbly soprano, "'My country 'tis of thee—'"

At the end of my performances, I could never resist a peek, a sly slide of my eyes over my left shoulder. Always, always, I would glimpse sage-green eyes in that dark, dark face.

Chapter 2

Edith McCormick taught me just how poor we were. Alex worked a full sixty hours in the mines, hammering at the coal seam above his head, but he had neither the experience nor the strength of a grown man.

"We must keep you two from starvin' to death," Mrs. McCormick said. "John's taken it upon himself to partner with your brother and teach him properly. And he'll do well, in time. But now your Da is gone, you've got to step up and be his helpmate."

Standing in her neat kitchen, where dough rose beneath cheesecloth, and Tommy McCormick worked the butter churn, and Katy McCormick peeled an onion, wiping her nose on the back of her hand every so often, I burned under scornful eyes. They thought me too spoiled, too coddled by my father to be of much use.

"I will," I said. "I can. I'd do anything for Alex."

"Would ye now?" Mrs. McCormick's face, flat and freckled, softened for a moment. I called her husband Uncle John, but she would always be Mrs. McCormick to me. "So, first, you must look at both sides of the meat at the company store. Check the color—be sure it's not green. They're as like to sell a dead raccoon as anything that's come from a cow or hog. I know you are only a little girl, Christian, but you must speak out. You need to let them know you won't be taken for a simpleton. They'll cheat you out of every cent you have if you let them. You just watch."

I nodded, filled with the sense of my duty to Alex, my job as his protector in all things domestic—sister, mother, housekeeper, laundress, seamstress, cook, friend.

Mrs. McCormick held up a spiked mallet. "Then you must beat the meat. Makes it more tender, at least so's you can chew it. My John's teeth have nearly fallen out, and he can't chew this tough stuff that the company sees fit to sell to us. Stretch the meat, so it lasts longer, too." Her deft hands guided a heavy, cast-iron rolling pin over the meat, flattening it into a pancake. "There, enough for three meals, not two."

The meat did not look like enough for three meals, but I nodded again.

She taught me to settle the dirt and scum in the water we bought from the company store with alum. "Where they dredge this up, I'll never know," she lamented. "And to charge us thirty-five cents a barrel for it, it's robbery plain and simple. Now, you'll need to let it sit for two weeks or so, in the sun, so you must always think ahead. Buy it before you're out or you'll be drinkin' brown slog. And catch the rain when you can." She glanced through the tiny window over the dishpan to the sky, her face lined with longing. "It comes so rare, set a pot or two out if ever you see clouds."

She showed me how to use the hanging shelves above the stove to keep the rats out of our staple foods, and to sprinkle arsenic in the corners to kill them. "Keep it far from the food," she warned. "You don't want to go killin' yourselves, now, do you?" She taught me to patch the holes in the cardboard walls of our house with newspaper and gummy glue, and to put wool into the cracks between the floor planks to keep out the wind. She even let me take two eggs a day from her hens, if I would come over at dawn to collect the eggs for her.

And she gave me Mary's old dresses that weren't worth remaking for Mary herself, a fact that Mary loved to point out to me on the playground in full hearing of her friends and anyone else who would listen.

I walked with Mrs. McCormick and picked coal from the tracks where it had fallen off the rail cars, stooping down in the shadow of her big body, so that the mine guards would not see us. Glaring at them, Mrs. McCormick muttered, "Who brings that coal up from below, you or my husband? And yet you search him each night to make sure he's not savin' a few bits to light the family fire, to cook the little food we have. And you beat the livin' bejesus out of him if he has more than just a speck of coal dust on him. Aye, 'tis a crime."

She was full of discontent, rambling on in a low, crackling voice, arguing with John D. Rockefeller as if he were in the room.

"The law says only eight hour days," she growled. "How about that, Johnny D? The law says it, and what do you do? You make them work twelve, fourteen hours, and you don't even pay them in American dollars."

"Where does John D. Rockefeller live?" I asked.

"In New York City. In a castle."

"A castle! I didn't know there were castles in America."

"Oh, I'm sure he has at least one." She drew out the words in bitter contempt. "But do you think he's ever left it to come out here and see what goes on in his precious coal mines? Never, not once, has he come to Colorado. Men are dyin' while workin' for him, takin' their last breaths bringin' up his coal, and he doesn't care."

I pictured John D. Rockefeller as a colorless, frowning old man sitting on a gilded throne, surrounded by curtains with red tassels the size of church bells. Women fainted at the sound of his name, men sank to their knees to honor him, and servants cowered before him, offering him wine and rich foods. His cold gaze never wavered. I decided I hated him, too.

"And safety!" Mrs. McCormick snorted. "There's laws, Johnny D, there's laws. But do you water down the dust, or vent the air, or bother with the firedamp, or give your men safety lanterns? No! And if they complain about bein' cheated on weight, your guards take them down to Ludlow and smash their hands and feet so they'll never work again. Aye, they're nothin' but your slaves."

So Alex was a slave, but he was not the kind of slave from a book by Scott or a poem of Burns. Those slaves suffered with quiet dignity, and earned their freedom from tyranny through daring, iron resistance. Alex just seemed tired. He acted older than Dad had ever been. The fire that had burned in our father—his desire to return to Scotland—singed Alex to ash with its fury, and the promise he'd given Dad drove him deeper into the ground than the mine ever could. His hair lost its red flame, turning to dull rust, and his pale, freckled skin looked mottled and blanched. He moved differently, too. No more the boy scouting the mesas for moths and lizards, clear eyes tracing the bounty of life, he walked with shoulders stooped, his gaze on his feet.

Nothing went as it should in our house. My cakes fell flat, my loaves of bread rose an inch before the yeast fizzled out of them. I beat the meat into a flat pancake, and it turned so tough we could not chew it. If I tried to boil it, the pan burned dry, and if I tried to fry it, it shriveled and curdled. I could keep up with the washing and darning, but that was all. Never did Alex's shirts or my clothes look crisp, but were either starched into suits of armor or limp like plucked chickens.

Alex said nothing about it, eyeing the miserable food piled on his plate and choking it down with stalwart resignation. He started bringing whiskey home in a silver flask. After dinner, he washed away the blandness of my cooking.

School was my refuge, those few hours away from housework and especially, the stove. I did not care that Mr. Rhine had retired—and with him, my place as favorite student. Miss Rice, my new fourth grade teacher, chose no favorites, but neither was she as quick with the ruler. A blonde woman who wore heavy glasses on her narrow nose, she did not distinguish between those who could be taught and those who could not. For the first time, Italians, Mexicans and Slavs penned the alphabet, drew equations on the board, and recited verses. Their names became a sort of music in our classroom—Giuseppe, Jerzy, Maria, Manuela, Gianni—and they were called upon as often as Ethel May or myself. Miss Rice had no patience for Jake Ruddy, who mimicked their thick, weltering accents, and even less for Theo Sky.

She stood behind him until he opened the lesson books, and she kept him in at recess until he knew arithmetic. Ignoring the muddy footprints near the door that Mr. Rhine would have ordered him to wipe up, she quizzed him on verbs and vowels. Setting a slate before him, she made him copy line after line of verse. Soon, he learned to read and write English.

Mrs. McCormick insisted that Alex take the bed in the main room of our house where my father had slept. For the first time, I was alone in the bedroom, Alex's narrow cot empty beside mine. Only a bullhide sheeting divided us from one another, but the sounds of the night grew louder.

The wind whistled, as it always did in Berwind Canyon, blowing the stagnant air from one mining camp to another, so that we breathed Tollerburg's cinders and smoke, and Tabasco breathed ours. Dogs howled, and cats or women cried out in the night. The pitiful bleats of sheep, lost on the ranches up the canyon, echoed in tandem with the coyote's bloodthirsty yip.

The mine engines, never idle, thrummed, and the locomotives hissed and rattled into the darkness. Footsteps scuffed on the gravel paths through the rows of houses, and voices—sometimes in English, more often not—split the darkness. I huddled in bed, no longer able to close my eyes and drift away on the steadiness of Alex's breathing.

Alex did not go to bed for a long time after I did. He sat at the table, shuffling through a deck of cards, laying out games of Solitaire or reading the newspaper that had passed through so many hands that the ink had rubbed into black smears. It was sheer foolishness, I thought. Why did we have to sleep with a curtain between us? We were both lonely.

One night, I woke to shouting and banging. I jumped from bed and wrestled my way through the curtain, but Alex was gone. No lights burned in our house, but I could see by the glow from the mine and tracks down the hill. Darting onto the porch, I ran for the steps, but a hand caught me before my foot touched the first stair. I stumbled into

Alex's grip. He held me against him, my back against his legs, his hands on my shoulders.

"Quiet!" he whispered.

"What's going on?"

He said nothing. Farther up the slope, lanterns blazed around a shack. At the edge of the porch, horses milled, kept under tight rein by sheriff's deputies with rifles slung across the pommels. Two mine guards stood to one side, a man pinioned between them. A woman swayed nearby, surrounded by children, screaming in a language I could not guess. Her screams turned to sobs, and she began to plead, over and over again, "Please, please, please, please, no, no, no, no, no!"

A mattress flew from the door of the cabin. Pots and pans ricocheted off the planks of the steps. Blankets, table, chairs, and stools leaped upward into the burning light and fell into the mud.

"Please, please, no, no!"

"What's happening?" I asked again. "What are they doing?"

"Be quiet, Kirstie." My brother slipped into the familiar name. "Don't wiggle."

More crying, more shouting. The children joined in, their voices not so foreign as they called, "Mama! Mama! Papa!" The man struggled to break free of the guards' grip, and one punched him in his stomach. He dropped into the darkness.

I whipped around and buried my face against Alex's stomach. He smelled as Dad had—of leather and working muscles and a neck that was never completely clean. I burrowed deeper into that smell and closed my eyes.

"Are you two all right?"

Peeking out, I saw Uncle John slip onto the porch from the shadows at the back of the house. He slid beneath the railing, appearing at Alex's shoulder.

"What is it?" Alex asked.

"One of the Poles, I think. Czeslaw, or something, his name is." Uncle John's gaze fastened on the brilliant circle of light up the hill. "Heard he was in the northern fields until last year. Some trouble with the gun thugs up there."

Alex's voice, already at a whisper, dropped lower. "Organizer?"

Uncle John said nothing. I did not know what Alex meant, but I thought of Mrs. McCormick—that great organizer herself—and her rants against John D. Rockefeller. Oh, Johnny D, I whispered to myself. Oh, why do you let this happen?

"You'd better leave before they see you here," Alex said.

"Edith wouldn't let me sleep if I didn't see to you and our Kirstie girl." He stooped down and smoothed my hair from my face. "Prettiest lass this side of Galway. Aye, here's my girl. You'll be fine by morning, you will. Take her inside, Alex. She shouldn't be havin' to watch this."

I ventured another look up the hill. The night had quieted, and now I only heard the panting sobs of the children. "Time to go," someone said, and the horsemen reined around, heading down the hill, toward us.

Alex pulled me into the darkness inside our house. Closing the door behind us, he stood against it, barring it with his body, until the horsemen passed.

I started to cry.

"Don't, Christian, don't." His face looked shrunken, tightened into a fleshless mask by worry.

"What did they do? Why were they being sent down the canyon?"

"Och, who knows?" His voice grew bitter. "Asked for a doctor, complained about the water standing in the mine, or the gas, looked the wrong way at a guard."

"It won't happen to us, will it? They won't come for us?"

"No," he said. "No, we won't be sent down. Don't worry. I keep my head down and don't cause trouble."

"Come sleep in my room tonight," I said. "Please." Then I shuddered, as I recalled the woman up the hill, repeating that word over and over.

He sat at the table, shoulders hunched, his eyes cast downward. "Christian—"

"Sleep in your old bed, just tonight. It will be like it was when Dad—"

"No, Christian, no," he said angrily. "You have to become hard, don't you see? You have to become like a . . . like a machine to live here! You have to be heartless, dead—"

"Don't!" I cried. These weren't the words of Scott or Burns, the words taught to us by our father, when we were Kirstie the Kind Heart and Alex the Brave. "You don't mean that—"

"Go to bed. You have school in the morning."

I said nothing, but I was certain that our father would never have wanted us to be heartless. *Despair is treason towards man, And blasphemy to heaven . . .* In my bedroom, I dozed off, but struggled back into the fear that the mine guards had spirited Alex off in the night without my hearing. Holding my breath, I listened for the shuffling of cards or the ripple of newspaper or the squeak of his chair as he turned a page of a book. When I heard nothing, I crept from bed.

He lay with his head against the table, cushioned only by his arm. Beside him was the silver flask, empty, a few drops spilled on the table. I picked it up and licked the rim. The taste of whiskey burned my tongue.

"Alex," I whispered, touching his shoulder. "Alex, you're wrong."

He shivered, as if I'd laid ice on him. "Go to bed," he murmured.

"We shouldn't be sad. We can't be, for Dad—"

"I try so hard!" he exploded. "Working, working all the time, but we have nothing. Nothing! Afraid to breathe, to look up, to lift my head—oh, God, look at me!"

I persisted. "We have to keep going. Something better will come—"

He grabbed my shoulders, and I winced from the rough grip of his hands. "One of these days, I'm going to take us out of here. You don't see it now, Kirstie, but one of these days, we're going to get out of here, leave this place behind us, nothing but a bad memory—"

"You're hurting me—!"

"And Dad!" He sobbed. "Buried in this godforsaken land. Why couldn't I do any better? Why couldn't I save him from—?"

"We've done the best we could—!"

"Go to bed," he said, no longer shouting or weeping, but tired, drained. "You'll have to be up early for school tomorrow."

I stood beside him for a few minutes longer, but he would not speak to me. Before my eyes, he seemed to grow smaller, weaker, folding up into the chair, and I knew he would never be a doctor or scientist. Going back to my room, I sat on the bed and let the tears run down my cheeks. When I caught my breath with a shudder, I kept my arm over my face to quiet it.

The next morning, the houses of Berwind were like tombs. Doors closed, window shades pulled tight, porches empty except for dogs and barrels and discarded tin cans.

Alex was gone by the time I woke. He had never come to bed—as far as I could tell, not even to Dad's bed in the main room of the house. I searched for the flask under his mattress and in the trunk where he kept his clothes. I couldn't find it, but the despair he'd left behind him hung in the air like smoke.

Before I went to school, I walked up the hill, my jaw set. Others were passing by the empty house, too. Most kept their gazes on the ground, except to sweep a glance at the trash and bric-a-brac stuck in the mud. Two boys collected, one silently watching for the guards while the other pillaged, picking up pages ripped from books, a doll's arm, a trampled pouch embroidered with red and blue beads.

In my imagination—so young, so untried—I saw it all. Mr. Czeslaw's hands broken beneath the pounding of gun butts so that he would no longer be able to work, his wife and children stripped of everything but the clothes on their backs. They would starve—the whole family—and die at the very mouth of the canyon, and their bones would be heaped atop the hundreds of other maimed and desperate souls who'd gone down before them, a lesson to us all. I saw the jawbones, skulls, and spines piled against the red soil and piñon scrub, guarded by thugs who spat at those lucky enough to pass by alive.

By the afternoon, another family had moved into the house. They were Chinese.

Chapter 3

When I was twelve, a violent storm swept through Berwind Canyon. Lightning pierced the mesa, leaving behind splintered trees and bushes that smoldered in the driving rain, and the thunder echoed against the sandstone and slapped the walls of our house. Rain and hail crept through the cracks in the floor and soaked our shoes. I begged Alex to sleep in his old bed, next to me. He said he would, but by the time he came to bed, I had been crying and shivering for hours.

"Quiet, Kirstie," he soothed, lying on the straw mattress of the cot next to mine. "It will pass. This storm will move on and we won't even remember it."

He was wrong. When he opened the door the next morning, he burst, "Good God!"

On our step, just beyond the threshold, lay a reeking heap of matted hair and cloth. It looked like a mauled dog curled up on some filth that it had dragged along with it.

Alex squatted down and reached toward the mess.

"Don't!" I cried. "It might bite."

He toed it with his boot. "I think it's dead."

It wasn't dead. Languidly, the heap stirred, arms reaching out from within the folds, head rising from the rotten fabric. A face lifted upward—eyes as black as the night, and skin the color of strong-brewed tea. The creature pushed at the black tangles of hair and gathered its dripping rags around it.

"Where am I?" She spoke through bloodied lips. "I run away and I don't know where I come to."

"This is Berwind," Alex said.

"Berwind? That's it?" She looked around her as if she had lost something. "I meant to get farther along!"

"Where were you trying to go?" Alex asked. "Tollerburg's up the canyon, and Tabasco's down. Ludlow's at the end, on the prairie. The Delagua Canyon mines—Hastings and Delagua—are yon. Where'd you come from?"

"Tabasco," she wept. "Tabasco. I wanted to go to Trinidad!"

We could see the houses of Tabasco perched high on the mesa a couple of miles down the canyon from Berwind. She had traveled almost no distance at all—and she had traveled the wrong direction. Trinidad was nearly twenty miles to the southeast of Berwind Canyon. We were to the west. Alex looked at me, lost for words.

"Are you trying to get home?" I asked.

"I ain't got one."

Her eyes met mine over Alex's shoulder. Her face carried a dead look, like that of an old mine mule, crippled by a lifetime of hauling and whippings. At once, I knew what had happened. Her family had been sent down the canyon, but she had escaped the starvation and pile of bones at the canyon's entrance. I wrapped my arms around myself, cold in the damp air.

"Can you spare something to eat?" she asked. "Something to drink?"

"Surely you have a home somewhere," Alex said.

She rose up on her knees, reaching for the fabric of his trousers. Alex backed away. "No, please, Mister!" she begged. "I had to leave Tabasco fast, and I didn't know where to go, and I ain't ate for so long, and they hurt me—!"

"Who?" Alex asked. "Who hurt you?"

She raised her hands to her face. "They done this to me!"

Alex stepped back again, his mouth pruned as if he might vomit. "You have to understand. We don't have anything. No money, nothing of worth. It's just my sister and me—"

"I don't want nothing!"

"You could go to the train depot. There's a train to Trinidad leaving—"

"I don't know nobody in Trinidad, or nowhere else—"

"Why were you going there, then?"

"I don't know!" she wailed. "Please, don't leave me here—!"

"Let her in, Alex!" I cried, my stomach churning, my lungs so tight I could barely breathe. "Let her come in!"

Alex's face filled with pity. "Oh, for God's sake! Come in, then. Close the door."

She rose first to her knees, then pushed herself up. Wobbling, she wrapped her arms over her chest, grabbing her elbows. Her hair hung nearly to her waist in wild tendrils—curls that ran riot over her eyes and around her ears, and twisted in tight ringlets. With one hand, she swept them aside, revealing a swollen, blackened eye.

Alex pulled a chair from the table for her, a proper gentleman. I hurried around the kitchen, pouring coffee and cutting bread.

"Where's your family?" Alex asked her.

"I ain't got one."

"Who's your father?"

"I don't know. I never had one."

"Did your parents die?" I asked. "Were they sent down the canyon?"

But her eyes had settled on the plate of bread and mug of coffee that I carried. As she reached for it, her muddy shawl fell, a dead weight to the floor. It was plain to see that she was at the age when most girls married.

She clapped the cup to her mouth.

"Good God," Alex said. "Don't drink that way. Nothing will stay down."

"I told you I ain't ate. I'm so cold."

"You aren't running from your husband, are you?" he asked. "What's your last name?"

"I don't got neither."

"Everyone has a last name."

"I don't know of one. What's yours?"

"I'm Alexander Scott. This is my sister, Christian."

She held out her hand to shake his. Her fingers and wrists were as delicate as those of a seamstress. "Thank you for being so kind, Mr. Scott."

Alex pulled his fingers from her grasp, as if she had stung him. "I have to go," he said. "I have to get to work."

I whirled around. "Alex!"

His look was that of a man unable to find his place, a man overwhelmed. "Heat some water," he ordered. "Fix her a bath. Find her something to wear. And, for Christ's sake, burn her clothes. And then, see her on her way."

"I have to go to school!"

"We'll have lice crawling through this house if you don't."

"I don't have no lice," she said, at the same time that I said, "I don't have any clothes to fit her."

"Just do it, Christian. Don't be stubborn." He grabbed his lunch pail and opened the door. A train whistle blared in the canyon bottom.

She called out, "Mr. Scott! I do so have a name. It's Pearl."

He stopped, his mouth working. Then, without a word, he shut the door behind him. Pearl and I stared first at the door, then at one another. She picked up the sopping shawl. Water streamed to the floor.

"My clothes have to dry first," she said. "They won't burn."

The water pooling on the floor sent me into the fury of helplessness. Alex had no right to leave me stuck with her. He could have given her a few coins and ordered her out. He could have sent her to the McCormick house. Mrs. McCormick would have her on her way to Trinidad in minutes. I grabbed the shawl and went to the door, flinging it out on the porch as hard as I could. It dropped into a ratty ball at my feet.

"It ain't like your floors are clean," Pearl said behind me. "Looks like you folks got flooded like everybody else last night."

"Who else did you visit last night?" I asked. "Did you go from house to house begging?"

"I ain't begging. I'm asking for mercy. That too hard for you?"

Her words shamed me—and made me cruel. I grabbed the kettle from the stove, swinging it toward her. "I don't have time to boil water for a bath. You'll have to use what's from the kettle."

She looked away. "That's fine."

I dragged the round tin tub inside the house and knocked the dirt and debris from it as best as I could. I dumped everything from the kettle into the rainwater that had collected, but I knew it would be cold.

She drew a hand through the water. "You go to school? How old are you?"

"I'm twelve and I'm in the sixth grade."

"You're pretty scrawny for twelve, ain't you?"

I wished I hadn't even added one kettle of hot water for her. Ethel May Farrington had already started wearing a corset under her camisole, and her mother had had to let out all her bodices. I was still as knobby-kneed as a six-year-old.

She went on. "I ain't never been to school. My aunt didn't let me go. She kept me home to take care of things. She's got the gout."

"You said you had no family."

She shrugged. "None I'd want to brag about."

"Did the mine guards do that to your face?"

"No, my aunt done it."

My stomach lurched, as if I'd heave up my breakfast on the spot. "No, she didn't," I challenged. "Your aunt wouldn't do that. Your family was sent down, wasn't it? You're just afraid to tell us."

"Why would I be afraid?"

"So we won't turn you in to the company. So you won't be sent down, too."

She laughed as if I'd said something stupid. "You're the one making up all the stories."

Humiliated, I went into my bedroom. Peeking through the door, I watched Pearl unhook her rag of skirt and remove her blouse. Purplish bruises swept over her back and thighs like the shadows of clouds on the mesa. Hand prints ringed her arms where someone had grabbed her hard and held her fast. When she stepped into the tub, her wild hair floated on the water, a mess of twigs on a pond.

I sat on the bed. I would be late, I must already be late. The mine bell had rung hours ago, it seemed. I heard Pearl moving in the tub and realized that I could walk out the door as easily as Alex had. Leave her, forget her, don't help her. But I could not move.

Finally, I took out an old calico dress of Mary McCormick's. It was so frayed on the cuffs and hems, so faded by washing that even I wouldn't wear it. But I wouldn't give her my best, which wasn't that much better. How could I, with Alex breaking his back in the mine just so we could eat? Laying the dress on the table, I said, "Here."

She splashed a handful of water on one dark shoulder, as if she were a lady bathing in a mansion. "Do you think they'd let me go to school?"

"Most kids finish by age fourteen or so." I went to the kitchen to gather my lunch, already packed in a tin pail. "Why did your aunt and uncle hit you?"

"I don't know." She slid down in the tub so that the water brushed her chin. "They're mean, that's all."

Suddenly, I wanted to get away, to be in a place where she didn't exist, with her battered, broken skin and cracked lips that spoke of something more than just a family row. I wanted to wake up again, with only Alex and myself, with only school to think about. "I have to leave," I said. "I'll be late."

Swinging out the door, I ran down the slope to the creek. I raced across the bridge, hoping Pearl would be gone by the time the school day ended. I took my seat just as Eddie McKelvey rang the school bell. My hands shook as I opened my books, and my eyes slid from the page as we started our silent reading.

It wasn't until I'd caught my breath that I began to worry that Pearl might steal everything we owned. Our food, our clothes, our pans and dishes, Dad's book of Sir Walter Scott, the family Bible with the names of all the births and deaths carefully printed in thick, black ink, the tablecloths of our mother's and the kilt of Dad's that were in the trunk beneath my bed. She could sell it all to buy her rail ticket to Trinidad. I shouldn't have left her, I realized. Alex would be furious.

I squirmed so much that Miss Rice asked, "Is something wrong,

Christian?"

"No, ma'am," I said immediately. Then, I began to connive. I could tell her Alex was ill, and I needed to go home. I could say that I'd forgotten to—

The door to the schoolroom opened. Miss Rice looked up from her desk into the light. "May I help you?"

A vision appeared in the doorway. Sunlight splashed against her dark skin and turned her corkscrew curls to the blue-black of a raven. Her eyes glistened, and her lips were dark as a ripe plum. Every student in the classroom seemed to breathe in, and then stop, until she took one more step into the school, and we saw by the bruises and cuts that she was only a girl.

Mary McCormick nudged me. "Christian, she's wearing my dress!"

The dress was so tight she could not raise her arms. Her wrists hung out two or three inches from the bottoms of the sleeves, and the buttons gaped across her breasts, revealing her stained slip. On her feet, she wore an old pair of Alex's work boots, with loose, flapping soles.

Miss Rice sized her up with one critical glance. "Are you a new student?"

"Yes, ma'am."

"What is your name?"

"Pearl."

"Pearl what?"

With a sidelong glance at me, she said, "Pearl Scott. Same as Christian over there."

Every eye in the classroom turned toward me.

"Is that so?" Miss Rice frowned. "Christian, are the two of you kin?"

"No, ma'am," I whispered, my face burning. "She's a stranger to me."

"Who are your parents?" Miss Rice asked Pearl.

She lifted bold eyes. "I'm a orphan."

"Both your parents are dead?"

"I don't know, ma'am."

"Then, your name isn't Pearl Scott?"

Pearl's steady gaze wavered. In the tender skin beneath her nose was a single, black mole that quivered when her lips moved. "No, ma'am, it ain't. It's something else, I suppose."

Miss Rice sighed, not bothering to correct her grammar. "Well, if you don't know your ancestry, we shall have to call you Pearl Doe. You can't take another person's name for your own."

"That's a deer," Pearl said.

"Pardon?"

"A deer. The mama deer is a doe."

Someone snickered, and Miss Rice slapped her ruler on her desk. "That's very inventive," she told Pearl when she had restored the calm. "How old are you, Pearl?"

"I'm . . ."—Pearl's fingers worked at her sides—"nine."

The classroom erupted in loud, mocking laughter.

"Nine?" Miss Rice questioned. "That seems very young."

She lifted her chin. "Yes, ma'am, I'm nine."

"Ninety-nine, more like it," Jake sang.

Miss Rice didn't even bother to pound the ruler, but stared at Pearl with open dismay. "All right. If you are only nine"—her voice lingered over the word—"you'll sit in that desk, in the third grade row. Third graders, let's hear Pearl read the first page of our lesson today. Maybe that will help us determine her grade level."

I twisted in my seat just enough to see Pearl from where I sat in the secondary grade row. Her desk stood before the door, in the pathway of the wind, but she had been placed directly beside Theo Sky. He leaned over and touched one finger to her *McGuffey's Reader*, pointing out the first word to her.

My heart throbbed as I turned back toward the front, knowing that Pearl would be ridiculed. I tried to tell myself that it was her own fault. She had followed me to school, to a place where dark-skinned students weren't even welcome. She had brought it on herself—she'd probably driven her aunt to beat her, too. That was the way it was, no matter what she said.

"Any time you wish, Miss Doe."

The rattle of the trip and the whir of engines at the mine broke the silence. A train bound for the coal yards in Ludlow whistled. The wind shuddered at the windowpanes. Read, I urged her silently. The first word of the sentence was undoubtedly just that: "The." Think, Pearl, I wished. Just say that one word, the word that almost every sentence starts with. Just pretend to read, and Miss Rice will be pleased.

Pearl whispered an answer no one could hear.

Miss Rice leaned forward. "Pardon, Miss Doe?"

"I never learned to read."

"This is a third grade primer! Surely you can read this?"

"I can't. But I know English."

"I don't understand," Miss Rice said.

"I can speak it just fine. I was born speaking it."

Miss Rice pointed to an alphabet that marched across the top of the blackboard in both print and cursive. "Do you know the letters, Miss Doe?"

"No."

"Dumb dago," Jake Ruddy snorted.

"Enough, Jacob," Miss Rice snapped.

The smaller children smirked at Jake's daring. Theo Sky stared straight ahead, looking past Miss Rice, as if he could see through the blackboard to a place far beyond Berwind Canyon. I wanted to weep as I waited for Miss Rice to order Pearl to leave.

But Miss Rice said, "If you don't know the alphabet, we'll have to seat you with our first grade students. Please move your desk over two rows, Miss Doe. That's two." She held up her fingers.

Pearl dragged her desk across the floor until she sat just behind the first graders. I could see her plainly now, whenever I turned my head just slightly to the left, huge behind children who were less than half her size. Every time I caught sight of her that day, she bent over the numbers or alphabet, soaking them in like so much dried-out clay during a rain.

At lunch, I took from my pail a slice of jerky, a crust of bread, and a piece of apple I'd cut the day before. Pearl sat at her desk with her hands folded as the other children brought out their meals. After Miss Rice said grace, she noticed Pearl. "Have you nothing to eat, Miss Doe?"

"No, ma'am."

"Why not?"

"I ate everything I had this morning, when I was hungry."

Jake blatted a laugh, but Miss Rice sighed. "I'm sorry, Miss Doe, but this is inexcusable. I suggest you not return to this school again until you learn proper etiquette. All children must bring a lunch, for their own health. It's the classroom rule."

With a bang, Theo Sky slammed the lid on his pail. He crossed his arms over his chest, leaning back in the desk so hard that the little wooden chair shrieked.

Miss Rice stood, grasping her ruler in her right hand. "Is something wrong, Theo Sky?"

"I don't got nothing neither." His deep voice rumbled.

Across the room, Russell Ruddy draped the cheesecloth over the corn cake his mother had sent with him. Daintily, he folded his hands on his desk.

"Russell?" Miss Rice asked.

"I'm not hungry, ma'am." He wiped his mouth with an

embroidered handkerchief.

"Well, if none of us is hungry, let's get on with our lessons. Lunch is over," Miss Rice sang, though we had yet to touch our food. "Clean up."

So we shoved our bread and cheese back into our pails and lined up to go to the outhouse and the pump, where we washed our hands and splashed our faces with freezing water. Theo Sky and Russell and Pearl stayed at their desks while we tramped through the mud for our ten-minute exercise. On the playground, a crowd gathered around me.

"Where'd she come from?" Ethel May demanded. "Why'd she say her name is Scott?"

"She showed up this morning on our porch." Hoping to cast away blame, I added, "Alex let her in."

Jake sauntered up, a full grin on his face. "Got yourself a friend, huh, Scottie?" he taunted. "Can't find one anywhere in the school, so you got to dig up a darkie."

"She's no Brit," Mary McCormick agreed.

"Why'd you bring her here?" Ethel May asked. "She must be dumb as a post not to know the alphabet at her age. And now we all have to starve because of her!"

"I didn't bring her here," I argued. "She followed me."

"Like a stray dog," Jake said. "Scottie and her dago doggie!"

He howled like a coyote, and the other boys joined in a shrieking chorus. The girls linked elbows and turned their backs, leaving me friendless and alone.

Running from them, I peeked into the schoolroom windows. The shadowy light silhouetted Pearl's tangled hair, Theo Sky's strong shoulders and square jaw, and Russell's delicate head bent into his sleeve. They were not speaking to each other, as far as I could tell. All three stayed firm and motionless as rocks in a fast-flowing stream.

That afternoon, I ran home from school as fast as I could, planning to lock the door against Pearl. I ran because Miss Rice had given Pearl a book with pictures and letters in it. Then, in front of everyone, she had asked me to teach Pearl the alphabet. I cried as I ran, because Ethel May and Mary blamed me for Pearl. I wept because Theo Sky's hand had touched the pages in Pearl's book, and he had never done anything but stare at me. I bawled because Russell Ruddy—stupid, sniveling, spoiled Russ—had starved himself for Pearl, and I knew that no one would ever sacrifice himself for me.

When Pearl arrived, she pushed hard against the locked door. "Let me in!"

"No!" I shouted back. "Go back to Tabasco! Go home!"

"Please let me in."

"Go away."

For a while, I heard nothing, but only a fool would think that she'd leave in broad, sunny daylight when she had slept on the porch through the hail. I crept to the window. There she sat, looking at the book Miss Rice had given her without opening it, just running her hand over the cover again and again, as if she had never seen anything as fine. With one finger, she traced around the outline of a fox in Robin Hood cap and jerkin playing a pipe while two rabbits dressed like children danced. Unable to bear such sadness, I opened the door.

Pearl entered, the book in her hands. "I forgive you."

"For what?"

"You can't help it if you ain't very nice. Mean folks don't never seem to know how to be nothing else."

I grabbed the broom and started sweeping the floor, my eyes filling with tears. No one had ever accused me of being mean. Pearl sat at the table. I jabbed the broom under the chairs and pushed the debris left by the storm through the cracks in the planking. She pulled up her feet and drew her knees against her chest.

"I have to move the table," I said.

"I can help."

"No, thank you," I said, shamed into politeness.

She gathered up her book and moved into a corner, sitting on the bare floor where I had already swept. Opening the book, she tried to read, moving her lips with every word, as if she couldn't keep them still. I propped the broom beside the door and began pulling the clothes from the indoor line, where they'd dried after the storm.

"This book here," Pearl said.

I rolled Alex's union suit into a ball to take out the stiffness, but she didn't continue. "Well," I said at last. "What about it?"

"I was wondering if . . ."

I folded Alex's extra shirt. "If what?"

"As far as I can tell—if the pictures is right, that is—this book don't got good words in it. It's got some stupid-looking animals—look at this rabbit in a pinafore—but it don't got no mine or tipple or coal in it. Not even a mule. Them words ain't in here, I don't think."

"So?"

"They in other books?"

"Well, maybe." I wiped my hands on a towel before I started cooking. "There's hundreds of books, you know."

"That's what I was asking. There's books about other things?"

"Yes." I thought of The Waverley Novels. Of Burns' poetry: *I see her in the dewy flower, I see her sweet and fair: I see her in the tuneful birds, I heard her charm the air* . . .

She crawled from the corner, clutching the book. "Then, if I learn to read this one, I can read others?"

"When you get better at it, I guess."

"I'd like to read one about a girl who lives in a house, with her own bed, and a fancy-painted horse carriage to take her to town."

I stared at her. Oh, the hours, the days that I had passed creating stories that featured my sister Elsie and Alex and me and Dad and my mother in Scotland where we lived in a fine house and—

She cocked her head, as if she might ask me what I was thinking. Then she nodded toward the kitchen. "I can cook for you, if you want," she said. "I'm good at cooking."

"That's all right."

As I pounded meat and cooked potatoes, her whispers drifted from the corner, growing louder, until she was speaking in a full, rich voice.

"Caaaa ssss ffff—" she said. "Caaa sssss ffaa—-"

"The cat is fat," I said, without looking at her.

She squinted at the words. Then, closing the book, she said, "Well, I ain't never read nothing so stupid in my life."

Chapter 4

That night, we ate dinner in near silence.

Alex and Pearl sat directly across the table from one another, but not facing each other. Pearl teetered on the edge of her chair, half-turned away from the table, as if she might need to leap to safety at any moment. She kept the book from Miss Rice on her lap. Even if she had judged it stupid, she wasn't willing to part with it, but reached down every so often to stroke the cover. Alex was wary, too, his chair cocked outward, face in profile, looking at anything but Pearl. I was the only one who sat straight on, staring directly at my plate, unable to swallow a bite.

I felt at a loss. Maybe her aunt and uncle had cast Pearl out, but Alex acted like we were harboring a snake in the wood box. He had said nothing to me when he came home from the mine and found Pearl at the kitchen table. He did not ask me about my day or sit in his chair and read the newspaper. He simply dropped his lunch pail beside the stove and went outside again to sit on the steps. He wouldn't even come inside until I'd called him twice for dinner.

Finally, after we'd nearly finished eating, Alex said, "I believe I've found your father. He's in Raton."

Pearl drew back, as if the words had struck her. "How do you know he's my pa?"

"There's talk," Alex said. "He worked Number 2 in Tabasco until three years ago. He has a family in Hastings."

"What's his name?"

"Rodriguez."

Pearl balked. "Half the kids in the schoolhouse is named Rodriguez, ain't that so, Christian? Why, down in Tabasco, there's a Rodriguez behind every bush, and Delagua Canyon floods with them every spring."

I held my breath, not daring to take her side.

"Aye, that's so," Alex said. "But in my homeland, Scott is the most common name of all. Still, Christian and I know our mother's and father's names, and our grandparents, and their parents, and so forth. Having a common name doesn't give you leave to quit your family."

"We can trace our family back to Mary Queen of Scots," I said.

Pearl's fork twisted against her plate. "I never seen my pa."

"Then, here's a chance. I'll write to him. And if he can't read, surely he'll find someone who can."

"He ain't wanted me before. What makes you think he'll take me now?"

Alex looked as if he had just kicked a dog. "You can't stay here. I've told you that."

"My pa done this to me." She unbuttoned her sleeve, and struggled to slide the fabric back over her swollen wrist and above her elbow. A thick, purple welt mounded along the skin of her upper arm. "He burnt me with a hot poker. Before my ma made him get."

"You told me you never knew him."

"Maybe I just don't remember, with him so mean and all." Pearl brandished her scar like some proud battle wound. "You want to know something else, Mr. Scott? My pa and ma never even gave me a name. Any name."

"What are you talking about?"

"I choosed my own name," she said. "Pearl. It's mine, all mine."

"What?"

"Aunt Lettie and Uncle Sam always called me Girl. Whenever they wanted something, they'd just say, Girl, come fetch the washing, or Girl, sweep the floor. Well, after a while, I got pretty tired of it. I thought I was good enough to need a name."

Alex simply stared at her, but I asked, "Why did you choose Pearl?"

Her eyes locked onto mine, hopeful. "Well, one day this woman come to see Aunt Lettie. She had this necklace that her mother'd given her. It was made of pearls, and she told us all about how the pearls grow inside shells in the ocean. And sometimes people find these old shells and open them and there's a pearl. A treasure just waiting inside a old shell." She hugged Miss Rice's book against her breast. "I thought, ain't it a miracle that there can be treasure inside things that's just plain and dumb, that you'd just as soon step on or kick? And Pearl sounds like Girl, too, so I could pretend they was calling me by my name whenever they shouted, Girl."

Alex's jaw worked back and forth, but I felt a bright opening in the thickness in my throat. She had chosen her own name, just as I had. She had become someone—no, something—else. "You never asked them to call you Pearl?" I asked.

"No, it wouldn't have done no good. They'd have taken it away from me."

"They can't take your name," Alex scoffed.

"No, but they can make it so it don't mean nothing special no more."

"You read that story somewhere, didn't you? You invented it."

"I can't read. Ask Christian over there."

"This is foolishness," Alex pronounced. Running a hand through his hair, he pushed back his chair with a loud screech of wood against wood. Taking his coat from a nail pounded into the wooden door frame, he slammed the door hard behind him as he left. As his feet crunched away along the gravelly path outside, I gathered up the plates and mugs. Unrolling the sleeve of her blouse, Pearl stood at the window and watched Alex make his way down the slope.

"He's going to send me off, ain't he?" she asked.

"I don't know," I said truthfully.

"I do," Pearl snorted. "Because he don't like me. Just like you."

"I didn't say I don't like you."

"You didn't have to. You never had to. I can tell." Pearl turned from the window. "Running off to school this morning without even telling me where it was. Not telling me about lunch."

"I didn't think of it." The ache within me turned to temper. "But you shouldn't have followed me and embarrassed me. Nobody would talk to me during recess, and—"

"What?" She laughed. "That ain't your problem. You don't care if nobody talks to you or not. What you're afraid of is that I'll learn the same as you know, so's that fancy teacher won't call on you all the time." She lifted her voice in a nasal twang that sounded remarkably like Miss Rice. "Christian, read page seven for us. Christian, tell us why there's stars on this old flag—"

Her mimicry took away my breath. "Why would I care what you know?"

"Because that'd mean that a dago girl is as smart as any old white girl."

I dumped the dishes into the dishpan, uncertain. Except for the Pavlovski brothers, the smartest always were those who knew English from birth. But none of them—not even the Pavloskis—had skin the color of Pearl's.

She pounced. "Oh, so I'm right, ain't I?" she taunted. "That's what you think. You and that yellow-haired teacher and all them freckle-face, blue-eyed boys at the school. In Tabasco, you'd search low and high to find a girl with skin as puny white as yours. Why, there's Italians and

Mexicans and Slavs and you name it in Tabasco, but nobody looks like you."

Stung, I washed the dishes, dried them, and put them on the shelves. Pulling a pair of Alex's overalls from my sewing basket, I sat in the chair next to the lamp. Pearl did not move from the window. Yet my hands shook and my stomach churned up what little supper I had eaten.

I didn't know what I thought. I didn't want Alex to send Pearl to hateful Mr. Rodriguez. All the same, we had so little to begin with, we might all starve if she stayed. But no one I knew had been so poorly treated that they did not have a proper name.

I sewed until my eyes burned and then carried the lamp into the bedroom, where I laid out my clothes for the next day on the foot of my bed and changed into my nightdress. I huddled beneath the blankets—the night seemed chilly to me—and folded my hands under my chin.

Pearl followed in a few minutes. She stood in the doorway, waiting for me to speak. I pretended to sleep.

Finally, she asked, "Are you praying?"

I opened my eyes. "No."

"Maybe you oughta." She looked around her. "Where do I sleep?"

"In here, I guess."

"Looks like somebody already slept there."

I'd forgotten that Alex had slept there during the storm. "No," I said. "Alex sleeps in the main room."

She removed her dress and settled down on the straw-stuffed mattress. She didn't pull up the blankets, but lay there, her skin melting into the darkness and only the white of her slip visible in the dim light. The night filled with the clatter of ore cars, bringing coal up from the mine, and the rhythmic snort of the waiting locomotives, and singing somewhere. "O Sole Mio," maybe, the favorite of the Italians, or some other foreign song.

"Listen to that," she said. "You ever wonder what all them words are they say? My ma used to talk some kind of language like that, when she didn't want nobody else to know what she was saying."

"Was she Italian?"

"No, maybe, I don't know. She never told me nothing about it." She paused, then added belligerently, "But she wasn't no Rodriguez."

I sent a question into the darkness. "Why did your aunt beat you?"

"I already told you. Lettie and Sam is mean folks. She had a belt she was awful fond of using, and he knew just where it hurt most. It's fun for them to get all drunked up and slap me around."

"Didn't you tell them to quit?"

She laughed. "You think that would have worked? I ask them to quit, they'd just gang up on me more."

I shuddered, but I wasn't ready to let it go. "There are some in the school who get a whipping every night. They come to school with bruises all over. But they don't run away."

"Well, maybe they ain't as smart as me. You ever think of that?"

I wondered—was she as smart as she thought, casting herself into the hands of people who had no reason to care for her? Alex could call the mine guards or even the sheriff, and she could be in an orphanage by morning. I could scream "Thief!" and have half of Berwind at my door, brandishing clubs and bricks. Instead, I said, "My father never beat me."

"Didn't he?"

Suddenly I could hardly speak. My throat was dry, swollen shut. Whether it was from talking of my father—oh, I missed him so—or from the effort of wishing Pearl away, I didn't know. "No. Or my brother."

"Your pa's dead?"

"And my mother. She died on the voyage over to America, along with my sister. I really am an orphan."

"Are you now? That's too bad. How'd your pa die? Blowed up or gas?"

"Pneumonia." I did not want to tell her how he had gasped for air in the night. I did not want her to guess how much it had hurt me to see him lying on the bed, weak and broken. I did not want her to know of Alex's tears.

Her voice lost its toughness. "That's a bad one. So many of them get it."

"After he died," I started, then stopped. "Well, after he died, I chose my own name, too. Sort of. Just like you."

"Did you now?" She rolled to her side and propped herself up on one elbow, curious. "What was your name?"

"Kirstie," I whispered, then spoke louder. "My father called me Kirstie, but that's just short for Christian."

"Christian suits you better," she said. "It ain't one of them sweet names, like Betsy or Daisy. It sounds stuck-up. And bossy, too."

Hurt, I said, "I'm not either of those things."

"No?" She laughed, stinging my pride again. "But your brother. He don't make you . . . do things when he's drunk?"

"Alex doesn't drink," I said fiercely, although the memory of the night he had sobbed at the table whisked into my head.

"Don't he? I thought they all did."

"Besides, I do plenty for him. I cook and clean—"

"I don't mean that—every woman does all that. I mean, since he don't got no wife, he don't ask you to do nothing?"

I had no idea what she meant. "I don't think so."

"You'd know if he did."

"Why is that?"

Pearl breathed in. "A while back, my uncle started telling me how pretty I was. I thought it was nice. Well, and he give me things, like shoes or a fan. And then, one night, he was drunk and he come to my bed and said I needed to pay him back for all the nice things he done for me. He said otherwise, he'd send me to that house up the canyon."

"What house?"

"You know, the one where all them women live, and the men pay for them. They take girls at ten years old up there, he said, and they work them day and night, because there's always men waiting after each shift. He said he'd get a good price for me up there, because I got plenty of flesh on me and don't look diseased, but if I did what he said, he wouldn't send me there."

A coyote yipped up on the hill, sending the dogs in Berwind into a thunder of barking.

"What did you do?" I asked.

"I did what he wanted. But when my aunt found out about it, she whipped me until I didn't think my skin'd stay on. My uncle lied and said I'd wanted him, and, well, when they let me go, I run as fast as I could. I thought I was headed toward Ludlow." She coughed a little, as if she were crying. "I don't know why I ended up here. How could I have been so wrong?"

"It was terrible out there—"

"I'd do it all again, just to get away from them."

Something came to me. "That's why you told Miss Rice that you were nine, isn't it? So she wouldn't send you away." I faltered. "To that house—"

"She seemed mean enough to do it, too."

"She's not mean."

"Your brother ain't going to do the same thing to me, is he?" she asked.

"What do you mean?"

"He ain't going to treat me nice, and feed me, and give me things, then ask me to do that for him, is he? I may as well be gone to Raton if so."

A sickness twisted in my stomach. I didn't know what Alex would do, I didn't know how he felt. That day, he had become a stranger. "Maybe my brother's got the wrong Mr. Rodriguez," I offered weakly.

"It don't matter." Her voice was rough with bitterness. "He'll just think up a lie to make me do what he wants. Just like Uncle Sam."

"Alex doesn't lie."

"He don't drink, he don't lie," she scoffed. "He must be some kind of angel."

She lay so still that I imagined that the darkness had swallowed her, or that she had willed herself into it. I wanted to go to sleep, to forget all she'd told me. Yet I couldn't abide her silence. My mouth opened, and I said, "My father used to tell stories about Scotland, where we're from. It's a beautiful place, with green fields and forests. The soil on the hills is black, and anything grows there. Anything. Not like here, where it's all dry and dusty."

She said nothing, but by her careful breathing, I knew she listened.

I rushed onward. "He talked of castles that stand yet today, walls of stone and mortar so strong no wind from the sea can tumble them. And of the heather—flowers, you know—which spreads over the hills until they are all purple. And there are deep lakes, hidden in pockets in the hills, that are as big as oceans."

"How'd he know?"

"He'd seen it."

"But you ain't?"

"I've seen it, yes. But I don't remember it at all."

"But you believed him?" She sat up in bed. "How did you know his stories—or any story—is true? If you never seen what went on, how do you ever find out if it is or it ain't?"

I wondered—about my father's tales, and the rules we recited in class, and the history of the United States in our schoolbooks, and Mrs. McCormick's rants about Johnny D, and the laws written on the message boards. Were any of them true?

"You can't tell lies," I said. "It's bad."

"It don't hurt nobody that I can see. Not like a belt or a fist."

"But if you lie, you can't be proud of yourself."

She laughed. "If that's all, I ain't got nothing to worry about."

And so it didn't surprise me the next morning when Pearl marched out to the table where Alex was sipping the coffee I had fixed for him and said, "My pa was killed ten years back. Fell under the wheels of a train. I forgot to tell you."

He squinted upward at her. "Is that so?"

"That's so," she said. "Now, I'm going to school. Then I'm coming back here." Her voice grew stronger. "I ain't asking for charity, Mr. Scott. If you want somebody to cook or clean or wash so Christian there don't have to, well, I ain't afraid of doing any of that. I'll scrub the floors to glass if you want."

I stood in the doorway to my bedroom, my hand clutching the frame, my lips pursed against my sharp breathing. If he were going to tell her to leave, he would do it now.

He said nothing.

Pearl stood there a while longer, waiting for something. A welcome, maybe, or a challenge to her lie, or even the command to leave. Something that she could grab and hold onto, carry with her, keep as her own. But it was something that Alex didn't—or wouldn't—give her. At last, she turned away and gathered up her precious book and put on her floppy old boots. After that, nothing more was said about Mr. Rodriguez or Raton.

Chapter 5

Pearl's arrival in Berwind didn't go unnoticed. Men flocked on the steps of the Colorado Supply Company Store to watch her cross the bridge, and the mine guards who lounged by the portals all day, guns in their beefy hands, noted Pearl's every step through Berwind. Whistling and whooping, they beckoned her: "Querida!" "Cara mia!" "Darlin', oh my darlin'!" She ignored them, chin thrust forward, arms cradling her schoolbooks, shoulders squared and hips swinging. I tried to imitate her, walking with the same jaunt, but the catcalls never followed me.

Jake Ruddy plagued us after school. "Hey, dago doggie," he'd taunt. "Your family come here thinking there's gold in the streets? I got some gold to show you, up in the hills. Come with me."

I'd shout at him to leave us alone, but he'd laugh. "Scottie here, she ain't never gonna find a man who wants her. She ain't never even had a friend. She's gonna have to marry a mine mule. They're blind—don't know what they're kissing!" He made sucking sounds, then winged in a girlish pitch, "'My sweetheart's the mule in the mines, I drive her without reins or lines, On the bumper I sit, I chew and I spit, All over my sweetheart's behind!'"

"Sounds like you had some practice at kissing mules, Jake," Pearl tossed over her shoulder.

"That'd be better than kissing a dago doggie."

"I bet you never kissed nobody," Pearl scoffed. "Nobody'd want you."

"That so? Come here, dago doggie. I'll show you what." Jake ran forward and grabbed Pearl's shoulders, but she was quick. She slashed his cheek with her ragged nails. Jake whipped his hand to his face and jumped back. "Damn it, what do you think you're doing?"

"Don't ever touch me," Pearl said in a deadly voice. "Don't you ever think you can touch me."

"Leave them alone, Jake."

It was Russell, limping along behind. He grabbed Jake's shoulder, but Jake whirled around and slugged him, catching Russell in the nose. Russell sank to his knees, clasping his fingers against his bleeding face.

Pearl dropped beside him. "Get out!" she screamed at Jake. "Go away!"

Jake did not move, shifting from one foot to the other as Pearl swabbed Russell's nose with a piece of cheesecloth she'd wrapped round her sandwich that morning. When Russell glanced up at him, Jake spat and sauntered off.

"Thank you, Miss Pearl." Russell's eyes brimmed with tears.

"He always that mean?" she asked. "You ought to tell your pa to give him a whipping."

Russell laughed, a sad, delicate snort. "Whipping doesn't bother Jake," he said. "Nothing does."

Soon enough, Theo Sky started lagging behind us, too. With him there, Jake loitered for only a minute, then skulked toward home, as sullen as a beaten dog. Theo Sky never talked to us. He simply shadowed us for a while, then veered off once we passed over the footbridge at the bottom of Berwind Canyon.

One afternoon, Pearl turned around and faced him directly. As sweetly as a lark, she sang, "Thank you, Theo Sky."

His strange light eyes flashed in the sunlight. He gave a quick bob of the head. "Miss Pearl. Miss Christian."

His accent thickened the words with vowels, so that my name became "Kree-stee-ahn." I opened my mouth to thank him, as Pearl had, but nothing came from it. I found myself staring at his hands, his fingers angular and his knuckles sharp. He put them in his pockets and walked away, moving quickly up the path and out of our sight.

"I think he's taken a shine to you," Pearl said.

"What?" I asked. "No, he wouldn't, it must be you, he didn't even talk to—" Finally, I quit tripping over my words and added, "He's Greek."

"I guess a Greek boy ain't all that different from any other. Besides, he ain't ugly, and he don't stink near as bad as most of them."

I laughed, but it was a nervous, unsettling sound.

"You know, he don't do no schoolwork," she said. "He just sits there and looks at you all day in school."

"Why would he do that?" I snapped.

She breathed out in disbelief. "Well, why don't you ask him the next time you turn around to make sure he's watching you?"

Tucking my books against my chest, I walked the rest of the way with my gaze on the ground before me, afraid that I was blushing, and more afraid that Pearl would tease me or even tell Alex.

But she had other ideas. One afternoon, she strode directly from the schoolhouse to the privy. I followed and lingered outside. The other students left—the McCormicks and McKennas in a tow-headed flock, disapproving looks cast toward the privy. Russell and Jake left, with the younger Ruddy boys trailing behind, and once they had gone, Theo Sky disappeared.

Standing alone, I stewed, tempted to leave as well. I walked a few languid steps down the hill, then turned around and walked back. What if she was sick? What if she died in that outhouse all alone?

"Are you all right?" I called.

The outhouse door cracked open. "Is he gone?"

"Who? What are you doing? Are you sick?"

She came from the privy, stench swelling behind her. "Hush up and come on," she hissed. "Be quick."

"But—"

She turned on me. "I nearly died in there. Now come on!"

We struck out on the path, swept up in the traffic that moved across the bridge to where the houses stood. Having spent so much time in the privy, Pearl was in a hurry, craning her neck and circling around others. At last, she plucked at my arm. "Look, there he is."

Ahead of us, Theo Sky sauntered along, unaware of us, his head held high and his arms at his side, his school books cupped in one palm.

"Come on." She pulled at my arm, dragging me on to the sloping path that led into Bricktown.

"Pearl," I gasped. "I don't—"

"I do," she said, and she was right. The others on the path, headed toward the brick shanties that the company had put up for the hundreds of Italian, Mexican and Slav workers, resembled her or Theo Sky more than they did me. Pearl darted and dodged, concealing herself behind three women who spoke in quick, singsong voices, and then edging outward, to where porches or barrels or drying racks hid us. I followed, clumsy and foolish, terrified that Theo Sky would turn around and see us.

At last, we came to the last company building in Bricktown, but Theo Sky kept walking. In the shadow cast by a pyramid of water barrels, Pearl and I huddled, panting from the effort of the chase, from giddiness, from confusion.

"Where do you think he's going?" I asked. "There aren't any more houses."

She watched him strike out on a narrow foot path that led upward, into one of the deep draws that surrounded Berwind. "Maybe there's another town up there," she said. "Come on."

"There's nothing to hide behind!"

"Then we'll just have to pretend we got business up there. Walk like you been here a hundred times before."

She straightened her shoulders and stepped out onto the path. I followed, stumbling over sandstone rocks embedded in the soil. This was no path tended by the company, but a lonely trail carved only by the passage of feet.

We moved into the draw, whose sandy walls rose up twenty or so feet. As we rounded two sandstone boulders that stood as sentinels at its mouth, Pearl came to a stop and grabbed my arm. Before us, between rugged ridges of sandstone, was a shack built of broken bricks, battered sheets of corrugated tin, and discarded timbers—from whatever could be salvaged—and a roughly-built pen filled with goats. Chickens clucked at our feet, pecking at the ground, and barrels and junk, gathered from the scrap heaps near the mines, scattered over the ground.

There, too, stood Theo Sky, facing us with a dark arrogance that left us in no doubt that he had known we were behind him the whole way through Bricktown. "What do you want?" he asked in his deep, heavy voice.

Pearl took one cool step, pulling me forward with her. "We was just seeing that you made it home safe, Theo Sky," she sang easily. "So nobody bothered you."

His brows furrowed an instant, and then he laughed. It was the first time I had ever heard him laugh—in fact, I had never before wondered if he could or would—and it filled his face with a bright openness.

Pearl laughed, too, and then I laughed, although it was a breathy, girlish sound.

"I am safe now," Theo Sky said.

"Good," Pearl said, keeping up the ruse. "We'll just go on home ourselves, then."

She wheeled around, still dragging me with her, and we walked in stately silence until we reached the wide streets of Bricktown. There, both of us burst into giggles as we ran down the slope and up onto the familiar pathways of our own world.

The British-born women of Berwind frowned at Pearl. Edith McCormick found me in the company store as I was choosing tins from the shelf. "What's this I hear about you takin' in that Negra woman?" she asked.

"She's not a Negro and she's not a woman," I said, though Pearl was as much a woman as Mary McCormick. "Pearl's the same age as me."

"She doesn't look it," Mrs. McCormick groused. "Where's she sleepin' in that sorry shack of yours?"

"In my room. In Alex's old bed."

"There's only a curtain dividin' those two rooms, Christian," she warned. "Saints alive, that girl looks like she's fresh from the cribs on West Main in Trinidad. Where'd she come from?"

"Tabasco."

"Well, what's she over here for? Send her home. Surely she can walk that far."

I gave the labels on the cans special attention.

"You know, Christian." She lowered her voice. "Alex isn't pullin' his weight down below, so John says. You can't imagine how it breaks John's heart—that boy's like one of our own. I'm afraid Alex'll be bringin' nothin' home soon enough. Then you'll be hard-put to feed yourselves, much less that girl. You best tell her to pack and get out."

"We're doing all right as we are." I did not offer that Alex had already earned less than we owed the company for housing, food and equipment for the past two months. He called it "getting the snake" when he brought home nothing.

"You tell Alex, now," she said, "that he needs to do what's right before that girl has a chance to cause you two trouble. It's a scandal, her livin' right in your house, and your poor father dead because he tried so hard to keep you two from want."

Anger flashed through me. "Dad always said to be kind to the poor."

I thought Mrs. McCormick would scold me for my smart tongue, but she retreated. "Well, so he did. So he probably did. But there's a difference between bein' charitable and bein' suckered. You and Alex don't want any more trouble in your young lives. You've had enough already."

But Pearl had settled into our house with no trouble at all. Every morning, she washed up and dressed, ate and left for school as if she had been doing it her whole life. After school, she worked at her books or mended the sorry rags of clothing that she had scraped up from my castoffs. She cleaned up the kitchen after dinner, then did her own washing and went to bed. After we bade each other goodnight, I would lie awake, hoping that she would ask me a question or make a remark or sneeze—anything—that would lead to shared secrets and stories. But Pearl knew enough of the perils of nighttime to lie so still in her bed that she vanished in the darkness.

Alex seemed most bothered by our new living arrangement. In

the evenings, during the hours between supper and bed, he acted as if Pearl were a half-tamed animal that might bite. He slid looks at her as he sat at the table or when she read in the corner. They walked around each other on opposing ends of the room, wary and skittish, never meeting each other's eyes. Alex moved like a tin soldier, stiff and jerky, while Pearl pulled her shawl around her shoulders, balling the fringe in her hands. They still sat at the table as if they were on passing railroad cars on two different tracks—only half of each face visible—and they spoke only the most common courtesies. Then, one night, after we'd eaten, and had all taken our places—me beside the lamp, Pearl in her corner, and Alex at the table playing Solitaire—he took an interest in Pearl's book. "What are you reading?" he asked.

Pearl didn't answer right away. She looked at me first, as if I should answer for her. When she spoke, her voice was so low we could hardly hear. "This here book."

"Where'd you get it?"

"Teacher."

"Let's see it."

She rose and dusted her hands on the back of her skirt, then handed the book to Alex. He flipped through the pages, not resting long on any. "You know all these words?"

Pearl tossed her head. "Teacher says I catch on faster than most."

"Is that so?"

"That's what she says. But, anyways, it's just some old poems and stories. Nothing special."

"Old poems and stories." His voice grew tender with memory. "Read something."

Pearl took the book. Casting a plaintive look my way, she said, "Help me, Christian."

I pulled my chair up next to hers. She smelled of a sweet, dark spice—cinnamon or nutmeg, something we did not even have in Berwind.

"*From breakfast on through all the day, At home among my friends I stay, But every night I go*—oh no, what's that?"

"Abroad."

"*Abroad, Afar into the land of Nod.*" Her voice was throaty, rough, as if it hurt to read. The book shook in her hands. "*All by myself I have to go, With none to tell me what to do—*"

Alex closed his eyes and leaned back in his chair. Pearl read louder. Every time her lips moved, the mole beneath her nose widened, or shrank, or sometimes disappeared. When she did not know a word, the skin around the mole grew pale, fraught. I liked the way her shoulder jostled mine when she turned the page, or how our hands collided when she pointed to a word.

"You do learn fast, don't you?" Alex asked, after she'd read two or three poems.

"That's what Teacher says." The light reflected against the membrane in her eyes, and her cheeks flushed. "Should I read more?"

"Something funny," he said.

"This one," I whispered to her.

She read. "*His face was the oddest that ever was seen, His mouth stood across—*"

"'Twixt,'" I said.

"*'Twixt his nose and his chin; Whenever he spoke it was then with his voice, And in talking he always made some sort of noise. Derry down.*"

"Durry down?" Alex asked.

Pearl looked to me. "That's what it's says, ain't it?"

"Dairy down," I said.

Her lips puckered, the mole quivering. "What's that mean?"

Alex looked to me. I shrugged.

"I don't know what it means," Alex admitted, laughing. "I haven't any idea."

We tried to remember all the poems and ditties that rang with the word. He sang a verse or two of "Derry down derry, oh! called me his dear." I had not seen him so light and free in years. He seemed young again, full of vigor and curiosity, as if he might search the world to learn the meaning of the word for Pearl.

After that, she read aloud—or found occasion to read aloud—nearly every night. She spoke as if she were giving her words to my brother, pressing the open book against her breast afterward, her treasure, her newfound source of joy.

Every day I fell more in love.

I watched her eat, drink, sweep the floor, fold the laundry. Nothing she did was too dull for me. She moved with a graceful stealth, as if sorrow haunted her always, and she had learned to jig and weave out of its way, like a young boxer.

When Alex had slept in the extra bed in my room, he'd kept it against the wall, as far from me as he could. Now the bed had inched closer to mine, until I could reach out and touch it. Sometimes I let my fingers walk to the edge of my mattress. They had only to leap across that narrow gap to stroke her hair or the knuckles of her fingers.

Once asleep, Pearl grew restless. Whether she was wrestling with demons or angels or with memory or fear, she slept in a tangle, her body arched, her elbows bent one this way, one that. Blankets surged from her onto the floor, and many a time, I crawled from my bed to wrap her up again. Sitting beside her, I wondered what caused such turmoil in the middle of the night, when Berwind was quiet, and the sky over the mesa no longer flickered with orange.

"What do you dream about?" I asked her one morning.

"I don't dream."

One day, she cooked for us, a meal that was unlike anything we had ever tasted.

Alex took a long look at his plate, his fork midair. "This isn't American cooking," he said. "What is it? Greek? Mexican?"

"Everything here come right out of Berwind Canyon," Pearl said. "Just things I pick up walking around."

"Is that so?"

He took seconds, thirds, and then kept poking his fingers into the dishes for bits and pieces. For years, I realized, he'd been starving, barely able to gag down my cooking.

Pearl teased him. "You better slow down or you'll weight the trip so much tomorrow, the poor old mule won't be able to stop until you're at the very bottom of the mine."

"The lowest level of a coal mine is hell," Alex said.

"And when you reach hell, you can rest at last."

"The miner's prayer."

And they laughed, as if they were great friends.

From then on, she cooked every night. She used spices—not just the sage I'd dried myself and sprinkled into our food, but powders and fragrant leaves she'd bartered for from the Italian women over in Bricktown. She crushed corn like the Mexican women and made flat, round tortillas. She coaxed the tough slabs of meat I bought at the company store into tender feasts, and cooked them over sweet-smelling mesquite wood she'd gathered up on the mesa. She seasoned potatoes with juniper plucked from outside, and she even fried up prickly pear.

Alex could not take his eyes off his plate—or from Pearl. He watched her circle the kitchen, his gaze tracing arcs up and down her body. When he read the newspaper, it was low enough that he could glance over the top, and he invited her to sit at the table at night, to read as he played Solitaire. We were happy again, the hole left in our hearts by our father now filled by Pearl.

That winter, the clouds dipped low over Berwind, burying the canyon with drifts of snow. Water rose in the mine tunnels, so the men stood in the damp all day only to be greeted by bitter cold when they came above ground. The sickness rolled in, killing babies and grandmothers and old, crippled miners. And even though Theo Sky spent most of his time piling coal on the fire, and Miss Rice moved our desks closer to the stove, the sickness crept into the school, too. Russell Ruddy was the first to fall, coughing into his sopping handkerchief and laying his feverish head on his desk. He left school in November, and Miss Rice sent his work home with Jake until the following March.

Early in December, Alex came through the door stumbling and falling about, unable to lift his feet. I laid aside my book and ran to him, crying, "What's wrong? What's happened?"

Pearl came from the kitchen, wiping her hands on her apron.

"Don't." Alex shoved me away. "I'm all right—"

I jammed my hands into his face, trying to feel his forehead. I pulled out a chair for him, guiding him into it as I would a loose bull, arms spread wide. "Are you sick? Do you have pneumonia?"

"I'm all right, Christian! Jesus!" He wavered across to his bed and sat down. Slumping over, he lay down with his feet still on the floor.

Kneeling beside the bed, I looked toward Pearl and begged, "Help me! Please!"

She did not move. "Looks like your brother drinks after all."

"No!" I cried. "He's sick. Dad had it, too! It's pneumonia, and Dad died—"

"Your pa didn't smell like a jug of swill after he got it, did he?"

For the first time, I smelled the sourness that rose from Alex each time he breathed. He seemed steeped in it. He had thrown his wrist over his eyes, breathing heavily, as if he might fall asleep. One of his boots twitched against the bare planks of the floor, grating against the fine layer of red dust that covered everything.

"Alex!" I shook him. "Are you drunk? Have you been drinking?"

"Leave me alone," he growled.

Panic overtook me. If I lost Alex, I would be alone in America, without a soul who cared about me. I'd be like Pearl, begging from door to door until someone was kind enough to let me stay. I shrieked at Pearl, "Help me!"

"This is how it starts, Christian," she said bitterly. "They start coming in all drunked up and feeling sorry for themselves, and it's the woman who has to pick up after them and get them fixed up enough to go to work the next morning."

"You'd know all about it, I suppose," Alex spat.

"My uncle was like you, drinking and cussing every waking minute. My pa, too."

"Which one? The one who fell under the train or—let's see—the one who burned you with a poker or the one you can't remember at all?"

The skillet smoked on the stove. Pearl grabbed a towel and lifted it from the heat. It came clattering down on the bare plank of counter like a fifty-pound weight, eggs and bits of sausage spewing on the floor.

I sat back on my heels. "No, you're sick, aren't you, Alex? You're—"

Pearl's voice assailed me. "Make him some coffee, Christian. I'll finish cooking dinner. He'll be fine once he sobers up. There ain't no reason me and you shouldn't go ahead and eat."

I was caught, unable to move one way or the other. I wasn't convinced he was drunk—how could Pearl be so sure?—and I resented that she simply stood there, eyeing him with a look on her face as if she'd caught a whiff of the latrine.

Alex felt it, too. "She lies," he said.

The voices in my head were so powerful that I did not know who he meant. Then Pearl asked, "What's that supposed to mean?"

He stood, swaying. "Filling our heads with troubles with your mother and father and uncle and aunt. Wanting us to feel sorry for you. I've been asking around. Nobody I've talked to has heard of a Sam and Lettie living over in Tabasco."

"Then you been talking to folks who don't know nothing."

"Oh, no, everyone I talk to has something to say about you," he said. "None of it good. What did your aunt and uncle do to you that was so bad that you had to run away? Don't you have a scar you can show us to prove that they were as rotten as your father?"

"Alex, don't!" I whispered, thinking of the bruises, and the belt, and her uncle's cruelty.

"What do you want?" she asked. "Want me to get my things and go? I will."

"Seems to me you came here with nothing."

"She can have the things I've given her," I cried.

Neither of them heard me.

"Is that what you want?" She struck again. "For me to go? I'll go, and you won't never see me again, if that's what you want—"

"What I want is for you to tell me the truth."

"Why bother?" she demanded. "You think you already know it. You think you're so smart, listening to all them jabbering on about me! What'd they tell you? That I'm just some whore, like my ma, that I'm just some piece of trash that ain't never been worth nothing—!"

"You're the one saying it."

"You ever seen a fox caught in a trap?" Her voice hardened into stone. "It wants to get out so bad that it chews its own leg off just to be free." She slammed down her fist. "That's what it was like, that's how bad it was—"

"You have no idea what it's like to be trapped," he shouted. "Going down that hole day after day, knowing it could be your last, and knowing that if it's not your last, it doesn't even matter, because tomorrow will be just the same—"

"Or night after night, waiting for some man to just take what he wants from you, slapping your face black and blue if you don't and his nasty spit all over you—!"

"Stop it, stop it!" I cried. "Alex, stop it! Pearl!"

"You can't come into a man's house," he lashed, "bringing your rubbish and filth with you—"

"Well, you like to look at it, just the same." She held out her arms. "Look, look, what filth do you see here? Or here? You can't stop looking at it, can you, but you think you're too good to have it—"

Alex lunged from his bed, swiping a chair out of the way as he went. Pearl grabbed the frying pan and brandished it before her. Our dinner slopped to the floor around her feet.

Alex's face blanched. "My God, what do you think I am?"

"Just like the rest of them," she said, breathing heavily.

He turned and went back to his bed. Half-falling onto it, he rolled away so that he faced the wall. Pearl jerked away, racing through the bullhide sheeting into our room. Sobbing, I fell into a heap on the floor. Alex snapped at me, "Be quiet."

"Who's telling you things about her? Why? Why do they care?"

"No more, Kirstie."

"Is it Uncle John? Mrs. McCormick doesn't like Pearl, but it's because—"

"No more, now! No—"

"Please don't send her away! Please don't! She's like Momma, she's like Elsie, I'd be so lonely—"

"Don't talk about them. Don't compare her to them. She's nothing like them." He straightened up. "Go away."

I wiped my nose on the back of my hand, gathered my skirt around me. In the kitchen, I swept up our meal and dumped it back into the frying pan, planning to feed it to the McCormicks' chickens in the morning. From the opposite side of the room, Alex made no more noise.

In our room, Pearl and I lay side by side, each on our backs, looking up. I didn't bother to mop up my tears or sniffles. I'd put out the lamp, but the night hadn't yet darkened into blackness. I could see the dark flow of her hair, her shape clearly etched against the sheets by the light of the fading day.

All at once, I was angry. What if she was lying—not just making up stories—but truly lying? She had lied about her father—why not about her aunt and uncle?

"Did you do anything bad?" I asked. "Before you came here?"

She was quiet for a long time. "I ain't ashamed of nothing I done."

I did not say anything—I didn't know what questions to ask—but my stomach twisted in knots. I did not know if I hated Pearl, or Alex, or loved them both so much that I would die without them.

Pearl heard my sobs. "He ain't no worse for it," she said. "He'll sleep it off and be good as new in the morning, except for a headache. And a man don't mine with his head, you know."

The picture of a man banging his head against coal struck me as funny. Laughter bubbled up inside me. My tears washed it away.

"What's wrong now?" Pearl asked.

"He wouldn't be here if it weren't for me. He would have gone home. He'd be in school, and happy, and—"

"In Scotland?"

"Yes."

"That's where you both want to be?"

"Yes." My voice was fierce, although I hadn't thought of Scotland in ages.

"That must be one special place."

"It is," I said, then added, "Unlike anything here."

She reached across the space between the two beds to lay her hand on mine. Under her dark fingers, my skin was the color of parchment. I turned my hand palm up and curled my fingers through hers.

Chapter 6

By the end of the school year, Miss Rice determined that Pearl had finished the sixth grade. Anyway, she was sixteen—we had counted the years she could remember and added some for good measure—and too old to be reading from the primers and adding with the youngsters. In the fall, we would both enter seventh grade.

That summer, Pearl and I spent almost every moment together. We poured over copies of *Ladies Home Journal* that fell into our hands after they'd passed through many others, their pages brittle and crumbling. For hours, I penned recipes that Pearl read to me onto old envelopes and stowed them in a cigar box, creating our own treasure trove of cakes and pies and cobblers that we would never have enough ingredients to make. Together, we hung the weekly washing on the community lines, doing a willowy dance as we pinned up the sheets to keep them from dragging on the ground. It didn't matter that Mrs. McCormick and Jane McKenna and the other women no longer spoke to me. They seemed old to me, now, used up, and their daughters looked to be tripping along on the path right behind them.

High on the mesa, Pearl showed me new plants. "This stuff that grows so tall"—she petted the furry green leaves of a mullein—"helps with colds and the green apple trots and all sorts of things, and when these little yellow flowers bloom late in the fall"—she touched a gumweed—"you can just eat them and they'll cure your sore throat. Yarrow you can use for just about anything. And you can make tea from chamomile, you know."

I started carrying Alex's knife with me, and we gathered plants to cook with and to brew for medicines before the sickness of another winter hit us again.

We chose a sand wash cut deep into the side of the mesa as our own special place, carrying our lunches up there nearly every day. Lying in the sun, we read to each other, devouring every tattered and dog-eared book from the lending library in Berwind. When we found missing pages, we just made up our own stories. Pearl acted out the characters, playing heroine, hero and even horse.

I gave her our book of Burns' poetry. "This ain't English," she complained. "Nothing's spelled right."

"It's the way English is spoken in Scotland."

"So Scotchmen have a different language, too?"

"Not a different language," I said, uncertain. "Just a different way of saying things."

"Ain't that what a different language is?" She huffed, but she put her heart into it, and soon she was reading Burns. I prompted her until she could read it with a clumsy Scottish bur. Throwing her hand over her eyes, she sang, "*At least some pity on me shaw, If love it may na be! And sa I must ga before the rooster doth craw.*"

"That's not what it says!"

"How do you knaw?"

Giggling, I said, "I knaw! I doth knaw!"

We laughed so hard that our voices echoed up and down the draw, through the canyon, maybe through all of Berwind. Delighted, we took turns yelling out other rhymes. "In the winter, it doth snaw!" "Look at the valley down law!" "Alas, my life is one of waw!"

One day, Pearl told me the story of La Llorona.

"Once there was a Mexican girl named Maria, living somewheres around here," she said. "She was the most beautiful girl in the country, but she was poor, and only poor boys wanted to marry her. But she said no, and wished and prayed for a rich man to find her some day.

"Well, one day a fancy Mexican come riding into town. He was dressed all in silver and black, and his horse had a solid silver saddle. He saw Maria, and even though she was dressed in some raggedy old skirt that was full of holes, he thought she was the most beautiful girl he ever seen.

"So they got married, and, pretty soon, she had a couple or three babies. And soon, she was fat and old, and her husband didn't love her no more. He went off, never even thinking of Maria or his kids.

"One day, when Maria was walking home from town, her husband rode by in a carriage with a beautiful lady. She got so mad that she grabbed up her babies and held their heads under water and drownded them. She felt bad right away, but it was too late. They was dead and floating away on the river.

"So now, she walks along the river at night, crying for her children. You can hear her calling for them on the wind, every night, if you listen real close."

I wiped tears from my eyes. "That's such a sad story!"

"But it's true. Ain't you ever listened to the wind? It's got all sorts of voices and sounds in it. Close your eyes."

Eyes shut tight, she turned her face to the wind, as if she was in a trance or under a spell. I buried my head in my knees. The air in Berwind Canyon was alive, always moving from one end to the other—the only thing that could move freely. Jagging around boulders and weaving in and out of crevices, the wind sighed, or screamed, or whispered. When it scattered over the plain in Ludlow, at the foot of the canyon, the wind carried a thousand cries from the canyons.

Then I heard it: "Ooo, ooo, I want my children back! Give them back! Ooo! OOO!"

I lifted my head. "That's you!"

She laughed. "You sure did jump."

One morning, I woke up and found I was bleeding. Creeping out to the privy, I pulled the door tight, although morning was a busy time. Had I injured myself somehow? Had I eaten something sharp—a sliver of glass—that had cut my insides open? I was so frightened that when someone banged on the wall, I shouted back, "You just wait!" The blood wasn't much, only enough to have stained the seam of my bloomers, but I was afraid, my hands sweating and my neck chilly and hot at once.

Finally, when the pounding on the door had become a howling call to tear down the door, I left, walking by the angry folks outside as if I didn't know they were there. I went back to the house and went into the bedroom, passing Pearl as she finished cleaning up from breakfast. Alex had long been gone to the mine.

She came in, wiping her hands on a dishtowel. "What's wrong with you? You was gone so long I thought maybe the privies had all tipped over again into the stream."

"I'm sick."

She put a warm, damp hand on my forehead. "What's wrong? You ain't coughing or fevered or nothing."

"No." I told her about my illness. "Can you stop it? Can you make it go away?"

Her eyes narrowed. "This ain't never happened to you before?"

"No."

"You little fool. It happens to all girls this side of heaven."

"What happens?"

"The curse. Becoming a woman."

"What curse?"

"You can have babies now. It's the natural way of things."

"I don't want to have a baby!" I cried.

"Well, you can't do it alone," she said coolly. "Ain't nobody ever told you nothing?"

I shook my head, tears welling up in my throat.

"I guess I known about it since I was a baby. My ma used to worry about it all the time, she took so many men. But I guess you ain't never had a ma to tell you, you poor sad thing."

And she told me about men and women, and how love worked. All at once, I understood why Mary and Katy McCormick whispered behind their hands as they waited in line for the girls' privy at school, and why the boys in the school had taken such an eager interest in Pearl.

"If every girl gets it, why is it called a curse?" I asked.

She shrugged. "I don't rightly know, except that maybe it's because you can't be with a man unless you're married to him, just in case you make a baby—"

"Who would want to do that without being married?" I asked, aghast.

Her brows knit as if she did not believe me, but she said, "Maybe being married is the real curse. Plenty of women ain't too happy with their husbands."

"I will be," I said fiercely.

"You think so?" She launched into a dramatic interpretation of "Oh, My Love Is Like a Red, Red Rose," one hand daintily posed against her forehead and the other holding her nose. In a high, nasal voice, she pronounced the word "love" as a sweeping, singsong "loo-ve" until I laughed and cried all at once.

Alex had started to spend more time away from home after his row with Pearl, but he rarely missed a meal. One evening, he would not eat, even though Pearl had cooked with mesquite and sage. We sat in silence—Alex and Pearl facing away from the table and each other, as usual. She perched on the edge of her chair, ready for flight.

My stomach turned, heaving before another battle, but curiosity made me bold. "What's wrong?" I asked Alex.

He did not answer, but pulled out his flask and took a swig.

"Today," he said, "I saw quite a sight."

Neither Pearl nor I spoke, waiting. At last, I ventured, "What was it?"

"A Slav kid, oh, about fourteen or so," he said. "He was ready to get on the trip when the boss of the mule drivers stopped him and told him he had to chip in for beer money. The kid said he wouldn't give any, couldn't give any. Sick mother, deaf little sister, no father. The boss said that was the second time the kid had refused and that he was getting mighty thirsty waiting around for him to pay his dues. He called over a couple of guards, and they started pushing the kid around, just roughing him up. Good, honest fun, you know. Well, stupid kid, he loses his temper and manages to catch one in the jaw with a fist. The guards took him aside and started slapping his face with the mule reins, back and forth, back and forth."

Pearl laid down her fork.

Alex lifted the flask to his lips. "Pretty soon, the kid has blood coming out of his nose, and his ears. He's crying, begging them to quit. They just laughed until they got him down on the ground where they could kick him."

Another deep swig. He set it down with a thump. I studied my plate, trying not to see the broken boy on the ground. "Didn't anyone stop them?" I asked.

Alex snorted. "Try to stop them and you'd be next."

Pearl picked up the flask, turned it around a couple of times in her hands, then poured a little into her metal cup. "You men got it pretty bad down there," she said.

Alex watched her drink the whiskey in one swallow. He didn't offer her more when she set down the cup.

"They treat mules better than you," she said. "They got horse doctors for them, but no doctors for people that's sick or hurt. Just a mine guard saying, take your bad luck and get out of here. That's why you men need a union."

"Jesus, lower your voice!"

She shrugged. "I ain't the only one talking about it. Plenty of folks don't like the way the company treats them."

Alex drank, a hefty draught, his face puckering as if he was swallowing poison. "It can't happen here," he scoffed. "We're too penned up in these canyons. A union man would never get through the gates."

Pearl persisted. "But you know what? The fox always gets in the chicken coop. No matter how careful you are, he digs his way under, or he slides in through a hole no bigger than your thumb. You ever try to shoot a fox? They move quick."

"Well, then maybe the union should hire foxes, because a bullet is a damned sight faster than a man."

She shrugged. "A lot of the men here in Berwind run pretty fast when they left the old country."

"You're talking about the foreigners. The union's an American institution."

She waved a hand in the air. "Dagos blow the mines, they set the timbers and rails, they get the stoop in their backs from the low ceilings and the dust in their lungs just the same as any white man. Why wouldn't they need a union, too?"

"Most of them don't speak enough English to ask for a drink of water," Alex said. "No, if the union comes here, it has to be for men who can understand the language. The Brits, the Americans. Those who are skilled and—"

"There's more ships sailing the ocean between the dago lands and here than between your Scotland and here," she scoffed. "Of the thousand miners in Berwind, how many speak English? Fifty? A hundred? If fifty men went out on strike, you wouldn't even know it."

Alex's jaw set like granite. "We've our pride."

"And that's about all you got. I didn't ask for no black skin and hair when I was born, and neither did any of those Italians or Greeks or Mexicans, I reckon. Maybe if we all poured bleach over our heads, you'd think we was good enough for you."

He said nothing, but his jaw clenched.

"Look at me." She held her arms out, palms up. "Ain't I just a woman? Can't I cook and sew and clean just as good as any other? You make me think I ain't no better than an old rag!"

His face curdled, his gaze locked with hers. Something passed between them, like a solitary note played high on the neck of a violin—something I was too young to understand.

"Don't you want me?" Pearl asked, her voice sweet and sad. "Don't you, Alex?"

Alex did as he always did—rose from his chair and grabbed his coat. But Pearl was quick. Pinning herself against the door, she demanded, "What don't you ever want to talk to me? Why are you so afraid of me?"

"Move," he said.

"No, sir, not until you tell me why you don't want me."

"I can't—" He glanced toward me, then said cruelly, "If all I've got left is my pride, then I better hold onto it."

Pearl's face drained of life. She stepped aside.

In August, just before school started, Pearl and I cooked a picnic supper. When Alex came home, I begged him to go with us up into the hills. "Please, Alex," I said. "It will be fun."

"No," he said. "And you're not going either, with all the guards crawling around just looking for lone girls."

"But we wouldn't be alone if you went with us."

Pearl kept packing the picnic, her movements slow, deliberate.

Alex's eyes flickered over her, as if searching for a sign from her. Feeling his eyes on her, she turned at last and said, "I wish you'd come, Alex. Christian's worked real hard on making all this food."

I opened my mouth to deny it—I had done almost nothing—but Pearl's gaze was locked with Alex's, and neither of them seemed to know I was there. He was the first to look away. "Aye, let's go."

We climbed high up on the mesa. From there, we could look down on a good part of Berwind, stretching five or six miles up the canyon, with its dusty shacks, mule barns, railroad tracks, turntables, engine houses and tipples stuck on flat ledges scraped into the slopes. The smoke from the slag heaps hung in the canyon below us, but from the mesa, we could see patches of blue and flat-bottomed thunderheads.

"Dad used to bring us up here," I said to Alex. "Remember? The Northern Lights?"

Alex said nothing, but Pearl asked, "What's that?"

"We'll show you when it's time," I said. "You'll like it."

After we ate, I wandered away from them to sit on some rocks higher up on the mesa. In the northwest, I could see the tips of the Spanish Peaks, whitened by snow. In the south, the plateau of Fisher's Peak rose ten thousand feet into the sky near Trinidad, where folks hurried about their business without a thought for those of us in the canyons. The sun was already setting behind the high ridges, and before long, the stars appeared in a sky that looked much bigger from the top of Berwind Canyon.

Leaning back against the rock, I closed my eyes and imagined where I would live when I grew up. A place where La Llorona didn't cry upon the wind, and men were not maimed by guards or beat up in the mines. No one breathed a last breath of cinder-filled smoke, no baby was born blue, no child parched with fever, no woman was afraid of her husband. I saw myself in a bedroom with a chenille spread on the bed and curtains of lace on the windows.

Alex's voice interrupted my wishes. "Read this."

There was silence, and then I heard Pearl ask, "This your own book?"

"It was our father's."

"And this Sir Waiter Scott—"

"Walter."

"Oh, I see it now. L. Is he one of your family?"

He snorted. "Aye, could be. In Scotland, a man tries his best to be related to the famous."

"I don't know if I can read something this fancy," she said, but after a minute, she settled on "It Was an English Ladye Bright," one of the most mournful verses in the book. Her voice was low and soft, trembling as if she were overcome by the sweet sorrow in the verses. "*Now all ye lovers, that faithful prove,*" she read. "*Pray for their souls who died for love, For Love shall still be lord of all!*"

I wiped away a tear and peeked out at them from behind the rocks.

"That's one sad poem." Pearl laid the book aside. "Seems like the Scotch poems is always sad. Always about saying 'fare thee well' or 'I'll ne'er see you again, my loo-ve.'" She spread out, lying flat on her back. Picking at her hair, she pulled strands of it from behind her back until she'd brought it all down around her shoulders and laid it over her breasts. She blended right into the rock and shadow, white and black, just like she was part of the earth, of the piñon and sage. "Ain't nobody happy there?"

"Our family was happy."

"Until you came here."

"Until we came here."

"I'm lucky, I guess," Pearl said. "I don't never want to go back to Tabasco."

Alex did not pursue it. "Living in Scotland isn't like living here. It's a—"

"A dream. I know. Christian told me so."

"Did she? I didn't know she remembered that much about it."

"If you want to go so bad, why don't you just pick up and leave?"

"I'm not a free man." He poked at the ground with a stick. "I owe so much at the store—"

"You can take whatever scrip you got to Trinidad, and they'll give you ten cents on the dollar real American money for it. Enough to get started toward Scotland. How far it is, anyways?"

"Is that what you planned to do? Whose money was it?"

The wind swirled, waiting for her reply. "I took some, but I don't steal."

I did not move, afraid it was all ruined.

Alex said, "A person has to have some dignity. Some sense of decency."

"That's why I come to you and Christian. You're right nice folks, even if you do read sad poems."

"Where did you come from, Pearl?" Alex asked. "Were you working in a house in Hastings?"

She sat up, gathering her skirts around her knees. "What answer do you want?" she asked. "If I say yes—and I ain't saying it—you'd think me a whore. If I say no, you'd think me a liar. I don't win with you neither way."

Suddenly, the sky north of us was bright orange. The lights flashed on the underbellies of the clouds, whisked through the darkness, then disappeared, as quickly as they had come.

"Look," I called, climbing out of my rock fortress.

"That's the ovens over in Hastings," Pearl snapped.

I glanced at Alex, but he just stared at the lights, a dark frown on his face.

Desperately, I said, "When our father was alive, he would bring us up here to watch. He said they reminded him of the Northern Lights in Scotland and told us stories. He'd nearly cry because he wasn't there."

"What's the Northern Lights?"

"They're lights up in the far north that bring wild and beautiful colors to the sky. In Scotland, you can go outside and the whole sky is brilliant white and glowing. Then, it'll change. Blue or red. Green, sometimes."

"What causes them?"

"I don't know," I said. "I don't think anyone knows."

Pearl gazed at the sky. "Once a boy told me that them ovens was the mouths of hell and that wicked children was sent to be burned every night."

"Did you believe him?"

"I didn't know. He'd been to school, and I hadn't. I figured he knew. And it made sense to me, you know. I'd seen men with faces all blackened and burnt by them ovens, and I knew sometimes they died from the smoke and burning hot. It struck me as right possible that they was burning more than coke in them ovens. Why not bad children and old ladies who don't have no use no more and babies that their mamas can't feed and such?"

Alex snorted, loud and harsh. "Leave it to you, Pearl, to believe such rot."

Pearl gathered her shawl up around her shoulders, girding for battle. "Ain't much difference between that and thinking those lights is the lights of Scotland, or heaven, or whatever you folks think it is. It's just some old coke ovens burning. Make up whatever story you want, it's don't change what's true."

Alex's face set, and I realized that they were talking of something other than I thought.

"Ain't that so, Alex?" Pearl asked. "Ain't those just the coke ovens, unless you want them to be something else?"

He made no reply, his gaze on the lights.

"Ain't it?" she demanded again. "Folks can say whatever they want about a thing, but that don't change what the thing really is. Ain't that so?"

"Aye," he begrudged her. "That's so."

"Then I ain't any of those things anybody says about me. I'm what you want me to be."

The lights leapt through the sky, retreated, and streamed forth again, dancing with the stars and darting through the whole of the sky. When Alex stood, he offered his hand to Pearl to help her up, and she looked at him with eyes that glowed in the Northern Lights.

Chapter 7

When we went back to school, we found that Miss Rice had married. A new teacher had taken her place, a woman by the name of Miss Holben. She had redecorated the schoolroom with scripture, covering half of the blackboard with neatly handwritten placards. On each desk was a pocketbook of Bible verses that we read from every day before lunch.

Miss Holben wore fine shawls around her shoulders during the cool, fall days, and in the mornings, she knitted as we read silently. She had even knitted a model of the sun and the seven planets to hang on wires from the schoolhouse rafters. It was the most foolish use of yarn I'd ever seen—the sun was a yellow ball made of enough yarn for a sweater, and the earth would have knitted into a fine pair of green mittens. A placard attached to the mobile read: "God is Everywhere."

Miss Holben wasn't particularly old, but she wore her hair in a bun pulled so tight the veins stood out beside her blue eyes. She never smiled, even when she testified about the joy she felt since she had dedicated her life to Jesus Christ. Miss Rice had said grace once a day, at lunch, but Miss Holben found it necessary to pray for everything from fair weather for recess to solving math problems. She called us all by our proper names, so that I became Miss Scott and Pearl Miss Doe. Theo Sky became Mr. Theo Sky, his name still only one word.

That year, the classroom flooded with faces that were darker than ever before. Italy, Serbia, Austria, Greece, Mexico—there were even four Japanese students who sat perfectly still all day and never spoke. The ranks of light-skinned, English speaking students had thinned. Russell Ruddy had graduated the year before, and when he left school, Jake had given up on learning, following his brother into the mine. The three younger Ruddy boys still attended, as did the McCormicks and McKennas and a few others who came from ranches up the canyon. Ethel May Farrington and I occupied the first two desks of the sixth, seventh and eighth grade row. Mary McCormick sat behind me.

And then there was Pearl.

Pearl ran afoul of Miss Holben almost immediately. She refused to pretend that she did not occupy the last desk of the secondary grade row. During the second week of school, she raised her hand. Miss Holben tried to press on with the lesson, scratching her wisdom in dusty chalk across the blackboard, but Pearl finally said, "Miss, I ain't got nothing to write with. Nobody back here does."

Miss Holben turned around. "Did someone speak?"

Pearl stood beside her desk. "It was me. I—we—back here in the back don't got nothing to write with. The slates is all in the front."

"You are not allowed to speak," Miss Holben replied. "No one is allowed to speak without my permission."

"I thought maybe you forgot," Pearl said. "And that you'd be glad that somebody pointed it out to you."

Miss Holben was certainly not glad. "I do not intend to teach those who do not have a rudimentary knowledge of the English language," she announced. "Those of you who speak a foreign tongue should be ashamed. You are in America now, where, through the grace of Mr. Rockefeller, your family has been given a home, and your father has been provided with a way to earn a living and keep his hands busy, safe from the grips of Satan and the pagan churches of your homelands. And still you aren't grateful enough to learn our country's customs and language."

"I ain't—"

"Do not speak again." Miss Holben swung back to the board. "Fourth graders, take out your readers, please, and turn to page—"

"It don't seem very Jesus-like not to teach the poor and stupid," Pearl insisted. "Besides, Miss Rice used to teach them just like everybody else, and some of them learned pretty good—"

"Did you just speak?" Miss Holben demanded. "And did you just blaspheme the name of the Lord? Come here, Miss Doe."

Pearl went to the front of the schoolroom. I leaned forward on my desk, half in and half out of my seat.

Miss Holben pulled a low stool, meant for a first or second grader, to a dark corner beyond her desk. "Since you want a seat at the front of the room with the others who speak English, then you can sit here. This is your new seat."

Pearl gave Miss Holben a cold look, then took the seat. The stool was so small that her knees bunched up nearly to her chin. I suspected Miss Holben had set it far enough from the wall so that Pearl could not lean back. From that corner, nothing could be seen. Not the blackboard, not the tattered map of the world, not even the other faces in the schoolroom. I craned my neck to try to see Pearl over Miss Holben's desk, but all I could see was the top of her head.

That night I told Alex about Miss Holben while Pearl served supper. "She won't let Pearl read or write, like Miss Rice used to," I complained. "She won't let us read extra books unless they have to do with Jesus or math. I wanted to read the new *Five Little Peppers* this year."

Alex's eyes sparked. "You just keep quiet. She's nothing but a company spy."

"Spy?"

"There's a strike up in a northern town called Boulder just now." He nearly whispered. "They're sure to win up there, and when they do, they're saying the southern fields will organize."

"I don't care what's going on anywhere else!" I cried. "I just—!"

"Quiet, Christian. She's looking to see who causes trouble, who has ideas of their own. She's looking to send them down the canyon. You just keep quiet and do whatever she says."

I said no more. That threat, that awful threat, again.

Pearl set plates of stew before us, her mouth trembling with tears.

"You have to just let it pass," Alex said to her, as if aching for his own lost days at school. "You just have to forget about it."

But Pearl did not forget. When Miss Holben asked the class the next day to name the first president of our nation, Pearl raised her hand right along with the rest of us. It bobbed in that dark corner, and most of the eyes in the room fastened onto it, then slid away, then popped right back. She didn't lower it either, but kept it up while Martin Harrington answered, and while Miss Holben, bent on ignoring her, asked the next question.

"Put down your hand," Miss Holben finally ordered, when Pearl's hand had not flagged during five questions.

"I know the answers," Pearl said. "I know all the answers."

"That makes no difference to me."

"It should make a difference. You're asking questions about America. I know them. I wasn't born in no foreign country. I'm an American, born right over in Hastings."

She may as well have poisoned Miss Holben. The color drained from her already bloodless face, and she spoke in a low, tight voice. "That's enough. Come here."

Slowly Pearl rose from the stool. "Turn around," Miss Holben ordered.

"No," Pearl said.

"Turn around!"

"If you want to hit me, you'll have to do it while you can see my eyes," Pearl said. "You can't do it the coward's way."

That was all Miss Holben needed. She brought the ruler across Pearl's mouth, and from the sharp crack, I knew she had used all her strength to deliver the blow. Pearl's body swayed a little, but her hands never moved toward her face. A thin line of blood formed along her lower lip, and a red slit spread from the corner of her mouth across her cheek.

"Sit down," Miss Holben said.

Pearl went back to her stool, but when Miss Holben called again for answers, Theo Sky raised his hand.

Miss Holben stammered a couple of times, trying her best to overlook him. Finally, her face ashen and tight, she asked, "What is it, Mr. Theo Sky? Do you need something?"

"No."

"Did you wish to speak?"

"No."

"Do you know the answers?"

"No."

Still, his arm did not waver. He had grown so much that year that his wrists hung from his sleeves, and his pants barely reached his ankles. He seemed larger, more imposing than ever. For the rest of the day, he held up his hand, sometimes changing arms, but never letting his rebellion flag. And even though Miss Holben did not glance his way again, he didn't stop. By the next morning, the Pavlovski brothers had joined him, so that every day, Miss Holben faced three hands that never faltered.

I sat at my desk, torn apart. Should I raise my hand and incur Miss Holben's wrath? Should I meekly say nothing, as Alex wanted? I had never broken the rules, never stepped outside the boundaries that were set for me. But Pearl hadn't read to Alex for a long time, and I was worried that if she didn't, they might start to fight again, that he might find reasons to start doubting her again.

At home, I offered her our copy of Sir Walter Scott's poems.

"Remember this?" I asked. "Remember up on the mesa?"

She ran a hand over the cover. "You better keep it for yourself."

Now that she had nothing else to snag her imagination, she started walking to the company store after school. Nearly everybody in Berwind went to the store for news. The place was especially popular with women. We called them the Widow Watch, because so many were young wives whose husbands had been lost in the mines and who were greedy for another man to feed them and raise their children. And soon enough, young men began to walk Pearl home, escorting her over the bridge at the bottom of Berwind Canyon and up to our front door like suitors.

Alex remarked on Pearl's new habits right away. "Men talk about women who do nothing but hang idle at the store. Watch yourself, Pearl. There's a passel of men out there who want the wrong thing from a woman."

"I reckon I can understand their wants just fine," Pearl said. "A man ain't that much of a mystery."

One by one, Pearl began to court Alex's friends. Some, like James O'Keegan, were looking for a wife to take on the house and give him children, but others, like Rory Capstan, simply had their eyes on a lively girl. They walked Pearl home late in the evening, and she, like a princess, invited them in for biscuits and coffee. Alex came home as they were eating and laughing, and usually joined them in a glass of whiskey.

He said little, but watched closely, as Pearl flattered and flirted and piled more food onto their plates. After her guest left, she sang as she cooked, while Alex nursed his flask.

Soon, Russell Ruddy started walking her up the hill. Like the rest of us, he had grown up, but he had never gained any more weight or muscle. His hair was the color of sand after a hard rain, and his eyes were so blue that I thought they must beam even in the dark tunnels of the mine. He dressed as if he couldn't find clothes to fit his skinny frame. His pants always hung from him, and his shirtsleeves slid over his fingers. He started bringing his violin with him when he walked Pearl home, playing for her at our table.

Russell played the violin in a lovely, careful way, as if it was made of thin crystal. He didn't fiddle dances or folk tunes, but played one string at a time, filling the air with dainty, old-world melodies. Those songs had a strange effect on me. They set off an aching in my stomach that made me both sad and yet burning with restlessness, as if there was something just beyond my reach that I wanted and needed so badly that I hurt for it.

"What's that song?" Pearl asked him.

"An old song from Wales," Russell answered. "Where my parents are from."

"It's such a sad song! Don't you know no jigs?"

Russell laughed. "Here, this one will make you happier."

He launched into a reel, playing it as well as he played the ballads. Pearl reached for my hands and pulled me up, locking elbows and swinging around me in a do-si-do. We started to whoop as we spun, yelping as we nearly collided with the table and chairs and woodpile. We laughed so hard our sides ached, and we both had to bend over double to clutch at them.

"I'd dance with you, too, Russ," Pearl called. "But Christian here can't play the fiddle."

Breathless, I sat down, but she danced toward Russell. Still fiddling, he turned in a circle, watching her as she wove around him. Pearl's hair, loose and waving to her waist, was silvery in the ticks of light from the windows. Her cheeks flushed to the color of roses, her lips were a deeper red. Russell kept his gaze on hers, his thin face bright with pleasure.

His fiddling slowed, lapsing back into a ballad, so that Pearl was no longer high-stepping and whirling her skirts like a Mexican señorita, but arching in a graceful sashay. At last, she brought her hands up in front of her, palms cupped, as if praying for rain, and simply swayed. The song came not to an end, but to one long, last note that hung over us, quivering in the air.

"My Lord, you're a beauty," Russell said, letting his violin settle to his side. Pearl smiled, her eyes glossed by happiness. Suddenly, Russell remembered I was in the room. Sliding an embarrassed glance toward me, he turned away and began to hastily pack up his violin.

The door opened, Alex home from the mine. He stopped, as if he'd walked into the wrong house, and stared at Russell. Then he noted Pearl—her high color, her quick breathing, the wild hair streaming down her shoulders, the dampness in her eyes. His gaze dropped to the violin, to Russell's slender hands snapping the gold clasps of the case.

"Look who's here, Alex," Pearl said cheerfully.

Alex barely nodded. Russell said goodnight and left, and Pearl went to the kitchen to cook. As she clattered and banged around in the kitchen, she hummed.

Alex listened for a while, turning the silver flask around and around in his hands. Finally he called out, "Russell Ruddy is not welcome in this house."

Pearl reared back from the stove. She took a stance in the narrow kitchen, between counter and stove, her eyes black and her face haughty and daring.

"Russ is my friend," she said.

"Nobody with the name of Ruddy is welcome here. If he asks again, you tell him to go."

"You ain't said nothing about Rory or James."

"That's because they're decent men."

"And Russ ain't? Why not? Who told you some lie about him now? The same folks that tell lies about me?"

Alex's gaze slapped at her. "There are things you don't understand."

"What things? Tell me."

"He's one of the worst miners, not able to bring up tonnage without his Daddy the foreman around to fill his ore car for him. And the Ruddys will send anybody who crosses their paths down the canyon."

"You don't know what you're talking about," Pearl said. "Russ is one of them honorable men you always talk about. A decent man, more then just about anybody else. He don't drink, he don't even smoke. He works real hard because his ma's sick and can't leave her bed—"

"That whole family has a sickness. None of them are as God intended men to be."

Pearl's voice rose. "Russ is a gentleman. He ain't always fighting and talking big—"

"Not in this house," Alex warned. "Do you hear me? Russell Ruddy—or any of the Ruddys—is not to set foot in this house, and neither are you if you're set on taking up with him."

"Alex!" I cried.

But he and Pearl simply stared at each other, until she flounced out the door. Her steps were so hard and fast that they shook the planks of the porch. I ran to the window and looked out. Already, she had disappeared.

Alex sought solace in his flask.

"What's wrong with Russell?" I asked. "Why don't you like him?"

"They're dirt, every last one of the Ruddy boys, and so is anyone who has anything to do with them."

"He doesn't do anything but play his violin," I argued. "I went to school with him, and he didn't ever cause trouble—"

"And at recess, did he play with the girls or the boys?"

"What?" I had no idea what he was talking about. "You can't make her leave because of him. Please don't make her leave. I love her so much, and you do, too. I know you do—"

"Keep still."

"Why don't you marry her?" I challenged. "You love her as much as I do."

"For God's sake, be quiet!" He glanced toward the door. "You're forgetting who you are, Christian. You're forgetting our family and our blood. We've a proud history—"

"But we don't live in a place where that matters, Alex. Nobody cares. I don't care!"

"Don't you ever say that again!" He hammered a fist into the table. "We have lost everything we ever had—Dad, Momma, Elsie, our home, our land! Everything! We have to hold on to something—"

"I don't even remember Scotland, and we're not ever going back, and I'm glad—"

Alex's voice quieted, its anger no less steely. "Think of Dad before you speak again, Christian. Think of how badly he wanted us to grow up with a sense of family and country."

He left the house, taking his coat. I ran into my room and lay down on the bed, sobbing. Don't be ashamed of me, I whispered into the falling darkness. Please, Dad, don't think I've forgotten. Then, anger boiled up in me. I was proud of who I was, but it didn't mean I wouldn't love those I chose to love. Yet I could feel Pearl slipping away from me, from us, as if she had never come, slipping away like my mother's and sister's bodies had in the sea, like my father had in the grave.

When she came home, long after dark, I asked her if she was all right.

"Don't talk to me," she said.

I started to cry again, but she stayed in her own bed, far from me.

On Monday morning, we assembled at school as usual, Pearl in her corner, Theo Sky with his hand raised before the bell rang. As usual, I couldn't see Pearl over Miss Holben's desk, but when Miss Holben paused in our lesson, her eyes on Pearl, I sat up, hoisting my feet up under me. I could see Pearl dreamily braiding her hair, bored and unaware of Miss Holben's eyes upon her.

In a snap, Miss Holben had reached into her desk and pulled out a pair of shears. Lunging into the corner, she grabbed one of Pearl's braids and cut close to her head. "I'm sick to death of you!" she screeched. She clipped again, lopping off the other braid in a ragged line just below Pearl's left ear. "'Turn thy eyes from looking at vanities, and give me life in thy ways!'"

Pearl was on her feet by now and ready to fight, but Miss Holben held the shears out in front of her. "I will have you whipped if you touch me," she threatened. "I'll have your family sent away from Berwind."

"That's my family!" I was on my feet and running toward the front of the room. "Leave her alone! She lives with me!"

Miss Holben brandished her scissors toward me. "That's nonsense. You can't be family with her. Go sit down."

"We are, too! We're sisters! We live together, even sleep together in the same—!"

"This is an affront to God. You are a wicked girl, Miss Scott."

Sobbing, Pearl dropped to her knees to gather her braids. Miss Holben snatched them from her and threw them into the stove. The flames seared upward as she jammed the braids inside, jaundicing her skin to violent orange.

"Don't!" I cried. "No!"

She drew herself up to her full height. "Sit down, Miss Scott," she said.

"No, she's hurt. I'm taking her home. Come on, Pearl."

"I won't allow you back in this school if you leave, Miss Scott." Her voice had reached a near scream. "I won't allow you to even walk near it! You are nothing but a wretched, disobedient—"

"No!" I shouted. "You're the wicked one! You're hateful and—"

All at once, Pearl twisted out of my arms and grabbed at the ball of yellow yarn hanging over her head. Wildly, she jerked, causing the knitted cosmos to list from side to side. One more tug, and the sun began to unravel. Miss Holben screamed, but her voice was lost in the shouts of her students.

Nearly every one of them was swatting at the planets floating above our heads. Two Italian boys overturned their desks to harvest the precious wool, and the red yarn ball of Mars wobbled across the floor, chased by some first graders, who scrabbled on hands and knees to claim it.

At last, the wires of the universe swung crooked and bent, with only the placard, "God is Everywhere," held by one pink piece of yarn. Pearl threw the yellow yarn up into the air, into greedy hands, and ran, leaving behind the schoolhouse and learning. We all followed her, spilling from the door into the weak sunlight, abandoning Miss Holben in the schoolroom to rant about heathens and sin. In the pockets of the lucky was the yarn of the universe, ready to be knitted into mittens and socks.

That evening, Alex had arrived home in a tizzy. "What in God's name happened today, Christian?" he demanded. "We heard that the schoolhouse had been pulled down by the students during a riot."

I was peeling potatoes in the kitchen. "No, it's still standing."

"Then, what—?" He poured himself a cup of whiskey. "You didn't have anything to do with it, did you? Did she?"

I put down the knife, afraid I would hurt myself. "She cut her hair off—"

"Who?"

"Miss Holben," I said. "She cut Pearl's hair, and—"

"What are you talking about? For God's sake, calm down."

I sat down at the table and told the story.

He set the cup on the table. The liquor in it swayed back and forth, slipping over the lip of the cup. "I told you to keep quiet in school," he said. "And not to call attention to yourself—"

"I would keep quiet!" I said. "I'd be a good girl. I always have been, you know that. But I wasn't about to let Miss Holben hurt Pearl!"

He rubbed at his forehead. "Is she hurt?"

"She has a nick on her scalp."

"Is she awake?"

"I don't know."

He went to the bullhide sheeting, pushing it aside with his hand. "May I come in?"

Her voice rang out. "I don't want you to see me! Oh, Alex, don't!"

The curtain swung closed behind him.

Turning away, I went to look out the front window. Now was the time. Now, let him forget our Scottish blood, our proud heritage. Let him realize we were not so different from anyone else in this canyon, trapped and downtrodden and wishing for something better.

But when he came out of the bedroom, he walked past me and out the door of the house without speaking.

That night, a winter wind blew down Berwind Canyon, bringing the dull, moist smell of snow with it. Lying beside Pearl, who slept in my bed, I pressed my hand against her shoulder. I wanted to comfort her, but only a numb "Shh" or a faltering "it's all right" came from my mouth. Fear rose in me that Miss Holben would follow through on her threat to send us down the canyon. Every moment, I listened for the bang of the mine guards' fists on the door.

Worse, I knew that the next morning, I would not rise from bed and dress and go to school, but that I would be just another of the girls in Berwind who had nothing to look forward to but marriage. Grief struck me—I loved school, I loved to read and write and learn. How could I live with being banned from the schoolhouse?

Pearl's night was more restless than mine. Even though the cut on her scalp wasn't bad, I kept a pad soaked in witch hazel pressed against the nick on her head. At last, she rolled onto her back and said, "Christian."

"What?" I whispered.

"Have you ever wondered about all them babies that die when they're born?"

"What about them?"

"Well, did you ever wonder if they die because they just ain't loved? You know, their ma and pa don't want them, and they're just going to go through life without a soul caring for them. Don't you ever wonder if that's why they die?"

"That's not true," I said. "Babies die whether anybody loves them or not."

"Every time I hear of a baby dying, I think, why wasn't it me? Why didn't I die the minute I was born? There's things that can't be loved."

"Not you. Never you. I love you."

"Tell that to him!"

She cried harder. I put my arms around her and pressed my cheek against her head and held her, thinking that I should have done this from the day she appeared on our doorstep, and that this was what I would do for the rest of my nights, as long as I lived.

In the morning, I took out the scissors and cut the last of her hair, trying to even it up some. She sat with her eyes closed, unable to watch. Miss Holben had missed one long strand in the back that Pearl had not braided. I clipped it off at the nape of her neck. It twined around my fingers, more than a foot long. I tied an old scarf around Pearl's head in the way of the Austrian women, and wrapped the hair I'd cut in a handkerchief.

"My hair ain't never been cut," she said, her eyes still closed.

"It grows back."

"But I'm ugly now, ain't I?"

"No, you could never be ugly."

"Nobody's ever going to love me. I'm too ugly."

"That's stupid. You don't love because of someone's hair or face."

"You know that's not true," she said angrily. "You know it."

Late in the afternoon, I heard about the mystery at the schoolhouse from Katy McCormick. Going to see it for myself, I lined up at the schoolhouse door behind Italian and Mexican women who clutched rosaries and waved crosses over their children's heads, and men who either chuckled or gritted their teeth as they gazed inside.

Somehow, Pearl's braids had not burned in the flames that leaped up from the stove. Instead, her hair had survived the fire to be woven into one pencil-thin plait, nearly three feet long. It hung from the stripped wires of the universe, just below the placard that read, "God is Everywhere." The lower end of the braid had been circled up to form a noose, which twirled slowly in the evening sunlight, gleaming silver.

As the women muttered their prayers and signed the cross, I tried to guess whether they saw the handiwork of God or Satan in the hangman's rope. One dark-eyed girl wrapped her own braids around her neck, as if captured in the noose, and made gagging sounds. She received a sound slap on her head from her mother and a snicker from her brother.

To my left, some of the Greek men lounged along the rock wall that surrounded the playground. Cigarettes dangled from their mouths or smoldered between their fingers. They watched the flurry at the schoolhouse with black, opaque eyes. Speaking in their own language, they did not bother to lower their voices. Among them was Theo Sky.

Leaning back, he steadied himself against the wall, hands braced on the ledge on either side of him, as if daring me to approach. My feet ground to a halt, my arms loose, like a rag doll, and I saw it all. Who else could have pulled that hair from the fire? Who else would have been close enough, or bold enough, to reach into that blaze and lift away the braids, pocketing them as the others tore apart the classroom? Who else would have the courage to return in the dead of night to that cold, hollowed-out room?

Unwittingly, my lips formed the word, "You."

He tossed his cigarette to the ground, a smug smile on his lips. My heart felt light, almost giddy. Who else, I sang silently, oh, who else? Who else would have given Miss Holben what she so richly deserved? Who else would have stood up for Pearl, like some hero from a work by Scott?

At home, I unfolded the handkerchief that held the hair I'd cut from Pearl's head. I was half-afraid that the hair now hung from the beams of the schoolhouse, that somehow Theo Sky had stolen into my dreams and taken it from me. I smiled to think of him plaiting that delicate rope with his bear-like hands. Kissing the hair, I folded it away, hid it beneath the needles and thread in my sewing basket.

Later, we heard that when Miss Holben saw the silvery black noose, she walked to the train depot and left Berwind, not even taking time to pack her things. It would be more than two months before another teacher took her place. But the damage had been done. Theo Sky reported to the mine for his first day of work, along with the Pavlovski brothers.

And Pearl, whose hair would grow back thicker, longer and wilder, eloped with Russell Ruddy.

PART II

O hush thee, my babie, the time soon will come
When thy sleep shall be broken by trumpet and drum;
Then hush thee, my darling, take rest while you may,
For strife comes with manhood, and waking with day.
Sir Walter Scott

Chapter 8

    Oh, the days that followed! Empty and dark, with heavy clouds hanging over the canyon. The wind blew, and rain and sleet angled against the house. The temperature dropped, freezing the last prairie asters of summer. News came that the strike in Boulder had failed, sending the southern fields into hopelessness once more.

    Russell's mother, Ava, demanded that the mine superintendent send guards to bring Russell home. Jake gathered a posse and rode the train to Trinidad, where he spent three days in a bawdy house on West Main. I careened between so much anger and sadness that I doubted my heart would ever stop shedding tears. If only Pearl and I had had one more summer to spend up in the sand wash, playing at heroes and heroines. If only we had had another school year when she could learn, from another teacher, a teacher like Miss Rice.

    Alex said nothing. Nothing about the bed that was now empty in my room, or about the torn-up miner's boots Pearl had left just outside the door when she ran, or the books that now lay untouched. Scott, Burns—they were as dead to us as their authors. He said nothing about my cooking, or why the wash was not done, or the floor swept. Pearl's scent of cinnamon began to fade from the house, and I folded up the pillowcase she'd used and stuffed it into a canning jar to preserve it, but the jar smelled too strongly of dill.

    Rumors flew through Berwind. It was said that John D. Rockefeller himself paid for Mr. and Mrs. Ruddy's honeymoon. It was said that they had settled in New York, or London, or Denver. Wherever it was, Pearl sent no word—not a telegram or letter—to Alex or me to let us know that she was safe or well.

The newlyweds came back to Berwind long after winter had closed in, and miners had begun to cough and children to sniffle with the yearly sickness. Pearl wore a finely-made navy blue suit, and a lavish hat that covered the bald spot on her head, and Russell wore the elegant suit of a gentleman. Somehow, during his absence, he had secured a job in the company offices as an accountant doing the bookkeeping for the Number 5 mine. The Ruddy clan—Tom and Ava, Russell and Pearl, Jake, and the three younger boys—moved into a home with six rooms and a covered porch.

"Don't think you can visit her," Alex said. "She made her choice, she's got to live with it."

"You made your choice," I said. "*She* had nothing to do with it."

His jaw clenched. "She 's a company man's wife now. When I saw her, she was wearing a fur stole."

"You saw her?" I asked, outraged. "When?"

"She and Russell were coming off the train. They looked pretty high and mighty to me."

"Did you talk to her?" I demanded. "What did she say?"

"I didn't say a word to her," he said. "She's a Ruddy now."

I went to visit her early the next afternoon. When I knocked on the Ruddys' door, I set off a howling. On the shady side of the house was a wire-mesh pen filled with dogs. Noses poked through the wires, all teeth and drool. After a moment, Pearl answered the door. She wore a stylish skirt with a matching scarf on her head to hide her hair, and she smiled at me and threw her arms around me.

"I never seen nobody I wanted to see more," she whispered, as if she already knew I was forbidden to come. "I'm not supposed to answer the door. Miz Ruddy gets mad when somebody comes by asking about my hair."

I held her until the tears in my eyes dried. "Who comes by?"

"Oh, some of the women and their babies. They want me to touch the babies and cure their croup or ailments. They think I'm blessed, able to work miracles or something. She hates the knocking at the door. Says it drives her to palpitations."

"It's probably those dogs."

"Oh." She glanced toward the back, where the baying and growling still echoed. "They belong to Jake. He says they're for hunting, but he's more keen on fighting them against each other."

I shuddered, half-turning, reluctant to go inside.

"Come in! Come in!" She opened the door wide. "I'm so happy you're here."

The house was darker than a mine. Mrs. Ruddy had ordered Pearl to hang thick drapes over the windows because of her infirmities. I had seen Ava Ruddy only once or twice, but I remembered that she walked with a twist in her hips, as if something had been injured there. The pain seemed to have corkscrewed right up into her face, leaving deep, sour lines. Given the number of Lydia Pinkham's bottles set about the house, I figured she must spend her day drowning her sorrow with tonic.

But there was a true dining room, and a parlor, and kitchen in the house, all of which were painted and papered. I sat at the dining table, and Pearl brought me tea. "Oh, you are a godsend. I been so lonely."

"What about Russell?" I asked bitterly.

"He's at work most of the day."

"Why did you run off? What was the hurry?"

Pearl dipped one finger into her tea. "Russ told me it didn't matter if I had hair to my toes or no hair at all."

This seemed like the worst reason for marrying that I'd ever heard. "Well, if it didn't matter to Russell, maybe there's someone else out there who doesn't care."

"No," she said. "No. Who did that at the schoolhouse? You?"

"No," I said, then lied, "I don't know."

She laughed. "Well, I bet you laughed good and hard when that old teacher took off."

"No," I said. "I didn't, because you were gone, too."

She played with her teacup, not looking at me. "When that old biddy chopped my hair off, it was like she done something to me—"

"It will grow back—"

"Like she'd chopped out a piece of my brain or my heart or something. I think—it sounds stupid—but I think I was proud of myself for the first time ever, being in school like everybody else. For the first time in my life, I wasn't just some dumb, useless old thing. I thought I could be as good as you and Alex. And then that teacher had to go and make a war of it."

The sorrow of her voice quieted me. I waited, my heart aching at her loss.

She pushed back her chair, a wan smile on her lips. "Want to see where we sleep?"

Upstairs, she opened the door to a room that smelled of cinnamon, of her. A brass, three-quarter bed and a dresser were the only furniture, yet the bed was beautifully made, the quilt smoothed across it and the pillows plumped against the headboard. Pearl ran her hand over the footboard. "Ain't it nice?" she said. "Ain't it pretty?"

"How does Russell afford all this?"

"Oh, he makes good money as the bookkeeper, I guess," she said, as if it had never occurred to her. "And Tom and Jake and the boys bring home some wages, too."

I sat down on the bed, heartsick and envious.

"What's the matter with you, Christian?" Pearl sat beside me. "You act like you ain't happy for me at all."

Words fell from my mouth, wild, unstoppable. "Why didn't you stay with me? We would have been together forever. If only you'd—"

"Don't be silly," she said, but her words carried no strength. "Nobody stays forever." She walked to the dresser and picked up Russell's violin. Polishing its wood with a corner of her skirt, she asked, "What's Alex got to say about me and Russ?"

"Nothing. He won't talk about it."

Her eyes flashed. "You tell him for me, tell him, I come to Russ clean. I come to him same as I would any other man, and for Russ, that was good enough. You tell him I got a real last name now. I'm Pearl Ruddy, and nobody can take that from me. It's wrote on the certificate. Look." She reached into a drawer of the dresser and brought out the marriage license. "See here. Pearl Doe Ruddy. It's my name. In writing, on paper, so it's real. And I got a birthday now, too. They asked me for one, so I choosed the day I first come to you and Alex, the day I first went to school."

"You broke his heart! And mine!"

"Ssh! Miz Ruddy'll have a fit!" Pearl glanced toward the hallway. "Well, what about my heart? Alex ain't never thought a dark-skinned girl's got feelings."

"You didn't wait long enough. I could have made him—"

"No, you couldn't," she said. "Do you know what he said to me when he seen me without hair? He said, I'm so sorry, over and over again, like I was some dumb animal that got hit by a club. My bald head just proved to him that I was dark-skinned all over. I knew he wasn't never going to see me no different."

I doubled over, my arms wrapped around my waist. She sat on the bed beside me.

"What was I to do?" she asked. "I don't got no family. I don't got no money. School wasn't worth nothing for me. What was I to do?"

"I don't know," I blubbered. "I don't know!"

"Russ is the best man I know," she said. "And look at him, he ain't even a miner no more, but somebody important—"

"He's a company man."

She bridled. "Don't you and Alex ever think about nothing but what's bad or wrong? Can't you just be happy for once?"

I blinked back my tears. "It's just like when Dad died. Everything is all . . . gone."

She put her arms around me. "I'm right here," she said. "It ain't that different. But it will be when the first baby comes. I can't wait to have that little one right in my arms and to love it until it can't see nobody but me. That's all I want just now—a beautiful little baby girl to call me Mama."

She told me again that it would be all right, but I knew it wasn't.

Because no baby came.

I went back to school in the fall for my eighth grade year. The new teacher, Miss Wainwright, spelled Berwind "BERWEND," but at least she wasn't hateful. She took a different stance from either Miss Rice or Miss Holben about the dark faces at the back of the room. "You should all be proud of your heritage," she told them. "Those of you who are Slavic should speak and read that language and put aside the learning of English. Those of you who know Spanish should not take time to learn another language. You can speak with your own people as much as you want."

And so the unteachables were once again left in ignorance, but this time it was for their own good.

I received my diploma from Berwind School in the spring of 1912. Alex bought a cheap metal frame for it and tacked it up on the wall of our house, but when I looked at it, I could only think that it should have been his. What was I to do with an education—and such a poor one at that? Ethel May Farrington was the only girl from our class to go on to high school in Trinidad.

The days passed, one after another, all alike, and I started doing what women who were looking for husbands did. Ice cream socials, and picnics, and Sunday baseball games. I went to the dances at the Meeting Hall on Saturday nights, walking over with Katy McCormick and standing in the corner watching the lucky girls sashay right into courtship.

One night, I saw Pearl and Russell dancing close during the slow, lovely ballads played by the Italians with accordion and violin. Russell held one of Pearl's hands tight in his, pressing it against his shoulder. They went round and round the dance floor, following a path that seemed traced only for them.

I felt a terrible envy. Were they really so happy that they did not notice the glares and whispers that followed them? I remembered how Russell had watched Pearl dance in our house, how he had followed her with his eyes, unable to let go. I thought of the spotlessly clean bedroom in the Ruddys' dank house and folded my arms across my breasts, my chest tight and sore.

Alex ignored them, watching instead a gang of Greeks who had collected around a table in one corner. I was aware of them, too. Almost two years had passed since I had last seen Theo Sky outside the schoolhouse, and he had grown again. This time, his height had caught up to the broadness of his shoulders, so that he stood tall and straight. I couldn't imagine him in the darkness of the mines, where a man had to crawl on his knees and pick coal while lying on his back against the damp floor.

He sat at the table, arm wrestling, his shirtsleeves rolled above his elbows. More than one man twice his size challenged him, only to lose to him. After every match, he shook hands with his opponent in American fashion, his face shining with the sweat and thrill of so many challenges.

Alex and his friends inched closer, watching with steely faces, their bodies rigid and tense. And soon, even Russell and Pearl found their way through the crowd to Theo Sky's table, Jake and the Ruddy boys following. They had watched Theo Sky wrestle two or three, and had turned away to leave, when Uncle John said, "Russell, try your chances with the Greek."

Russell shook his head, but Uncle John crooned, "Come on, Russell, a stout lad such as yourself, with a wife and all." He nodded his head at Pearl. "Mrs. Ruddy."

"Come on, Russell," Rory joined in. "The Greek'll play fair, won't you, Greek? He won't take your mining arm from you, just in case you need it again. You'll always be the company's star."

The remark caused a twitter of laughter through the crowd. Even Theo Sky smiled. Pearl spoke. "Let him alone."

"Excuse me, Mrs. Ruddy," Rory mocked.

"Come on, Russ," Pearl said. "Let's go." And Russell followed her, meek as a trained lamb. Once they'd passed through the crowd, the laughter burst forth—men poking fun at Russell's muteness, at his thin body, at his henpecking, dago wife.

I started to follow, angry with them all. Why, oh, why had Pearl married someone as weak as Russell? And why couldn't everyone else let them be?

But it wasn't over.

"I'll take on the god-damned Greek." It was Jake. "Let me through."

The laughter ended. The Greeks murmured, shuffled, moved closer to Theo Sky, but he held up his hands to quiet them, then placed his elbow on the table, his right palm extended. Jake clasped the hand. At the signal, their muscles tensed, and they struggled against one another. I could see Theo Sky strain against Jake's power, the veins in his neck and forehead raised and popping out. Jake seemed not to sweat at all, but neither could he bring Theo Sky's arm to the table. Rory and Uncle John rooted for Theo Sky, forgetting their hatred of the Greeks in their ill will against the Ruddys. "Don't let him take you, Greek," Uncle John said. "Keep it steady."

As I watched, a strange excitement filled my heart. I wanted to see Theo Sky's dark arm lying atop Jake's at the end of the battle, his hand squeezing the blood from Jake's fingers. I wanted to see him crush Jake's hand in his own. Maybe it wasn't a girl's place—many of the others had gone back to dancing or had been removed by their parents—but I wanted to see the very end, the moment when the pain crossed Jake's face, and the cost of the victory washed over Theo Sky's.

It came suddenly, when Theo Sky flattened Jake's arm with a crash that echoed through the room. The Greeks jumped and shouted, and Jake stood and pocketed his sore hand. Theo Sky held out his hand—the one that had just defeated Jake—to shake, but Jake balked.

"Hey!" One of the Greek men called after him. "What is this? No shake hands?"

"I won't shake hands with a filthy Greek."

The Greek whipped around the table so quickly that a chair clattered to the floor.

"Take it easy, Greek," Jake said. "I paid you."

"Was fair fight, you shake hands," the Greek protested.

"That damned dago had grease on his palm," Jake said. "I can smell the damned lard on him."

The Greeks rumbled, ready to fight, but Theo Sky held up both hands. "Look," he said. "My hands are clean. I wash after I eat."

Laughter spread through the spectators. Jake spat and walked through the crowd and out the door, leaving the Meeting Hall. The Greek flashed one last resentful look in his direction before calling, "Next. Who is next?"

"No," Theo Sky said. "No, not tonight. Next dance."

With a sweep of his arm, he parted the crowd and pushed through, following Jake's path out the door of the Meeting Hall. And I found myself carried outside, too. Stepping into the night and the cold, I stopped in the hazy light from the light above the door. A goodly number of men had gathered, warming themselves around fires in old barrels. Beyond, the slag heap smoldered, leaving a wet, rotten smell in the air. The smoke hung thick, and it took me a long time to spot Theo Sky. He stood alone at a fire pit, holding his right arm in his left.

"Theo Sky," I said.

He started, surprised. "Miss Christian, why are you here? Where is your brother?"

"Are you all right?" I asked. "Did Jake hurt you?"

"Never!" He laughed. "He is weak. Stupid, too. But why are you here? It's bad for you to be here. Too many men, too much drinking—"

"I wanted to know if you were—"

"So you are finished with school?" he asked.

"I graduated this past spring."

"So now you are smarter than before."

A woman squealed near us, startling me. I watched as she grabbed the coat of a man leaving the dance. "Don't go," she cried. "You can't leave me." She dragged her feet, begging the man to stay with her. He kept walking, towing her down the slope toward the bridge. They tumbled down the slick slope, the man cursing, the woman shrieking, then both of them laughing at their antic.

I could not bring myself to look up into Theo Sky's light, wondering eyes. Instead, I looked into the flames.

"So, you are married now?" he asked.

"No," I said flatly.

"Why not? There is one thousand men in Berwind. It's not hard to find a husband."

I said nothing, humiliated by how I must appear—homely and small and unlovable.

"You will marry one of your brother's friends, I bet. *Analatos.*"

"What's that?" I asked.

He laughed, but cut it short. Two dark shadows approached us, the faces under their brimmed hats coming into view only when they stepped up close to the fire. Theo Sky shifted so that he stood in front of me, casting a shadow over me. Peering around him, I saw two mine guards. My hands began to shake, my head to reel.

"Hey, Greek," one said. "You took ol' Jake down pretty good. You work that hard in the mine, it might get you somewhere."

Theo Sky said nothing, standing with his weight on one foot, his shoulders straining upright, as if trying to make himself bigger, to cast a wider shadow.

The other guard picked up the banter. "Maybe you'd make enough so you Greeks don't have to raise goats no more."

"Ah, but then, who'd he take to bed with him? You snuggle real close and tight"—he chirped the word to make it sound like a thrust—"with 'em, don't you, Greek?"

He did not waver. In the darkness beyond us, shadows crept closer. I glanced behind me, afraid that more guards were sneaking up on us, surrounding us. My movement caught the attention of one of the two at the fire.

"Hey, look, he ain't so pitiful after all. He's got a girlfriend."

The other guard stepped around the fire to look at me. "Where are you supposed to be, princess?" he asked. "Not out here with no Greek. From the looks of you, I bet you're supposed to be teaching your little brother the two-step so's he can dance it at Sunday school tomorrow morning. What's your name?"

"Don't tell him," Theo Sky rumbled, his words barely audible.

I said nothing, afraid my knees would buckle, my body collapse.

A man emerged from the shadows, another Greek. In silence, he offered a cigarette to Theo Sky and lit it for him. Murmuring something, he blew smoke into the freezing air.

"There they go again, talking their gibberish," a mine guard said. "It's time somebody learned them how to talk right."

Theo Sky flicked his cigarette into the fire and took my arm. Clenching it in a painful, iron grip, he turned me around and began walking me toward the meeting hall.

"Don't," I protested. "It hurts."

He only grasped tighter. "A girl shouldn't be out here, in the dark," he hissed. "Why do you do such stupid thing?"

"You're hurting me."

"I won't hurt you, but they will. You are stupid to think they won't."

"Don't do anything," I pleaded. "They're just looking for a fight."

"So what?" he said, jerking his chin upward. "I am not *analatos*."

We came to the door of the hall. Tipping his hat to me, he swung angrily down the hill. My feet moved forward a few steps, but I hadn't the nerve to follow him into that darkness that swallowed him up so quickly, that night where mine guards roamed and hunted.

Analatos. I understood now. Coward.

I ran inside, to where Alex stood in a dark corner nipping at his flask. Mary Thomas had already started to sing in her pretty opera voice, "O Sole Mio," a tune the Italians would want to hear again and again until the evening ended.

Chapter 9

In the fall, I turned sixteen.

"What are you plannin', Christian?" Mrs. McCormick asked. "To take care of Alex forever? It's not natural, you know. A girl your age needs a husband. Look at my Mary—that girl has married a saint in young James O'Keegan, long life to him. There's plenty of men in the mines lookin' for a woman who can keep a house clean and cook a decent meal."

"And who's frisky enough to keep 'im 'ome on Saturday nights," Jane said. "If you catch my meanin'. And for some women, that's all they want as well."

"Jane McKenna!" Mrs. McCormick scolded. "You'll be poisonin' this innocent child's mind with your wickedness!"

"Oh, and who's poisonin' her 'ead by callin' men saints? Take it from me, love, ya don't want a saint, ya want one with some muscle and skin to 'im."

"Oh, Mary's young James is that, too. How do you think she got in the family way so soon after their weddin'?"

They laughed, delighted even more when I blushed like the girl-child I was.

Rory teased me as well. "When you gonna put some meat on your bones, Red? You're not gonna catch a husband lookin' like an old stick-pole. Better feed her up good, Alex, or you'll be stuck with her forever."

Alex only chuckled, but I knew he had tired of me as well. I could have told him that, although I didn't know what I wanted, I was sure of what I didn't want. A man whose mind was as dull as the utter darkness in which he spent his days, a man who could talk of nothing but cards and fights, whose time at liberty was given to mind-numbing drink. That's what I saw in Berwind—men as dead as the machines that mastered them during the day.

On Friday nights, when Alex invited friends over to play poker, the men seemed unable to see me. As I sat in the corner, sewing or darning, they told loud and boisterous stories, careless of their speech. Yet one night, I realized they were speaking in low, steady rhythms like the murmur of the engines at the mine, and I started to listen.

"So what's the union gonna do different this time?" Rory whispered. Born in Georgia, he claimed the darkies on the plantations had had it easier than the men in the Colorado mines. "Knock at the door and say, can I come in? These camps is all closed down here in the south, worse'n in the north."

"'Tis a dollar to join," Uncle John said, taking a card dealt to him.

"But who's to say they ain't gonna take that dollar and hightail it out of town?" Rory asked. "Look at the company—always collecting for doctor's fees and buryin' costs. And do you think you can find anybody who knows a lick about it when you need one or the other?"

James spoke. "This isn't the Western Federation of Miners. It's the United Mine Workers of America. It's a powerful lot, it's helped miners in West Virginia and Pennsylvania—"

"Aye, but I bet they've never seen it as bad as it is in Colorado!" Uncle John raged in a throaty brogue. "In '04, they shot them dead in the streets up in the northern camps. Or they beat them to within an inch of their lives and took them by train to the Kansas border and left them just beyond. No food, no water, only the beatin' sun on their backs!"

"They gun down strikers like dogs in them other places, too," Rory said. "Got the Baldwin-Felts cuttin' notches in their belts for every striker they kill."

"What's Baldwin-Felts?" Uncle John asked.

"Nothing more than killers," Rory said. "It's a private police force they brung in to them other states to protect company property and make the scabs behave. That's what they done in every strike that ever happened. Bring in more immigrants and give 'em a shovel and say, Mighty glad you came, now go bust your dago heads in the mines, and those of you that live can strike next time. Bastard Greeks came in as strikebreakers, every last one of 'em, and now look—you can't find a mine that don't have a gang of 'em working there."

"The union's taken a bold step, they have," Uncle John said. "Settin' up shop right there on Main Street in Trinidad and passin' out membership cards."

"That's not all," James whispered. "Sure, the UMWA's passing out cards to miners at liberty, but that's just to keep the company guards watching that street in Trinidad. There are union men right here in the mines. Aye, right here among us, in Berwind and all the camps. Here's the game—they turn in the names of company men to the mine guards, saying they've joined. So the company sends their own down the canyon. It's a great scam."

"Is that so?" Uncle John said. "Maybe they'll chuck the Ruddy boys out of Berwind."

"Nobody'd be dumb enough to believe they'd turn against the company." Rory chuckled. "They'd lick Rockefeller's boots clean if he was to come here. I can just hear them now. More tea, sir? Want a turn with Russell's wife? That is, once Jake's finished with her."

The men laughed. I glanced toward Alex, but he kept his head down, his face hidden from view. Futilely, I tried to train my attention on my handiwork, but my hands shook and my eyes watered.

"Aye, you did well to wash your hands of that one, Alex," Uncle John said. "Every man in Berwind panting after her, and she doesn't have enough sense but to choose a half-man."

"Ah, what are you sots playing at? Women and stupid tricks." James gestured impatiently. "I'm joining the union. What about you? Are you going to pay your dollars and claim your rights as men?"

"Who're the union men in Berwind, James?" Rory asked. "You?"

James looked hard at his hand, shuffling two cards. "No."

"Who then?"

No one spoke, eyes averted, fingers clenched tight on their cards, mouths set. Alex took a sip from his flask.

James finally answered. "Has to be somebody who speaks English. All the UMWA men in Trinidad do. Lawson, Doyle, Fyler, McLennan—they're American or Irish or Scot."

"So, are they giving out union cards only to white men?" Rory hoped.

"To whoever pays a dollar," James said grimly. "Come on, Alex, are you joining?"

Alex leaned back, shook his head. "Not yet anyway."

"Better not be so hasty, lads," Uncle John warned. "There's plenty of mine guards can sniff out a man's intent to join. Keep it quiet or you'll be sent down the canyon, too, dollar or no."

I thought about what a dollar could buy—meat, new shoes, a length of calico for a skirt, a sack of flour to replace the one that I'd found bugs in last week, all of those things and more. But while I was busy tallying up what we couldn't afford, the conversation moved on.

"The Greek's fighting tonight," Rory said. "He's taking on a Starkville guard over at the machine shop. Are you coming, Alex?"

"The Greek again?" Alex asked.

The thread in my needle knotted in a botched stitch.

"Which Greek?" I asked.

My question caused an uncomfortable silence among the men.

They had forgotten about me, still as I was in the corner. Rory chuckled at my interest, while James looked at me with surly eyes. I could tell he regretted his words about joining the union.

I didn't care. "What's the name of the Greek?"

"Why'd you want to know that?" Alex asked.

"I want to go."

The men chortled, but Alex turned cold, seething eyes toward me. "Women don't go to the fights, Christian," he said. "Where'd you get such an idea? The sport's for men." He turned back to his friends. "Do you have money on him?"

"The Greek?" Rory said. "I do. But they say the Starkville man is twice his size."

"They say that about all the guards, but they're dumb as oxen, and the Greek's wily," Uncle John said. "It sounds like a good evening's fun."

Alex did not glance at me again before he left, and I knew I'd humiliated him. As I finished my chores around the house, my heart smoldered. Women claimed such small space in this canyon. We lived out our lives on paths beaten between the company store and our stoves, the washboard at the creek and the community clotheslines, the weekly dances and our marriage beds. Stewing myself into idleness, I stared at Alex's swaybacked cot and at the trunk where his clothing lay folded—by me—in neat piles.

Furtively, I opened the trunk and straightened the clothes. I knew well which shirts fit my brother snugly and which trousers had been hemmed so often that they had grown too short. It was only a matter of choosing the smallest of the garments. Winding my hair into a ball, I shoved a tweed cap on my head and darkened my hairline with a touch of bacon grease. At last, I donned a dusty coat of Alex's that hid the daintiness of my body.

Then I struck out down the hill, over the bridge and into the man's world of Berwind.

A long line of men sauntered toward the machine shop. I fell in among them, trying to keep my arms loose and swinging at my sides, my face half-hidden in the collar of Alex's coat. At the door, a Greek younger than Theo Sky collected a quarter from me. Behind me, men crammed into the shed, pressing forward in droves, until there was hardly room to shuffle. Cloaked in the heavy coat, my skin grew damp and my face felt smothered by the collar. Cigarette smoke clouded the light from a single bare electric bulb that swung low in the center of the long, narrow shed. I could see nothing of Alex and his friends or of Theo Sky, but Alex had not exaggerated when he said that women shunned the fights. Not a single female stood among the eager, jostling crowd.

Elbowed aside, I took refuge beside a small, ratty table set up against the back wall of the shed. Around it, men shouldered and bumped one another out of the way. Waving their money, they loudly placed bets and swore at a hapless Greek, who was painfully slow to understand their words. The men insulted him freely, but he only nodded at them and took their money, undaunted.

"You place bet?"

Another Greek stood before me, his hands outstretched, his words sharp and impatient.

I shook my head.

"You place bet now, when is no fight. Fight start, no bet."

Again, I shook my head.

"No bet, then get out. Go!" He shooed me from my refuge near the table.

A loud rumble filled the shed, and I guessed that the contenders had come to the ring. Dimly, I heard a voice calling out, announcing the contestants. Moments later, a bell dinged, and the shed filled with a sound as thunderous as an oncoming locomotive, the shouts and catcalls of the wild crowd. I stood on tiptoe to see the action, but a hundred heads blocked my view. I would never know what was happening.

The crowd pressed forward again, even though it seemed every bit of air had been sucked from the shed by so many packed bodies. My feet nearly lifted from the ground, I was carried along, as the men began to swirl around like the hands of a clock, searching for a glimpse of the fight. Breaking free at last, I ducked beneath elbows and wedged myself between bodies until I was able to see the makeshift ring through a gap between shoulders.

Inside the ropes, Theo Sky was taking a beating. The Starkville mine guard, more massive than Jake, was pummeling Theo Sky's head. Crouched down against the fury of the blows, Theo Sky shielded his head with hands clad in worn boxing gloves. Regaining his footing at last, he jabbed at the guard, and I caught my first look at his face. Blood from his torn, pulpy lips dripped down his chin and spattered his bare chest. One eye was already swelling purplish. The Starkville man swung again and found his jaw. Theo Sky's head snapped backward like a ball on a string. A whip of blood flew from his nose to fall across the straw.

My stomach turned, and a hot darkness seared my head. I turned to run, but fell against the wall of men behind me. Cursing, a man shoved me aside. His face shone with sweat and excitement, as did the faces behind him. Pushing and scrambling, I clawed my way through the crush of bodies and out the door into the cool night air.

As many men were outside the shop as had been inside. They loitered in groups, peering hopelessly through the grimy windows of the shed. "What's happening?" someone yelled at me. "Who's winning?"

Staggering past him, I grabbed for the walls of the shop at the same time that my stomach parted with the evening's meal. Bent over double, I retched into the dirt at my feet.

"What's wrong, kid?" another man taunted. "Can't take the fights?"

I wiped my mouth on my sleeve, but immediately vomited again.

A chorus of laughter followed. "Maybe you oughta stay home on fight nights," another man called. "At least until you're old enough to grow a beard."

"Here." A third man wrapped his arm around me and held something to my lips. I smelled whiskey and felt the burn of it on my lips. With disgust, I spat it aside.

"Christ!" he exclaimed. "Spoil a good flask, will you!"

"Where you from, kid?" the first man asked. "How come you're such a sissy boy?"

I cowered against the wall, aware that if I spoke, they'd know what I was.

"Hey!" someone yelled from the doorway of the machine shop. "The Greek's done a turn-around! He's beating the bejesus out of Wells!"

"You don't say!" The men lost interest in me, pulled as if by a magnet back to the door of the shop.

Clutching my stomach, I lurched away, Alex's trousers and coat ballooning around me as I ran down the slope to the creek. Splashing through the water, I barreled along the well-worn path toward the houses in Berwind. Twice, I checked to see that I wasn't followed.

At home, I scrubbed the vomit from Alex's coat and hung it on a peg, then replaced his trousers and shirt, glad to rid myself of the disguise. My body ached, and my stomach felt as queasy as it had inside the machine shop. After washing the filth from my hands and face, I sought the solace of my bed. Yet every time I closed my eyes, I saw Theo Sky's head snap backward, as if the muscles in his neck were nothing but putty. Why would he do such a thing to himself?

Early in the morning, I heard Alex's voice, slurred and bold. "It calls for a celebration!"

"That it does! The Greek took a beatin', though. You wonder how the lad stands it."

"Ah, his brains are pro'bly nothin' but jelly. It's a blessin' he don't need them. Here's to the Greek!"

"To the Greek!"

I covered my ears with my hands and closed my eyes. Daylight could not arrive soon enough.

Chapter 10

After Alex left for work the next morning, I boiled enough precious water from the barrel to fix myself a bath, then dressed in my best blouse and skirt. A felt hat on my head, I slipped from our house and walked to where, so long ago, Pearl and I had followed Theo Sky along the main street of Bricktown to the small canyon beyond.

It was a long, harrowing trip. With every step, I felt faint, dizzy, as if I was an old woman, followed by the urge to bolt, which electrified me as if I was a hunted rabbit. Twice, I turned back and started for home. Twice, I changed my mind, the vision of Theo Sky's battered body haunting me.

When I finally arrived at the Greeks' shack, my lungs felt too tight to draw a decent breath. Yet, when I tried to listen for movement inside, the sound of my breathing deafened me. What was I doing here? What if Theo Sky wasn't here, and I blundered onto a group of men whose faces and eyes were so dark and—?

I knocked on the door. "Theo Sky?" I called, so breathy that someone standing next to me would not hear. "Hello?"

No one answered. Pushing open the door, I went inside. The room was cool, and it smelled of tobacco and candle wax. I could see almost nothing but shadows, and I dared not move until my eyes adjusted to the dim light.

The room held only three cots, but a pile of bedrolls, and I knew the Greeks slept in shifts, just as they worked the mine in shifts. No one was there. I wondered where the sleepers were, and the possibilities sent me stumbling frantically toward the door. Leaning against it, as afraid to open it again as I was to be inside the shack, I tried to still the whir of my brain.

Outside, I found my way past the pen built of saplings where the brown goats bleated plaintively at me. From the back of the hovel, I heard the scratching and clucking of chickens. And there, sitting on a wooden bench in the sun, was Theo Sky. The blows from the mine guard were clearly etched across his skin—on his arms, his bare chest, his face. His nose was badly gashed on the right side.

The dry piñon snapped beneath my feet, and the chickens chased after the sound, hoping for a grasshopper or snake or lizard.

Theo Sky jerked forward, hunched in pain. "Miss Christian! What are you doing here?"

I had no answer. In the half-dreams of my restless night, I had not planned what I might say to him. The chickens cackled.

Alarmed at my silence, he pushed himself upward into a half-crouch. "Why are you here? Who is with you? You bring guards?" He glanced toward the corner of the shack and called, "Who is there? They have come to take me?"

I shook my head, his fear shaking my tongue loose. "I'm alone."

"Where is your brother?" He struggled to rise. "You bring your brother? His friends? What?"

"No, no, just me."

The tension in his body did not lessen. "Why?"

"I heard about the fight," I said. "I came to help you."

"Why do you do this?" he demanded.

"I wanted to help you."

"For what?"

"Because I knew you were hurt—"

I stopped before I said more. From my basket, I took some herbs that Pearl had taught me to use. "Let me make you tea. It's from the chamomile. It'll—"

"No drink."

"Have you eaten?"

He shook his head.

"Where are the others who live here?"

He shrugged. "Gone."

"When will they come back?"

He made no reply. I had to hurry, I knew, I had to do this and go. I thought of the Greek who had shooed me from the betting table the night before. I did not want to incur his displeasure again. "Let me wash your cuts for you."

He said nothing, so I knelt in front of him and took from my basket the rags I'd soaked in boiling water and iodine just before I came. But as I lifted the rag, my nerve failed. I could not bring myself to touch his face. The heat of the sun had warmed the skin of his chest, releasing a rough, hot smell like pine in summer. I shifted again, creeping closer, still on my knees. Then, my hands cold and stiff, I clapped the first compress on his chin. He winced.

My mouth worked under its own power. "Why do you fight? Are

you trying to get money to go home? Or so you can move on to another place?" I knew I should not be pestering him this way, but I couldn't stop myself. "This is so stupid!"

At that, he came alive and grabbed my wrist so tightly that a pain shot to my elbow. "Let go!" I cried, but he pulled me closer and trapped me between his thighs. I could not rise from my knees. "Let me go!"

"You came to help me," he said. "Then help me. Don't talk!"

Furious, I squirmed, but I could not budge his powerful legs. I reached up to push him away, but could not bring myself to touch his bare flesh. What had made me think I would be any safer with him than I'd been last night outside the machine shop?

"I shouldn't have come!" I gasped. "I'm shouldn't be here—!"

He softened. "Don't be scared."

"Let me go! Don't touch me!"

The muscles of his legs loosened. I caught my breath, blinked away my tears. My arms and legs were paralyzed. I couldn't bring myself to touch him, but neither could I run. My face felt stiff, stretched in a silent cry of fear.

"Go on," he urged. "My face still hurts."

I pulled a fresh rag from my basket and wiped awkwardly at the cut on his nose. He shut his eyes against the sting of the iodine. Pouring more on the cloth, I dabbed at his lip.

"You trust me?" he asked after I'd finished.

"I don't know," I whispered.

"You must. You come here alone. You don't know what you will find. Maybe Greeks will sell you to the mine guards, yes? Maybe they will take you up in the hills and leave you to die after they have finished with you? That is what your brother tells you. But you trust me good enough to come?"

"I wanted to help."

"I know this."

"I didn't think of anything else—"

"You didn't? Then you are not as smart as I think. There are men—Greeks, too—who would hurt you even in day time."

My entire body quailed, and I slipped off my knees. Sitting flat on the ground, I drew them up in front of me. His knees, still on either side of me, closed against me, but this time, they did not squeeze. They only steadied me, pocketed me. "Why do you fight?" I asked again.

"We make good money."

"It's not worth it! You could die doing this. That guard was so much bigger than you, so much stronger! The way he hit you—"

"What?" He pulled away from me, alarmed again. "You know this Wells fellow? You are his friend?"

I bit at my lips, so angry with myself, so frightened now that I'd let my secret slip. What must he—must anyone—think of someone who had acted as I had? Finally, I mumbled, "I was there. I dressed up in Alex's work clothes and went, and I saw—I was only there for a few minutes—but I saw him hit your nose, and it bled, and I was so sick—"

He stared at me as if unable to fathom my words. "You went to the fights? But you are a girl."

"No one knew. My brother's clothes—"

The look of bewilderment on his face dissolved. He laughed, then wrapped his arms around his ribs to stifle the pain. "You dressed as a man?"

"Yes."

"You! So tiny! So skinny and short! No one can think you are a man!"

He laughed again, unable to restrain himself. Finally, the pain in his ribs drove him to chuff breathlessly. "A girl who thinks she is a man! Think of that!"

I wanted to hide my face in shame. "Is it always like this?" I asked. "Are you always hurt this much?"

"No. Last night was worse night of all. This Wells was too fast, I too slow. But you came to see me? How did you know it was me fighting?"

"My brother's friends called you the Greek, and I guessed—"

"So you did not know. But you still went to see fighting? Even though it might be ugly, old Greek with one eye and ears like pancake and no teeth and—"

"Stop!" I couldn't help but laugh.

"So, you dressed up as your brother and sneaked out? Just like today, you sneak away on your brother?"

I didn't want to answer. I brought up my hands, but there was nowhere to lay them but on his thighs. Quickly, I dropped them. "How can you do this? You might die!"

He shrugged. "So what? I might die in the mine some day. Gas blows up, walls cave in, timber falls, water floods—who knows?"

"Why couldn't you just arm wrestle? You gathered a whole crowd around you at the dance. Remember? The night you wrestled Jake?"

"Arm wrestle!" he scoffed. "Men watch arm wrestle for a minute, no more. No, everybody wants to see blood, beatings. They watch from start to end and they place big bets on it. Did you bet on me?"

"Of course not," I said primly.

"Why not? Did you think I would lose? That I am not strong enough? Fast enough?"

"No, I didn't think—" I considered. "But you won, didn't you? Alex said so—"

"Did your brother bet on me?"

"I think so." I tried to remember the conversation between Alex and Rory.

"Then he is smarter than I think."

I ignored the jab. "So it's all about the money? What will you use it for? To go back to Greece?"

He judged me shrewdly. "Why do you come here? Why do you care so much? *Americanidha* don't talk to Greek."

"American what?"

"American girl. Why do you talk to me? Why don't you marry?"

I felt my neck burning, and I knew my face was scarlet. My upper lip tingled, as it had when he'd stared at me in school. "No one's asked," I admitted.

"Why not? Your skin is the color of eggshell. It is pretty."

He took my hand and admired it—my jagged fingernails and my swollen, chapped knuckles. Every inch of my arm to my shoulder felt hot, as if I'd stuck it into a fire. The warmth cascaded through my breasts and down, down to my legs.

"In Greece," he said. "A girl's father chooses the man for her to marry. She don't have to wait to be asked. She don't even meet him until her wedding day. Will your brother do that?"

"I'll marry who I want," I declared.

"So you will catch a husband like American girls do?"

"How's that?"

"So, here is how. Man walks you through the evening, all clean and smelling of flowers and smiling nice, talking pretty words, holding hands, going dancing—tra-la-la—all sweet and safe, then kissing you only on lips, and you slap his face and run to your father, and he gets his gun and says, you will marry her now—"

"I won't do it that way!"

"No? So how do you catch a husband?"

"I'll, I'll—" I stammered into silence. Desperate to say at least something—anything—I blurted, "Maybe I'll ask him to marry me."

He laughed with delight. "So you will kiss him, and he will slap your face. Then he brings his mama to make you marry him, right?"

My nerve failed. This time, I did not even try to reply, but simply let him laugh at me.

He turned my palm upright, tracing the lines across it with his finger. "American girls are so different from Greek. Greek girls stay with her mother, don't speak to boys, don't even look at a man unless she is married to him. American girls play with a man like he is a puppy. They dress like a man and go to fights."

I didn't know if I wanted Theo Sky to think of me as a carefree, sassy American girl—I wasn't about to tell him of my Scottish birth—or as a proper, marriageable young woman, but I knew I could not bear to attend another fight. "I won't do that again."

"Good," he said. "No more trousers. I like you as a girl."

With a sly smile, he raised his hands and closed my face in them. I pulled away, but now he had my chin clasped as tightly in his palms as he had my shoulders between his knees. Urging me forward, he kissed me on the mouth. Without allowing me to catch my breath, he kissed me again.

He leaned back. His lip had cracked open, and a tick of blood pooled on his lip. "You have never been kissed before?"

My face flamed—my lips, my eyes, my cheeks, every inch of my body—so fiercely that I could barely utter, "No."

"Good," he said happily. "So you are going to slap my face now? It won't hurt nothing. It is already broke. You will bring your brother back with his gun? He will see it is Greek who kisses you and shoot me dead. Then you won't catch a husband after all."

I could not laugh, although I knew he wanted it. Instead, I shook my head, swallowing at the twitch at the back of my throat that made me want to cry and sing all at once. My eyes burned, without tears, my lips burned, parched. It was as if I was suddenly someone else—not Kirstie, not even Christian. The American girl of his imagination, maybe, someone new, remade, or just released.

"American girls are not afraid of nothing," he said. "I like this."

I thought he might kiss me again, but he only looked at me with those light eyes that had so bedeviled me in the classroom. The heat of his skin, the smell of the witch hazel and medicines, the sun—all of it made me dizzy, frightened, thrilled. All at once, I sensed he knew what I was thinking.

"I would kiss you again," he said. "But my mouth hurts too much." He smoothed his finger over my lips. "You would like that, I think?"

A slow, steady flush of warmth ran through my entire body. My head bobbled, whether in agreement or refusal, I did not know. I had no control over it. His knees slowly gripped, tightening to trap me again.

"Answer me," he said. "You would like that?"

Every possible feeling raged through my mind—I wanted to run, to be far away, I wished I had never come, I wanted to laugh, I was afraid to open my mouth, for I knew some stupid answer would come from it. And then, without any thought at all, I lifted up on my knees and kissed him, aiming for the part of his lips that wasn't split or bruised, and landing mostly on his cheek. It was a cockeyed peck, nothing sweet about it at all.

He looked at me as if he were too stunned to speak, and then he laughed hard enough that he doubled over, clutching his stomach. "You scare me," he said. "No, not scare. You make me think, Oh, how does this happen?—"

"Surprise," I said. "I surprised you."

"Yes, surprise. I like this. But the others will be back soon. You must go."

"I know." Suddenly shy, I busied myself with gathering up my ointments and bandages. "You'll need to wash your cuts with iodine—"

"But you will come back, Miss Christian?"

"Are you planning to fight again?"

"Well, why not? Because if I do, you will come back, yes?"

I did not answer—if I said yes, wasn't I sending him back into that makeshift boxing ring? If I said no, it started the argument all over again, and I would be telling a lie, anyway. But before I left, I mustered the courage to reach out and touch his bare shoulder with the very tips of my fingers.

Chapter 11

Nothing looked the same. As I clattered my way around the kitchen, or scrubbed clothes against the washboard, or pumped water at the community sink, I saw only the squalor of it all, my life wasted in drudgery, my mind deadened by patching together new skirts from old, or measuring how much flour I needed, or judging whether Alex's socks would last another winter. I fidgeted with the sewing and the cleaning, making stitches so sloppy that they had to be plucked out, and sweeping the floor again and again, never catching all the dust.

My jaundiced eye fell on Alex as well. What had happened to the boy who drew knights on fine chargers and yelped with joy when Scott's heroes banished the villains? Where was the brother who had taught me about snakes and crickets and spiders during long walks on the mesa?

Mostly, I studied myself. Ponderously, appraisingly, for hours. Looking in the hand mirror, marred by black where the silver had worn away, I ran a finger over my lips, reliving all the sensations Theo Sky's touch had aroused in me. Oh, how could I not look different, be different, even sound different, given my newfound knowledge of his mouth on mine, of the touch of his hands against my face, of the strength of his thighs and arms?

One day, in a stroke of boldness, I asked Pearl about it. We were walking toward the sand wash. Pearl seemed tired. Her cheeks had lost their dark rosiness, and her nose was rough and reddened. Her hair looked dull in the sunlight. She pushed it back with hands so chapped that the skin had cracked in a latticework of tiny cuts.

"Are you happy, Pearl?" I asked. "You don't look it. Mrs. Ruddy is working you too hard."

"I ain't so bad. Russ is doing good at the counting office." She looked away, toward the horizon, where a storm was brewing. "All we need now's a baby. Then we'd be happy enough."

I walked ahead of her, pausing to admire a cholla, which had burst into blooms as delicate as hearts. "What's it like? Being with a man?"

"What do you mean?"

At once, I wished I hadn't spoken. I wished I were at the O'Keegans' house listening to the women prattle on about Mary's babies, or at home, gutting a rabbit or scrubbing the slop jars, or one of the other jobs I hated. But I'd gone so far, and I couldn't turn back. "What's it like to be with a man?"

"You got a man, then?" she asked, and I saw for a moment the Pearl who relished Sir Walter Scott's romances. "It's time, you know."

I picked at the berries of a juniper growing nearby, tearing them from the twigs. I wanted to tell her, yes, I've been kissed, yes, I've touched his skin, yes, he is beautiful and strong and . . . "No," I said. "There's no man. I'm just curious."

"No man?"

"No."

"You shouldn't of asked me, then."

"Why not?"

"Oh, God, Christian," she cried, "I ain't had nobody to tell about this and it's ripping my soul in pieces! Russell, he sometimes comes home all swollen, but he can't, or he won't. He don't want me." She brought her hands up to her face. "Maybe he's just like Alex. All he can see is the dago, and nothing pleasing or fine."

"That's not so. He married you."

"Every month, the blood just dries up in me and flows away, and I think, no baby, no baby again! I want a baby so bad, Christian. I want one to love and to love me." She wrapped her arms around her chest. "They laugh at me in the store. They point at me like I got a boil or a goiter because I ain't got no baby yet."

"Have you talked to Russell—?"

"Oh, he tries! He tries so hard—and I done everything I can. But he don't want me! The only one who wants me is Jake. He says to me, he says, You two need some help? Need me to show you how to make me a nephew? Sometimes I get so mad!"

I said nothing, afraid to move, to breathe, to ask. My mind felt sticky, slow, but I could imagine the Ruddy house—the men lazing around the table, Mrs. Ruddy feigning illness, Russell with his violin, and Pearl fighting off Jake's hands. I heard the barking of Jake's dogs, and I smelled Pearl's cooking, and I saw the sly grins of the younger boys, who were raising themselves into an ugly manhood.

"You haven't—?" I asked.

"Oh, no," she said. "I'd never let Jake touch me. But the other day, it was the worst. He kept pestering me and pestering me while I was cooking, just coming up behind me while I was at the stove and kind of leaning into me, so that I couldn't hardly breathe. I was stirring stew with a big, metal ladle, and he said something that just set my blood to boil."

"What was it?"

"Oh, never you mind. A girl who ain't been with a man shouldn't hear that kind of filth." She started walking again. "Well, finally, I whirled around and smacked him in the face with the ladle. Stew shot all over the place, and he had this big, red welt where I'd burned his cheek. He started yelling like a madman, and I was yelling at him, and Miz Ruddy come out and she started in yelling at me that I better clean up the mess."

"Oh, Pearl," I whispered.

"Well, I wouldn't clean it up. I told Miz Ruddy that if they keep letting Jake act like a hooligan, then I ain't about to clean up what he brings down on himself." She half-laughed, in a painful rasp. "It was a fight the likes I'd never seen."

"Who won?"

"Oh, I never win." She laughed. "But I sure can make trouble for them."

"What did Russell do?"

"Oh, Russ." She shrugged. "Russ has got the kindest heart. He just led me to our room and let me cry it out."

"That's all?" I spouted. "He should have gone after Jake with a hoe or something!"

"Russ ain't like that." She shook her head. "You know, that stew was still all over the place the next morning, and the plates and cups and things they'd used to eat that night was still sitting on the table, as dirty as if pigs had been there. So I let Jake's dogs in to lick everything up. And then I put the plates back in the cupboard. I served every single one of them, excepting Russ and me, from those plates the next night."

"You need to get out of that house," I protested. "Forget Russell."

"He's my husband," she lashed. "He give me his name and all, and he ain't ashamed to be seen in public with me. Not like—"

She looked away. The sky had turned slate gray, and lightning snapped near the top of the mesa. "Don't tell Alex none of this," she said. "He'd say it ain't no more than I deserve."

"Alex loves you," I said. "He would be sad for you, just like I am."

She shook her head. "Do you read to him in the evenings? Like I did?"

"No. I never did. He never asked me to. Only you."

"Them days with you and Alex," she said. "Them days was the happiest I ever spent. I liked so much being there with you, in a house where there ain't always fighting and carrying on."

"Let's run away together," I said.

She laughed. "Where'd we go?"

"I don't know. Anywhere—"

"Scotland," she said.

"Scotland?"

"Sure. You and Alex always did want to go there, and it's far enough away from here. Just take me along. I'll be a foreigner there, just like all the Greeks and Italians are here."

I laughed. "I'd be just as much of a foreigner as you. I've been here for too long."

She rubbed her hand over her arms, her smile fading. The thunder rumbled again, and I could see rain coming our way, just beyond the mesa. "I got to go," she said. "With all them men to feed, I ain't never away from the stove for long." She kissed me on the cheek. "You don't worry about me. It ain't going to kill me."

With that, she hurried down the slope. I stood in the wind, no wiser or happier, until the lightning drove me to safer ground.

Three weeks later, I heard about another fight. It seemed right—time enough for the gash beside his nose to close and the bruises to fade to yellowish-purple stains. Alex and Rory brayed about it in the early morning hours, but I could not tell who had won or who had lost. All I gathered was that it was another bloody contest.

After Alex left for work, I waited until the bell at the mine had rung, and the men coming off the night shift had disappeared into their houses or the stores or saloons. Then I picked my way through Berwind, walking as fast as I could.

Theo Sky was not outside. I crept into the shack, barely closing the door behind me, and standing with my back against it, ready to wheel out again if any other Greek appeared. After my eyes adjusted to the dim light, I saw him lying on one of the cots. He seemed to be asleep, and from what I could see, not nearly as bruised as he had been by the Starkville guard.

I knelt on the floor next to him. He lay on his back, one arm at his side, his other hand laid across the scruffy undershirt he wore. His breathing caught every so often, as if a dream was rumbling through him or he needed to cough.

"Theo Sky," I whispered.

His eyelids flicked. "You came."

"How badly are you hurt?"

"You went to the fight last night?"

"No."

"I almost . . . just was winning."

I wondered if the Greeks made more money if he won or if he lost. Why didn't they take turns fighting, if it was the quickest way to earn home? Why didn't they each suffer for it, if they wanted it so?

"Where are the others?" I asked.

"Don't worry," he said. "They won't come here."

At once, I knew that he had told them about me. I could hear their teasing: Oh, she is a true American girl, bold enough to come here, and to be alone with a Greek—

"Where are you hurt?" I asked.

He gestured to his ribs. "I think . . . here."

"Let me look."

Gingerly, he swung his legs from the bed and sat up. Rolling up his shirt, I found a fist-sized bruise just below his right rib. I pressed gently, and he gasped in pain. "I don't think your ribs are broken," I said. "I can't feel anything amiss."

"Then what? It hurts awful."

"They're bruised. Terribly bruised. How many times did he hit you? Let me wrap them."

Like a child, he lifted his arms and let me pull off the shirt. Yellowing bruises, the remnants of others fights, trailed up and down his chest and abdomen. How long had he been at this? Why had I not known? Then again, I rarely listened to Alex and his friends talk. What a fool I was—sitting in my corner, smiling and humming and being as mousy and dreamy and dumb as a maiden sister was expected to be.

I poured liniment into my hands and rubbed them together to warm them. The sharp smell of camphor and menthol made my eyes water, but before I could bring myself to lay my palms on Theo Sky, I hesitated.

"Go on," he said. "What is wrong?"

I lifted my hands and touched his ribs.

Oh, the feel of his skin. Warm from lying in bed and smooth against the tender tips of my fingers. The hair of his chest was as dark as that on his head, and it trailed all the way down to his trousers. I rubbed gently up his rib cage, around his sides, over the middle of his back. Moles dotted his skin, black-brown against his dark skin. His spine was firm under my fingers, the muscles of his shoulders tight from years in the mine.

He coughed.

"Am I rubbing too hard?" I asked.

"No," he said. "No, it is okay."

But I was not all right. I could not breathe, I could not speak, I could barely see. My eyes watered, but not from the menthol oils. I wanted to close them and let the smell and the heat of his skin lull me into sleep and sweet dreams. Still kneeling on the floor, I held one end of a cotton strip against his side and wrapped, up and around his chest. Sometimes, my cheek bumped against his shoulder or chest as I pulled the strip around. He sat motionless, arms half-raised.

When I was done, he lay back in the bed and pulled the blanket over him.

"Are you cold?" I asked.

"I'm okay," he said again.

He closed his eyes, as if he didn't want to see me. I felt the same—afraid, happy, shaken, dazed. Unable to sit still, I rose and walked around the room. My hands tingled, and the burn went right up my wrists into my elbows. I scratched idly at them, spreading the smell of liniment over my skin. Lifting my wrist to my nose, I sniffed at it as if it was perfume.

In one corner of the room was a kitchen—stove, counter, shelves—so similar to the one in our house that I knew it had been taken from a company home. A skinny kind of mandolin stood in another corner, beside a guitar. On the wall hung a long-faced, pensive saint in a white robe, a crown of thorns piercing the thin skin of his forehead. It must have been Jesus, but I had never seen the Savior so dark and hollow-eyed. Below it, on a small wooden table stood a cross, candle, and photographs of dark-haired, black-eyed women and children. Some of them were beautiful in dark, embroidered dresses, shawls over their hair. So there were women attached to the Greek camp.

Behind me, Theo Sky spoke. "There is a picture there of my mother. See it?"

An older woman with dark eyes looked out from a gold frame. "I think so."

"And the girl with babies? That is my sister, Elena. She is the wife of Dimitrius. He works in Number Six."

"Why didn't she come with him?"

"And live here? Like this?" He laughed. "She stays with her mother."

"Doesn't he miss her?" I searched the woman's face. She had a broad forehead and sharp chin, and her eyes were dark and deep. A toddling girl sat at her feet, and on her lap was a chubby baby boy. "The children?"

"Maybe. He don't talk much."

"But you've been here for years! How old are they now?"

"No, Dimitrius only comes last winter. To make money, he says, for his family. But I tell him, no money, no fortune. Nothing in America but bitter."

No wonder the Greeks were scrambling to go home. Looking at the photo of Elena, I imagined every day as an agony for her. Was he safe? Was he still in love with her? Did he still long for her touch, her lips, her hands, or had he forgotten—?

"Why did you come to America?" I asked.

"I am youngest in my family," he said. "Mother said, we cannot feed him and he is too little to work. So I come with my uncle to America. When we got here, I wanted to work, because I was ten years and that is old enough for America. But my uncle said, no work. You are too smart. Go to school and learn to talk American. Then you talk it for us all. I don't want to go, but he made me. And I learned it good, yes, Miss Christian?"

"Yes, you did." I looked over the photos again. "Where is your father?"

"He is dead. He died when I was very young." He gestured. "Look, find that bag on the table."

I picked up a small leather pouch, its drawstrings pulled tight. Handing it to him, I helped him to sit up and watched as his big fingers undid the drawstrings. Inside was dirt, as red as any in Berwind Canyon.

"This is from my land," he whispered, pouring a tiny pyramid of it into his palm. "We bring this with us. So we never forget old places. It smells of home. See? Smell it."

He lifted his palm, and I sniffed at the sand, but I could smell nothing beyond him.

"What do you think?" he asked.

I wanted to please him. "It smells good."

He carefully dumped the dirt back into the bag, and I tied the drawstring for him.

"Tell me about Greece," I said.

"I am not Greek."

"What?" I laid the bag of soil on the bed beside me.

"I am Cretan. From Crete."

"Where is that?"

"It is a island. In Mediterranean Ocean. It is near Greece, but is not Greece. I am not Greek until I come to America. Neither is all these others here, but it don't matter. Americans think we are Greek, so we don't say nothing, because Americans don't know nothing. But we know the truth."

I wished for the faded map of the world that had hung in the Berwind School. I had never heard of Crete, and now, I wanted to know where it was, and what it was. An island, like Scotland. "It does matter," I said. "You should tell them."

"Ha!" he scoffed. "In the mine, we are not even Greeks. We are goat-herders, even dagos sometimes. They call me goat-herder. Good morning, goat-herder, they say. Goodbye, dago. But they never call me by name."

"I'm sorry, Theo Sky—"

He straightened, then winced and pulled at the binding around his ribs. "My name is not Theo Sky. I am Theros Skyrapoulos. When I come to America, the men at Ellis Island could not say it, could not spell it, so they gave me papers that made me Theo Sky."

All the years, I had called him Theo Sky, without thinking, without questioning—and now it struck me that it was a nonsense name, a child's name, after all. But I liked the name he had just given—so complicated and full of letters. It would not roll off the tongue as Theo Sky did, but stick to all but the most nimble. "What is it again? Theros Sky—"

"Skyrapoulos. You will say it?"

"Yes," I said. Then, in a voice that trembled, "Theros Skyrapoulos."

He reached up and smoothed back a lock of my hair that had escaped and fallen into my eyes. "You are nice, Miss Christian. Why do you have the name of God?"

I laughed, surprised. "What?"

"Christian. Name of God."

"That's Christ. No, Christian was my grandmother's name. It has nothing to do with God or the church."

"No?" he asked. "It is nice."

He shifted, lowering himself onto the cot, stretching out on his back with a grunt as his sore ribs touched the straw pallet. Patting the bed, he said, "Lay down beside me."

I hedged, feeling that now familiar burn of restlessness and giddiness and want and shame.

"Come on," he urged. "Don't be scared. I am too tired to hurt you."

Still, I hesitated.

"Please," he said.

Tentatively, I stretched out on the very edge of the bed, keeping myself as far from him as possible.

We lay side by side, looking upward to the tin of the corrugated ceiling. Grayish cigarette smoke and dust from the dirt floor swirled in the light near the windows. The walls creaked and whistled in the afternoon breeze. The metal framing of the cot dug into my back, and I crossed my left arm over my stomach to keep my hand from slipping and dragging on the floor.

We did not touch. We did not talk. He drifted off into a low, lumbering sleep that was interrupted every so often by a sharp jolt. I did not sleep—my mind was too busy and my body too tense—but I closed my eyes and willed myself to listen.

To the sound of his breath, and mine, and the thump of my heart, and the pumping of my blood. I had not slept this close to anyone since I had shared a bed with Pearl, and I remembered how sweet it was to wake up in the knowledge of her arms and legs and face so near mine. I lay in the bed until I heard a goat's bleating, as if someone was approaching.

I slid from the bed. "I have to go."

Without opening his eyes, he reached out for me. Taking his hand in mine, I smoothed my fingers over the scratchy, thick palm callused by his rough work in the mines. I waited for him to speak, but he didn't. Neither did he open his eyes. Finally, I lifted his hand to my face.

I didn't kiss it. I simply held his fingers against my lips, and then I spoke his name.

Chapter 12

So many times that summer, I made my way over to the Greeks' shack—more times than I could count. Every time I heard of a fight, I'd go. Hoping to escape the notice of the guards, I wrapped a scarf around my hair and wore simple skirts made of the same calico that almost every woman in Berwind bought at the company store. Each time I came to the hovel, I expected the Greeks to be gone, traveling toward Crete. Each time, Theros was still there.

Sometimes he was sleeping peacefully. More often, he would be sprawled helplessly across his sleeping roll. I'd brew tea to soothe him, and I'd spoon broth into his broken mouth. Once strengthened, he would whisper, "You should have seen. I was winning until the end."

"Shh," I'd say. "You'll crack your lip open again."

I always called him by the name that he had given to me, like a promise or present. It seemed to take him home, to remind him of who he had once been, where he had once lived, where he wanted to be.

"Crete is like heaven," he told me. "Big cliffs, falling water, tall trees. Tall mountains with snow, but where I lived, it is green. Ocean is such beautiful color and the water so warm. It is most beautiful place on earth. A nice place to die."

"Oh, you have to get back before that!"

He laughed. "It is a sad thing in America when Greeks die. Without women, we don't have no one to sing *mirologhia*."

"What is that?"

"When Greek dies, women sing for his soul to reach heaven. It is sad singing, crying out for him, but also hope for him to come to God. Soul hears it and understands and goes to God. When there is no one to sing, who knows what happens to soul?"

"Do you believe that?"

He looked at me as if I'd asked a stupid question. "Yes."

I told him how I had recited Burns' poetry to my father as he lay dying. Surely his soul had been raised up, welcomed into heaven to the sound of such beautiful language. Theros asked me to recite some, and I said, "*Flow gently sweet Afton, among thy green braes, Flow gently,*

I'll sing thee a song in thy praise; My Mary's asleep by thy murmuring stream, Flow gently, sweet Afton, disturb not her dream."

He snorted. "That is silly stuff, yes?"

"Maybe," I admitted. "My father loved it."

"And you?"

I did not know if he was asking if my father had loved me, or if I loved the poetry as well. Choked up, I simply said, "Yes."

I sat with him and fed and washed him, but I could never leave off nagging him to stop. It hurt me to see his face ravaged by someone else's fists, to see his eyes swollen shut. "Why is it always you?" I asked. "Let the others get the stuffing beaten out of them for once! Then maybe they'll change their minds about going home."

His eyebrows arched. "I don't care," he said. "You do?"

"Yes, I do! You're always hurting, you're always missing work, you could be—"

"If I don't fight, what reason do you have to come visit?"

I stumbled, stammered, fell silent, and he laughed. "You think about that, Miss Christian," he said. "Think about it hard."

He needn't have asked. Nothing kept me from thinking of him. The smell of sage reminded me of his eyes, and the ointments and balms I used clung to my hands even after I'd scrubbed them clean. Nearly every day, I mixed medicines or teas from yarrow and chamomile or some other herb from the mesa. Every moment I spent with Mrs. McCormick or Jane McKenna or Mary O'Keegan, sewing or canning or doing the laundry, I remembered that I had done what no decent girl would do—keep company alone with a man, touch him, bathe him, kiss him. Often, my hands fell idle, and I longed to be kneading the muscles of his back or tracing the veins down the length of his arms. My face smoldered, until I was certain that the others could sense my guilty knowledge of his body.

But Mrs. McCormick was more concerned with what was happening in Berwind. The canyon had always been closed to visitors and curiosity-seekers, but now, more barbed wire was strung around the mines, unraveling in sloppy fences over the mesas and down into the valleys. Signs tacked to the fence posts warned against trespassing and reminded us all: PROPERTY OF JOHN D. ROCKEFELLER, COLORADO FUEL & IRON.

Searchlights shone along the streets of Berwind from sundown to sunrise, piercing the paths of the town, and the row of privies near the creek, and even the porches of our houses.

"Those lights shine all night in my windows," Jane lamented. "I haven't slept a wink in weeks."

"That's probably for the best," Mrs. McCormick said. "Those Baldwin-Felts fellows they're bringin' in from West Virginia make our mine guards look like Catholic school girls." She lowered her voice. "I heard their favorite game is to find a girl that doesn't speak English and tell her her husband's hurt and waitin' for her up the canyon. And when she goes with them, they take her just as they please."

The faces of the pretty brides from overseas came into my mind, and I saw them standing together in the aisles of the company store or carrying laundry from the stream to the clotheslines. They were little more than girls, some even younger than me.

"Holy Mother Mary." Jane shuddered, and my body chilled. "Keep your young Katy and Emmy safe, for heaven's sake."

"And you, too, Christian," Mrs. McCormick said sternly. "Don't ever be caught alone by those fellows. Stay right where you should—and if you ever need to walk anywhere by yourself, you come take my Tommy with you."

I nodded meekly, pretending I did not travel the most desolate paths in Berwind to the Greeks' shack.

On a day late in July, I found Theros lying on the floor of hovel. A sleeping roll was half-bunched beneath him, half-lumped over him in a feeble attempt to cover him. He lay on his side, with both his arms up over his head, hiding his face from me. His shirt was unbuttoned and tangled around his waist, his feet were bare.

Kneeling beside him, I swallowed my panic. "Theros," I whispered. "Let me see."

When he rolled over, his face was hardly recognizable. Both eyes were blackened, his lip was torn at one corner, and his nose looked crooked. His right temple bled, poorly stanched by a stringy piece of cotton. His jaws swelled, as if he held walnuts in his cheeks. The knuckles of both hands were bloody and ripped.

"My God!" I cried. "Did all this happen in the fight?"

He did not reply.

My hands shook so hard I spilled iodine down my skirt. He needed stitches in his forehead, I was sure, something I'd never attempted before. "You need a doctor," I said.

"No," he growled.

"I can't do this. I've never handled anything so—"

"Start on what is worse."

"No," I said. "I'll be back."

"Miss Christian, no!" he called weakly, but I ran, barreling down the slope toward Bricktown and into Berwind. I went straight to the Ruddy house, knocking on the door before I even caught my breath or wondered what I would say if Jake or one of the others answered.

But it was Pearl who greeted, me, squinting in the bright light of the morning. She took in my strange costume, my frantic breathing, and reached for my hand. "What is it?" she asked. "Alex?"

"No." I shook my head. "Come with me, please, won't you? Please, come with me."

"Sure." She cast a look into the darkness behind her, checking for Mrs. Ruddy. "She's sleeping, I think. Or drunk. Hard to tell which these days." Grabbing a scarf, she wrapped it over her shoulders and hair in imitation of mine and followed me.

We did not speak as we climbed up the slope toward the draw where the Greeks' camp was hidden. Pearl glanced behind her only once. Inside the hovel, she took in the room with a sweep of her eyes, then said, "Theo Sky?"

When he heard the voice, he tried to sit up. One of his eyes had swollen completely shut, so he wrenched his head about, trying to see. His elbow slipped out from under him and he fell back onto the floor.

"Don't!" I said. "Stay still!"

He flailed, trying to roll over and push himself up. "Miss Pearl! Why you are here? Who else is here—?"

"No one," I said. "I promise. No one saw us. No one followed. It's just the two of us."

Pearl knelt beside him, hands on her thighs, eyeing his wounds. "What trouble have you gotten yourself into, Theo Sky?" She reached out a cautious hand, as if approaching a wild animal. "I ain't seen you since we was in school together. Remember way back then? A hundred years ago, I think. You was always nice to me."

Words tumbled from me. "He needs stitches, and—"

"First we got to get him out of the dirt."

Her words settled me, and I found my bearings. Together we heaved until we were able to help Theros onto the nearest cot. He fell back against the straw pallet as if he had no strength left. Pouring steaming water from the kettle, I bathed his face, mopping up the blood and grime. When the rags would no longer rinse clean, I tossed them into my basket. Pearl gently dabbed away the trickles and seepage from the cleaned skin.

"How many teeth did you lose?" Pearl asked him.

"None, right now," he moaned.

"We'll use alum," she said. "It might settle them back in their sockets, so you can still chew on something tougher than oatmeal. Who did this to you, anyways?"

She looked up at me, but I shook my head.

"You got a needle and thread?" she asked. "And some whiskey? And Christian, you hold his hands down tight. I don't want him swatting at me."

"I don't hit woman," he said through gritted teeth.

"Oh, you might, you just might. This ain't going to be any fun, you know."

Her hands were so deft and quick—seven stitches in heavy black thread that we had soaked in alcohol. I could never have managed it. My hands would have trembled. I would have been too slow, trying to prevent pain and probably causing more. I would have had to blink back tears, to keep myself from vomiting.

"You need to leave those in for a while," she said as she finished. "A couple of weeks, at least."

He lay back, face pale, body limp, as if he could no longer bear it. The black stitches jutted out, angry and red, just at his hairline. I put clean cheesecloth soaked in witch hazel across them. Pearl watched him for a few minutes, until his breath evened out, and then, lifted her gaze to mine. How could I explain it, how could I make her understand what I'd done?

But it was a relief to tell someone, to tell the story only I could tell. Standing outside by the goats' pen, we talked until the sun moved from the eastern side of the hovel and left us in shadow.

"So Theo Sky does all this to get home?" she asked. "I ain't never heard of nobody being that desperate."

"His family's there. All of their families."

"I suppose," she said. "Does he have a sweetheart back there? One of them arranged marriages you hear about in the old countries?"

My throat closed. "He was awfully young when he came here—"

"Oh, they arrange them things before the babies is even out of diapers." She shrugged. "You wouldn't think he'd want to go home just to see his ma. He grew up without her. You think he'd be man enough by now that he wouldn't need her no more."

"Look at the Ruddy boys."

She laughed. "You're right there. So why do you come over here? Why do you care if Theo Sky kills himself before he gets home to old Greece?"

I stammered a single word. "Because—"

She eyed me. "Because what?"

My courage failed. "I want to help him. He's nice, and—"

She laughed. "You're in love with him, Christian. That's why you're here. Because you love him and always have."

My insides bubbled up in laughter and happiness. What a joy to hear it, admit it, to live it at last. "You're right," I said.

"I knew it this morning, when you showed up at my place all crazy-eyed and babbling." She laughed. "And I was sure that if I missed with the needle and Theo Sky let out even a tiny, little, old ouch, you'd take a hatchet to me."

I laughed, a high, silvery note. "I'm so glad you came. I couldn't have done it—"

"No." She frowned. "One person couldn't have, by themself. He's got some grit to him, I grant that, to do this over and over again."

"This is the worst I've seen."

She laid her hand on my arm. "You be careful, Christian. Alex is like to knock you two ways from Tuesday if he finds out you're chasing after a Greek. You know how he feels about those who ain't got pure white skin. And there's probably some Greeks who don't like Theo Sky taking up with a Scotch girl any more than Alex would."

"They think I'm American."

"Don't matter much, the way I see it. You ain't acting like most girls—American or not. Coming over here on your own, taking care of him—what do they think goes on in there when there ain't nobody there but you two?" She tossed her head toward the hovel. "You be careful they don't start wanting more from you."

Her words sobered me. "I will."

She kissed my cheek. "I got to go. If Miz Ruddy wakes up and I ain't there, there's hell to pay."

I watched her leave, shushing the goats that bleated as she hurried down the slope. Inside the shack, Theros lay on the cot, sleeping off the whiskey we'd spooned into his mouth, hoping to numb the pain of the needle. As I settled on the floor beside him, he opened his battered eyes into narrow slits.

"You are still here?" he asked.

"Yes." I dabbed at the drops of blood seeping from Pearl's stitches.

"Miss Pearl?"

"She's gone."

He tried to hoist himself up on his elbows. "Why did you bring her here, Miss Christian?"

The anger in his words stunned me. "I needed help. I—"

"She is married to Russell Ruddy!"

"She won't tell him. I trust her. She's like my sister—"

"A woman tells her husband everything—"

"I trust Pearl," I said again. Then, all the worry of the morning bore down on me. "Why do they make you do this? Your uncle, your cousins? They don't seem to care if you're with them, or if you're lying dead here in Colorado because you fought one too many times! It's not worth it! Just stay here in Berwind, just be a miner, forget about going home!"

"You think I do this to go home?"

"What other reason is there?"

He shifted, as if he might rise, but lay back, exhaustion in his face. "Look in the pocket of my shirt."

His shirt was twisted around him, the tails securely tucked beneath him. As I leaned across him to loosen it so that I could reach into the pocket, my cheek brushed against his chest. I fumbled with the shirt, picking out a small green card.

The words "United Mine Workers of America" marched across the top, above an oath of loyalty to the union. His name—Theros Skyrapoulos—was written in full across the dotted line in odd, geometric shapes.

Everything spun—the room, the stiff writing on the card, his body stretched out on the cot, the earth beneath me.

"You've paid your dollar," I said.

He took the card back, his hand closing over it, as if he didn't want me to have a clear view of it, after all. I waited, suddenly frightened.

Licking his lips, he said, "When I fight, Dimitrius takes bets from guards. He pretends to be stupid, unable to count money. And he can't talk so good, neither. Guards watch close. They yell at him, scared to lose their dollars."

My gaze went to the photograph of Theros' sister and her children. Dimitrius was her husband. The seemingly dimwitted Greek who fumbled with the money at the table, unperturbed by the tempers flaring around him.

"Then, after bets, they watch fight. All eyes are on me. I choose to fight the biggest, strongest, so fight is not . . . I forget the word—"

"Fair," I said.

"Yes, that is it. But while guards watch me fight, my uncle Spero, he talks about union. Greeks come from Tabasco to watch, from Delagua, Tollerburg, Hastings, Starkville—from every camp. Sometimes even Raton in New Mexico. Uncle talks to them all about union."

How, given the crowd in that shop, could his uncle possibly be heard above the noise? But I knew. "He speaks Greek, doesn't he?" I said. "So the guards don't think anything of it."

"Yes," he said fiercely. "Italians, they have opera singer. Pretty redhead, Mary Thomas. She is Welsh woman, but Italian singer. She sings 'O Sole Mio' ten times a night, while men drink and women weep. Guards leave, bored by song, by stupid Italians. Then men talk union. Your people, they have men from union right among them. Greeks, they have me and Spero and Dimitrius."

"Why didn't you tell me?" I demanded.

"Why would I?" he asked, his voice ratcheted by fury. "I don't know if you would tell your brother, I don't know if you would tell mine guards, or other girls, or who. Miss Pearl—she is a Ruddy!"

"I would never tell anyone," I rasped. "No one knows I come here—except Pearl, and she only knew today! Every time I do, I'm scared to death that . . . and then, I find out you've been hiding this from me—!"

"What does that matter, why I do this?"

"Because I should know! If I'm going to take such chances, I have a right to know!" I grabbed at my bottles and rags, throwing them haphazardly into my basket. "I should go."

"What? Are you afraid of me now? You don't like me now? I tell you the truth. That is all."

"No, not—" I felt the shame running up with the blood into my face. "So the others know what you're doing? And they think I'm just a stupid girl who comes over here to take care of you because, because—"

"They think you are looking for a husband."

My stomach cramped as I imagined the Greeks laughing, joking among themselves. Sweet American girl, thinks she finds a big strong Greek to . . . My God, how had I been so stupid?

"You believe in union, don't you, Miss Christian?" Theros asked.

I said nothing. What did it matter?

"This is true story," he said. "Listen to this. One day, we sell some goats to this farmer up at the end of the canyon. We got money from the farmer, American dollars. So we went to Trinidad and go to real store, not company store, where Americans shop. We buy boots with steel toes—we have enough money for all of us to buy new, nice boots. Not like at the company store, where we can buy only one, two pair."

I bent over, huddling on the floor.

"When we come back to Berwind," he went on. "The guard stopped us at the depot. What is in this package? he asked. We said boots. He said you can't buy boots at other store, only company store. He said we can't have boots. So he takes them. And next day, guess what? We went to the company store and there is our boots on the shelf, for sale, for so much more than we pay. Store owner comes to us and says, I have boots for fit your big stupid Greek feet, and laughs at us."

"It happens to everyone."

"No!" he roared. "Your brother never has his boots taken. Never! Not once! Right? Answer me!"

His voice echoed against the walls of the hovel. "No, he hasn't," I admitted.

"That's what union is about. It is about every man being treated as a man, and talked to like a man. It is about a man from Greece or Italy or"—his knowledge of geography failed him—"Slavia who come here and wants to be American. Union is about letting Greeks be like your brother, like American man."

"My brother is Scottish," I flared. "So am I. I'm not American, I wasn't born here—Alex and I came here on a boat, across the ocean, just like you did!"

Outside, the goats bleated, and a train whistle sounded in the distance. At last, Theros spoke. "You have white skin, like all Americans. Your brother gets good, no, best, rooms in the mine with other white men. No matter that he don't mine too good."

"That's not true—"

"Fifteen men joined union last night," he said defiantly. "Greeks from Hastings, who want to be American men, too."

"Fifteen? I'd think it would be a hundred, as hurt as you are!"

"Why do you think this way?" He flipped one bandaged hand. "We fight to beat the company that says no, you are not good enough to be American men. We fight so no one takes our jobs, takes our money, our things. We fight to be men. It don't matter if one dies, because others still fight. It don't matter if I get hurt—or die—if union comes to Berwind."

"Don't say that."

"And then you bring Miss Pearl here!" he said, restarting the argument. "You know what Russell Ruddy does? In his big office? He sits there and says, Throw this man out, he is with union—"

"No," I said. "Pearl won't tell. I trust her. Anyway, she thinks you are trying to go home." Unable to let it go, I added, "But you should have told me what you were doing the first day I came here! Alex could be in trouble because of me, and my—"

"So you think I am a fool," he said fiercely. "You think I am stupid. You think I am dago who isn't as good as American. You think your brother is better. That is okay. I don't care. Leave, if you want."

He dropped his head, studying his lap, like a child who believed that if he couldn't see me, I couldn't see him. I gathered the rest of my things and left, closing the door behind me.

But that evening, as I washed out the rags I'd used to clean up his head and hands, my tears dripped into the water. My whole body ached, as if I were as battered as Theros. My pride ached, too—all those days I'd pranced over to that shack, with the Greeks laughing at me as I went. All the times I'd felt lovely and needed and happy when I returned. Vanity, foolish vanity. School girl daydreams.

Why hadn't I realized from the beginning what he was doing, and in realizing it, talked him out of it or at least stayed out of it myself?

Alex came home and asked me what I was doing. When he saw the pinkish water in the pan, he went outside to the rusted sinks near the privies to wash. He was embarrassed, I realized, because he thought the blood was my monthly flow.

I was glad not to have to talk.

But as the water in the pan swirled from pink, to red, to rusty, the blood seemed to become something else. The voices of so many, the discontent and heartbreak and anger of so many. I felt the tally of all the slights, the injustices, the outright crimes against every person in Berwind pressing up against me, resounding in my head.

Do you believe in union, Theros had asked, and I thought, yes, yes, I have to. My father believed in dignity for all. He had died trying to preserve Alex's and mine, and were he here, I sensed he would not be so much shocked by what I was doing as pleased. Why had he versed us so well in Scott and Burns if not to teach us to stand up for what we believed in? *Lay the proud usurpers low! Tyrants fall in every foe! Liberty's in every blow! Let us do or die!*

Dipping another cloth into the water, I knew I would not stop.

Chapter 13

    The next day, I hurried to the Greek camp through heat that pressed down on Berwind Canyon, smothering the town with the stink of the slag heap. Slipping into the shack, I waited until my eyes adjusted to the musty darkness. No one was there.
    My lungs heaved in the dank, sweltering air. Theros had been barely able to move. Surely he had not gone back to work—to crouch on his knees, swinging the pick against the hard rock wall, and shoveling the broken rock into the cart. I called for him, frantic, afraid that the guards had come for him, that he had been taken down the canyon and beaten senseless. As weak as he had been, it wouldn't take much to kill him.
    Outside, the sun beat down on my head. The goats were gone, the gate of the sapling enclosure swinging in the breeze. I could hear their bleating echoing from farther up the draw. I ran, my shoes filling with sand. Coming around a jagged sandstone formation, I found him, sitting with his back against the sandy wall. The cliffs rose high above his head, shading him from the sun's fury, and the air was much cooler. Scrub clung to the steep slopes, and tufts of grass grew on the knolls and between the sandstone boulders. Before him, in a flurry of brown and white, the goats plunged their noses into a pool of cool, fresh water that collected in the sandy bottom. A couple of shovels and some buckets lay scattered around the dugout spring.
    He turned his head, peering out of one half-closed eye. Without speaking, I knelt beside him. His face had puffed into a lopsided, purplish ball, and his seeping stitches had stained the white bandage. He sat with his arms crossed over his chest, huddled into himself. One of his legs was fully extended, but he had drawn the other up, favoring his left side.
    "I am too hurt to carry the buckets," he said, as if no angry words had passed between us. "So I let the goats out."
    "I was wrong," I said. "I'm sorry."
    His lips curled in a secretive, satisfied smile. I set about tending to him, first pulling away the bandage over the stitches. The black thread crept across his forehead with the gangly legs of a spider. I dabbed at it with a clean cloth soaked in iodine. He closed his eyes.

"When I was little boy," he said, his words rough and slow. "I watched my mother's goats all day for her. I followed them up hills, down, through mud and rocks. They are stupid animals, no good for nothing. I cursed them and yelled at them and hoped that wild dogs kill them, but I know that if I lost even one, my mother would beat me for a week. So I become good at what I do to save my skin."

I put a fresh bandage over the stitches, and he opened his eyes. At the spring, one of the nanny goats butted her kid to keep it from nursing. The kid let out a piteous bleat.

"That is right?" Theros asked. "To save my skin?"

"That's right."

"You see, I learned English good in school."

"You didn't like school, did you?"

He shrugged. "I liked school good enough, but not teachers. So I quit. So now, I am nineteen years old and still in second grade." He leaned forward and peered into my face. "Look, Miss Christian, you are smiling. You are not mad no more? You don't think I am stupid no more?"

"No, but now I think you need to become better at fighting to save your skin."

He laughed, but turned toward me, serious and urgent. "You know of Louis Tikas? You have heard of him? He works at union office in Trinidad, talking to men about union. He has another name, Greek name. But when he comes to America, it has too many letters. So he chooses—this name, Louis, that name, Tikas. Now Americans can spell it, can say it, but we know his Greek name. He is our *strategos*, our—what do you say—?"

"Leader?"

"Yes. The guards and Baldwin-Felts watch him, follow him, say to him, We will kill you. And he has already been shot by them, up north, in the fields there. But he is great man—he does not quit. He is from same place as me, from Crete. We speak same language, from same heart." He touched his chest. "He speaks English, too, like me."

I smiled at his proud words, filled with a sweet longing. "Does he ever come to Berwind?"

"Oh, no, no." He laughed shortly. "No, he would be killed. No, Spero and me, we are the ones who work for union in Berwind. No, see,"—he struggled to describe it—"Louis, he hands out cards on the street, he talks about union in loud voice. To everybody, whether they are miner or no. Spero, he is quiet, talks to a few here, few there, but then few become many. So guards watch Louis all day and all night, but they don't know nothing about what is really going on."

"Is he why you joined the union?"

"He tells me he is proud of me and writes to union men in Denver about me. He says that union is only way to win our industrial freedom. So that we can be equal to all other American men, like the United States government says. That is what he calls it, our industrial freedom."

At once, Mrs. McCormick's rants against John D. Rockefeller echoed in my head: You've done it now, Johnny D. Your employees are ready to fight you to the death for their industrial freedom.

"Does he think we'll win this time?" I asked.

"This is the biggest, best union ever," he said. "We won't lose." He turned to me. "You see, Miss Christian, this is why union is so, so"—his English failed him—"much for me."

I covered his hand with mine.

Nearly every day, I went to see him. But it was becoming more dangerous to step beyond the quiet streets of Berwind and strike out into the canyons. The company had doubled the number of guards, and the Baldwin-Felts security agents poured into Trinidad and the coal camps. They didn't even bother to conceal their guns, strapped to their waists with belts notched once for every striker they'd killed in West Virginia or Pennsylvania or Montana. They paced day and night, standing on the bridges and spitting streams of tobacco juice into the creek when the women washed clothes, prowling around the field at baseball games, and ruining our dances and socials and any other public assemblies.

I made every effort to fall beneath their notice. Every day, I walked the same path in my calico skirt and bland white blouse, my flaming hair hidden beneath a dark scarf, my skin pale and plain. I looked straight ahead, never meeting their eyes or responding to their glances.

Then, one day, as I was following the scrubby path home from the Greek camp, I glimpsed a flutter of movement between the sandstone cliffs of a narrow ravine. My heart leaped. Few roamed that far from Berwind proper, and no one had business in the wild, secret places between mesas. I stopped, terrified—another Greek? a mine guard? He heard my step as I stumbled over a rock, and his head snapped upright, alert, cagey.

It was Russell Ruddy.

I knew from the twitch of his mouth that he recognized me, though I wore my scarf and carried my basket of ointments like a housewife on her way to buy eggs from a farmer. But there were no farms or ranches nearby, and the only destination at the end of the path

I was on was the Greek hovel. Before either of us spoke, I saw he wasn't alone. A boy about my age slipped out from the crevice in the sandstone. He looked familiar, and I thought he'd once been in school with me. He didn't notice me, but went to stand close to Russell. When he saw me, he took a quick step backward.

Russell's head bobbed a couple of times. Whether it was a greeting or a reflex, I wasn't sure. He strode quickly down the path, the boy skittering along in his dust. I did not move for several seconds, my mind reeling. Should I go back and warn Theros? Should I go home and tell Alex? Should I seek out Pearl and beg her to silence Russell?

I ran toward Berwind, cast into indecision by my fear.

At home, I listened for horse hooves or shouts, for the dreaded knock, but heard only the hum of the mine machinery down the hill. The pulleys groaned, the bells rang, and the trams clattered as they were hauled to the tipple. A train whistle echoed down the canyon.

When Alex came home, I eyed him warily, skirting around him as I served dinner, afraid that Russell had spoken to him, and equally afraid that Russell hadn't, and that I would have to live another day with the fear of discovery. But Alex himself seemed jumpy. He barely ate, and he anxiously tilted his head when he heard noises outside.

At last, he said, "I'm having company tonight."

"Who?" I asked, my voice so shrill that he started.

"James, John, the usual." Alex went to the window, peering out nervously. "Tonight, I was thinking, maybe you'd like to go visiting over at the O'Keegans and see the new baby."

"The new baby!" I had forgotten that Mary McCormick O'Keegan had given birth to her second. "Doesn't it look just like the other one?"

He started to scold. "Christian—"

"I'm not a friend of Mary's. I never have been."

"It's out of courtesy. Edith is going, too."

Unable to trust myself, I set about scraping food from the plates, the knife gritting against the metal. "Why don't you want me here, Alex?" I asked. "What are you planning?"

He looked out the window again. I waited, listening to the shouts of children and the calls from mothers and the other sounds of a pleasant evening. A tune played on accordion drifted down from the direction of Bricktown, and the whistle of the early train to Trinidad, filled with miners at liberty and ready for a bawdy night in town, tooted shortly.

"Does it have to do with the union?" I challenged him.

"Jesus, Christian!"

"Tell me the truth, Alex."

"You just stay out of it—"

"What do you think Mrs. McCormick will talk about tonight? She'll spend the whole evening raving at Johnny D—"

"This isn't some kind of game—"

"I know that!" My temper flared, but I stopped myself from spilling my own secrets. "But it's not just the men who should know. If you go on strike, I'll go, too! And so will Mary and Mrs. McCormick and all those babies! If you get sent down the canyon, I will, too! You should invite every wife and woman and child in the neighborhood over here tonight!"

Lowering his voice, he said, "As far as I'm concerned, you don't have anything to do with it. You don't know about it, you don't talk about it, you don't even listen—"

"I'm not leaving!"

"All right, calm down," Alex said. "But you'll sit there and be quiet. Not a word. Understand?"

I bit my tongue. It was the best offer I would have from him.

A pack of men gathered in our shack. Rory and Uncle John settled into their usual spots, but James was missing. The other men were strangers to me—a Welshman with beetling eyes and coal black hair, a man whose slow, lingering drawl gave away his American birth, another whose tall, gaunt frame barely fit through the door of the cabin. They carried with them small barrels and blocks of wood for chairs.

"We're all here?" Alex asked, as they sat at the table.

"Aye," Uncle John said.

Seven men had come for the evening's poker game, and Alex patiently doled out cards. Antes of a few pennies were half-heartedly pitched into the center of the table.

It was the oddest entertainment I'd ever seen. No one spoke, no one gossiped. Smoke rose from the ragged butts of cigarettes into the dwindling light from outside, and some of the men nipped from flasks pulled from their pockets. The smell of pomade, clay and chewed tobacco mixed in the stuffy room, for Alex had closed the windows and drawn the curtains before the gang arrived. A few pulled at their collars and shed heavy overshirts, but no one complained.

The dour game had barely begun when James burst through the door, harried and wan, a stranger by his side. He scooted in and slammed the door behind him. "This is Ned Binford," he said breathlessly. "He's just now arrived from Denver."

Binford looked like the friar from the legend of Robin Hood—stout and short, with slouching shoulders and a rolling belly. Nearly bald, his remaining hair fringed wildly around his ears. The men murmured a greeting and slid aside to allow him a spot. Noting me, Binford tipped his hat and said, "Ma'am."

"This is my sister," Alex said.

Binford said nothing, but I sensed that he did not approve of a woman in the room. Sitting at the table, he was silent as Alex dealt both him and James into the game.

"Did you have trouble comin' in?" Uncle John asked Binford.

"No, no," he said. "There're plenty of back doors into this place. Down one gully or t'other."

"But they've gone and dropped razor wire by the roll along most of the washes around camp," James huffed. "You have to slither through or you'll be sliced to pieces."

"Have they now?" Uncle John wheezed. "Seems they don't trust us."

Some of the men chuckled, but fear gripped my heart. Was that what Russell Ruddy and his friend had been doing in the ravine? Dropping razor wire so that no one could come or go from Berwind? And if there was razor wire farther up the ravine where Theros and I had met, someone might have seen us together. Noticing Binford's eyes on me, I quickly picked up my sewing.

Binford leaned forward, his double chin nearly on the tabletop. "Let's get to this."

The circle tightened, heads bent over cards, shoulders tensed and riding high. Binford spoke in a quiet, smooth voice as calm and mesmerizing as a flowing stream. "We believe, at District 15 headquarters of the United Mine Workers, that the southern fields are fully organized, in every CF&I mine from the New Mexico territory to Walsenburg. All forty-four of them." He held up his hand to curb the men's enthusiasm. "But that means the work is just beginning."

He rifled through his cards and tossed two down.

Wordlessly, Alex dealt two more.

"These are the demands that the UMWA will make of Colorado Fuel & Iron," Binford said. "First, pay for dead work. No more dragging and laying track in the tunnels, no more timbering, no more mucking for free."

"Yes, sir," the tall man said.

"Two, no more scrip. American money is dollars and cents, and that is what all American workers should receive at the end of a shift." Eyes on his cards, he meticulously sorted them. "Three, a union appointed checkweighman to make sure the company weighs each and every ore car fairly. No more cheating a man on weight."

"When I started work here in Berwind Number 3," Rory complained, "I was pulling 5,000 tons. Now the company scales weigh half that. Same car, same hours on the job, and I ain't working any less, I can tell you."

Binford nodded. "I've heard that more than once, son. Just don't give up hope. Next, safety laws. Colorado's had laws in the books since the beginning of the century and not one company follows them. So you breathe in the dusty air and cough yourselves to death before you're thirty." Once again, he fingered his cards. "And the right to live where you want and buy goods at any store—"

His words were cut short by a knock on the door. Alex looked at James, then at Binford. "See who it is, Christian," Alex hissed at me.

My hands shaking, I raised the corner of the curtain enough to spy the silhouette of a lone man. I shook my head. "I don't know."

Quickly, Binford opened his coat and pulled out a pistol. He laid it in his lap.

"Miss," he whispered to me. He tipped his head toward the door. "If you'd be so kind. Open it, and then stand aside quick."

Drawing in a deep breath, I unlatched the door, fully aware of Binford behind me, armed and ready. A man I'd never seen rushed into the room. Breathlessly, he said, "I've just come from Trinidad. They've gunned down the Italian who passes out the union cards. The little one, name of Lippiatt."

"Good God." Binford's face went pale. "When?"

"This afternoon," the man said. "A gunman by the name of George Belcher. He's one of them Baldwin-Felts boys out of West Virginia."

Binford studied his cards, as if looking for answers. "Lippiatt was a good man."

I swallowed, trying to calm my breathing. If they found out what Theros did, if they learned what I was doing—

When Binford spoke again, his voice was laced with urgency. "This, then, is the last demand, men. The union's calling for the open shop, which gives a man the right to work where he wants and under the conditions he demands. We want full recognition of the UMWA by the company as an equal partner in the operation of CF&I's mines. The Italians, Slavs, Greeks—"

"Greeks!" Uncle John protested. I looked up from my sewing.

Binford coolly surveyed the faces around him. "A union's only as strong as its numbers," he warned. "We need a united brotherhood, we need every man ready to see this thing through. If that means joining with Greek or Negro or Chinaman, so be it. Every man who wants a better life is welcome in the United Mine Workers."

Another chimed in. "But the Greeks—"

"Have a leader by the name of Louis Tikas," Binford said. "The kid's been around, through the strikes in the northern fields. Hell, he's no more than thirty and he already led a walkout in a little town up north called Frederick that brought the operators to their knees. The Greeks have organized right quick around him down here in the south. He's a good man to have on our side."

My heart seized. The same homeland, Theros had said, the same heart.

Binford studied his cards. "The UMWA is holding a convention in a few weeks in Trinidad. There we'll formally make the demands."

"And if the company doesn't accept?" Alex asked.

"Then we'll strike."

"So it will happen here?" James asked.

"I do believe it will," Binford said. "And mark my words, boys, this strike will be the one that makes labor history in the state of Colorado and even the nation. It will never be forgotten."

For a moment, silence prevailed. Some of the men stared at the cards in their hands, and some at Binford himself. Then James laughed aloud, and a few of the others joined him.

A knock on the door stifled the jocularity. At once, the men fell silent, half-turned toward the door. Binford pulled his pistol from the pocket of his jacket, and the other union man did exactly the same.

"Miss, if you please," Binford asked.

I lifted the curtain and peeked. Three men, each armed with a carbine, stood on our porch. "Guards," I whispered. Then, one of the men shifted, and I glimpsed a meaty hand in the dying light. "I think it's Jake Ruddy."

"Who?" Binford asked.

"Jake Ruddy," Uncle John said. "Part of a whole family of company men."

Another knock, louder and angrier.

Binford cast a few cents into the center of the table. "Remember, we're playing poker."

The door thundered, struck from outside by a gun butt. As Alex passed me to answer the door, he whispered, "If anything happens, just get out of the way." Opening the door, he demanded brusquely, "What is it?"

Jake stepped inside. "I heard there was a meeting of some sort here tonight."

"We're playing poker," Alex said tensely.

"Come join us," James called cheekily.

Jake's two companions leaned inside the door, their hands on their rifles. "Do I know all of you?" Jake nodded toward the American. "Who're you?"

"I work in Berwind Number 1," the man said, not offering his name.

Jake's curiosity settled on Binford. "And who're you?"

"I'm down from Tollerburg," Binford said easily.

"He's my cousin," James added airily.

"Everybody's a cousin where you come from, O'Keegan," Jake said. "Whole shiploads of starving cousins." James balled his fists, but Alex put a hand on his shoulder. With a laugh, Jake passed by Binford, and questioned the man to his right.

"Either come join us or leave," Uncle John said. "We're waitin' on you."

Nearly everyone in the room held their breath. Jake's gaze fell on me. "Evening, Scottie," he said cordially, tipping his hat as if he were an invited guest. "I didn't see you there."

My mouth went dry. So Russell had told Jake that he had seen me near the Greek camp, and here was my comeuppance. And—oh, God—what had they done to Theros?

One of the mine guards, a burly man with a drooping mustache, stepped forward. "This meeting needs to come to an end."

"It's no meeting," James snapped. "It's a poker game."

The guard snatched James by the back of his shirt and jerked him out of his chair. The chair skidded across the floor, knocking into the woodstove. The others jumped to their feet, but the second guard leveled his gun at them. "Keep it civil, gentlemen," he drawled. "There's a lady in the room. Now, if you'll all come outside, we'll settle it there. Keep your hands where we can see them."

One by one, the men left, abandoning their cards and pennies and coats and hats. Ned Binford passed by me, his pistol stowed in his pocket. Alex hung back, arms folded over his chest.

"You, too, Scott," Jake said.

"It's my house," Alex protested. "I've a right to—"

The guard with the mustache jabbed Alex in the small of the back with his rifle. "Get out," he growled.

I stood, too, intent on following, but Jake barred the door with one arm. "Where're you going, Scottie?" he asked. "You ain't joined the

Yoo-Em-Dubbelyoo-Ay."

I stepped backward as he closed the door.

"What's wrong?" he asked. "Still scared of your own shadow, like you was in school?"

My heart pounded. "You're the one who has to bring along mine guards when you come visiting."

"I ain't visiting you, you sorry old maid." He wrapped steely fingers around my arm. "But say, you ain't as ugly-looking as you used to be in school. Why don't you come out some evening with me and my friends?"

Fear shot through me. With what was happening outside, no one in Berwind would have the courage to come if I screamed. I writhed against his grasp, pulling at his fingers with my free hand. "I hear you have a special fondness for stew, Jake. You like it all over your face."

His face contorted, as if it were being pulled inward by his rage. He jerked me so I fell against him. "What'd Pearl tell you? What'd she say about me?"

His hair smelled of the sweaty leather band of his hat. A vicious strength rose up in me, and I twisted against him. "Nothing that surprises me."

"Listen to this," he spat. "She's my brother's wife, and every night, you know what they do? Every night, they take off each other's clothes and—"

He whispered a short, sharp word in my ear that I had never heard used in conversation before. I tried to jerk away from him, but his grip tightened.

He laughed. "I bet you don't even know what that means, do you?" His lips touched my temple. "Want me to teach you?"

I jammed my hand into his face, but he twisted my arm behind my back.

"Your brother's little green card is gonna deliver him right to the Pearly Gates," he said. "And you can't do nothing about it. But don't you worry. I'll turn it in and get good pay for it. A hundred dollars for each dead union man."

A sharp pain ran up my arm, but I rasped, "No better than you could read in school, Jake, you'd never be able to figure out whose name is written under the oath."

"So, you've seen plenty of them cards, have you, Scottie?"

I bit my lip, my eyes filling with tears, knowing I'd said too much.

"You know something, Scottie? It's all a big joke. There ain't no such thing as the United Mine Workers of America, and those men who've been paying dues have just been handing their sorry little dollars over to company men all along. That's right. We got a big, old list of who's joined and each of them is a dead man."

"That's not true—"

"Come on," he growled. "Let's go see what's become of your big, brave brother."

He opened the door and prodded me outside. I could see nothing in the shadowy, dusty street beyond our house, but the dull thud of flesh against solid flesh rippled through the night and, somewhere, someone drew in terrible sob-like breaths. Jake pushed me forward, and I stumbled to the edge of our porch. From there, I could see two Baldwin-Felts agents holding James between them, while a third beat him over the head with a pistol.

A scream came from me, but Jake put his hand over my mouth. "This is what happens when you double-cross the men you work beside every day," he spat. "This is what happens when you think you're so damned much smarter than anybody else."

"Alex!" I cried. "Alex!"

Across the street, Alex and the others stood motionless, pinned down by the aimed carbines of the two mine guards. They were silent, their faces stricken with terror.

"Give me a turn," one of the Baldwins said.

The two exchanged places, the one who had been beating James tucking his pistol into his belt. With new force and energy, the second Baldwin pummeled James with his fists. James' body sagged, his arms and legs at unnatural angles, his face a dark mask in the night. The Baldwins let go of his arms and he fell into the dirt, where the third man began to kick him.

A commotion echoed from up the slope. Mary O'Keegan barreled down the hill, Mrs. McCormick and Jane McKenna close behind her.

"Leave him alone!" Mary screamed. "Let him go!" Dropping to her knees in the dirt, she flung her body over her husband's.

"Get her out of here!" One of the Baldwins hefted her up as if she weighed nothing at all and shoved her toward a mine guard. As the guard took her arm, the men in the shadows broke loose. Some careened down the slope, running for Berwind, and others ran uphill toward the mesa. Alex and Uncle John shot forward into the fray.

Jake let go of me and jumped off our porch, throwing himself at Alex. The dust swirled upward as the men roiled in the dirt, Jake raining punches into Alex's face. Alex brought his hands up to his face, trying to protect himself.

I ran down the steps. Grabbing at Jake's shirt and shoulders, I tried to pull him from Alex. "Stop it!" I screamed. "Stop!"

He shoved me with one arm, knocking me backward into the porch steps. I grabbed onto the rail as the ground went out from under me.

"What's going on here? What's happening?" The light of five or six lanterns split the dark. "Hey! Stop it!"

Men flooded up the slope, maybe twenty in all, coming from Berwind. At once, the Baldwins strode away, their greatcoats flapping around their knees. The two mine guards and Jake vanished into the darkness.

I ran forward again, trying to find Alex in the dust and confusion. By the time I reached him, he had pulled himself upright, his hands on his thighs, his breath coming in a wheeze.

"Alex!" Uncle John called. "Help me!"

Leaning heavily against me, Alex hobbled to where John bent over James, whose face was torn into a black, bloody mask. Together, Alex and Uncle John heaved James into a sitting position. His head lolled back, his eyes rolling in unconsciousness. Mary sobbed his name over and over, wringing his limp hands in hers.

Uncle John slapped at him. "Are you all right, lad? Come on, talk." He pushed a flask against James' lips. The whiskey ran down and dripped from his chin.

"Get him inside quick!" Mrs. McCormick ordered. "Katy, get some bandages!"

Uncle John grabbed James beneath his armpits, and Alex took up his feet. Jane put her arm around Mary, who was crying so hard she couldn't stand on her own. I followed Alex, who leaned against the door jamb, half-bent, a trickle of blood at the corner of his mouth.

"Take him home, Christian," Mrs. McCormick ordered. "Jane and I will do here."

The door of our house stood wide open, left that way by Jake. After I helped Alex shuffle inside, I slammed it behind us and locked it. The heat of the previous day had escaped, chilling the air inside. The chair where James had sat still sprawled next to the stove, and tin cups, cigarette butts, and flasks littered the table. The sorry penny ante spread across it, the cards scattered on the floor nearby.

"Give me a drink," Alex said, wiping at the blood on his mouth.

Grabbing the bottle, I poured it into his tin mug, but when I held it to his mouth, he grimaced. I helped him to his cot, and he folded up, falling so fiercely that the metal springs of the bed hummed under his weight.

"See if it's still there," he wheezed.

"What?"

"In my boot, in my sock." He waved toward his right ankle. "See if it's still there."

I unlaced his boot and folded down his sock. Bent from the curve of his ankle was a green UMWA membership card. So Alex had joined the union. His name scrawled across the line, as if he'd forgotten how to form his letters in the years since he'd been at school. Remembering the way that Theros' name had marched defiantly across that line, something inside me twisted.

"It's still here." I tucked the card away. "Let me see what's wrong."

Filling a pan with hot water, I washed his face and hands and cleaned the blood and grit from his hair. Jake's fists had left ugly red marks up and down his chest, and his chin was cut. Remembering James' face, my stomach rose up in a dry heave that I choked back with a swallow.

"Where did Binford and the other union man go?" Alex asked.

"They ran," I said, pouring liniment into my hand. "They went toward the mesa, I think."

"And let us take their beating for them."

"Why did they go after James? Did he say something—?"

"Kirstie," he said desperately. "Kirstie, there's something you need to know—"

I froze, the liniment pooling in my hand.

"That beating that James took," he whispered. "It wasn't him they were after."

"Who, then?"

"They wanted me." He swallowed convulsively, as if the words were lodged in his throat. "I've been passing messages—"

"You're organizing, too?"

"Too?"

"I was thinking of Binford," I said quickly.

"I'm not organizing. I'm just passing messages, that's all. Meeting times, names of those who've joined, that sort of thing—"

I heard Theros' voice: *Fifteen men join last night.* "But James brought Binford here tonight, and he—"

"I think they've known for a while that it is one of us," he said. "And James' mouth gets him in trouble—"

"Oh, God, you should have told me long ago."

"I won't do it again," he said. "It's too dangerous. Take that card and burn it. I won't do anything that might—"

"Burn it!" Rage flared up in me. "After what just happened? After what they did to James? There are men out there who risk their lives every single night for the union, who are—"

"What's in God's name has come over you?" he asked, wary. "Who are you talking about?"

"That Italian organizer, Binford, and the . . . the Greek man he mentioned," I said. "Oh, don't you see? It has to work. It's gone too far, too many men have been hurt or worse. How can James go back to that mine and forget about this? How can we forget about that Italian organizer in Trinidad who was shot?"

"Och, what a mess," he said, lying back on his cot.

"Dad would have joined, Alex," I whispered. "He would have."

I knew he would say no more, that he would not have the gumption to argue with me. Silently, I rubbed his shoulders and back and ribs with liniment, but my mind sped onward. If they suspected James or Alex, how much longer before they saw through the ruse of Theros' boxing matches?

In the kitchen, I poured clean water into the basin and scrubbed at my ears and neck and everywhere else I could feel the rancid taint of Jake's breath. When I was done, I pulled the rocking chair next to Alex's bed.

I kept one lamp lit even though the night had quieted again. The clock next to Alex's cot ticked loudly, its second hand springing forward and then falling back a little, as if afraid of what the next moment would bring.

Wild thoughts ran through my head. If Alex died because of his work with the union, I would be alone, the only one of my family left in America. Without money, without a home, without a way to reach Scotland, even if I wanted to go back. I thought of Pearl, and how she had once spoken of running away, but we were both women, each one as poor and stranded as the other.

Suddenly, the door handle rattled, and someone leaned against it from outside. I jumped to my feet and ran to the window, peeking out of the curtain. Behind me, Alex roared back from sleep. "Good God, who's that?" he cried.

Pearl stood outside.

She nearly fell into the house when I opened the door. "Jake said he'd killed Alex!"

"No, no, he's all right."

Her tears still flowed. "I ran! I didn't care if he knew where I was coming!"

I looked beyond her, into the dark street outside, my heart jolting with fear. "He didn't follow you, did he?"

Alex sat uneasily on the edge of the bed. "What brings you here?" he nearly shouted. "Looking for union cards, so you can help out your dear husband and his brother in turning in names to the company? Are they with you? Come back to finish the job they started?"

"Russ wasn't there," Pearl said. "You know that."

"What about Jake? Did Russell send him down here so he could enjoy a nice, quiet evening with his wife?"

"Don't you dare." Her voice rose to a shriek. "Don't you dare say a word against him!"

"He's no better than the rest of them," Alex scoffed.

"Russell give me his name. He wasn't ashamed to make me his wife. He don't think of me as no dago."

"Aye, Russell gave you a name, but what about a baby?"

"Why do you care?" she spat. "You wouldn't have married me even if I'd gotten down on my knees and begged. Because you was afraid of me, afraid your old friends'd think you'd married down if you took me. You was too proud of your family's past, of your fancy Scotchman blood. Well, I spit on that past, I spit on it! It don't mean nothing!"

"And your marriage to Russell does?" he demanded. "What kind of love is it, Pearl, when a woman runs away and marries a man she doesn't want out of cold-hearted spite? Russell's not going to give you a baby. Surely you know that by now. Not as long as there are others like him."

"What?" I asked. "What's this about Russell?"

No one listened to me.

"Don't be mean, Alex, please," she pleaded. "I come here because I was scared. They told me you was dead, and that's all I cared about. That's all. That I'd never see you again."

"And you came back here, thinking it's all forgotten—"

"Maybe not forgotten. But I come back here thinking that you might be man enough to forgive me! What did I do wrong, Alex?" Pearl pressed her hands to her face, her body shaking. "I didn't do nothing wrong but fall in love with you—"

"Nothing wrong?" he roared. "Why did you marry that fool? Why did you choose a family that makes its living by preying on others—?"

"The rest of them do that," she snapped. "Russ don't. He's sweet and . . ." She stopped, tears flowing. "Oh, God, Alex, ain't I been punished enough? Ain't I suffered enough?"

"Where is Russell?" he demanded. "What did he think of his wife running out of the house tonight? He isn't going to be banging on our door in five minutes, ready to drag you home, is he?"

"He wouldn't do that to me," she sobbed. "He wouldn't—"

Without mercy, Alex watched her crumple to her knees. I started toward her, but he said, "Don't, Kirstie."

"Help her," I said, helpless myself.

"She doesn't deserve it," he said coldly.

"Alex!" I cried.

Still, he hesitated, his face etched with fury. Pearl sobbed, without restraint. At last, he reached out and laid his hand on her hair. Pearl clasped his knees, her head in his lap. "Oh, Alex," she cried. "You don't know how unhappy I been—"

I went to my room and pulled the curtain. Taking off my skirt and blouse, I lay down on the bed and closed my eyes, thinking I would never be able to chase away the brutality of the evening or the dread of the next day. But within minutes, I lapsed in a dark, exhausted sleep.

I woke to the sound of roosters from the McCormick house next door, and knew instantly that something was different. Something was echoing in my heart, and it brought with it both joy and worry. I slipped into clean clothes and went into the other room. Pearl lay on the cot beside Alex, cuddled with her back against his chest.

"Pearl." I shook her shoulder, the flesh warm and soft. "It's morning."

Her eyes opened, and she reached out a hand, silently, wordlessly.

I went outside and sat on the porch steps. Before me, the street was calm, empty, the violence of the night before visible only in a few scuffs in the dust. The sun had just started to lick the darkness above the mesa. On the prairie below, it would be morning already. In the canyon, we would wait a little longer.

The door closed, and Pearl sat beside me. "You fixed him up good," she said.

"I've seen worse."

"You sure have." She fingered the fringe on her shawl. "I saw Theo Sky just the other day, in the supply store. When he saw me, he bowed just like a gentleman from merry old England and swept off his hat, doing this funny little thing with his hand"—she pushed her own hair off her forehead—"so that I could see that his stitches were healing pretty good."

My heart lifted at his cockiness, but worry overtook me almost at once. "Did Russell or Jake say anything to you?"

"About what?"

"About him."

"No, why would they?" As soon as she'd spoken, she whipped toward me and grabbed my arm. "He's part of it, too, ain't he? He's wrapped up in it, too? Oh, Christian, you and Alex have to get out! And Theo Sky would do better crawling over the ocean back to old Greece. That union ain't going to do you no good. It ain't going to do nobody no good."

"What did Alex tell you?"

"He told me he's joined up and is helping the cause. I told him, don't. Just watch out for yourself and forget all them others!"

"Russell saw me coming back from Theros'—from Theo Sky's—place. He was with another man up one of the canyons, and he just stared at me. I'm afraid he'll turn me in, or tell Jake—"

She said nothing. The rooster crowed again, and a train whistle sounded from down the canyon, near Ludlow. At last, she said, "Don't worry about Russ. He's got his own secrets to keep."

"What do you mean?"

Again, she hedged before answering. "He don't like women."

It took me a long moment to respond. "What? You mean he doesn't—?"

"No," she said. "He don't want me, he don't want you, he don't want the most beautiful woman ever to walk this earth. Some men is like that, I guess, though Russ is the first I known."

"But"—my voice was timid, girlish in my own ears—"but you can't—"

Theros' touch on my hands, the heat of his body next to mine as we lay side by side on his cot, the tingle when he kissed me—

Indignant, I asked, "Why would Russell marry you?"

"He needs a wife, don't he?" she said. "So nobody thinks about what he really is." The anger dissipated from her voice. "He's the only one in that family who's worth something, and they know it. He's their ticket to something better. And so everybody in that family's always trying to make him into something he ain't. His pa wants him to be superintendent one day, and his ma is always going on about how happy she is her first-born son has a wife and a grandchild pretty soon." Pearl pressed her hands to her face. "Poor Russ. He used to try when we was first married. He'd tell me how pretty I was, and how he liked the sound of my laugh, but—"

"But you can't be happy with all that—"

"I ain't," she admitted. "But he's good to me. He loves me in his own way. He's always there to talk to me and to calm me down when Jake gets me so riled up I could eat dirt. I ain't about to forget that."

"That's not love," I said. "It's just wrong—!"

She looked out at the street. "That's just it. I knew what Russ was when I married him, and I didn't care. Not then. I just wanted to get out and be clear of Berwind—"

"You knew?"

"He told me," she said steadily. "But I thought he'd change. I thought I could change him. I'm pretty enough, ain't I? And it's dangerous being what he is. Somebody's always teasing him or threatening him. Even Alex does it. So do the ones who . . . they want money sometimes"—her voice trembled—"to keep quiet."

"Oh, Pearl, why did you marry him?"

She grew fierce. "I wanted a name. I wanted to be somebody that nobody could look down on. I thought then that I'd had enough of men pawing at me that it didn't matter." The words caught, and she whimpered, "But it does, it does."

"Stay here," I begged. "Don't go back." My shoulder ached with the memory of Jake's rough touch, and the queasiness came back to my stomach. "Jake might—"

"I can handle Jake. He's like just about every other man I ever known. You worry about yourself and Alex and Theo Sky." She rose and dusted off the back of her skirt. "You know, I didn't never believe that story about him wanting to go back to Greece. Who'd want to go back to that old place when you could be here?"

I let out a thin, teary laugh, and she kissed the top of my head.

"I'll be back," she whispered. "I been wanting to see Alex for so long! Oh, Christian, you don't know the half of it. Day after day, thinking, if I walk by the mine at this time, or that one, or if I go down there to their house and ask for a cup of sugar or something stupid like that, then maybe, maybe he'd talk to me—"

"I love you, Pearl. We both do."

She kissed me again, then stepped off the porch into the gray light. Wrapping my arms around my shoulders, I kept a vigil as Berwind woke, and the men went off to their shifts, and the women tossed the contents of the chamber pots into the lime pits, and the children filled the street with their shouts and games. For the rest of the summer, I carried Alex and Pearl's secret as solemnly as I carried my own—like a tightly-bound package, wrapped round and round and knotted with twine.

Chapter 14

The United Mine Workers' convention was held in early September. At the West Theater on Main Street in Trinidad, eighty-two-year-old Mother Jones declared, "When I get Colorado, Kansas and Alabama organized, I will say, God almighty take me to my rest if you want to, but not until then." The miners who managed to escape from the coal camps and attend the convention chronicled the injustices they'd suffered in the camps, and the organizers spoke of the union's resolutions. At the end of it all, the vote was in favor of a strike. Colorado Fuel & Iron's operators were given one week to meet the union's demands.

We already knew that Johnny D's men would not comply.

"The top union man is a bloke by the name of John Lawson," James related as he sat at the table in our house. His face had taken on a different shape since his beating—not as handsome, but lopsided and jowly. "He's president of District 15, from an old Scotch family in Pennsylvania. He'll be running the strike, managing it all himself. That's how important this strike is!"

"How long do you think we'll be out?" I asked.

"They're saying one month," Rory said. "One month, and the company'll be beggin' us to come back. Once word reaches New York and ol' Rockefeller hears he's losin' money, he'll turn right around and shake Lawson's hand and say how-dee-do."

"Well," Uncle John offered. "Even if it does go beyond a month, the union's givin' a million dollars for it. A million dollars! We'll be livin' like kings."

"Where will we be living?" I asked.

"Ludlow," Rory said.

"Ludlow?"

"That's the little town right at the end of the canyon," James said. "Oh, the town isn't much—a post office and a couple of stores and some other sorry buildings. But every road and every rail from Delagua and Berwind Canyons, and from Denver and Pueblo in the north, and Trinidad and Raton in the south passes through there. It's a brilliant scheme—the UMWA is calling it the 'Crossroads of the Kingdom of Coal.' We'll be sitting right where they can't ignore us."

"The union's bringin' in tents from the West Virginia and Michigan strikes," Uncle John added.

"Tents?" I asked. "We'll be blown to death by wind. It's all open prairie down there."

"Don't take it so hard, Kirstie girl!" Uncle John laughed. "You heard James. We won't be gone for more than a wink of an eye, and then we'll come back home, and they'll have to build us palaces fitted out with gold, if the union says so. You've nothin' to worry about, lassie."

"The union's calling it our great emancipation," James said. "Like the slaves, you know."

"Some of them have already gone," Rory said. "The Greeks cleared out of Berwind the day of the convention. Word has it they've taken off for the northern fields."

"They're gone?" I asked, attracting all their attention.

"They're probably too cowardly to stand up with us," Alex grumbled. "They're strikebreakers at heart, not strikers."

The next morning, I raced through Berwind, running carelessly to the Greek camp. When I came to the door of the shack, I burst in without knocking.

The hovel was empty—stripped of the sleeping rolls, the rough table with the candles and photographs, the portrait of Jesus. Outside, droppings stank in the empty pen, and I heard the faint bleating of the goats from far up in the draw, where they'd been turned loose and left to fend for themselves. It was as if the Greeks had never lived in Berwind.

I sat on the floor and hugged my knees. Ugly possibilities ran through my head—if he were killed, if he left for another place, if the union wanted him in Denver. I sank down onto the dirt and sobbed.

During that last week in Berwind, I cleaned our house, dusting the dimmest corners, turning the straw-filled mattresses of the beds, scrubbing down the floors and walls. I put my kitchen in order, washing the pans, plates, and knives in boiling water and soaking the sticky molasses jug. I beat the rugs with all my might and aired the blankets in the golden warmth of the sun. Nothing escaped my hand—not a single cobweb or fly speck on the windowpanes, no matter the cracks that snaked up most of them.

My housekeeping was a farewell to Berwind and all I'd known there, a rite as solemn as the washing and dressing of a body for a funeral.

Alex silently gauged my handiwork. "Some of the others are doing as much damage to their places as possible before they go."

"We'll have to live somewhere when we come back."

He made no reply. He had taken the news of the strike not as one about to realize a great victory, but as one who stood to lose everything. Pearl had flatly refused to leave Berwind with us, no matter how much Alex or I pleaded with her.

"They'd hunt me down like a runaway dog," she had said. "Jake's already promised as much." Her breath caught in a sob. "Oh, and what he'd do to Alex—I can't stand to think it."

"It's a free country," I said. "You have the right to go—"

"It ain't a free country in Berwind yet." She kissed me. "You go down to Ludlow and strike good, so that the likes of Jake and his pals don't dare show their faces ever again."

My last night in Berwind, I suffered from strange and frightening dreams. I dreamed that I heard Pearl reading Burns' poetry to Alex and me—*Oh, love will venture in, where it daurna weel be seen; Oh, love will venture in where wisdom once has been*—but when I looked, she was asleep in the bed next to me, shaking and twitching so desperately in the throes of her nightmare that I threw myself on top of her, begging and crying for her to wake. I saw a vision of Ludlow, where we were to live, its tents flapping in the wind until they beat hard enough to sail away into the blank of the sky. I searched for Theros, racing from tent to tent, entangling myself in the canvas and being pulled along, like a handkerchief in the wind. When I woke, light was streaming down on me, and my blankets were twisted around me.

Berwind was already awake. Around us, sounds echoed through the canyon—rushed footsteps, knocks on doors, shouts of fear, calls of distress. "The guards are going from home to home, asking who's staying and who's going," Alex said. "Be quick, Christian. We need to go."

Alex had found a handcart to take our possessions to Ludlow. He loaded it while I dragged our family's old steamer trunks to the door and piled the bundles I'd packed through the week in the middle of the floor. We had so little, yet the heap mounded tall. Maybe it was that those who had nothing saved everything.

"It's started raining," Alex said as he came inside. "Hurry along, now, it'll take us an age to get there."

Already the rain fell steadily, darkening the blankets I'd wrapped around our things. Alex looped rope once around the heap on the cart, then tied the chairs and bed rails to the side. His efforts caught the attention of two mine guards. I stood at the front of the wagon, between the two shafts.

"You folks leavin'?" one of them asked. "You joinin' the wops and dagos in their lousy tents on the plains?"

"You look like you need some help," the other said. He rammed the back of the cart. My ankle turned as the cart slid into me, and I stifled a cry of pain. Alex reached for the guard, but was met by the barrel of a shotgun in his chest.

"Don't reckon that's too smart, Mr. Scott," the guard said coldly. "You ain't a CF&I employee no more." He spat, then wandered up the hill, stopping at the McCormicks' house to taunt them.

"Come on," Alex said. "Let's go."

He grasped a shaft in each hand and started down the path leading to the creek. I walked beside, reaching up to balance the load whenever the cart lurched. The rain fell harder now, stinging my face and hands. Down the lane, a woman who had no conveyance sat hopelessly, her household goods thrown asunder by the guards. Blankets were trodden into the mud, and a few torn pages of a Bible sank in pools of rainwater.

"Please, señor, can you help?" she asked Alex, but he kept moving.

At the main road, we turned east, toward the mouth of the canyon. It wasn't long before our cart mired in the wet sand. I pushed with all my strength, slamming my body against the wood until I felt bruised around my ribs and thighs, but the cart did not budge. At last, Alex came back. "You pull," he said. "I'll push."

I took up the shafts while he laid his full weight against the back of cart. It broke free of the mud, slopping water and gravel around my feet. Staggering like a drunken man, I struggled to balance the weight of the cart and steer it forward. Alex hurried around to steady our goods.

Only a half-mile down the canyon, Tabasco's employees spilled onto the road. Soon, no one could move at all, and the wheels of the rickety wagons and carts sank in the mud. Those lucky enough to hire horse-drawn wagons to carry them out of the canyon plowed on impatiently, edging through narrow gaps. A man on a bicycle slogged by, mud sluicing from the spokes, a silver bell tinkling as he went. Within a few feet, the bicycle tires lodged in the slop, and he waded off on foot.

I sat on one of the shafts and lifted my skirt to rub my ankle. Already, it had swollen and bruised. I unlaced my boot and tucked the leather lacing inside. The rain had turned to sleet, and came down in sheets. My ears ached so badly from the cold that I felt dizzy and faint.

For another five hours, we crept down the canyon, moving forward a few feet at a time only to be blocked by another unfortunate soul whose cart had tipped, shattered from the weight, or lost a wheel.

The wind gave us no rest, but whipped at our bundles, threatening to overturn our cart. Pain slashed through my ankle, so that I leaned my head against the sopping bundles and gritted my teeth whenever I stepped forward. Alex's gait seemed unearthly slow, forced as he was to sway this way and that. At last, the canyon opened onto the plain near Ludlow, and we could see the heaps of coal in the rail yards and the crisscrossing of tracks and roads. Along the highway to Trinidad, curious observers and newspaper reporters had gathered for the show, many in automobiles, many with umbrellas above their heads and lap robes draped over their legs.

We pressed on until we came to the prairie just north of town. From there, I could see one lone tent standing amid the cholla and sage. Dumped on the plain were small piles of chairs, baskets, bundles, chicken crates, and the other stuff of living. Lost dogs wandered, their wet fur plastered into mats. Families perched around their goods, heads bent against the driving wind and sleet.

"Where are we to go?" I asked Alex.

"I don't know." Water dripped from his face, which was blotched red and purple with cold. He moved his arms stiffly, as if they had frozen straight while he hoisted the shafts. "I'll find out. Stay here. Do you have a dry blanket, something to wrap up in?"

I shook my head. My clothes were as wet as the ground beneath me. Even though I'd worn my boot unlaced, my ankle had swollen enough to make the leather bulge. I feared I would need to cut the boot away and knew that I didn't dare, for I had no idea where I'd get another pair of boots.

Around me, strikers arrived—from Tollerburg, Berwind and Tabasco in Berwind Canyon, and from Delagua and Hastings in Delagua Canyon. Children scattered across the prairie, squalling for relief. Men tried to shelter their wives and young ones by spreading quilts over trunks or by wrapping their babies in their own coats and carrying them along. Occasionally, a voice would reach me, usually in a foreign tongue, but with the same ring of desperation and disbelief. Where were we to go? Where were the tents, and why had we been left to suffer in the cold?

Alex came back, moving slowly as an old man. "There's only the one big tent," he told me. "The railroads have held up the tents being shipped from West Virginia, out of loyalty to CF&I. The women and children are to sleep in the tent, and we men are to find our own places tonight."

"It'll freeze tonight."

"All the same, we're to find our own."

I stood slowly, trying to balance on both feet. But my ankle would not hold my weight, and I sank down on the shaft of the cart.

"What happened to you?"

"The cart hit me this morning when the mine guard pushed it."

"Och, Kirstie, you should have said so." He wiped his hand across his mouth, but the rain still dripped from his nose. "I would have laid that guard low."

"It's better you didn't."

In an apologetic voice, he said, "They're settling the women with children into the tent first. You'll have to wait a little longer. I'm sorry."

The wind whipped my sodden hair across my face, but I hadn't the strength to peel it away. I started to cry, ashamed by my weakness, but unable to stop. Today, an end had come to everything we had known. Berwind, Pearl, Theros—just how much had we lost? Would we someday speak of Berwind with the same hazy nostalgia that my father had felt toward Scotland? Just now, Berwind seemed a paradise, given our plight on this lonely, empty prairie.

The rain turned to snow. Our great emancipation had begun.

PART III
LUDLOW, COLORADO

The union forever, hurrah! boys, hurrah!
Down with the company, up with the law;
For we're coming, Colorado, we're coming all the way,
Shouting the battle cry of union.
　　　　　　　　"The Union Forever" by Frank Hayes
　　　　　　　　Sung to the tune of "The Battle Cry of Freedom"

Chapter 15

Imagine this.

A great prairie stretches for miles with little relief—an arroyo here, a grassy hill there, the windmill of a nearby ranch. Sage grows in wiry clumps, and cholla and prickly pear spike upward. To the west, locomotives weave through a maze of steel, trailed by miles of freight cars that spill dingy black coal. In the rail yard, everything is metal and mechanical, built to store, load, dump, or move coal. Sweeping up beyond the bridges and rails are the twin canyons of Berwind and Delagua, their wind-carved mesas and rocky, cedar-covered slopes casting late-day shadows. To the northwest, you might glimpse the rugged snowy caps of the Spanish Peaks, but to the north, there is only prairie. Flat, unbroken, its soil brick hard. To the east, the low, scrubby Black Hills, so called because they bristle with cedar and piñon, barely dent the straight, blank line of the horizon. To the south, past more rails and steel bridges, and past the water tower of the town of Ludlow itself, the great mesa near Forbes sweeps forward, blocking any view of Fisher's Peak, in Trinidad, twenty miles beyond. Overhead is sky so radiantly clear that it hurts your eyes to look into it.

This is where the UMWA built its largest tent city.

For days, women and children pitched rocks onto the flats beyond the tent colony, and rammed wheelbarrows heaped with uprooted cholla and sage into the deep Delagua Arroyo, shouting in delight as the prickly skeletons plummeted to the sandy floor. Once a patch of land was cleared, the men built another tent, until there were one hundred and fifty in orderly rows. Each was numbered with red paint on white canvas, next to the framed wooden door. Each tent had a wood stove and chimney, and each row of tents had its own privies and piles of coal.

Voices echoed through the long streets, a storm of sound that wafted on the wind. Music from guitars, accordions or wooden flutes, the whining of bright red gramophones carefully wound to play Caruso or ragtime. Dogs howling, roosters crowing, babies crying, children screaming. Pounding, sawing, the beating of rugs, the clatter of pans, the crackling of fires. Peddlers plied their wares up and down the wide avenues, selling everything from chamber pots to parasols, and a fair-haired American man with tripod and camera took picture postcards of immigrant families posed outside their tents. For a few cents more, he would mail them to Italy or Russia or wherever home might be.

For a while—a brief while—we were free, just as the union had promised. Free from the steep canyon walls, we roamed at will. Free from work, the men collected near the meeting tent, or at the baseball diamond, or the steel exercise bars. They juggled or did tricks with lariats or tested their skills on a unicycle that someone had bought in Trinidad. They laughed and smoked and drank from flasks readily shared, sitting with square shoulders and backs that didn't ache from bending low in the mines.

Women weighted down the clotheslines with brightly colored shirts and union suits, or herded children across the prairie to school in the community tent. They haggled with the peddlers, flirted with the fair-haired photographer, and took from sealed crates the treasures of heritage—fans of ivory and silk that had belonged to a Croatian grandmother, crucifixes struck of silver, hand-cut Battenburg lace, and the furs of the last European wolves. They sang and talked and believed, for a moment, that they, too, could be free.

At least twenty times a day, someone hummed "The Union Forever." We all joined in, then, whether British, American, Italian or Slav.

Alex and I lived in Tent No. 18, near the center of the colony. We put our beds—Alex's cot and my brass bedstead—as far apart as possible, and hung the bullhide sheeting that we'd used in the doorway in Berwind between. Still, there wasn't enough room for all of our goods. Alex's trunk rested atop the bureau where I kept my clothes. We crammed our dining table so close to the stove that the resin in the wood blistered. The canvas walls gave us no buffer from the sounds of the trains on the rails or the noise in the public square, just a few tents beyond ours, where endless announcements were blurted through a bullhorn in a number of languages.

"Well," Alex said, as we looked around at our sad surroundings. "We'll hope for the best."

Day after day, he joined the other men at Ludlow's gates in hoisting hand-painted signs of protest. The marches were all orderly, sharply done, and led by a representative from each nationality. We had elected James O'Keegan as ours, in honor of the beating he had taken for the UMWA in Berwind. Meanwhile, a chorus of women gathered near the picket to sing union songs.

Every woman, whether married or single, cooked in the commissary kitchens. Mrs. McCormick acted as our leader, setting us to husking and chopping and pounding beside foreign girls who hid their hair under embroidered scarves, and wives branded by the bruises of a marriage-by-mail, and mothers whose children clustered in the folds of their skirts like ducklings. At first, we whispered among our own—English with English, Italian with Italian, Pole with Pole. We'd rarely shared a path in Berwind, much less a kitchen. But working in such close quarters, our hands touching, our shoulders brushing, it was only a matter of time before our languages merged into a choppy, crude English—gimme spoon, you have knife, pork no more today.

It wasn't long before the company guards and Baldwin-Felts agents started in on us. They paced the platform of Ludlow's train station and bullied each man, woman and child who tried to board. When the men played baseball or walked to the depot or post office, the guards gathered in jeering, smoke-haloed knots, their carbines in their fisted hands. More than once, our supplies arrived off the rattletrap union-owned trucks in pieces—flour or sugar spilling from a sack riddled by bullets, sides of meat bleeding again from a fresh wound. Searchlights from Hastings, a half-mile away, bore down on Ludlow at night, keeping everyone trapped in their tents. Soon, automobiles wheeled past the colony, sporting men with rifles.

Alex, Uncle John and Rory tore up the floor planking in our tent and began digging.

"What are you doing?" I asked, kneading my hands to bring some warmth back to them. I had been to the community line to retrieve our laundry. The clothes were half-frozen that day, sticking stiffly from my basket. My twisted ankle, which still gave me a limp, ached.

"We're puttin' a pit below your floor," Uncle John said.

"Why?"

Alex lifted a shovel of dirt from the prairie. "When the guards come shooting, you can climb in and be safe. We've already done one for James and Mary. Come down and see."

"Climb in?" I thought of a rabbit or mouse, holing up underground, quivering as its predators circled above.

"Sure."

The men moved out of my way, and I descended the makeshift ladder. The pit was deep enough for me to stand at full height—though I doubted Alex could—but I could nearly touch all four walls from the ladder.

I leaned back against the wall. Dirt gave way behind me and crumbled onto my shoulders. Cold, dull air settled around me, and I could hear nothing except my own breathing and the pulsing of my blood. Breathing in the smell of soil, I imagined the roof collapsing—my head crushed, my bones broken, and my ears and eyes and nose clogged with dust and dirt.

I burst upward, into the tent.

"Whoa, there, Kirstie girl!" Uncle John laughed. "You'll break a leg."

Alex's mouth twitched. "What's the matter?"

"I couldn't see, I couldn't breathe—"

"Everyone in the colony's to dig one," he said, annoyed. "It's a good idea."

I struggled to catch my breath, silently vowing I would never, ever use the pit.

"Now if only we had guns to defend ourselves," Uncle John mused. "Then we'd be set."

Rory snorted. "The union's got guns, don't think it don't. But will they give 'em to us? Not until somebody's outright killed."

Which happened during the second week. A mine guard's bullet found its mark, killing a striker by the name of Mack Powell. Those who had guns in the colony went hunting, and the president of the union, John Lawson, called a meeting in Ludlow's public square. We gathered outside the commissary, near the pole where the American and Colorado state flags flew, and union notices cascaded down a bulletin board in nine languages—English, Spanish, Italian, Greek, German, Croatian, Polish, and Russian.

Standing in the bed of a union truck, Lawson towered over the other union officials, tall and rangy, with large hands and a wide, grim face. I stood beside Alex in a crowd that pressed close, smelling of damp wool coats, smoke, greasy meat, and the acidic smell of cold.

"We need more guns," an Italian yelled. "To keep our mothers and childrens safe! The guards come to wipe out Ludlow!"

Shouts of agreement filled the air. "Aye!" Uncle John raised his fist. "Give us weapons!"

Lawson held up his hands. "No more guns," he countered. "We can't afford to stir up trouble. The whole country is watching this tent colony. Not Forbes or Starkville or Suffield or White City in Walsenburg or any other tent colony we've set up. They're watching Ludlow. They're looking to see what this strike is all about. America needs to know that the United Mine Workers are hard-working, honest folks who just want a square deal. This is about the rights of men, women and children to live in peace and prosperity and freedom, not about vengeance!"

"Let me speak," a small, white-haired woman clamored. "Let me have a say!"

Around me, voices rose in excitement. "It's Mother Jones! She's here! She's come to lead us on!"

Someone lifted her up onto the bed of the truck. Bracing against the wind, she looked frail, as if her bones were those of a chicken. Her voice, though, was strong. "We'll win this time!" she shouted. "We'll win, yes we will! The earth was made for you, not for Colorado Fuel & Iron! These canyons have been here a long time before the company came here, and they'll be here when the company falls! But you have to stand up and fight for it!"

"Say it, Mother," a striker yelled. "Say what you told us at the convention! No dagos!"

"That's right," she called. "There's no such thing as a dago in America. Once you stepped off the boat and onto dry land, boys, you became Americans, true, full-blooded Americans!"

The applause thundered through the crowd, whistles shrilling.

"But you have to act like Americans," Mother Jones added. "You, men! You picket, you keep this place clean and looking like a right American town, you keep yourselves sober and sharp. No drinking, no sinning, no spoils."

She paused until quiet returned.

"And you, the women of the camps. This strike depends on you most of all. If we win, it will be because of you! And if we lose, it will be because you didn't do enough." She planted her hands on her hips. "So keep mending those socks and shirts one more time! Keep making that meat last one more meal! Keep your children clean and warm, and your man happy and full. And keep fighting! Sing your union songs to make your man's spirits soar! Wave your signs in the Baldwins' faces! Keep your heads high! Women don't need the vote to raise hell, we can damn well do it all by ourselves!"

A full five minutes passed before John Lawson could restore order. Women hugged one another and shrieked in jubilant voices. I didn't know how much some of them understood of Mother Jones' message, but we all knew the words home, children, and men.

Finally, Lawson managed to quiet the crowd enough to call, "I've sworn in a number of deputies. They'll keep peace in Ludlow—enforce curfew, settle disputes, protect our boundaries. They'll be patrolling Ludlow and keeping the guards out. It's our Greek men."

The crowd exploded in complaint. "The Greeks? What the devil?"

"Oh, just watch, we're all dead now!" Rory roared.

Lawson held up his hands. "Louis Tikas, our Greek organizer, is in charge of his men. You can trust him. Come up here, Louie."

A short man climbed onto the truck and shook hands with Lawson. He was elegantly dressed in a tailored coat, his legs in black leather leggings. His eyes and hair were coal black, and a heavy mustache hid his face, making it hard to remember what he looked like besides dark, dark.

Breathlessly, I stood on tiptoe and searched the crowd until I spotted Theros. Taller than the other Greeks, he slouched against a union auto. His face, turned toward Tikas and Lawson, was no longer blemished by bruises or cuts, his eyes no longer purplish or half-swollen. His hair had been clipped short above the ears and at the collar. He looked trimmer, too, as if his skin fit him tighter, more evenly. Even his clothes were different. He no longer wore miners' overalls, but a dark coat over a white shirt, black breeches and knee-high black boots. On his chest was pinned the tin star of a deputy.

The meeting ended with the singing of "The Union Forever." As the crowd left, I stole away from Alex, moving toward the truck. I met Theros as he stepped away from the other Greek men. He looked around him, searching, I supposed, for my brother. Then he spread his arms in a buoyant gesture.

"Miss Christian!" His word rushed out. "Look, it has happened! We are here! We are out of the canyon!"

"So we are!" I laughed. "I've never seen a bigger sky, have you?"

"You are right." He looked up, as if he had not yet noticed it. "Everything here is big! So much room for us to live."

"And so much air to breathe—"

"But you know what?" He fingered the tin badge, boyishly proud.

"I am American now. Louis Tikas and me and some others go to Denver and sweared to be American citizens. So now Skyrapoulos is American name."

"American?" I asked with a flash of envy. "You used your full name."

"I made them spell it, every letter." He mimicked a clerk. "S-K-Y—is it done? No!"

I laughed. "You've bought new clothes."

"Ah, no, these are Cretan, from the old country."

"So when you were Cretan, you wore American clothes. Now that you're American, you wear Cretan clothes."

He laughed. "Least I don't dress like a girl," he teased. "I know one girl who dresses like a man." He waited for my laughter, then asked, "Where is your tent?"

"It's No. 18."

He waved his hand. "Greeks live in those big tents, not in the colony, but to the west. You have seen them?"

"How many Greeks are here?"

"Who knows?" He shrugged carelessly. "Ten, maybe, or ninety. Men come and go and come and go. Everything is always changing now." He touched my shoulder, so quickly and lightly that I might have imagined it, but for the spark of heat that ran down the muscle and into my heart. "But when I was gone so far to Denver," he said, "I don't forget how good you were to me in Berwind. I remember how you came over every day when I was laying around. I remember how much I like your hands and your mouth. I think you are nicest girl. Prettiest, too."

Without waiting for my reply, he gave a rogue's smile, half-bowed and walked away, joining the other Greek men at the truck. They had been watching us, I saw, and at once, began to question him. He simply shrugged. As my face colored into its usual fire, I drew my coat around me and turned away. Smiling into my collar, certain that nothing could ail the world, I went toward home.

Alex came home in a foul mood that evening, still grumbling about guns and the Greeks. "Old Mother Jones says fight, but John Lawson says don't," he lashed. "The Baldwin-Felts men are bringing in machine guns from West Virginia every day, and Lawson goes and gives all the guns to the Greeks, who'll shoot anything that moves, friend or foe."

"How do you know that?" I filled the dishpan and started to wash dishes as he sat at the table, whittling on a chunk of wood. "Surely Lawson wouldn't make them deputies if he didn't trust them."

"Oh, he's thick as thieves with Louie the Greek," Alex said. "We went to the headquarters this afternoon to talk to him. And there they were, just chatting away. Arm us, we said, we speak English, we take orders, and he says, Can't, boys. There's not a gun to be bought in the state of Colorado. CF&I has cleaned out every store between the borders. So where did they get the guns they gave the Greeks?"

"Don't you think they want this strike to work out just like you do?"

"Come now, Christian. They haven't any understanding of what it's all about. They just know violence, and they'll bring it down on us. Lawson hasn't lived around them. He doesn't know. Louie the Greek's got him bamboozled."

Furious, I dried the dishes, and carelessly clattered them onto the rack. I would not win this argument, and it touched too close to my heart for me to speak. Hefting the dishpan, I stepped outside to dump the water.

The night was nearly silent. A foreign phrase floated light as a spore on the wind, and a low laugh rose and fell. The light of the moon, shining above the glare of the searchlights, fell down on Ludlow. I breathed in, trying to let go of my anger. Because of Theros, I was a stranger in Alex's world, woefully misplaced in my own heritage. But I was equally barred from Theros' world of boxing matches and black Cretan clothing and tin stars and rifles. They were men, bent on men's acts. I was neither wife, mother, nor inspiration like Mother Jones. I wasn't truly Scottish, but I wasn't American. What was I?

I lowered the pan, holding it one-handed by the rim, braced against the front of my skirt, so that I could wipe away a tear. Almost at once, the Hastings searchlights flashed across me. It caught the dull metal gleam of my dishpan, and I heard tiny popping sounds, as if someone had heated corn kernels. I dropped the dishpan.

A hand grasped my arm. "What are you doing?"

Alex yanked at me, dragging me back toward the door of our tent. "Good God, get back inside!" He pulled me through, then slammed the door behind us with such force that the canvas walls quivered. Pulling me to my knees, we crouched near the stove, Alex's hand on the trapdoor of the pit. "What were you doing?" he demanded again. "What in God's name were you thinking?"

"I don't know! I forgot—!"

"That we're sitting on this godforsaken prairie without a single thing to hide behind? Aye, you'll get your feather-brained head blown off."

He listened, but silence had overtaken Ludlow again. With a punishing squeeze to my arm, he released it and rose.

"For God's sake, take a look at this!" He picked up the block of wood he had been whittling. "This is what Lawson told us to do. We're to march around with wooden sticks on our shoulders and hope it scares off the mine guards. Hope they think we're armed, and that they haven't the smarts to take a closer look. Because we don't have a single weapon to protect ourselves with!"

Dizzy, I sat down. My hands itched from the soapy water that had dried on them in the chilly wind. I shook, so cold I could not feel the warmth from the fire.

He threw the wood across the floor, where it bounced against the canvas wall and crashed to the floor. A trickle of dirt from outside spilled onto the wood planking.

"Och," he said. "Why'd we ever leave Berwind?"

Chapter 16

The Death Special rolled past Ludlow on a cold, rainy day in October. Picketing at the gates of the colony, we shuddered, for we had never seen anything like it. High, thick steel plates replaced the ordinary sides of the truck, even shielding the motor. In the open bed were two mounted machine guns. Walter Belk and George Belcher, the Baldwin-Felts agent who had shot the Italian organizer on the streets of Trinidad, each manned a gun.

Our voices trailed away. Mothers grabbed at their children, and the men on the picket line stopped in their tracks, their signs toppling to the ground.

"What in the world?" Mary Thomas, the Welsh soprano who led the daily singing, gawked at the road. Turning to us, she said, "Ladies, we'd better sing before we scream."

And so, in trembling voices, we sang "The Union Forever," as the automobile crept by, moving so slowly that we could hear the grind of rocks beneath its tires. The men leered at us, carelessly swinging the guns back and forth.

That afternoon, the Death Special attacked the UMWA tent colony at the Forbes mine, riddling the tents with bullets. Four died, including a young girl from a ranch near Ludlow, whose head was pierced by a bullet as she was walking home from school. An eighteen-year-old Italian striker was left lying in the dust, nine bullets in his legs. He lived, but did not walk again.

In the days that followed, Alex and I and the McCormicks joined a mournful pilgrimage to Forbes—only a half-mile away—to view the blasted barrels, the mangled canvas, the wooden tent frames splintered by machine gun fire. Seated on a stool before the colony, an old man spoke to anyone who would listen about the one hundred forty-eight bullet holes in his tent.

"I hid under the bed," he told Alex. "For hours, it was, and them bullets just kept flyin', hittin' the pans and the stove and bed springs. I was scared out of my wits." His hands shook as he tried to light a cigarette. At last, Uncle John struck a match and lit it for him.

A week after Forbes was destroyed, Alex and I woke to a desperate knocking in the early dawn. Alex stumbled from his cot, clothed only in his union suit, and tore open the tent door. I leapt from my bed, fear coursing through me. Anything could happen to us in Ludlow. Wrapping a shawl around my shoulders, I groped my way out from behind the bullhide sheeting.

Rory rushed in, bringing with him a blast of fierce October wind. "Come on, Alex," he said. "There's trouble."

"What is it?"

"They gunned down three strikers yesterday on Seventh Street in Walsenburg. And now a train full of Baldwins is headed this way! The train was made at the CF&I mill the same as the Death Special. Steel sided cars with machine guns mounted right to it!"

"When is it coming?" I asked, breathless.

Before Rory could speak, James appeared. "Look at this!" He reached inside his great coat and pulled out a rifle. It was ancient, with dull metal and a scarred wooden stock. It smelled of oily pennies. "What do you think, man?"

Alex fondled the rifle, checked the chamber, raised it to his eye. "Where'd you come across this?"

"An old farmer up near Aguilar who swears the company took his land. Hates anything to do with CF&I. Come on now! The Greeks have gone to take the Walsenburg shooters."

I busied myself stoking the fire, my hands trembling. Alex buttoned his flannel shirt and rummaged for his trousers. "Where do we go?"

"Wherever the hell we want." Rory patted the rifle. "We got a ticket."

"Berwind," James fingered bullets from his pockets, seeming to count them over and over. "To visit some of our old friends?"

"Berwind?" I said. "But—"

Alex interrupted me. "Pack us something to eat, Christian."

As I filled canteens and packed bread and jerky in a satchel, I smoldered. Surely Alex had no intention of putting Pearl in danger. Surely he would stop the others.

Someone knocked at the door, and Alex shot forward to open it. Outside stood a small boy, no more than twelve, looking at us with startled, blue eyes. "Mr. Lawson wants the women and children to go to the safety tent in the arroyo," he said. "He doesn't want anyone to stay in Ludlow."

Alex and James eyed each other warily.

Rory whistled. "It's lookin' to be an all-out war today."

We left the tent, Alex walking close by my side, my elbow clutched in his hand. Around us, the colony was awakening in chaos as the news spread. Tent doors swung open, men shouted to one another, dogs barked, women's voices shrilled, and children cried. The streets leading to the arroyo were strewn with the signs of a hasty exodus. Dropped gloves and hats flopped in the bitter wind. A rag-sock doll lay face down, trampled in the dirt.

"Wait," I said.

"What are you doing, Christian?" Alex asked. "Come on!"

I picked it up and propped it against the door jamb of a nearby tent.

The arroyo fell away from the prairie in sheer, sandy walls. Trash from the tents spilled down one bank like the tailings from a mine—tin cans, chipped crockery, animal skins, broken casks and splintered cart wheels. East of that, an icy footpath snaked down the steep sides to the muddy bottom, where a large, flapping tent had been hastily pegged into the soft, wet sand. An old wagon stood before it, filled with water barrels and packages of supplies. A fire burned in a shallow pit, four or five coffee urns buried deep in the coals. Beside it, a woman ground beans.

"You want some?" she asked.

"No," James clipped. "We're off."

Alex turned to me. "Stay here until it's safe. I'll come back—"

"Let me go with you. We could—"

He breathed quickly, heavily. "No, Christian, don't."

He swung away, striking out at a brisk pace, with James and Rory just behind. I watched until they disappeared around the bend just beyond the railroad bridge, fuming at my own helplessness, my uselessness. I couldn't warn Pearl, I couldn't protect her. I couldn't even protect myself, but was forced to hide out in this ditch. Mother Jones had urged women to fight, but with what? Our sewing needles, our skillets, our brooms?

The woman at the fire shivered. "Go on in," she told me. "You'll have your turn out here soon enough."

Inside the tent, I was greeted by startled, blinking eyes. Along the walls, women sat in knots, their children sprawled on their laps or lying on old blankets, sacks, or their mothers' skirts spread wide as a bed. Some of them wiped away tears on the scarves wrapped round their heads, and their voices fell dully against the canvas siding. Everyone trembled from the cold.

"News?" one girl called.

I shook my head. A mother with four children pulled one onto her lap and waved the others aside to make room for me. After I sat, she offered to share her lap robe with me.

Soon, Mrs. McCormick ducked through the flaps. "Oh, you're here!" she cried. "Thank the Lord you're safe! I told John to—"

"What's the news?"

"Nothing yet." She picked at her ragged gloves. "I just sent Mary and her young ones to Trinidad. John Lawson is sendin' them to the homes of sympathizers there. She didn't want to leave James, but with this shootin' everywhere, I couldn't stand to have those little ones here—"

"Lawson will take care of her."

"I hope so." She surveyed the huddled forms in the tent. "This is a mournful bunch."

"Some of them come from places where this happens all the time."

"Where, the northern fields?" She snorted, but her defiance turned to despair. "Ah, Christian, we can't go back, we just can't! We can't fail! We'd be poorer than when we came down. At least we had hope when we walked out, eh?"

My heart lurched—had all this been for nothing? "So you think this is the end?"

"I think our men better do their best to keep Ludlow safe," she said hotly. "They better stop that train."

We passed the time trying to stay busy, but there was little to ease our minds. The lyrics of songs died in our throats, and attempts at conversation circled around until we were back to contemplating our fate. Snow began to fall, whipped against the tent by the bitter wind. The woman who had been outside tending the fire came into the tent, and we took turns ducking in and out of the tent to fetch cups of coffee and dry, spare sandwiches that we slapped together from pieces of meat and bread. All the while, I was haunted by thoughts of Pearl, trapped in Berwind, surely as frightened as we were.

Near noon, a man opened the tent flap and called, "I need someone to come along and help with nursing. There's some men hurt out here."

His words jolted us. "Who?" someone cried, as others murmured prayers.

I looked around the tent—at the mothers, the grandmothers, the wives. "I'll go."

"Oh, no, Christian," Mrs. McCormick said. "What would I tell Alex?"

I waved her away and wrapped myself as warmly as I could in my coat, scarf and hat. Someone handed me a blanket, another gave me a shawl to wrap around my shoulders. In a gunnysack, I packed bread, sausage and cheese, and makings for coffee. The striker's name was Joe. He hefted a milk can of water. Together, we tramped through the arroyo to the steel rail bridge, keeping close to the sandy walls. The snow pelted my face, melting into a cold stream that dripped into my collar, and my shoes sank in the soggy sand.

"Walk quick, Miss," Joe warned me. "And if you hear gunfire, squat down. Don't run."

"What's happening?" I asked, huffing as I tried to keep up with his quick step.

"Don't you worry none," he said. "There's men stretched all the way from here to Walsenburg along the tracks. Just waiting for that train."

"Are they armed?"

"Those that got guns, anyway."

"What's going on up in the canyons?"

"They're shooting up the camps," he said. "Berwind, Tabasco, Hastings. Cleaning out the mine guards. The scabs have taken shelter in the mines, trying to keep out of the line of fire." He laughed and spat tobacco juice. "Let 'em find out what it's really like up there."

My heart beat violently. I could nearly see Pearl, in the Ruddy house, ducked down low, out of sight of the windows. But those walls were only wood and cardboard, easily pierced. I imagined Mrs. Ruddy stranded in bed, hysterical, probably trying to blame Pearl for it all. And Jake—God knew where he might be.

The hospital tent was emblazoned with a red cross on one side. The door flapped, already torn away by the fierce wind that whistled through the steel supports of the bridge. Inside were two camp cots. A woman in a plain brown dress with a red cross pinned to the back bent over a man lying on a cot.

"Oh, I'm glad you're here." Dark-haired and dark-eyed, she had a round, lovely face and slender shoulders. Her words carried the flat, hard consonants of an American. "How much nursing have you done?"

"Some," I said, hesitant to tell her.

"No schooling?" She pinned a red cross to my sleeve.

"No."

Joe had started to serve coffee and water to a few men sitting along the back wall of the tent. They grabbed at the food greedily. "What can I help you with, Mrs. Jolly?" he called.

"Just keep them fed," she said. "Keep them warm, if you can. Come on, Miss Scott. Let's teach you to be a nurse."

Through the afternoon, I patched up the men—an arm grazed by barbed wire, a hand slashed as the striker pitched a barrel into the burning pile on the tracks, a cut forehead—far more cautious about keeping my hands and bandages clean than I'd ever been with Theros. None of the medicines and remedies was homemade, like mine, but packaged and purchased at a drug store—iodine, Mercurochrome, plasters, powders, liniments and tonics.

Cold and weary, the men told me stories of hiding behind boxcars near the rail yards, of crouching beside piles of coal, of casting black powder bombs along the tracks, and of waiting endlessly for the steel train.

"Is it still coming here?" I asked, bandaging a striker who had come in with an elbow gashed on a barrel.

"Oh, you betcha!" He spoke with a heavy accent. "It comes from Walsens Berg tonight. But we has torn up the tracks, see? No train now."

The first bullet wound came late in the afternoon. The tent flaps flew open, and Louis Tikas and another man hefted a third into the tent. Lowering him onto a cot, Louis called for Mrs. Jolly. "His name is Giuseppe," he panted. "Shot over by the section house."

Blood soaked the leg of Giuseppe's overalls, dripping onto the floor. I grabbed cotton dressing to stanch it, while Mrs. Jolly cut away the trouser leg with a pair of shears. The flesh under the fabric was flayed, with a ragged hole in the middle of the thigh. Giuseppe writhed in pain, speaking frantically in Italian. Joe clamped his hands around each of Giuseppe's ankles to hold him still.

Mrs. Jolly flinched. "He needs to see Dr. Beshoar."

"It's too dangerous," Louis said. "We aren't sending the trucks out anymore. There's too much shooting." He tenderly touched her arm. "Do what you can."

He left, as urgently as he had arrived. Mrs. Jolly told us what to do, instructing Joe to pour whiskey down Giuseppe's throat, while I dropped metal instruments into a pan of boiling water. Standing at her shoulder, I handed her tools. With a set of long, thin pincers, she dug into his thigh while Joe more or less flattened himself across Giuseppe's chest. Giuseppe screamed with rage and pain.

The pan of water that I held between two towels lapped like a windblown lake.

"Steady, now," Mrs. Jolly said. "If you pass out, there's no one to pick you up."

She poked into the wound. "If it's only a single ball, I'll be able to get it. If not—"

Her voice trailed away as Giuseppe screamed again, then began to sob in heaving, broken cries. Her hands did not shake, yet her forehead beaded with sweat, and she swayed a little as she probed. Carefully, she pulled out a blood caked ball from the thigh. She dropped it, still clasped in the pincers, into the pan of water. "Put the dressing against it and press until the bleeding stops," she ordered me. "Don't mind if he yells."

But Giuseppe had passed out, overcome by the whiskey and pain. As I folded a fresh piece of cotton, Joe came to me. "I'll take over," he said. "You better go outside, Miss Scott. You're looking awful peakedy."

I stumbled into the bright, grayish light and cold air. Mrs. Jolly was just outside, smoking a cigarette. Offering me one, she said, "I was taught to nurse by the nuns at Minnequa Hospital in Pueblo. But I've never had to do anything like that. My God, it makes me wonder what we've gotten ourselves into."

All at once, my stomach turned, and I ran as far from her as I could before I vomited. Sinking down against the sandy wall of the ravine, I covered my face with my hands. I did not know if I was hot or cold. The air in the tent had felt so stuffy and warm, but outside, the bitter cold and snow chilled me, so that I sweated and shivered all at once.

What had we gotten ourselves into?

"Oh, so, look who is here."

The voice came from just behind me. Theros stood halfway up the side of the ravine wall, leaning against the steel strut of the bridge.

"Don't," I pleaded.

He slid down the embankment, coming to kneel just in front of me. "What is wrong?" he asked. "Miss Christian, you are shaking so! Don't be scared. Everybody goes here, goes there, shoots here, shoots there. But nobody aims. You would need to run and catch a bullet to be killed today."

I shook my head. He leaned back on his heels. He carried a rifle much shinier and newer than James' relic, one that would surely inspire envy in Alex and all the Brits. Looped over each shoulder was an ammunition bandolier, filled with hundreds more bullets than James' paltry stock.

"What is wrong?" he asked again.

My words curdled in my mouth, and I started to cry. Theros put his arms around me, pulling me against him. My cheek touched the cold metal of the bullets on his bandolier, and I put my hand up against his chest to shield my face.

"Your brother?" he asked. "Something has happened?"

As I choked out the story of Giuseppe and Mrs. Jolly's hasty operation, a volley of shots sounded along the bridge above us.

"Get down!" He pushed me down onto the sandy floor, using his body to shield me.

Silence fell again, but he did not release me.

"You are too bold for a girl, Miss Christian." Gently, he pushed a strand of hair from my eyes, his fingers light but cold against my cheek. "Too brave."

"Not brave enough. I nearly passed out—"

"If you were a coward, you would be some other place, crying and screaming."

He helped me to straighten up, and I leaned against the wall. There were men all around, I realized, squatting by bonfires built in the sand or lined up near the hospital tent to get coffee. Most seemed glad simply to be out of the fray, but a few talked in loud, tough threats. Far down the arroyo, other Greeks sat along the canyon walls, quiet and tense, waiting like coiled snakes.

"Where is the train?" My voice sounded shrill, desperate. "Shouldn't it be here by now?"

"It will come," he said. "Today, tomorrow. Someday."

"Did you go to Walsenburg? Did you find whoever shot the strikers?"

He shook his head. "I am here today."

"Aren't you afraid? All those guns, all the bullets—"

"For a minute. You either shoot or be shot at." He watched the men filing through the arroyo, his light eyes sharp, assessing. "Just stay away from the man who carries the jar of nitroglycerin—the kind to blow the mine, you know. He runs around, shaking his jar like it has milk in it. He is a fool."

"Too bad he's not on their side."

He laughed. "See, it's not so bad, yes? You don't need to cry."

"Not right now, anyway."

"And most days, it is good in Ludlow," he said. "It is good, it is free down here. You can go to Trinidad any day without getting a pass from the mine guard. You can buy at real stores with real money. The UMWA gives us real American dollar each week. Even women get money, yes?"

I wrapped my arms around me for warmth. "Fifty cents a week."

He shook his head. "Women with money! This don't happen in

Crete. Only in America. And you know what? For the first time, me and other Greeks, we walk down the streets in Trinidad and sit and talk. Like real American men, not like mules in the mine, who never see the sun. There is Greek bakery and coffee shop in Trinidad. You know it?"

"I've never been to Trinidad. What's it like?"

"Little town, lots of people." He held his hands in a vee-shape and pointed with his chin toward the left. "On this mountainside is stores—drug store, clothes, hotels, places to eat, theaters. Big places, built of stone with big windows. On other side, across the river, there's lots of big houses, all white and fancy. Everything is on a hill, so it's up, up, to walk, no matter where you go, because train depot is at bottom, by the river."

"I'd like to see it."

"Then go." He dropped his hands. "We are free now, we can talk to anybody we want. Free to see people we like when we like. It is good now, it is the best than ever before. You think that, Miss Christian?"

As if we were not sitting in a ditch awaiting death, and the cold had not numbed my face so completely that a smile felt unnatural, as if each breath of air didn't sting my lungs with the smell of gunpowder and smoke.

"In the mornings, when I wake up," I said, "I wonder what the day will bring. Oh, I don't think about something bad, like this, but I wonder if something . . . new will happen."

"See?" His passion boiled over again. "This is what we fight for. This is why we will stop that train, and every other train that comes after it. We will stop them until we are all dead."

I laid my head against my knees, tears rising again in my throat.

"No, no, don't do this," he said. "Where is your brother today?"

"He went to Berwind."

"Berwind?" he said slowly. "That train of Baldwins will come here. Where tracks are. Where Ludlow is."

His slight smarted. I said nothing, annoyed at him and at Alex.

"Miss Scott!" It was Joe, calling me back to the tent. "We need you!"

I stood quickly. Feeling light-headed again, I leaned against the bank of the arroyo.

Theros laid a hand on my arm. "Just think, we will win today, and it will be over. We will win by tomorrow."

I longed for him to promise, but I knew he would only say that we would either win or die. I said nothing, too unsure of myself. Gathering his gun and satchel, he tipped his hat and strolled down the arroyo to join the gang of Greeks.

I went back to the hospital tent. Between Joe and me, we gave Giuseppe enough whiskey to keep him still and quiet through the night.

The next afternoon, a steel-sided train filled with Baldwin-Felts agents and machine guns chugged into Ludlow not from the north, but from Trinidad in the south.

Terror broke out in Ludlow all over again. The men, some of whom had come in to rest, ran helter-skelter, charging down the tracks. Women scurried back to the safety tent. Mrs. Jolly and I kept a close eye on Giuseppe, our only remaining patient, listening all the while to the sounds of gunfire that rang through the arroyo. If we needed to leave, we would have to take him with us.

As the sun dropped behind the mesas in the west, we heard the roar of the locomotive and the blare of the whistle. After that, the sounds came in short, quick punctuations: volleys of gunfire, the screeching of metal on metal, a boom that echoed through the arroyo, another barrage of gunshots. Finally, everything quieted.

"I wonder what's happened," Mrs. Jolly asked, taking stock of the medicines she had left.

We didn't wait long before we knew. Early in the evening, Ludlow's men began to drift in, singing and hollering, already well on their way to celebrating. Just after dark, Alex came to the hospital tent to find me. I left Mrs. Jolly with Giuseppe.

Outside, Mrs. McCormick whooped. "Look here, Christian! They're all safe! And wait until you hear what became of that train!"

"We shot at it from along the tracks, Kirstie girl!" Uncle John hugged me in delight. "It started to back away, but the cowards were movin' so fast, it clipped a telephone pole in Forbes. Brought pole, line and all down on it. The Baldwins spilled out, runnin' every which way. I don't doubt we cut down a few of the bastards."

James shouldered his rifle. "Ludlow'll be celebrating for days!"

Laughing like jokers, James, Alex and Uncle John passed around a flask, their boasts growing louder and bolder.

"Oh, you should have seen it," James crowed. "I shot the hell out of the old house. Some scabs living there now. Should have seen them run for the mine when I blasted through the windows. Scattering like mice!"

I hung back, forcing Alex to dawdle. We fell into place behind the McCormicks and James, walking up the arroyo toward the tent colony.

"Any news of Pearl?" I pulled my coat closer around my chin. "Could you see the Ruddy house?"

"James manned the gun most of the day, having his fun with it. I barely had a look through the scope." He held back, letting the others forge ahead. "But I'll tell you this, Christian. They think they've won something today. But the Baldwins—they're piling in as fast as they can in those hills. They have machine guns, scopes, wagons of ammunition. I saw it. We're surrounded."

All at once, a bone-weary ache overcame me. I didn't want to hear any more stories of battle or doom. I only wanted to go home, warm myself, and sleep.

We walked through the colony in silence. Yet, as we approached our tent, we could see a light burning within the canvas walls, casting a shadow of a lone person in the tent. A haze of smoke drifted down to us from the chimney.

"What the hell?" Alex roared. He ran toward the tent. I followed, reaching the door just after he had jerked it open.

A scent reached me that I had not smelled for a long time—an aroma of sage and juniper and all the sweetness of the plants on the mesas.

Pearl stood at the stove, a fully cooked meal beckoning us to her.

Chapter 17

"I come down on a cloud," she said. "It was the most wonderful thing."

She spread her hands, palms up. The gesture jarred me from my stupor, and I ran to her and wrapped my arms around her. The worry of the past two days emptied in great bursts of tears. "You're safe," I whispered. "You're alive."

"Hush now, Christian, hush now. Sure I am." She wiped away my tears with her fingertips. "What a sight you are! Ain't there no soap down here in Ludlow?"

I could feel the gummy dirt on my face. My hair hung heavy with grease, and I smelled of wood smoke and sweat. My clothes were soiled by dirt, spilled coffee, and even blood, and my shoes and stockings were caked with gritty mud. I managed a weak laugh. "I've been gone for two days. There was no water to spare."

Pearl reached out her hands to Alex. "I sure am glad to see you."

He whispered something I did not catch, a word that drifted to her and made her smile. "I'm home," she said.

He kissed her forehead, and she threw her arms around his neck. I busied myself near the stove, lifting the teakettle and pouring a steaming pool into the basin.

"Let that cool for a few minutes before you wash, Christian," Pearl said. "It's awful hot."

"It would feel good."

"Until you scald your skin right off." She moved away from Alex and pulled out the chair from the table. "Sit down, Alex."

"Have you left Russell, then?"

"Yes." She laughed, her wild, unsettling laugh. "I left them all, every last one of them. I spit on the way out the door. I ain't going back." With a quick turn, she looked me up and down, her eyes coming to rest at my feet. "Them's the ugliest shoes I ever laid eyes on. Where'd you get them?"

"They're union shoes," I said. "I hurt my ankle the day we left Berwind and had to cut off my boot, it was so swollen. The union gives these out free."

"They look like men's."

"They are."

She laughed, doubling over with her mirth. Infected, I followed suit, tears and smiles mingling on my face. Alex joined us, and soon all three of us were laughing in great shouts of relief.

"I'm so glad to be home," Pearl said, wiping her eyes. "Wash quick, Christian. You, too, Alex. I fixed this special."

Pearl's meal spread generously before us, savory and rich, even though she'd created it from the supplies I'd left in the tent. Both Alex and I ate as if we'd been starving. Pearl buzzed around us, as if we were her guests.

"It was a miracle," she said, once she'd filled her own plate. "I was all scared and lonesome up there in Berwind, thinking I'd never see another day, what with all the shooting and screaming. Oh, folks was running this way and that, and everybody yelled, go get in the mine, it's the only place you won't get shot. And I just decided, I ain't going down them dark tunnels, where I can't see what's under my feet."

Alex laughed. "There are more rats in the houses in Berwind than in the tunnels."

She churned her food with her fork. "Besides, there was Miz Ruddy to think about—"

"Her!" I cried.

"She's been laid up sick in bed with the dropsy, you know. Well, I knew she couldn't walk that far, or else she'd scream like a mountain cat as we went, and we'd be shot anyway."

"But weren't you afraid of the bullets?" I asked. "Weren't your windows shot out?"

She smiled, sheepish. "I sat under the table, with Russ' old mining hat on my head and a mountain of old crates piled around me to stop the bullets. I probably looked like a lunatic."

We laughed again.

"Only a couple of our windows was broke," she said. "Your old house was worse. Not a one wasn't broken."

"James did that," Alex said. "All of our houses—theirs, John's and Edith's, the McKennas'. Right up the row."

Pearl laughed. "When you go back, I bet the company will charge you for them."

He laughed loudly. "I'll pay them in scrip."

I asked, "So, you walked out of Berwind while there was gunfire?"

"Well," she said, "I was just sitting under my table with the dogs a-yapping and Miz Ruddy cussing her head off. But then, something told me to go outside, to look up to the mesa." She laughed, a low, sweet cadence. "And there's this bright silver cloud, just hanging on the slope. It must've been sent by—I don't know—Jesus or somebody. As I watched, it just kept coming my way, floating toward the house. Just drifting, slow as the night, right toward me."

Alex laughed. "A cloud?"

"It's true! It was all silver and bright. Like no cloud I'd never seen before." She shook back her hair. "When it got down to the house, it just filled it up. Floated in through all the windows. All I could see was silver light, and I knew it was safe to go. And once I started moving, it just kept up with me, and I headed right toward Ludlow. This time, I knew the way, because that cloud drifted along with me, telling me so."

We all sat entirely still, willing ourselves into belief. Alex's fork was halfway to his mouth, and Pearl's hands were lifted near her heart. Outside, a band had started up in the public square. Someone began blustering through the bullhorn.

The noise brought me back to the tent, the weather, the shooting. "But the hills were crawling with men," I said. "And the fighting! Pearl, how did you make it through all that?"

"I was blessed, I guess." She turned to Alex. "And I tasted that cloud."

"What do you mean?" he asked.

"You told me once that the clouds in old Scotland tasted of salt—"

"Our father told us that," I said.

"Well, I tasted my cloud, and it was of the softest rain and the newest of the spring grasses, and the sage and the smell of snow. You was right. The clouds taste. They taste good."

Alex gestured with his fork. "Not as good as this."

I reached for Pearl's hand. "I've missed you," I said. "Oh, how I've missed you."

"You folks only been gone a month, but it seems a lifetime."

As we ate, Alex retold the story of the steel train, and I told of helping the men in the hospital tent.

"That you both come home safe is a miracle, too!" Pearl said at the end of it. "There must be a host of heavenly angels hanging over this tent."

We laughed at that, but even the thought of heaven's vanguard wasn't enough to dispel the discomfort of our situation. Our tent, already encumbered by the bodies of two people, could barely hold another. The air seemed stale and hot. Around the table, our knees knocked when we sat. Hands grazed against each other as we reached for forks or knives, elbows clunked as we cut our meat. We did our best to keep from crashing into one another as we cleared the table.

"Where's Jake these days?" Alex asked.

She shrugged, pouring water to wash. "I don't know. Down here, maybe, shooting at Dago City. That's what he calls it. I don't know. He don't come home much no more."

Alex let it drop, his attention on Pearl. Her hands were plunged into suds, the front of her dress spotted with water. Her hair had broken loose and hung in sweet, curling drifts around the side of her face, and one black, tender strand coiled down her neck to her shoulders. Watching Alex, I realized that he was still a young man, at the age where men fell in love and married and became fathers. He was not so many years older than Theros.

I picked up my coat and slipped it onto my arms.

"Where you going, Christian?" Pearl asked.

"Out," I said. "I'll be—"

"You be careful," Alex said, but he did not try to stop me.

"This time, I got my own clothes," Pearl said as I opened the door. "So I don't have to borrow yours."

"After the fun you made of my new shoes, I wouldn't let you borrow them anyway."

Her laughter followed me outside. "You're still mean!" she called.

I walked through the darkness to the public square, packed and bustling even at this time of night. Children out of bed late and reveling in the freedom of the darkness, women welcoming home their soldier husbands, men marching in from the hills and arroyos and tracks where the battles had taken place. A band of Italians played quick, light dances on accordion, violin and mandolin. Meat and coffee roasted over a fire in a pit. Union trucks belched into the square, spilling those who'd taken refuge in Trinidad from their flat beds. The bullhorn squealed endlessly, passed from hand to hand.

I found James, Mrs. McCormick and Uncle John waiting at one corner of the square. "We're hoping Mary comes home tonight," Mrs. McCormick fretted. "They said they won't bring many more trucks up from town because it's too dark."

"Where's Alex?" Uncle John asked me.

"He'll be along in a while," I lied.

"Look over there!" James shouted. "Wild men, they are! Crazy!"

Across the square, the Greeks danced furiously to music that was much livelier, much wilder than the Italians' offering—music that they woofed out in low, raucous voices. Dressed in their black breeches and black leather boots and leggings, with colorful sashes around their waists, they bent at the knees, then leaped upward in powerful bounds. Hands on their hips, they whirled until their bodies were nothing but blurs. Every now and then, they paused and shouted—a quick, feral bark. Theros swayed to and fro in the midst of them, a clean white shirt on his back and a green sash whipping as he danced. Occasionally he broke step to drink from a flask or clap another on the back or wrestle him to the ground.

"Ah, they've good cause for celebration," Uncle John said. "They left a trail of bodies from Ludlow to Walsenburg, all right. Burned Barnes Station, the section house, shot the hell out of the guards there. They're a fine lot of killers."

"They have a fine lot of guns," James groused.

I folded my arms across my chest, a terrible thickness in my throat. Yearning buckled my knees, made my heart skip achingly into the very center of my breast. I wanted to laugh, to spill out the news of Pearl's arrival, and dare anyone to throw the first stone. I wanted to cry, because everything seemed so impossible. I wanted to return to the hours I'd spent in the arroyo the day before, when Theros and I had talked. Then, he hadn't been a wild, foreign man leaping in a dance I could not follow. He hadn't been a killer. Then, I could see myself walking down a street in Trinidad with him, or sitting at a café, in the sun, talking without a care.

Around us, the crowd shuffled and jumbled and yammered and yelled. The story of the steel train was told and retold, growing more thrilling each time—the speeding train bearing down on the colony, the strikers ambushing it with a hail of gunfire from every last man, the guards dropping face-first dead in the snow, the train reversing so fast it derailed in Forbes in a mighty crash of steel and steam.

And still, I watched the Greeks, unable to take my eyes away.

Near midnight, Mary O'Keegan and her daughters rushed forward, returned from Trinidad. James wrapped her in his arms and began to sweep her about in circles. Uncle John swept up Mrs. McCormick, and they kicked into a jig, which no more fit with the Italian music than the Greeks' solitary celebration. So many people waltzed and skipped and twirled in the square that the union man with the bullhorn had to shout through it for a good five minutes before he gained our attention.

"Hey!" he screeched. "Listen! We have just received a telegram from Denver! Governor Ammons has called out the Colorado National

Guard! Troops will be here for peace-keeping duties in three days!"

The mood curdled. The Greeks fell to the earth, flying no more, and the spinning dances of Italian, Welsh, Slav and American ended in stumbling steps. The music petered away with a few ugly squeaks. A few booed or hissed, venting their disbelief. At once, I could hear children crying to be taken to bed, and couples arguing, and men's voices heated up with alcohol and anger. The day's victory faded as fast as it had been won.

"Peace-keeping!" James shouted. "That's a lie!"

"Three days!" Mrs. McCormick mourned. "No time at all!"

I went back to our tent. I tapped on the door frame, but heard no answer. Opening the door, I found Alex sitting on the foot of my bed. He was just tucking in one of the bricks that we heated in the stove and put at the end of our beds. Pearl was stretched across it, in a white nightgown, in a deep sleep.

When he looked up at me, his face was serene, even hopeful. "You'll have to squeeze to fit in," he said.

"When you share a bed with Pearl, you're used to it."

"Aye, I suppose."

He turned away, and I knew that my words had set him to wishing, but not, I was sure, as much as I was. I remembered that hot afternoon in Berwind, lying next to Theros on a cot too narrow for both of us, breathless with need, and so close to him, yet so afraid—

I swallowed against that too tender memory. "The governor's called out the militia."

The spell broke for Alex, too, and he smoothed the blankets over Pearl's feet. "Let the Greeks loose with guns, and what do you expect?"

I bit my tongue. Who had attacked Berwind and the other camps? Who shot out windows and aimed at scabs as if they were cans on a ledge? They weren't Greek.

"What do you think will happen?" I asked.

He shrugged, stood, and went to his own side of the tent. I heard him fumbling for his flask. I did not look at him, for I knew I would see the years of sorrow and disappointment pile on him again, lining his face with worry and despair.

But when I slipped under the blanket and into Pearl's warmth, I fell asleep, and slept well. I dreamed of flying, of leaping into air that was thin and pure, silver as a cloud. I laughed as I flew, twirling in the dazzling mist, soaring so high and so fearlessly that when my feet finally touched the ground, it felt unfamiliar beneath them, like a place I had never been before.

Chapter 18

We were to welcome the militia with a parade. We were to show our pride, our determination, our orderliness and our willingness to cooperate. Wear our best, use our best manners, be on our best behavior. Like true Americans.

We readied ourselves for the parade as best as we could in our cramped tent. Pearl washed my hair, scrubbing deep against my scalp with her fingertips, and rinsing it twice with vinegar to make it soft as a baby's. She brushed it with a care that I hadn't given to myself in years.

"Your hair's grown so long," she said. "And the color—there ain't nothing on God's earth that's the same color. Not gold or copper, not flame, not blood. It's all that and more."

When she finished, she held a hand mirror before me. I rarely took the time to moon over myself, but that day, I studied my eyes and mouth and freckled skin. I looked stately and older than seventeen years. My cheeks had fleshed out, so that my chin was not so sharp. My mouth no longer looked too heavy-lipped for my face, but like a woman's. My hair fell in glorious, soft curls on my shoulders.

Alex appeared, dressed in Dad's green jacket and red, green and blue tartan kilt. A smile stretched across his usually somber face.

"You look right handsome, Alex," Pearl offered.

He straightened the high, square shoulders of the jacket. "Dad was a bigger man than me, though."

"He'd be proud," I said.

He reached behind him. "Here, Christian. I've kept this for you. I wanted to give it to you for your wedding day, but this seems a better time."

A thick woolen scarf trailed from his hand. The fabric was soft and rich, as downy as the sheep's wool from which it was made, and the pattern was the same vibrant tartan as Alex's kilt. I took it from him, kneading the fine wool beneath my fingertips. Tears unexpectedly filled my eyes.

"You wear it from shoulder to shoulder." Alex laid it on my left shoulder so it fell across my breast and cinched it in at my waist, under my arm. "See? That's the traditional way. Or shawl-like, if you've a mind to."

I wrapped the scarf over both shoulders. "This was Momma's?"

"Aye, it's the Scott tartan." His eyes watered. "Lord, Kirstie, you look just like her."

My own memories of her were dim, but at Alex's words, pride and joy blossomed in me.

He handed me a blue hat. "And here's a tam-o'-shanter to go with it."

"Let Pearl wear it."

"Oh, no," she protested. "I ain't no Scotchman. I'm going dressed in my best American."

"What's that?" Alex asked.

She laughed. "I don't rightly know."

The day had dawned surprisingly mild and pleasant. The welcoming parade streamed across the prairie for a quarter of a mile, behind the American flag and a two-colored banner that read LUDLOW. The children of the tent colony, dressed in white tunics, marched first, singing, "The Union Forever." Then a brass band lumbered along, playing American patriotic songs.

Each nationality marched under its own flag. James waved the Union Jack as he strode, with Alex and two others manning a hand-painted banner that read "Miners of the British Isles."

Dressed in her blue bridal suit, Pearl walked beside me.

Almost at once, she caught Mrs. McCormick's eye. "Your husband's joinin' the strike, then, Mrs. Ruddy?"

"He ain't," Pearl said. "But I signed up as a official, registered UMWA striker just yesterday."

Mrs. McCormick sniffed and looked across the prairie, where the colony's residents were fanning out into a half-circle to greet the Colorado National Guard.

Jane McKenna craned her neck, trying to see to the north, where the trains were puffing on the tracks. "They'll be wearin' fancy uniforms," she sighed. "Epaulets and gold braid and all."

"They're not likely to be friendly, Jane," Mrs. McCormick huffed. "John says they fought in the Spanish-American war, some of them. He thinks they'll rival our Greeks in killin' for sport."

"Oh, they'll try to break the men, all right," Uncle John said. "Break the strike by breakin' the men. Mark my words, that's the way it always works in Colorado."

The prairie was alive with color and motion. Mexican women

swirled like butterflies in their bright, flashing skirts while the men bent giant sombreros against the wind. The Italian wives came wrapped in layers of delicate lace, and the Germans wore their lederhosen and suspenders. The Greeks lagged behind, the Cretans in their black, others in white kilts and open-necked shirts. On their heads, the Cretans wore tasseled hats, and a few had strapped sabers at their waists. Shamelessly, I searched for Theros, but I could not spot him among the hundred or so men clustered around the blue and white flag of Greece.

"Look, here they come!" James called.

With the sound of thunder, the cavalry galloped toward us. Sunshine glinted from the polished metal of bridles, saddles and brass buttons, and the horses pranced in exquisite, sleek-bodied waves. The soldiers' uniforms were the color of the dried grass beneath our feet, with leather leggings wound from their knees to their boots. On their heads were wide-brimmed campaign hats; at their sides were shiny, new rifles.

"Look how young they are," Pearl giggled. "Better give them pop-guns, not rifles!"

The horsemen spurred their horses to wild speeds, pounding up a wreath of dust, and then halted in even, straight lines at the far end of the prairie. From the opposite end of the field came foot soldiers, swinging their rifles with grace and clicking their heels so often that we started to mimic them. Along the roads, spectators from as far away as Denver tooted the horns of their automobiles. The fair-haired photographer, whose camera had already caught Alex and me in our Scottish finery, captured pictures of the scene. And all the while, the flat cars slowly rolled past on the tracks, laden with wagons, rolls of brown canvas tenting, crates of ammunition and cannons.

"This doesn't look like a peace-keeping force to me," Alex grumbled. "They've brought Gatlings."

An older uniformed man rode forth on a horse with a silver saddle. He saluted his troops and halted in the center of field. Peering over the crowd, he raised his hand for silence. Thanking John Lawson, Louis Tikas and the other union officials for the welcome, he introduced himself as General Chase and announced his first two directives. All strikers were to bring their weapons to the gates of the colonies for disarmament by the troops. All saloons in the strike zone would be closed.

A hush fell. The breeze licked at the flags, snapping them, and the horses pawed and neighed. The Union Jack dipped, and James quickly arighted it.

"Och, what's all this?" Alex muttered. "We aren't under martial law."

Louis Tikas stepped forward from the crowd. "We will do as you ask," he said simply.

But only thirty-seven rusted and broken guns were surrendered at Ludlow that day. None in the sorry lot resembled the one that Theros had wielded on the day of the steel train. Nor did James' ancient rifle appear in the pile.

I was pouring Alex's coffee the next morning when a knock shook the door frame of our tent. "Private Lewis and Sergeant Crandall of Company K," a voice called. "Please open your door."

Alex unlatched the door, but he did not allow the troopers inside. The boys were dressed in full khaki, with bands of blue tied around their campaign hats.

"We've been ordered to search for arms," Private Lewis told him, peering into the tent.

"We have no arms," Alex said. "They were collected yesterday."

"You folks speak English," Lewis said in disbelief. "We were told no one in these tents was American."

"If you folks would just let us in," Sergeant Crandall said. "We'll be quick."

"Did you boys disarm the mine guards yesterday?" Alex asked. "Did you take the guns from the Baldwin-Felts? Or only from the men in the tent colonies?"

Crandall straightened his shoulders and spoke half-heartedly, "We have orders—"

"Get on with your business, then."

They stood in the doorway like children invited over for cake. At last, the sergeant poked around Alex's bed, obviously uncertain what to do. Lewis looked under Pearl's and my bed, then opened the drawers of the bureau where I kept my clothes. I thought at once of the lock of Pearl's hair, of the books of Burns' verse and Scott's prose, of my mother's scarf nestled there amid sachets of sage. I breathed, "Please don't."

"What are you doing?" Alex whipped away the hanging blanket so that he could see. "Get your hands out of there!"

"I'm sorry, sir. We have orders to check everywhere." Lewis looked young, no more than my age.

"What's the matter?" Crandall moved from the stove, where he had aimlessly rattled our pots and crocks and poked here and there in the coal bucket.

"You come here to paw through our things and you can't see what's the matter?" Alex demanded.

"We have orders not to harm or take anything," he said. "Unless it's guns."

"Martial law hasn't been declared, has it?" Alex asked. "Oh, the governor called you here, but he never said we answer to you, and until he does, I consider myself a free man in this country. You have no right to search here."

Lewis pointed to the trap door. "What's that?"

"It's a cellar," I said. "A place for storage."

He lifted the door and peered inside. "Nothing but junk down there," he reported to the sergeant. "Do you want me to go down in?"

"No," said Crandall, casting a look of fear at Alex. "Never mind."

They left, but none of us moved, even after we heard them knock on the door of the McKennas' tent. At last, Pearl whispered, "You ain't got nothing they'd want, do you?"

"No."

"Where's the gun?" I whispered, wondering, too, where the Greeks had hidden their weapons.

"James has it. He's built some kind of secret case for it under the floor." Alex went to the shelves and pulled down his whiskey. "Well, they didn't find this, did they, even though it was sitting in plain sight?"

He poured himself a generous dose. I picked up a piece of sewing, but my hands shook so that the stitches were tortured and overlapped. They had touched nearly everything, and I could feel their fingerprints like a stain on my clothes and books and bedding. I could hear their breathing, smell them in the stagnant air of the tent.

I could not help but agree with Alex. When the military trains had rolled into Ludlow, our freedoms had just as quickly rolled away.

Chapter 19

We had something that the militia wanted, after all. The day after Private Lewis and Sergeant Crandall searched our tent, another knock sounded our door. Pearl and I eyed one another warily. Alex had already left for the picket line.

A single soldier stood outside our tent. "Hello, Miss," he said. "Is this the tent of Alexander Gordon Scott from Berwind?"

"Yes," I breathed.

"Is there a lady here by the name of Mrs. Pearl Ruddy?"

I felt Pearl pull back behind me, as if she would hide behind the bullhide sheeting. "Yes," I said.

"I'm Private Donald. Mrs. Ruddy, would you please come to the train station with me?"

"Don't leave me, Christian," Pearl pleaded. "Stay with me."

The militia had set up temporary headquarters at Ludlow's train station, commandeering two small offices at the back. Each office had once housed a single railroad employee, but was now serving a handful of militia officers. Already, the offices were in disarray with the administrative burden of a field army. Papers and typewriters perched on ledges or heaped haphazardly on uneven surfaces, and telephones had been patched into the lines that ran parallel with the railroad tracks, their wires looping up the walls and out the windows. Officers bustled in and out of the station, giving reports, taking orders, conferring in voices that carried through the entire station.

Private Donald led Pearl and me into the second office, where an important-looking officer sat behind a scarred desk. In a chair in front of the desk sat Russell Ruddy, dressed in an elegant brown suit, his hat in his hands. Both men stood as we entered the room.

"Russ!" Pearl exclaimed. "What are you doing down here? Are you joining the strike?"

The officer at the desk cleared his throat. "I'm Captain Philip Van Cise," he said. "I'm in charge of Company K, which is currently overseeing affairs at the Ludlow tent colony. Are you Mrs. Ruddy?"

"I am," Pearl said.

"Your husband has requested to talk to you." The captain rose. "I'll leave the two of you alone. Please take your time."

"Christian, stay with me." Pearl grabbed at my arm, but Russell gently reached out and touched her shoulder.

"Alone, Pearl," he said. "Please."

"Your friend can wait just outside, Mrs. Ruddy." Picking up his campaign hat, Captain Van Cise smartly crooked his elbow, tucked my hand through it, and escorted me to the lobby. "You can wait here, Miss," he said, showing me to a bench. With a polite nod of his head, he left me and took up a post near the office door.

I sat where he left me. The militia office had a large window that looked out on the lobby, and even though the blind was half-lowered, I could see Pearl and Russell from the bench where I sat.

At first, they faced one another straight on, Russell with his hat still in his hands, and Pearl fingering the fringe on her shawl. Putting down his hat, Russell gestured with his hands. Pearl's head bowed some, and he stepped closer, his head bent close to her ear.

She listened to him for some time, but when he raised his arms and wrapped them around her, she pulled away. Lurching out of the office, she bumped into Captain Van Cise in her haste. Russell ran after her, catching her by the arm as she reached the lobby. Almost at once, a small crowd gathered, watching eagerly.

"Please, Pearl, don't walk away," he said. "You need to come back, you have to come home—"

"All you want is somebody to take care of your old ma," she snapped. "Well, she can just tonic herself to death for all I care."

A few in the crowd tittered, and Captain Van Cise interceded. "Mr. and Mrs. Ruddy, please step back into the office. This is no place to discuss—"

"I'm not talking about Ma," Russell said, without hearing the captain's words. "I need you with me. You have to understand—"

"Need me for what?" she cried. "So we can just pretend some more? So nobody'll think you're . . . well, guess what, Russ? Just about everybody knows."

Russell's face blanched, as if he'd been violently wounded, stricken to his soul. Putting his hat on his head, he walked out of the station.

Pearl ran through the opposite door and across the wooden platform to the dirt road leading back to Ludlow. I followed, trotting in her wake.

In our tent, she set about baking, banging pots together and jabbing firewood into the stove. I took up sewing, trying to outlast the storm, to be a silent, welcome friend. Yet as she was breaking eggs, she dropped eggshell into the batter. "Damn it!" she said.

"What happened in that office with Russell?" I coaxed. "What did he say? Did he threaten you?"

Digging in the batter with one finger, she said, "Not Russ. He wouldn't do that. He just said he was so sorry I'd come down here, that I was gone."

"Then why did you run from him?"

She banged down the spoon. "Oh, God, I shouldn't have done what I did! I shouldn't have shamed him that way! He ain't never done nothing mean to me!"

She started to cry, and I helped her to lie down and shushed her until she fell asleep. But as I finished baking the bread, I thought again of Russell's face. He had looked desperate, like a man who had lost his only friend, or maybe even his true love.

The first few days of the militia's presence brought a fragile peace to Ludlow. Militiamen and strikers played baseball when the wind did not howl or the snow fly. Girls flocked to dances in the big tent, hoping to catch the eye of one of the sometime soldiers of the Colorado National Guard—a grocer, perhaps, so they'd never be hungry again, or a dry goods merchant, so they would always have clothes.

The sweet-faced boys of Company K—who we came to call Blue Bands, because of the blue ribbon around their campaign hats—lived in a colony of brown, tepee-like tents that sat catty-corner to Ludlow, across the intersection of the dirt road to Ludlow and the road to Delagua Canyon. Mostly college boys called to duty from their classes, they patrolled outside Ludlow's barbed wire fence and offered presents and giddy conversation to the girls of the colony. Pearl gathered a heap of trinkets from the troopers as she hung laundry on the community line or hauled buckets of water from the well, and even I found myself laden with bits of ribbon, buttons and paper fans.

"Some of them boys is dumb as pie." Pearl laughed. "They don't know why they come here or what the strike's all about. Some of them don't even know where they come to. They think this here is the state of New Mexico."

"Don't you be fooled," Alex said darkly. "It won't last long."

The news of Pearl's arrival had nearly trumped that of the militia's, passing through the canvas tents like the crack of a summer thunderstorm. But it was Pearl's meeting with Russell at the station that brought Mrs. McCormick to our door, demanding that Pearl move into a tent set up near the edge of the colony for women whose husbands had not joined the strike.

"She sleeps with me in my bed," I argued. "It's all perfectly respectable."

"It is not," Mrs. McCormick insisted. "We're to keep this colony clean and moral, and since she's made it clear that she has no intention of being a proper wife, she needs to live with the other single women and widows. Why did she decide to come down here, anyway?"

"She wanted to join the strike."

Mrs. McCormick huffed, not even bothering to acknowledge that one. "That's another thing—suckerin' the union into payin' her way while her husband is still workin' for Johnny D! The union should send her right back up to him. I've half a mind to have my John take this up with the union officials."

"Don't, Mrs. McCormick." My resolve broke. "Please."

There were plenty who welcomed Pearl. The foreign women who had seen her hair hanging in the schoolhouse clamored for her attentions. They planted themselves outside our tent door during the day, calling for Pearl to sit with them and to touch their children's heads for luck.

One woman begged Pearl to lay hands upon her swollen stomach. "I come from Italy when my husband sees picture of me," she said. "We meet at train station, marry in one hour."

"Is that so?" Pearl said, her tea-colored hands alighting on the woman's belly as gracefully as two birds. "Do you love him?"

"Oh, he no bad sort. No drink. No hit much." She grabbed Pearl's hand. "He say strike is short, that baby is born in house in Berwind. No in tent with drips in roof."

"When's the baby coming?"

"Today, tomorrow. Baby is born in Ludlow." Shyly, she added, "You are good luck. For him to be strong and handsome."

Pearl took everything in stride, not simply spreading hope but also good advice. She delivered shoes to women as often as she delivered babies. She offered remedies not only for illness, but potions to calm a drunken husband. She brewed a foul-smelling potion from chamomile and Lydia Pinkham's tonic for a girl, not more than fourteen, to wash away an unwanted child. In return, the women brought her gifts—linens from the Old Country, cakes baked with precious eggs, silver chains, fragrant soaps. They hauled buckets of water, emptied slop jars and scoured sticky food from the bottoms of pans for her.

"Miz Ruddy ought to have this crew helping her," Pearl remarked. "She'd think she'd died and gone to heaven."

"Let's hope she has," I said.

I thought Pearl might scold, but her face twisted inward. "I wonder what Russ is thinking now," she mused. "I hope he's getting along good enough."

Mid-November bore down on Ludlow with a dreariness we had not yet seen. The sound of coughing echoed through the colony as children and the old suffered from winter colds. Snow fell, and the sun hid behind heavy, gray clouds. The union's stash of shoes and coats dwindled. At the gates of the colony, where warmth-giving coal had mounded during the first days of September, a few chunks lay scattered under the snow. Fresh meat no longer arrived at the commissary every day.

Rumor had it that the negotiations in Denver, where CF&I and the UMWA bartered for our lives, were so bitter that the two sides no longer met. In New York, John D. Rockefeller told the newspapers that the strike in Colorado was not serious enough to command his attention.

Then, just as Alex had predicted, the militia turned against us.

It started with simple discourtesies—a woman pushed off the boardwalk in the town of Ludlow by a soldier, a man and his wife searched as they stepped from the train, and strikers turned back at the post office without their mail. A week later, mounted soldiers rode down strikers gathered at the depot. Military blockades on the roads to Ludlow halted the union supply trucks and forced the drivers to return to Trinidad.

The outrages were reported at weekly meetings in Ludlow, where John Lawson and Louis Tikas begged us to keep the peace. "The Colorado National Guard isn't the enemy!" Lawson shouted through the bullhorn. "Colorado Fuel & Iron is!"

But in Company B, which was assigned to Berwind Canyon, the faces beneath the yellow-banded military campaign hats had begun to resemble the mine guards we'd known in the canyons. Commanded by Lieutenant Karl Linderfelt, a veteran of the Spanish-American war, the Yellow Bands became the scourge of Ludlow.

"It's nothing more than happened before," Alex pronounced bitterly. "The soldiers want to see the strike end, so that they can go home and get on with their lives. Well, I'd like to get on with my life, too."

Pearl busied herself with a skillet at the stove, undoubtedly wondering what would happen to her if we returned to Berwind Canyon—with or without a union. I took up my coat and went outside to give Alex and Pearl time alone, hoping that the clean, cold air would calm my nerves. It wasn't pleasant outside in the gusty wind, but it was away from the unspoken thoughts in the tent. I headed toward the arroyo.

As I slid down the icy path, Theros was winding his way up.

We both stopped, as if we were strangers who might squeeze around one another with muttered apologies. His eyes were clear in the light of late afternoon. He wore a hat pulled low over his dark hair, but a stubborn lock curled over his forehead.

Laughing at our predicament, he asked, "Miss Christian, you are walking where?"

"I need fresh air."

"I will walk with you." He stretched forward to take my hands and help me down the steep slope.

The arroyo had been claimed as part of Ludlow, and it was filled with activity no matter how bitter the weather. We strolled among women who were gathering mesquite driftwood for fuel, and children who played in icy pools left by the snow. Others strode purposefully through the arroyo, aiming to catch one of the union trucks that picked up passengers from the roads north of the tents. A few vendors rolled ramshackle carts through the sand, peddling everything from hot coffee to children's toys.

We walked to the west, toward the steel bridge. Our feet slithered in the icy mud, until our shoes were caked by sand as heavy as bricks. Theros thrust his hands into his pockets for warmth. I kept one hand on my scarf, to keep it from blowing off my head.

"Miss Pearl lives with you now?" he asked.

"Since the day of the steel train."

"How does she come here?"

"She walked." I looked sidelong at him. "Through a cloud."

"A cloud?"

I told him the story.

He laughed, but his forehead creased. "She does not belong here. She is a company man's wife."

I flared into belligerence. "She belongs with us, not with the Ruddy family. She's always been more like Alex and me than like them."

"Maybe." He looked down the canyon, as if weighing my words. "In Greece, a girl stays with her man, no matter what. He may beat her, he may starve her, he may drink, but she stays."

I gathered my coat around me. "That's not right."

"Smart men don't do those things. In Greece, marrying is between families. If a wife leaves, she is disgrace to her father and mother and sisters and uncles."

"And the husband?"

"The same. A man who leaves his wife is shameful and bad, no longer one of his family. He has forgotten his *time*."

"What does that mean?"

"His—you must learn Greek." The wind plucked at the brim of his hat until his light eyes and forehead were clearly exposed. "Doing right. Doing what he should, but better than that—"

"His honor."

"Honor—yes, maybe that is the word."

"So you think Pearl should go back to Berwind?"

"Oh, no, it is different in America," he said. "If you don't like your wife, you say goodbye. Don't like husband, you walk away on a cloud. Nobody fusses, nobody cares, nobody's mother cries. You think that is better, right?"

"I think it's better."

He shrugged. "So, I will, too. I'm an American."

We both laughed, as if the whole situation were a joke. A train thundered across the steel bridge, heading north for Pueblo, its cars fully laden with coal. Women and children ran along the tracks beside it, chasing wildly after the cars.

"They are getting coal," he remarked as two boys scrabbled in the dirt beside the tracks. "Catching what falls off the cars. There's no more coal from the UMWA."

"What?" I turned to look at him, and the wind caught me full in the face. "They're not bringing in more?"

"People take too much, burn too much." He kicked at the muddy sand. "And where can union buy more coal anyway? From CF&I? But, there is no money anyway."

My breath caught in my throat. "What do you mean?"

"They don't think we are here for so long," he said. "They don't think there would be so many of us. Twenty-thousand, now, they say, on union lists! We use up all the million of dollars that the UMWA has, and for what? CF&I says, no deal for you. So now what?"

"But they can't just quit taking care of us—"

"Look at Ludlow." He swept his hand over the arroyo. "What do you see? Dark hair, dark skin. Listen. What do you hear? Not English." He laughed dryly. "Union wants strikers to be light skin and yellow hair, with blue eyes, like china dolls. No accents neither. Then men from the newspapers will come and take pictures and tell everybody how sad it is that these people suffer. Help them, they will say. Send money, send food to these beautiful, sad people. But who cares about dagos?"

I said nothing, fearful that he spoke the truth.

He ran up the steep embankment until he could reach the girders of the bridge with long, outstretched arms. "Come up here, Miss Christian," he called. "There is no wind."

He sat, and I joined him, wincing at the bitter feel of the frozen ground, which never saw sun, beneath me.

"Just don't be scared," he warned me. "When the trains go over this bridge, it makes terrible roar. We hide up here to wait for the trains."

"You steal coal, too?"

"Not like them." He waved his hand in the direction of the women and children. "One man jumps on the train as it slows down, before it comes into Ludlow. He shovels coal onto the track for others to shovel up quick from ground, then jumps off when the soldiers start to shoot. Everybody runs then."

My heart clamored. "What if you're caught or—?"

"Then I am caught." He laughed. "Every day, Louis is called to the depot and told by the soldiers what Greek must go to jail. He comes back and tells us who." His hair fell down into his eyes, and he swept it away with one hand. "Five times now, the bet is for me, but I am not taken to jail."

"What have you done to make them bet on you?"

"Stolen coal, fight, maybe worse." He shrugged. "But if I go to jail, I won't get out. I know that. Louis tells us General Chase says there is no more habeas corpus. You know what that is?"

I shook my head. "Is it Greek?"

"No, it is American. It means men can be left in prison forever. We say, no matter. Greeks never have habeas corpus anyways. One Greek has been in jail since the day the strike begins."

The steel above our heads began to hum, as if it were quivering in the stiff wind. The sound drilled and crashed around us, pounding so hard that sand rose in a shining cloud around us. I clapped my hands over my ears, knocking my scarf from my head.

"The train!" he shouted. He put an arm around me until the barrage whittled away to the steady beat of the cars over the rails. He laughed, for I supposed my face was washed of color, my eyes wide and popped, my mouth hanging open in surprise.

Reaching for my scarf, he lifted it over my ears. "Women wear scarves like this at home. But proud *Americanidha* like you wears hat. Little blue one. Like on the day of the parade."

"You saw me?"

He wrapped a strand of my hair that had come free around his finger. "Yes, I saw you! How could I not see you? Other Greeks say, Why does that girl talk to you? Why is she nice to ugly, nothing you? So pretty, they say."

Where had he seen me—posing for the photographer's camera or marching along with our countrymen? I hoped the sunlight had caught the shine of my hair, that he had seen how the green of the scarf brought out the color of my eyes—

"It was Scottish," I stammered. "My hat and my scarf. My brother gave it to me. It was our mother's." Then, the words rushed out. "I looked for you. I didn't see you."

"I am not as pretty as you," he teased. "I don't have pretty blue hat."

He leaned toward me and kissed me. His lips were cold—mine, too—but they sent a shock of warmth through me, the taste of them like juniper, bittersweet and raw. He kissed me again, his mouth fleshy and full, his tongue seeking mine.

A cry of surprise came from my throat. This kiss was far different from the cocky, I-dare-you kisses that we had shared in Berwind. Blood rose to my arms and legs, my throat and ears, and I felt that deep, breathless yearning down in the pit of my stomach. Wrapping my arms around his neck, I kissed him back as fiercely as he'd kissed me, again and again, wanting more.

He jerked away, choking out, "You are too sweet, Miss Christian."

"Come back—"

"Oh, no, no, no," he said. "I need to stop. You are so . . . beautiful woman."

A bright whirlwind ran through my arms and legs and head, lifting me into lightness. My throat ached, pulsing with desire, and I felt that I needed either to laugh or cry. He sat hunched forward, his hands around his knees, and suddenly, I felt uncertain. I pulled my coat around me, straightened my scarf, and stared sightlessly at the people passing below, suddenly aware that they might have spied us in the gray shadows, and not caring if they had.

"You make me feel wild," he said.

His words brought a flood of relief, and I laughed, a hand over my mouth.

"So wild," he said, reaching for me.

And with that, we started kissing all over again. But this time, my back was against the ground, our bodies pressed against one another, his shoulders and legs on mine. His hands searched beneath my coat, stroking my side, my breasts, my hips, and my own hands sought the breadth of his shoulders, the curves of his chest, the firm muscles of his arms, the heat of his flesh. His lips trailed behind my ears, down my neck.

"I wanted to do this when you come to see me in Berwind," he said. "But I was always too beat up."

I ran a finger over his lips. "I wanted," I said, and then checked myself, afraid of saying too much.

"What?" he asked.

"I wanted to touch you when you weren't hurt," I said, in a quivering voice. "I wanted to run my hands over your skin when it wasn't bruised or broken."

"So, go ahead now," he said. "I don't care."

I laughed, but he stopped me with a kiss, uttering low, mixed-up words that might have been English or Greek or neither. From my own throat came sounds that were whimper, laugh, cry and song all at once.

By the time we left, the sun was setting, and the sand of the arroyo glistened in the orange-yellow light. We walked back to the path leading up to Ludlow in silence, our shoulders touching, our fingers hooked together.

At the foot of the path, he stopped. "We will walk again," he said. "Tomorrow, maybe? You'll come?"

Happiness shot through me. "I'll come."

He leaned down and kissed me on the lips, lingering, almost lazy, as if daring others to take note. Looking over my head, he assured me, "No one looks. They are all old and stupid and ugly back there."

I laughed again, hysterical, unstoppable. With a tip of his hat, he wished me goodnight and swung down the arroyo. At the bend, he waved with clumsy, boyish glee before he disappeared.

At home, I found Pearl alone in the tent. She stood at the table, mixing stale bread crumbs into ground meat.

"There you are!" She wiped her hands on a towel. "Me and Alex was so worried!"

"Why? What happened?" Breathless, I sat down at the table without removing my coat or shoes. Laughter threatened to spill from me again.

"You missed all the upset." Returning to her work, she slapped the meal against the wooden board. "General Chase come driving past the gates of Ludlow in a open car, all dressed up in his best uniform. And who do you think was with him?" She paused, but rushed ahead before I could speculate. "Mr. Jesse Welborn, the big boss man from CF&I!

He's the president or something, almost as important as Mr. Rockefeller himself!"

My stomach knotted. "When did this happen?"

"A few hours ago. And following right behind them was the Death Special, with them Belk and Belcher fellows—them Baldwins, you know—hugging the machine guns like they was babies." She folded the dough into cheesecloth. "Alex says General Chase has gone over to CF&I. He thinks he's planning to clean out Ludlow and all the other colonies."

Cold spread through my body, and I realized that high spirits were all that had kept me warm. The afternoon sitting in cold wind and shadow and wading through wet sand had chilled me through. I began to shiver.

"Where'd you go?" she asked. "Alex went out to find you. He thought maybe something had happened to you."

At once, panic filled me. How easily he could have discovered Theros and me. I reached up and touched my lips, which were swollen, then caught Pearl's sharp eyes on me. "I was walking," I lied.

"You could have tiptoed to Trinidad and back in all that time." She cocked her head. "You was off seeing Theo Sky, wasn't you?"

A laugh ricocheted up in me and turned to hiccuping.

"Well, I'll be," she said. "Tell me all about it."

When Alex returned, he found us sitting side by side on the bed. Pearl danced up and into his arms, kissing him on the cheek.

"What's come over you?" he asked.

She smiled and winked at me, her eyes bright and saucy with our secret.

Chapter 20

The day before Thanksgiving, I woke from a deep, dreamless sleep to a frantic commotion—barking dogs, children's whines, shouts from neighboring tents. A knock sounded on the door of our tent, and I struggled from the blankets and into a skirt and blouse. Pearl sat up in bed, startled and with hair dampened by perspiration.

"Christian!" she called out. "What's going on?"

"Wait here." I found a shawl and passed through the bullhide sheeting.

Alex had answered the door, clad only in union suit and trousers, too sleepy to be belligerent. Two Blue Bands stood at the door.

"That includes you, Miss," one of the guardsmen said. "And whoever else is in this tent." His face was serious and intent. The other militiaman fingered his rifle and kept his gaze on something outside, in the street.

"What?" I said. "I didn't hear."

"This is in connection with the murder a few days ago. They're searching for the guilty parties. Everyone in Ludlow is to go to the field south of camp."

"What murder?" I asked.

"On Main Street in Trinidad last Saturday. A Baldwin-Felts agent by the name of Belcher was shot dead, point-blank. A single bullet to his skull. A wop by the name of Zancanelli has been arrested, but it's thought that others from Ludlow were involved."

"Belcher," I whispered. George Belcher had shot the Italian organizer in August and had manned the Death Special's machine gun against the Forbes tent colony. He was known in Ludlow as a violent brute. "We weren't in Trinidad last Saturday," I protested. "We were here."

"It doesn't matter," the soldier snapped. "Ludlow's to be completely cleared."

"But why the women and children? Surely they—"

"Everyone, Miss. We have orders to escort everyone to the gates and to search all tents. You need to hurry."

Alex picked up the argument. "John Lawson's agreed? He's permitting this? A search while we're out of the tents?"

"I don't know, sir." The soldier shifted impatiently. "My orders are from Captain Van Cise of Company K. I don't know anyone named Lawson. Now, you folks need to move or risk being detained by the guard."

The threat pushed me into action.

"We can take warm clothes, can't we?" I asked.

"Yes, Miss."

As we dressed, we could hear protest rising in Ludlow like a cloud of steam. Occasionally, the crash of glass or the crack of a tent frame echoed through the air, or a hoarse order was shouted. I wrapped my mother's tartan scarf around my waist under my coat and stuffed my paltry treasures into my skirt. The blue tam I gave to Pearl.

"Take our money," I whispered to Alex.

Outside, we melted into the swarm of Ludlow's residents who had been rooted out from their homes, shirts half-buttoned and loose hair tangled by the wind. Accompanied by a company of militiamen, we trudged to the parade ground, where the men were sent to the left, and women and children to the right. There, we huddled together and passed mittens, hats and scarves to the less fortunate. Around us, a cordon of soldiers massed silently, their bayonet-mounted Springfield rifles ready. The Death Special trolled slowly around the field, its guns manned by Baldwin-Felts agents.

The wind tumbled hats and shawls across the prairie. Men bent nearly double to hide their faces from the stinging cold, and women huddled over their children, shielding them in their arms. Pearl and I embraced each other.

"I wish I'd thought to bring a blanket," I said.

"What do you think they want with us? You don't think they'll make us all go back to Berwind, do you?"

"No, of course not. We're not under martial law."

But my words were weak, deadened by dread and doubt. What was to stop the militia from marching every last striker back to the coal camps? Or from loading us on trains and shipping us to another place, another state, as it had with the strikers of '04? What would stop the soldiers from tearing our tents to ribbons and leaving us homeless?

From the far end of the field, several automobiles spilled a host of high-ranking militia officers. A cadre of horsemen rode alongside, raising a flag of dust. "Something's happening," I said to Pearl.

"Major Boughton requests that you form straight lines," Captain

Van Cise blared through a bullhorn. "Women, remain where you are. Place your children in front of you. Men, line up to the east. On your feet, now. Everyone."

Mothers pulled their children from the ground and pinioned them against their legs. Pearl grabbed my hand. We formed ragtag lines across the prairie. We faced the men, catching eyes in the opposite line that mirrored all the fear, desperation, and anger that we felt. Across the prairie, Alex stamped his feet, craning his neck in a futile attempt to keep Pearl and me in his view.

Accompanied by John Lawson and Louis Tikas, the militia officers walked slowly past us. The soldiers showed interest only in the men, and even then, they questioned only the dark-skinned, swarthy ones. Alex and the other British miners were ignored.

Yet we stood, and stood, and stood, while the wind blew and the temperature dipped lower. Children cried ceaselessly as the cold bit through their thin clothes and shoes. Noon came and went, and still, no relief. Suddenly, a little girl broke free and raced across the prairie.

Her mother screamed at her to stop, in Spanish and English. The other mothers tightened their grips on their children's arms, crouching in horror, crying out to the little girl. A hundred voices joined in, the calls echoing across the prairie.

The commotion brought an end to the questioning on the other side of the field, as Lawson and Tikas and the militia officers turned to follow the child's path with their eyes. The little girl ran toward the mounted soldiers, causing the horses to shy and prance. Her mother screamed and dropped to her knees.

A young soldier slid from his saddle and seized the child. Holding the struggling girl in his arms, he carried her back to the woman. "*Gracias*," she wept. "Thank you. *Gracias*."

Now it seemed that nearly every child sobbed, and every woman begged for relief. The men began to stir, murmuring in low, threatening tones. But the officers went back to their work, combing through the dark-skinned ranks, badgering the same foreign men again and again. John Lawson stood with his hands on his hips, his legs spread. Louis Tikas began arguing with the officers, gesturing wildly with his hands.

I strained to see the Greeks. From where I stood, Theros' tall body appeared silhouetted against the mesa, his head above the other men's, his shoulders straight. Five times he had escaped arrest. Let this be the sixth.

An officer with a bright blue band around his campaign hat sauntered down the length of the ladies' line, searching. Some drew back, afraid. He stopped in front of me. "Miss Scott?" he asked. I made no move. "Mrs. Ruddy?"

"Yes." Pearl clutched the back of my coat so tightly that I felt I was being strangled.

"I'm Lieutenant Doll of Company K." He waved toward the far end of the prairie. "Would you follow me please?"

We walked along as if to a death knell. Pearl and I held hands, squeezing the blood out of each other's fingers. Sweat broke out on my back, though I was still bitterly cold, and Pearl's trembling vibrated up my arm. As we passed, the women fell silent, except for a few gasping tears or prayers. Alex came up beside me, escorted by a couple of militia officers with bright yellow hat bands, his face crabbed up in fear. We were marched through a throng of militiamen mounted on horseback. Four autos were parked in an uneven line. One was the Death Special, its machine guns pointing directly at the people on the prairie.

Just beyond stood Tom and Jake Ruddy.

Pearl grabbed Alex's arm. "I told Russ I wasn't going back!"

"Please listen, Mrs. Ruddy." Lieutenant Doll signaled. "Go ahead, Mr. Ruddy."

Mr. Ruddy spoke. "Pearl, Russell's been hurt. Bad."

"Russ!" Pearl moaned. "What happened?"

"He was down in the mine," Jake said. "The wall caved, and a timber come down on his head. They don't have nobody but scabs working the mines just now, and they don't know nothing. Knocked him clean out for about two days. Now he's awake, but he ain't doing so good. He's like, it's like . . ."

Jake turned away, and Mr. Ruddy spoke again. "He's like a child, Pearl. He don't know how to do anything anymore. Feed himself, get dressed, any of that. You need to come home and take care of him."

Tears slipped from her eyes. "No," she sobbed. "Oh, no! What was he doing down in the mine? Why wasn't he in the office, doing the books?"

"He was doing a foreman's job," Mr. Ruddy said. "There's almost no one left who knows how to do anything. Listen, Pearl, I know you wouldn't have left, except that somebody made you." His eyes skimmed over Alex before he turned to Lieutenant Doll. "She didn't go alone—"

"What's this?" Lieutenant Doll intervened. "Mrs. Ruddy, did you leave Berwind of your own free will? You weren't forced to leave Berwind, were you? Threatened somehow or drawn out of your house and made to leave?"

"No!" She shook her head fiercely. "I come down here because

I wanted to."

"Come on, Pearl," Jake joined in. "They was shooting the hell out of the house. Ma says you looked outside to see what was going on, and all of a sudden, you just took off, leaving the door open and the water boiling and her lunch not even fixed." He turned to the officer, his voice rising. "She must have been kidnapped, Lieutenant. She wouldn't have left otherwise."

"Kidnapped?" Alex demanded. "What nonsense is this?"

"Mr. Scott, were you in Berwind on the day Mrs. Ruddy left?" Lieutenant Doll asked.

"Yes, but we were on the hills, shooting at—"

"Ah, you're a fine talker, Scott," Mr. Ruddy interrupted. "Playing at war and for what? Because of you, my son is nearly dead! You and your precious union!"

"You were every bit a part of it," Alex said. "Favoring your friends over honest hard-working men—"

"Stop it!" the lieutenant ordered. "All of you, keep quiet. Now." He motioned for the two Blue Bands to come forward and stand just behind Alex. "I don't care one whit about your politics, either of you." Dully, as if he were tired of us, he spoke to Pearl. "We've heard reports that the United Mine Workers have been kidnapping residents of the coal camps and bringing them down to Ludlow, where they're forced to stay and support the strike. Do you know anything about this, Mrs. Ruddy?

"No," Pearl said.

"Mr. Scott didn't offer you anything to come to Ludlow, did he? Money or . . . jewelry or anything?" His eyes flickered over Alex's patched overalls and my union shoes.

"I never seen him that day up in Berwind. I come down because I wanted to."

"But your husband stayed in Berwind?"

"He don't believe in the strike."

"Pearl, you gotta listen to us," Jake begged. "He's crying for you. He won't shut up, just moaning and shedding tears and calling for you. We can't get him to do nothing, not eat or clean up or sleep. Ma's at the end of her rope."

Pearl covered her face.

"Russ is in a bad way," Mr. Ruddy added. "He's not long for this world, the way he's carrying on. You need to come home now."

"He cries day and night," Jake tried again. "Just calling your name, asking where you gone. He needs you back."

"It sounds like you should go home, ma'am," Lieutenant Doll

said.

Pearl shrieked and sank beside the Death Special, shrinking into the earth. I was afraid she might simply dissolve into dust, be taken into the ground before our eyes. I knelt beside her and cradled her head against my breast.

Over my head, the words flew as viciously as bullets.

"She's in Ludlow because she chooses to be," Alex insisted. "Lieutenant, you must see that this is a trick to get her to go back—"

Jake spat back. "She's in Ludlow because she thinks you're man enough to keep her. And she's dead wrong."

"Well, Russell isn't man enough, is he?" Alex challenged.

Jake burst forward, shoving his way toward Alex. The two soldiers from Company B each grabbed an arm and pulled him back.

"Enough," Lieutenant Doll commanded. "Hold off or I'll take all of you to the jail."

"Martial law hasn't been declared," Alex protested, struggling against his captors. "You can't arrest me—"

"Pearl," I whispered. "Pearl, it's all right. Don't cry. It will be all right."

Lieutenant Doll squatted down. "Mrs. Ruddy," he said kindly. "I can't make you go back to Berwind. No one can. But these gentlemen are right, ma'am. Your place is with your husband."

She lifted her face, washed clean of dust by her tears. "Is it true? Is it true, Jake? Is Russ really hurt that bad?"

Jake's expression lost its swagger. "Yeah, Pearl, he is. Come home."

"No," she wept. "I ain't going back to Berwind. I can't—"

No one moved. We just let her wail, as if we were afraid to pierce through her sorrow. Then Lieutenant Doll straightened up and said, "This has gone on long enough. Mr. Ruddy, sir, you need to leave now. Mrs. Ruddy has made her choice."

"Then she's staying here with him?" Jake spat. "She's married to my brother!"

"How are we to talk to her again?" Mr. Ruddy demanded. "When she's back in Ludlow, we can't get anywhere near, not even to let her know—"

"If you need to contact her again, you come to me," Lieutenant Doll said. "I'll help you find her."

Mr. Ruddy and Jake moved away, heading back toward the train station. They walked brokenly, painfully, as if they were afraid to press their heels too deeply into the dirt.

"Where should we go?" Alex asked Lieutenant Doll.

"You stay here." He glanced toward the prairie. "Something's going on out there."

A dozen troopers from Company K were escorting several dark-skinned men toward the headquarters. The men's faces were contorted, as if the anger of the morning had slowly ebbed, lost its strength, and fallen into dismay. One wept. Quickly, they were loaded into one of the flag-bearing cars. They stared out the windows at the Death Special until the cars sped away in a flurry of dust and horseflesh.

And still the people stood on the prairie.

Another hour passed before Captain Van Cise shouted through the bullhorn, "You can go back to Ludlow now. Walk slowly, don't run or make sudden moves."

The mass on the prairie broke apart. Men hoisted exhausted children onto their shoulders, and old grandmothers were carried away, too frail to walk. Alex lifted Pearl from the ground. She clutched his sleeve as if she might fall. I slipped my arm around her waist.

More than six hours had passed since we had left Ludlow.

Our tent had not been badly damaged in the search—our mattresses had been flipped, our drawers shoved closed without care, the trapdoor of the pit left open. Some of our food had been spilled, but nothing had been broken.

Alex sat on his bed and pulled out his flask, while Pearl sat at the table. I set about cleaning up, saving what I could, cooking what was left. I did not think I could eat, anyway, with my stomach so knotted and roiled with anger.

After a long while, Pearl broke the silence. "Oh, God, you don't think it's true, do you?"

I did not know if she was talking to me or to Alex, but I knew exactly what she was talking about. We had all been thinking about it since we had come in off the prairie.

Alex made no sign of answering, so I said, "I don't think Jake would lie about something as terrible as that."

"I should never have left! Oh, I never should have said what I did—!"

"Why?" Alex's words boiled up and out of his mouth. "Why do you care about him? He tricked you, he lied—pretending to be a man, pretending to be a husband—"

"Don't you say one word against him!"

"Somebody needs to! You talk like he's a saint, when he's nothing but a—"

"I won't hear it, Alex. You hear me! I won't listen!"

Alex slammed down his flask and whipped out of the tent, leaving the door open and banging in the wind. Pearl leaped to her feet and dashed behind the bullhide curtain. She began to tear apart our little nook, jerking open the drawers of the bureau and throwing clothes on the bed. Dropping to her knees, she dragged the calfskin valise she'd brought with her from Berwind out from under the bed.

"What are you doing?" I cried.

"I have to go, I have to leave!"

"Where would you go?" I shoved the curtain aside. "Back to Berwind? To Russell? Oh, Pearl, you can't—"

"Don't!" she shrieked. "Stop it!"

I caught her flailing hands in mine, clamping down on her wrists. Like a flower pulled from its stem, she withered. Slowly, I eased her to the bed. Tears streamed from her eyes. "Oh, God, I don't know! I can't go back to Berwind! I won't!"

I stroked her hair, let her tears soak through the thin cotton of my blouse. "Alex didn't mean it," I said. "He just gets upset when he can't fix a problem—"

"He ain't never going to love me!"

"He does love you, though," I said, but my uncertainty weighed on me too heavily. "But he's jealous, he's . . . What happened in Berwind? Why'd you leave?"

She lay down on the bed. "Alex don't understand! He don't have no idea about none of it! He's thinks Russ is the bad one, but he ain't! He's the first man who treated me gentle. He acted like I was something that could break if I was spoken to too mean or rough." She glanced up at me. "Alex didn't treat me like that until now—now that it don't make no difference. I can't be his anyways, can I?"

I winced. Surely Alex didn't love her now simply because he didn't have to worry about marrying her. Surely he wasn't so low and weak. Yet my eyes went to the trunk where he kept Dad's kilt and jacket, where he had kept Momma's beautiful scarf. He'd been so proud to be Scottish again.

"You understand, don't you?" she said. "You know what it's like to want to be loved and not have to pretend that you're somebody different." Her words caught in her throat in a strangled laugh. "You and Theo Sky—meeting every day, kissing under the bridge. You don't never tell him he can't be Greek, do you?"

"So why did you leave Russell if he's so good to you?"

She put both hands atop her stomach. And suddenly I understood why she had left Berwind and Russell Ruddy, and why she could never go back.

"Oh, Pearl," I breathed. "When is your baby coming?"

Her face showed joy, fear, anger, frustration—all in one quick spasm. "Oh, God, Christian! It's so good to let somebody know! I been about to bust, keeping this quiet!"

"Why did you keep it quiet?"

"Because I didn't know," she cried, her eyes glittering. "I been waiting for something to happen. Maybe for the strike to end, or for Alex to say that he wants to move to another town. You always said he wants to go back to Scotland—we could start out together there. Nobody'd know us."

"Is it his baby?"

She laughed her wild laugh. "It ain't Russell's, that's for sure."

"When do you think you'll have it?"

"Four, five months."

"That's April, the end of it. Or early May."

She laughed again. "There's so many pretty names for a girl born in springtime. I think I'll name her Lily. *The lily it is pure, an' the lily it is fair.*"

I smiled at her memory of Burns. "Why a girl?"

"It's like there's butterflies in my belly. A boy'd be fiercer, I'd think."

"A baby born in Ludlow will have to be fierce either way.'"

"What's wrong?" she asked. "Ain't you happy for me? Ain't you happy for Alex? We finally got what was supposed to happen."

But you can't just forget, I argued silently. You can't just erase the past. I kissed her forehead. "Yes, I'm happy for you. Do you want me to go find Alex, so you can tell him?"

Her eyes flickered in hesitation for just a moment before she said, "Sure."

I picked up my coat and left, desperate to quiet all the voices that ran together in my mind. But in every street, on every corner, people flocked. Around me, tent doors flapped open, revealing the destruction left by vengeful militia officers. Conversations as raw and painful as broken bones drifted on the air—about a jug of molasses that had been shattered by a soldier, about justice for the day's folly, about the UMWA's faltering negotiations, and as always, about the Greek fighting men.

They had brought this on, with their love of guns, they had not been brave enough or they would have stopped it from happening, they had failed us, they had saved us, they would do both again tonight, or tomorrow, or the next day.

I stood at the edge of the arroyo, searching for Alex, but also watching for Theros. I needed to know he was safe, that the militia officers had not doubled back and taken the Greeks as well. I wanted to sit under the bridge, unafraid of the trains passing overhead, or what was to come. I needed to talk, to spill my words into the evening air, to feel his arms around me.

Clouds rolled across the sky, and the chill of the early evening began to settle into my bones, driving me from the arroyo. As I was passing by the community well, I found a crowd. The photographer who'd snapped Alex's and my picture on the day of the militia's arrival crouched behind his tripod, his head draped in the heavy black tarpaulin.

Before the well, Louis Tikas posed, barbed wire looping from his arm and spilling across the ground.

"What's going on?" I asked a woman who waited nearby with a bucket.

"While we were all lined up out there on the prairie, the soldiers threw rusty barbed wire down the well. The water's no good now, if that's what you've come for. It's poisoned."

The cameraman's bulb crackled a blinding white light into the deepening evening. Louis Tikas pulled more barbed wire from the coils at his feet. The other Greeks clustered near a union automobile parked a few feet away. Almost at once, Theros came to me.

"Look at this," he said, his voice thick with anger. "They don't even leave us water to drink."

"Can we go somewhere?" I asked.

He glanced toward the arroyo. "Not to the bridge," he said. "It is too dark. Come on."

We walked through Ludlow to the union tent. On one side were pallets that had been used to bring in stores for the colony. Theros pushed his way through the piles until we were nearly boxed in, away from the wind and out of sight of others.

He leaned back against a stack of pallets and drew me to him. "What is wrong, Miss Christian?"

"How could they do that to us?" I asked, overwhelmed by it all. "How could they herd us out onto the prairie like we were cattle or something? And it's all going to happen again, isn't it? It's going to keep happening! Not one of us is safe!"

"In the mines, we are treated like we are not people," he said. "Now, here, too. But don't worry. Some of us will go out tonight. We will make it right—"

"You can't do that!" I cried. "Nothing will ever be settled if you do that!"

"But if we let them keep doing this, we will all be dead for nothing."

"Don't you see? We'll never get even, we can't! And it isn't right anyway--!"

My words ended in a harsh sob. Theros put his arms around me, pulling me close. "Don't cry," he said. "Don't be so sad—"

"Pearl is going to have a baby," I blurted.

He said nothing for a moment. Then, skeptically, he asked, "It is Russell Ruddy's?"

I said nothing.

"Then it is Jake's?"

"No!" I protested. "It's my brother's."

"That is some surprise. I didn't think your brother liked anybody who wasn't the same as him."

"You mean with the same color of skin?" I asked heatedly.

He shrugged, unwilling to answer me.

"We both love Pearl," I said fiercely. "But I don't know how we'll live with a baby in our tent. He'll need space and good air and a warm home and good food. He'll need a place where he can sleep at night without being scared by gunshots. We don't have any of that here."

"What did you have in Berwind?" he asked bitterly. "The same."

We could not go back to Berwind, I realized. Alex and Pearl could not live together, raise a family, make a home in the same place as the Ruddy family. Even if she was free of Russell—even if he died—she and Alex could not live under the vindictive eyes of the Ruddy clan. They would have to take their baby and live somewhere else.

"We can't go back," I whispered, tears falling. "We can't go home."

He held me until I stopped crying. When we parted, it was with a single, solemn kiss.

That evening, I said nothing to Alex about the well and the poisoned water. We had worries of our own. I wondered if Pearl had told Alex of the baby, if he'd greeted the news happily or with dismay.

I knew soon enough. The next morning, I woke to find myself alone in bed. Pearl had gone to Alex.

Chapter 21

Three days later, on the last day of November, it started to snow.

By dusk, the snow had thickened into white sheets. By midnight, the wind heaped it into solid walls. By morning, the temperature dropped, and pinpricks of ice formed on the insides of the tent wall. For five more days, the storm battered Ludlow. Tent frames twisted and collapsed. Families huddled in their pits, awaiting rescue, or sliced through the canvas walls and burrowed through the drifts like gophers.

Our tent withstood the snow, but the roof drooped bluish and frigid over our heads. The fire flickered from lack of air, and the tent filled with smoke. When Alex tried to open the door, he found it wedged shut. We stood on beds, chairs, and the table, pressing upward on the canvas with a broom or our hands, hoping to dislodge the snow, but it did not budge. Our arms ached from the effort, which left us drenched in sweat.

"We'll have to cut our way out," Alex said. "Unless they come for us soon."

Trapped, cramped, tired and cold and hungry, we did not move. We did not talk. We did not eat. Alex drank until his flask ran dry. Pearl slept. I tried to keep busy—sewing, mending, tinkering—but my hands fell idle in my lap and I found myself staring at the gray, frosted walls.

Every doubt I'd ever had was unleashed in my mind—about myself, Alex, about Theros, about Ludlow, but mostly about Pearl. She had never told completely believable stories, from the day she'd come into our lives. Every story she had ever given us—losing her way in Berwind Canyon on the night she came to our house, her father's cruelty, her uncle's terrible crime, and on and on—had to be questioned. We had to decide whether or not we would believe it. Even now. She said she'd walked down the canyon when the cloud gathered her up in its protective cloak. Yet she'd carried a satchel of fine clothes with her.

I could not help but think we were being played for fools.

After nearly a week, a shoveling crew came by our tent. We responded like prisoners freed from a dark cell. Alex pushed open the door as soon as he heard the knock, crazed, desperate. I shielded my eyes from the glare of light, so unfamiliar that it made me dizzy. The cold air stung our faces and nostrils. It smelled as good as a spring day, after so many days of being trapped with the putrid smells of slop jars, rancid grease and unclean hair.

"Look at this!" One of the men spoke. "Six feet of snow, they're saying, all from this one storm."

I asked about food and fresh water.

"You need coal?" he asked. "I got a gang of kids bringing it in buckets, and you can melt snow. Got plenty of that. But we sure could use men to shovel. The Greeks were rounded up before the snowstorm. We're short about a hundred and fifty men from the colony."

"The Greeks?" Alex asked. "They're gone?"

I spoke at the same time. "Where were they taken?"

"The jail in Trinidad. Even Louie the Greek was hauled in. Their tents—you know, they live in those big ones west of the colony—have collapsed, and there's not a one of them to be found."

The shoveling crew moved on, taking Alex with it. I stood in the open door, staring out into the strange, blank whiteness. The wide, muddy path had disappeared, and a tunnel bored through the snow, so narrow that a man could not fit without rubbing both shoulders against icy walls. Swells of cold wind rushed along the snowy canyon, and the noises of the men soon fell dead, muffled by the drifts. Yet the sun shone brilliantly, and bright diamonds of red and blue sparkled on the canyon walls.

No habeas corpus. The words sang through my head. I looked to Pearl, who had crawled from bed to peer outside. She shuddered once, and went back to the warmth of her blankets.

"I ain't getting up until all of that's gone," she said.

The next day, drays came from Trinidad, pulled by Belgian horses foaming with sweat. Women swarmed around them, screaming at the vendors for their slowness, for the poor quality of their wares, accusing them of siding with CF&I. I elbowed and shoved my way through the haggling crowd only to find the dray empty. Within minutes, the eggs, milk and bread had been traded away not only for money, but for treasures of lace or silver from the Old World.

"Christian!"

Alex was hailing me from near the gates, his shovel in hand. He broke away from the gang of men who were clearing a path to the main road. "What did you get?" he called.

"Nothing. There were so many women. With children and all."

"So you let them take it all?"

I shrugged. Alex and I walked together down the center of the road, which had been forged only wide enough for a horse or two. Quickly, our breathing grew shallow and strained, and our feet slipped on crests and ridges hidden by the brilliance of the bright sun.

"You've heard Pearl's news, I suppose." He leaned, chuffing, on his shovel. "From the day she knew Pearl was here, Edith has been saying, There's a baby, I'll wager there is. How do you women know?"

"We just do, I guess. Although I'd rather Mrs. McCormick didn't know. Whose baby does she think it is?"

He waved me aside with a laugh. "Pearl says it's a girl, but I'll hold out for a boy. My young Gordie, after Dad."

His face, even through the ice-crusted beard and frosted brows and lashes, looked as if it had been touched by angelic fire—bright and glowing and so alive. Happy, I thought. He is happy—perhaps for the first time since he'd grown up. Tears formed in my eyes, but evaporated in the cold.

"Is it that easy?" I asked. "After all that's passed between you and Pearl? After all your talk of our proud heritage? The baby might take after Pearl, you know. No matter what, it won't look like us."

He scowled. "We've forgotten all that."

"Have you forgotten Russell, too?"

He plunged his shovel into the snow, tossing a scoop up toward the banks that rose above our heads. Most of the snow came back down on the path. "We'll talk to a lawyer, once this strike is settled," he said. "Surely she can get the marriage annulled if he can't support her anymore."

"Then you believe Jake and Mr. Ruddy?"

"Aye, I reckon they were sincere."

I had spent too many days trapped in my own dark doubts and too many nights lying awake, sick with fear, to foresee that Alex's plan would work. I could think of a hundred—no, a thousand—reasons why, the first of which was the look on Russell's face when he saw Pearl at the train station.

"When do you think the strike will be settled?" I asked. "We're almost to the new year."

"I think this storm will change it all," he said. "Once the newspapers report that Rockefeller's employees are stranded and starving in six feet of snow, the public outcry will be too much for him."

I thought of Theros' words—*who cares about dagos?*—but said nothing. Alex and I walked on, caught up in our own thoughts. Soon, we had come to a spot where the drifts had been scattered by wind, a spot where we could survey the world beyond Ludlow.

The militia tents had fared no better than ours. They tilted from the drifts, their stabilizing poles broken. Telephone and telegraph lines had snapped and slithered to the ground, and the poles listed at awkward angles. Near the town of Ludlow, train cars stretched one after another on the tracks behind stalled locomotives. Everywhere, the snow was dappled with the drab brown of militia uniforms, as the soldiers dug out the tracks and the roads.

"Well," Alex said. "At last they've got them doing something useful."

The soldiers finished their work after ten days. The snowstorm had wreaked havoc on every living thing. Carcasses of horses or cattle were found humped and frozen where they had bent their heads against the blinding snow. Automobiles angled out of ditches, the passengers' bright Sunday clothes sheathed in ice, their lifeless faces scribed with surprise. Coyotes skittered around the edges of the tent colony, looking for food, and people kept their children close by their sides.

In Ludlow, the tents were rebuilt, the paths cleared, and, soon, the familiar sounds returned—children shouting as they sledded on dishpans down the mountains of snow, the bullhorn in the public square, the guitars and penny whistles and accordions, the scream of locomotive whistles echoing from the mesas and from the snowdrifts in endless rounds.

Then we learned that the first train to pass through Ludlow on the newly cleared tracks had carried strikebreakers bound for Berwind Canyon.

As soon as the sun broke above the horizon the next morning, I walked to the Ludlow depot, a few quarters jingling in my pockets. The platform swarmed with militiamen. At the ticket window, two Blue Bands from Company K barred my way. "Where are you going, Miss?" one asked.

"I need to go to Trinidad," I said.

He shifted his rifle. "No strikers are allowed on trains, unless they're under military guard. General Chase's orders. So, go home."

As my feet sank through the crusted snow, I grew more determined. Clear blue sky spread above me, but the rising sun brought no warmth, and the air chafed bitterly at my lungs. At the gates of Ludlow, the picket was just forming—groggy, shivering men and women with faces wrapped in scarves against the bitter wind. Listless and dull-eyed, they watched as another train crept past the colony and switched to the spur leading into Berwind Canyon.

I passed through the tent colony without stopping and slid down the icy banks into the arroyo. A thin trail had been carved by countless feet through the drifting snow, leading to the roads north of Ludlow where fortunate strikers might flag down blockade-running union trucks. Luck was with me that morning. A rusted truck shuddered at the edge of the road, belching billows of black smoke into the air. With fourteen other strikers, I boarded it. Almost at once, the truck accelerated and careened wildly across the patchy ice. I gripped the sides of the bed to keep from being bucked out. The driver raced along back roads, avoiding the main highways. When we were halfway to town, a bullet pinged against the metal sides and the driver swerved back and forth to dodge the sniper.

In Trinidad, the truck slid to a halt a good distance from the depot. "This is close as we come," the driver shouted. "So we don't get shoot at."

Achingly, we stood and brushed loose snow from our coats. Many swayed from the truck, as if seasick. One child vomited, as likely sickened by the fumes from the truck's engines as by the wild antics of its driver.

Trinidad was just as Theros had described it when he had made a vee with his hands. In the clear morning air, the blue-white glory of Fisher's Peak rose ten thousand feet into the sky to crest at two stair-step mesas, framing the town. On the steep inclines below, the town spread downward, dipping all the way into the valley where the Purgatoire River flowed and the railroad tracks stretched. Then it rose again, its lovely Victorian houses climbing up to the top of Simpson's Rest.

Following the others, I traipsed up the hill along Commercial Street. Even this early in the day, the boardwalks teemed with strikers in red neckerchiefs with their wives and families, Baldwin-Felts agents with greatcoats flapping around their holsters, at-liberty militiamen, townspeople on daily errands, and overall-clad farmers and ranchers. Everyone on earth, it seemed, was in town, snatching at the food in the stores, bartering for warmer clothing.

The city trolleys clattered along the narrow tracks, carrying foreign women who sold soaps and needlework from open baskets and dainty Trinidad ladies dressed as if for church. At the intersection of Commercial and Main Streets, I looked upward to buildings built of stone that was engraved and chiseled and smoothed into perfection. Some were built of Trinidad sandstone, others from granite. I touched the building beside me, marveling at the slick, mirror-like marble.

The striker beside me gave a low whistle. "Look at that."

Across the street, the majestic Columbian Hotel, with its graceful, arched windows and hand-cut stonework, had become a fortress. Soldiers loitered on the flat rooftop, their arms crossed over rifles, their hats shading their faces against the winter sun. They paced back and forth, hawkish eyes on the street below.

"Better move fast, Miss," the striker whispered. "General Chase's sharpshooters don't like nobody to stop and gawk."

Without speaking further, my companion disappeared into the crowd. I went across the street and walked north along Main, past the elaborate Opera House and warm storefront windows lavished with colorful merchandise. Slipping onto Chestnut Street, which had yet to be cleared of snow, I climbed uphill to the Las Animas County courthouse and jail.

On the steps of the tan brick building, I found myself amid a rowdy picket of women and children. Clutching signs that demanded, WHERE IS MY HUSBAND? and GENERAL CHASE, LET MY DADDY GO, they unleashed a catcall of demands every time a militia officer passed through the front doors of the courthouse. Children ran after the troopers, shouting insults at their backs.

"You're from Ludlow, ain't you?" A woman signaled to me. "Who are you looking for?"

"No one."

She laughed. "If he ain't married and you ain't married to somebody else, it ain't a sin."

"Where do I go?" I asked. "Who do I talk to?"

"Oh, honey, that's a funny one. Those soldiers in there think a woman's for one thing. The girls who go in there, well, they don't come out the same."

I shivered. "Then what do I do?"

She gestured with one hand. "If you go down that alley, there's a broken window. The men keep watch—they'll know you're there. But be careful. The soldiers come along every couple of minutes, and you don't want to be caught."

I slipped behind the courthouse. The shadowy alley, strewn with trash, was bitterly cold and caked by ice. Above my head, the walls rose three stories. I searched for the broken window, but saw nothing. Then, my foot caught on a patch of ice, and I looked down. Nearby was a barred opening no more than a foot wide and nearly buried in a window well. Jagged glass framed the tiny window. Yellowish shards thrust from the ice, frozen into daggers.

Carefully, I knelt down. "Is anyone there?" I cast into the

darkness of the basement. The smell of rotted wood, unwashed bodies, and full slop jars drifted from the window. I drew my scarf over my nose and mouth, retching at the stench.

"Who is it?" said a voice.

"I'm looking for Theros Skyrapoulos. He's from Ludlow—"

"He in here." A low murmur rose from inside.

"Miss Christian?" A single hand appeared and clasped a bar at the window. Dirt creased the skin of his knuckles, and his fingernails were caked with black grit. "You are crazy."

"What did you do, Theros?"

"Nothing. It is funny. No one bet on me this time."

He tried to laugh, but his voice sounded weak and hoarse. He coughed violently, and his knuckles turned white as he battled to keep his grip. I thought he must be standing on a box or overturned slop bucket. "Are you sick?" I asked.

"I am not dead, not yet. Snow blows through this window and we walk in it. Guards throw water on us when we try to sleep. We wake up in coats and shoes of ice. The food is for dogs."

I balanced perilously on the ice. "I heard you were all taken. Even Louis—"

"What day is it?"

"The twelfth of December."

"No! We have been here ten days. No, longer than that."

"There's news from Ludlow. Strikebreakers are arriving in Berwind Canyon."

"What!"

"Governor Ammons changed his mind. The militia's bringing them in. The soldiers are riding on top of the trains to escort them. They have machine guns and—"

I heard him speak to the others, but I could not tell if his words were English or Greek.

"Strikebreakers!" he said at last. "That is why they arrest us. They want us here, not at Ludlow, when the trains come. So we cannot stop them."

An ache jolted my heart. "Do you think you'll get out?"

"Miss Christian." His other hand appeared, and he tried to pull himself up on the bars. His voice trembled, as if he was trying not to cough or cry. "Miss Christian, touch my hand. It's so cold."

I reached forward. "Mine are cold, too."

Still, our fingers locked, his icy and dead-feeling. He tried to grasp my palm, to take my entire hand in his, but he could not reach far enough across the windowsill. "You are so sweet," he said. "Your hand is so—"

"What are you doing?"

The voice came from behind me. Jerking my hand away, I spun around on my heels, still kneeling, and lost my balance. A sliver of glass pierced the heel of my hand, and I clasped it against my breast. Blood ran warm down my wrist. A militia lieutenant loomed over me, hands on his hips. "Get up from there," he ordered.

My teeth chattered violently as I rose. Theros' hands slid from the bars.

"Who were you talking to?" the lieutenant ordered.

I made no reply, unable to think clearly. My hand felt as if it had been sliced in two.

"Come with me."

He herded me to the front of the building, jerking my arm with every step. We passed through the picketing women. "Oh, Lordy Lord!" one of them cried. Inside the courthouse, he pushed me into an office filled with soldiers. Militia clerks were jammed at desks, piles of paper before them. A well-dressed colonel, hair pomaded and boots polished black, lazed with feet on his desk, a half-smoked cigarette in his hand. Heat poured from a clanking radiator in the corner.

"She was at the window, Colonel Drake," the lieutenant reported. "Talking to the Greeks. I think she was giving one of them something."

The colonel dropped his shiny boots from the desk and folded his hands before him, looking me up and down. "To the Greeks, huh?" he said. "You don't look like you'd know Greek. What is your name?"

"Christian Scott." I cupped my palm, trying to keep blood from dripping on the floor. The clerks forsook their paperwork, their eyes bright. One winked, then set his chin in his hand, freely enjoying my discomfort.

Colonel Drake seemed no less amused. "And you're from which colony?"

"I'm from Ludlow."

"Well, well, Miss Scott. That's a surprise. The ladies don't look like you in Ludlow." He pompously ran a hand over his hair. "Who did you come here to see? What did you give him?"

My thoughts whirled. Naming Theros or any of the Greeks would unleash relentless torment on them. Already, they had no hope of release. Quickly, I named my own father, praying that no one in the jail shared his name. "Gordon Alexander Scott."

Without taking his eyes from me, Colonel Drake flipped his

hand, and a clerk paged through a roster. "He's not here," the clerk said, interest piquing his voice, as if a prisoner had somehow eluded him. "Are you sure he's been arrested? By which company? Where? In Ludlow?"

"I don't know any of that." I doubled my fingers against my palm, trying to hold the blood. The heat from the hissing radiators turned my stomach. Droplets of sweat beaded my nose and forehead, and I sought to loosen my scarf and unbutton my coat with my uninjured hand.

Colonel Drake leaned toward me. "No, sweetheart, there's nothing but that bunch of Greeks and a few wops down in the jail just now. Your daddy's probably just gone off for a few days. Check the houses on West Main, where the girls and their madams live. You understand?"

The clerks tittered, and a soldier blurted out one, nasty "hah."

"I'll go look," I said.

That caused more laughter. Colonel Drake lit another cigarette. "What do you have in your hand?"

I held it out, unfurling my fingers so that the blood pooled in the palm. A few drops fell on the carpet.

"Sergeant Holmes, get this lady a clean cloth." He scooted his chair back, his eyes narrowing. "You look like a starving rat. All the women in those tents do. Let me buy you a good meal. Then we'll talk more about your father."

"He isn't here. I know that now."

The sergeant had come up behind me. Reaching around me, he took my outstretched hand. I lurched, jerking to one side. "Don't touch me!"

"Hey, hey!" the sergeant shouted. "You'll have blood all over the office!"

Keeping my wrist in a tight grip, he wrapped the handkerchief around my hand. He pressed in behind me, his breath teasing the hair on my neck, his other arm tight around me, barely below my breast. Colonel Drake smiled, keeping his gaze on my face, waiting. I cursed myself as the heat of anger and embarrassment rose into my cheeks, but I forbade myself to step away from the sergeant.

Colonel Drake laughed. "Lieutenant Anderson, escort this proud young lady to the train and put her on a northbound. Make sure she doesn't disembark until Ludlow." To me, he added, "And Miss Scott, next time I catch you poking around, I'm going to find room for you here somewhere, maybe even in the cell with all those Greeks. You understand?"

"That seems like a safer place than in here."

Laughter erupted around me. Colonel Drake laughed so hard

that I was certain he wouldn't let me go, that he would keep me around to amuse him. But Lieutenant Anderson grabbed my arm and herded me out of the courthouse, parading me through Trinidad as if I was a prize, greeting other militiamen with a smug smile, pushing strikers and townspeople out of the way, jerking my arm if I didn't keep step with him.

Fear rose in me. Rumors of girls taken into the canyons were rampant, and certainly a solitary woman could vanish from the busy streets of Trinidad without much notice. But at the station, the lieutenant loaded me onto a car with two other women, an old man who looked as if this trip out of Trinidad might be his last, and five young militiamen. "See she gets to Ludlow," he told a bored-looking sergeant. Then, with one last wink at me, he strode off toward downtown.

The sergeant posted himself in the row just behind me and traded tales of days at liberty with the five boys. I huddled against my seat, as close to the window as I could possibly squeeze. The wide gash in my hand bled heavily, soaking the handkerchief. I pressed against it to stanch the cut veins. Suddenly, something swept across the tender skin of my neck just under my right ear. I slapped at it and caught the sergeant's fingers. He had plucked a pin from my hair, so my bun hung heavy and lopsided.

"You have such pretty hair," he said, hazarding another stroke that unfurled half the bun.

"Leave me alone."

But he kept on—a hand on my shoulder, another swipe at my hair, a whisper in my ear. The other five boys picked up the taunts, talking openly about what they'd do with me.

When the train screeched into the Ludlow depot, I leaped to my feet. The sergeant blocked the aisle.

"You're coming with us now," he said, running his hands up and down my arms. "We'll have a good time, won't we?"

The other militia boys chortled, and I slapped the sergeant with my bandaged hand. His hand shot up to his cheek and then pulled away, blood on his fingertips. "Jesus Christ! What did you do?" He whirled around and asked the boys, "Did she cut me? What did she do to me?"

I rammed him from my path and ran down the aisle, nearly falling as I scrambled down the steps of the train, and only stopping long enough to vomit on the platform. All I wanted was to reach the safety of the flimsy white tents of Ludlow.

Chapter 22

Pearl sewed up my hand.

"Are you sure you don't want no whiskey, Christian?" She bit off a length of thick, black thread and soaked it in the cup she was offering to me. "It'll hurt something bad."

I closed my eyes. The pain shot up my hand into my elbow, my shoulder, my head, and I started to cry. Pearl's words—something about Theo Sky, the militia, the colonel at the jail, oh, she was indignant—bounced away from my ears, unheard. I did not care enough to follow them.

She tucked me into bed, put an extra brick next to my purple, wasted feet, my shivering back. She kissed my forehead and told me to sleep.

"You want any whiskey, you just let me know," she said. "There ain't no reason to be brave."

But in Ludlow, we had to be brave.

On Christmas Day, the residents of Ludlow sang hymns celebrating the birth of the baby Jesus. Later, John Lawson and some of the other union officials gathered to give the children presents of a doll for each girl and a slate for each boy and a bag of penny candy and nuts to every resident of Ludlow.

All the while, train loads of strikebreakers funneled through Ludlow, heading for Delagua and Berwind Canyons, and for Forbes and the mines south of Trinidad.

Then, January, 1914, dawned, each day, cloudless, brutal and frigid.

We harvested sage and piñon from the hills to burn in our stoves, and at the commissary, we stirred gruel for breakfast, lunch and dinner. There was no more meat—all the game near Ludlow had been killed, and the union provided little more than a gristly piece or two each week. Our clothes turned to rags, then threads, and our shoes drank in ice and snow. Our faces grew drab and wizened, frozen by the bitter winds.

And day after day, we buried our own.

During the frost-filled nights, babies were stillborn, or were cut down by croup or fever, or simply grew weaker and more waxen until they were carried away in caskets no bigger than breadboxes. Children—stick-thin, runny-eyed, and with noses rubbed raw by the rags they used to wipe their noses—coughed themselves to death. Old people stooped lower and lower until they moved no more.

Even the militia suffered. The poor, feckless boys of Company K, who had expected to stay in the strike zone for a week or two, had now celebrated the most festive Christian holiday in cramped tents where fuel and food were scarcely more plentiful than in Ludlow. Their uniforms had begun to rot, threadbare and stained. Their manners soured, and they joined the Yellow Bands of Berwind Canyon in galloping past Ludlow in the dead of night, whirling their whips so that we woke with a vicious start.

And still, the strike continued.

Near the end of January, Mother Jones came back to the strike zone to revive our spirits.

I first heard of the news from Mrs. McCormick. We were kneading the daily loaves of bread in the commissary, our faces and hands whitened by flour dust.

"So see here," Mrs. McCormick said. "She's tried to come into Trinidad four or five times, now. But every last time, she's been escorted back to Denver by the militia. This time, she didn't dare come into the Trinidad train station. So, lo and behold, she talked the train crew into lettin' her off a mile outside the city limits. And she walked into town!"

"At her age," Jane marveled.

"She checked into the Toltec Hotel, napped a bit, and was eatin' her breakfast when General Chase's hooligans caught up to her and arrested her. They'd searched every depot between Trinidad and Walsenburg for her."

I shuddered at the memory of the barred, broken window and the smell of human filth that wafted from it. "Surely General Chase didn't put her in the jail."

"Oh, no, I don't think he'd dare," Mrs. McCormick said. "You know, a man died in there just a few days ago. No, he put her in San Rafael Hospital, under the care of the nuns." Her laugh turned bitter. "Guarded day and night, she is. By two militia sharpshooters."

"Does General Chase think she can run from them?" Jane asked, wide-eyed. "Surely she's not spry enough for that."

"Don't bet on it!" Mrs. McCormick gloated. "Johnny D must be downright afraid of Mother Jones. Think of it—all his millions and one little granny can give him nightmares!"

We laughed, relieved that we still could.

Within a week, newspapers around the country picked up on Mother Jones' plight, printing a cartoon of teeth-gnashing militia guards tormenting a bedridden, angelic old woman. The caption read, "How They Treat an 82-Year-Old Woman in Colorado." John D. Rockefeller, far away in New York, refused to remark on the matter. But in the tent colonies, the women planned a parade through the streets of Trinidad to demand the release of Mother Jones.

We painted signs: WE'RE FOR MOTHER JONES, FREE MOTHER JONES, DON'T YOU HAVE A MOTHER TOO? From the crack of dawn, union trucks raced out of Ludlow, carrying scores of women, children, banners and placards. Women gathered in Trinidad from all the tent colonies, even from as far away as White City in Walsenburg, forty miles to the north. We were to march from the bottom of Commercial Street to General Chase's fortress in the Columbian Hotel on Main.

Alex kissed Pearl goodbye at the depot. "You look beautiful," he said to her.

She laughed. "It's pure happiness at being out of Ludlow."

She was beautiful, with her hair tied back in a simple tail and her stomach rounding beneath her heavy coat. Her face, fleshed out and baby-smooth, shone with a rosy softness.

"Look at this!" she exclaimed as we lined up near the depot. "You would never have thought so many went out on strike!"

Around us, foreign women peered out from beneath colorful scarves and cheap felt hats. Strident American women in button-down coats, sure and strong, headed the parade. Everywhere, children tripped alongside their mothers. For a moment, it felt like the first days of October, when the weather had been mild, and the strikers had been given over to baseball games and lazy lunches at the commissary. Hope had followed us like a guardian angel then.

"Come on, women!" came the call. "Take up your signs, and let's go free Mother Jones!"

My arm linked through Pearl's, we joined the ranks behind a child carrying the two-colored banner of Ludlow. In our hands was the sign we'd painted: THE UNION FOREVER. We strode along, pressing up the steep slope of Commercial, singing and brandishing our messages. Along the route, striking men and townspeople urged us on.

Yet as we approached the intersection of Commercial and Main, where the Columbian Hotel stood, the women at the head of the column halted, banners and flags drooping, and the singing died. Blocking the intersection, mounted, armed soldiers formed a solid wall.

"Keep steady," the leader of the parade called. "We aren't breaking the law. We have nothing to fear. Link arms! Stay with your sisters!" She began to sing in a quavering voice, backing toward the militiamen and motioning in wide circles for the others to follow. But many women broke away from the parade, shunting their children off to safety in the crowd of men. Pearl and I pulled closer together and moved forward.

Suddenly, the pounding of horse's hooves echoed through the street. "Get back!" the horseman yelled. "Go home!" It was General Chase, his hat pulled low over his eyes. He spurred his horse between the soldiers and the women, twisting and jerking the reins. The horse snorted and pranced sideways, frightened by his wild movements. "Get back!" he shouted again, kicking a girl near the front of the parade.

She screamed, and all at once, mayhem spread through the streets. General Chase's horse shied and rammed a parked buggy. As he fell to the cobblestones, he called to his men, "Ride the women down!"

The cavalry obeyed at once. Drawing swords, they charged, slapping at us with the flats of their blades. I grabbed Pearl's hand, trying to pull her off the streets. "Come on," I cried. "Pearl, come on!"

The flag of Ludlow toppled across our path, and I jumped over it, landing on my tender ankle. Pearl was not so fortunate. She tripped and fell, dashing her head against the cobblestones and rolling away. A horse stamped by, its hooves striking like a blacksmith's irons on the pavement, nearly trampling her. "Pearl!" I screamed. "Pearl!" Limping, I tried to push through the flailing legs and hands of fleeing women.

But I had no luck reaching her. Beside me, a trooper brought his sword down around the head of a woman who had sunk into a heap on the street. His sword gashed her ear and the hand that she'd raised to protect herself, and blood cascaded onto her shoulders.

"Leave her alone!" I slapped at his horse.

It sidestepped as he levied the blows, and its rump swung into my shoulders. I fell on my hands and knees. As I tried to rise, my ankle gave way. Scrambling away from the horse's hooves, I crawled along the street.

"Get up!" a voice shouted in my ear.

"I can't, my ankle!"

A man lifted me up and set me on my feet, then ran off to aid another. Grabbing a hitching post, I inched my way to the spot where Pearl had fallen. She lay there yet, her hands thrown out beside her as if in surprise. Blood spilled down her temple, staining her hair. I pulled her up until she sagged against my shoulder. "Come on," I said. "Move!"

"Christian," she breathed. "Help me."

But I could not rise. Still, I hooked my hands under her arms and pulled with all my might, trying to scoot across the cobblestones. My ankle burst with sharp pain as I pushed, and I crumpled helplessly against Pearl.

"Here," another voice said. "Let me."

Theros stood before me, already lifting Pearl into his arms. He stretched out a hand to me and pulled me upward, and I wrapped my arm around his waist. Awkward and overburdened, he struggled to the boardwalk on Commercial and slipped into an alley. We left the screaming and terror in the street behind, the sound deadened by high brick walls. He staggered along, with me limping at his side, until he came to a screened door at the back of a store. "Open," he grunted.

We came into a small storeroom, a pantry filled with tins of coffee and baking powder, sacks of sugar and flour, and iceboxes. Leaving me, Theros carried Pearl up a flight of stairs. I crawled along behind, my ankle throbbing with pain, until he came back for me.

Wordless, I wrapped my arms around him and buried my face against his neck. For a moment, he did not move, but simply held me against him, his warmth and strength around me. Then he carried me to the room where Pearl was and set me on the narrow bed next to her. Before I could speak, he ran out, thumping down the stairs again.

"Where does it hurt?" I lifted her arms and legs, checking for bleeding or broken bones. Helping her out of her coat, I turned down the quilt on the bed for her.

She lay down without coaxing, seemingly dazed. "Oh, God, you don't think anything could happen to my baby, do you?"

"Lie still. It'll be better."

Theros appeared, carrying a tray with cloths, fresh water and two glasses filled with a colorless liquid. An open bottle stood beside them. He set the tray on the table. "Here, Miss Pearl," he said, handing her one glass. "Miss Christian."

"Theo Sky!" Pearl tried to laugh. "Why are you here?"

"This will make you feel all better. It is Greek ouzo."

I sniffed the drink, then set it on the table. Pearl sipped from her glass as I poured the water into a basin on the nightstand. "Oh, it tastes awful," she said. "So sweet."

"It is like your whiskey," he said.

He stepped back, leaning against the wall to give me room to tend to Pearl. Dipping a cloth, I wiped away the blood on her cheek, the smudges of dirt on her chin and forehead. The cut on her temple had swollen into a reddish welt. Gently, I pressed against her cheek to see if the jawbone was cracked.

"That hurts," she whispered.

"But it's not broken, I don't think. Are any of your teeth loose?"

She tested them with her tongue, then shook her head.

"Just rest, then," I said as I helped her under the quilt.

"It's warm here." Her eyelids fluttered. "I'm so sleepy."

I pulled the quilt up around her shoulder and stroked her hair until her eyes closed and her breathing fell into a long, even cadence. When I glanced up at Theros, he tipped his head, beckoning me to follow him.

We went into the room next to where Pearl lay. Larger than the first room, it also had a washstand and a bed draped in a patchwork quilt. A scarred chest of drawers crowded into one corner. Directly across from the door, an attic window let in bright sunlight. Two wooden chairs and a table had been placed before it.

He opened his arms, and I rushed into them. Kissing my hair, he said, "I am so glad to see you."

"How long have you been out of jail?" I asked.

"A week or so now." He went to the window and looked out at Main Street. Shouts echoed upward to us, along with the clatter of horses and wagons. Downstairs, I could hear the slamming of doors and the boom of furious male voices. "They let us go, for no good reason than they arrest us for, but Louis told us to stay out of Ludlow for a while. He says to lay low—that is the words he uses—so there is no more trouble."

"I need to find my brother," I said.

"He is here?" Theros asked. "In Trinidad?"

His contempt annoyed me. "He came with us this morning. I need to find him and tell him we're all right."

"You cannot go out there. They will arrest you—"

"But—"

"There is nothing for it. He must be left to worry." Glancing down, he said, "You are bleeding."

I looked at my hand. The rag I'd wrapped around it that morning was bloody and tattered. "I cut it at the jail," I said. "The day I saw you. I fell on it again today."

He went back to Pearl's room to fetch the water, bandages, and the bottle of ouzo, then sat at the table next to me. "Is this the American way?" he demanded. "Throwing old ladies in jail? Killing women and children on the street? And for what—because men ask to be treated like men. To be treated like Americans." He unwound the soggy bandage from my hand. "I tell you this, Miss Christian. When Louis was in jail, they offered money to him to give up the UMWA. The soldiers said, leave, go live away from here, we will pay you."

"What did he do?"

"He is still here, yes?" He washed my hand and wrapped a clean cloth over the cut. "Still waiting to be killed. The night we went to jail, Lieutenant Linderfelt beat Louis on the head with his pistol, saying he would kill him. He only stopped when Lieutenant Doll took the gun away, but it will happen again. Maybe to all of us. Louis should have taken the money and run away."

"You don't believe that."

"Why not? He could buy a coffeehouse. He could spend all his days laughing and playing cards with others. He would not die until he is old, old man."

"Would you have taken the money?"

"Yes," he said savagely. "And I would go to Denver. It is a big city, with no mines, lots of places to go to movies and dance and drink. You have never seen it, you don't know."

I caught his fingers and held them. "You wouldn't have taken it."

"Why not?"

"Because you have *time*. Honor."

He laughed, genuinely surprised. "Ah, Miss Christian, you remember good." Sobering, he shook his head. "Maybe you are right. I wouldn't take the money. I am so stupid that I stay." He tied off the bandage. "There, your hand is better now?"

I meant to answer, but my tongue felt thick and slow, and my throat rasped with desire. Leaning forward, I put my hands on either side of his face and kissed him. He pulled me closer, his hands like dark heat on my skin.

Voices bounced up the stairwell, and he moved away from me. Dimitrius appeared at the door and spoke to Theros in Greek. Sighting me, he bobbed his head and said, "Good afternoon, Miss," in perfect, stilted English.

"I have to go," Theros said.

"No—"

"I will be back." He stood to follow Dimitrius. "You will wait for me? You and Miss Pearl will be safe here."

With that, he was gone. I sat in one of the chairs, shifting the sailcloth curtains to watch for him, but I did not see him. In the street, chaos still reigned. Cavalrymen whipped their horses up and down the cobblestones, chasing away spectators and breaking up clusters of women or strikers. Occasionally, soldiers on foot escorted a striker or two down the street, certainly on the way to jail. More often, they flanked a woman, her elbows in their hands.

What threat had we women and children posed to mighty General Chase? What fear could any of those well-armed, mounted soldiers feel from such a poor, hungry crowd? I watched for Alex, desperate to send him a message that we were all right, that Pearl was not hurt. By dark, I had not seen him.

I lit a kerosene lamp and crept back into Pearl's room, treading lightly on wooden boards that squeaked from age. She slept peacefully. Quietly, I went down the dark stairs, favoring my ankle. A canvas curtain divided the pantry from the store, which was a small high-ceilinged hall, with tipsy round tables and spare, wooden chairs. Plate glass windows stretched from ceiling to floor, overlooking the street. This was the Greek bakery where Theros and the others gathered to talk and drink coffee.

A closed sign hung in the window, swinging lightly in the draft from the door. Behind the counter, near the bulky brass cash register, glass shielded pastries and loaves of bread—baked, I supposed, only that morning. The aromas of cinnamon, yeast and herbs made my mouth water. As I bent toward the bounty, a face appeared outside the window. Someone was looking inside.

I extinguished the lamp and hunkered down on the floor, my breath ragged. The lights from the street shone into the room, casting long, dark shadows. I hid my head in my arms, frightened that whoever had peered in the window—whether thief, soldier, or Greek—would come back and find Pearl and me, alone.

After a long while, I heard the back door close. Theros came into the bakery from the storeroom. I called to him, and he came to me, kneeling down beside me, folding me in his arms. "Why are you here?" he whispered. "Come with me."

He carried me upstairs to the second bedroom. "Miss Pearl is still sleeping?"

I nodded, and he said, "Wait here, I will get us something to eat."

He brought back a feast for us—cold slices of lamb wrapped in thick, doughy bread, cheeses, pastries soaked in honey, and hot, sugary coffee. I had not tasted food of such richness in months, and I ate as if I were starving. Theros ate some, washing it down with ouzo.

"Will others come here tonight?" I asked.

"Don't worry. You will be safe."

"What about the militia?"

"They won't come. There is too much down there for them to worry about."

A cry echoed through the street below, followed by the pounding of hooves. Theros shifted his chair so that he could see through the half-open curtains, one hand on his rifle. "See, they are hunting tonight," he said.

"Not you, I hope."

"Who knows?" His voice was bitter. "They hunt whoever they think is weak."

With a shudder, I remembered Colonel Drake's attempts to intimidate me. If I had acted scared or cowed—or foreign—he would have taken what he wanted from me. I joined Theros, standing just beside him and peering down at the street. Unable to put weight on my ankle, I leaned against the chair.

"When I was in jail," he said, in a low voice, "there was two Slavs in the cell with us Greeks. One day, the soldiers come for one. He is gone for a big while, then he comes back, crying, his clothes dirty. We try to understand him—he has no English—but he does this with his hand." He pretended to ply a shovel, then pointed index finger and thumb, forming a pistol, against his temple. "He digs, then shoots. We think and think, and we think men are shot by these soldiers, then buried by prisoners in the field outside of the jail."

"No, surely not." The echoes died in the street, leaving only the thin eerie popping of the lamp's flame.

He shrugged. "Well, one day, the soldiers come and they wanted Greek. I said to others, let me go. They don't know I know how to speak. So the soldiers take me outside to this flat field and hand me a shovel. Dig, they said. They made a big show to teach me. They talked about whether I have a wife, some kids, they say that I am big and stupid, that I am ugly bastard. I dig for a while, when I heard this word—privy. And I know what I am doing. We dug plenty of those down in Ludlow before the strike. When I finished—it is deep and wide, too—they said, Tomorrow, we kill you, and this is your grave. They laughed—fine joke. They think I will cry, like that Slav does. But I said, I have dug you new shithole. And they know they cannot fool me."

"What happened?" I asked.

"They beat me until I couldn't stand. You think you know English, you son of bitch, they said. We teach you English. Then they threw me back in the cell."

I reached for him. He turned to me with a sudden twist and buried his face against my breasts, the heat of his breath searing through the cotton of my dress. I kissed his hair, his eyes, his cheeks, his lips.

He stood, so abruptly that the chair skidded across the floor. Lifting me from my feet, he said, "Come with me," and carried me to the bed. Kneeling, he untied my shoes and pulled them from my feet. I cried out when he touched my ankle.

"Your hand, your ankle," he said angrily. "Look what they have done to you."

"No, don't think of it," I whispered. "Not tonight."

I reached for his shoulders, urging him toward me until our lips met. He pulled the pins from my hair, combing his fingers through it until it fell heavy and free. I tugged at his shirt, feeling for the buttons, as he undid the stays on my dress. Our clothes fell away, one layer after another, until we lay from shoulder to ankle, pressed against one another, skin against skin, the softness and sharpness of our bones and teeth and mouths between us.

His lips warm against my shoulder, he kissed a pathway across my collarbone and into the tender hollow of my throat. I swept my hands across the dark skin and hair of his chest. I had touched him so often in Berwind, rubbing salve or ointment over his skin, but now, he didn't wince, he didn't groan at my touch. It made me greedy, light-headed, and I wanted to feel every inch of him—his legs, his arms, his chest, his back—at once.

He kissed my breasts, taking each into his mouth, and I closed my eyes, reveling in the sensation. I ran my hands over his hair, the curves of his ears, the sharp stubble of his chin to the ridge of his Adam's apple, then down, through the thick hair of his chest to his thighs.

When he entered me, the sharp sting of his thrust made me cry out, but he covered my mouth with his, silencing me. I clasped his shoulders, rocked up and against him, let him take me deeper. Beneath his weight, I was lifted away from myself to a place of light and breath and deep, sweet knowledge.

I called out his name at the same time that he began to moan, our passion coming together in delight, wonder, beauty. After, he lay atop me, his head buried against my neck, his breath hot against my skin, our legs caught round each other, a mesh of heavy and solid flesh.

For a long time, we lay in each other's arms, silent and content. At last, he said, "Since I first see you in Berwind, I think, this is the prettiest girl I have ever seen. This is the girl I want."

"I have always wanted you," I said. "Since I met you."

"Oh, no." He laughed. "You hated me in school. You were too smart for me. Too good for me."

I kissed him. "But I thought of you. Not always kindly, but day, night, all the time."

"Good," he said with true satisfaction. Rolling away from me, he lay on his back, his arms around me. "Greeks call this *kefi*."

"What is that?"

"Great happiness, so much that you can only think it, not say it, because words are too stupid."

"You can only feel it," I said. "I know. I have it, too."

He kissed me, his fingertips moving over my skin, learning it. With my lips and tongue, I sought out the tender spots on his neck and chest until our desire grew strong and we came together again.

That night, we slept in the warmth of each other's bodies—far, far from Ludlow.

Before dawn, I woke to the rumble of voices downstairs. Sitting up, I clutched the blankets around me. Theros was already dressing, pulling on trousers and shirt. "Stay here," he whispered. "I will see who has come." He took the rifle from the table and dashed down the stairs.

I couldn't wait in such a state—my clothing scattered about, my hair twisted around my shoulders in a mass of curls. After he left, I pulled on my clothes and bound my hair with whatever pins and combs I could find. Frantically, I remade the bed. Opening the door, I crept to the stairs and tiptoed halfway down, then sat, unable to go farther. Men's voices resounded through the landing, but I could not hear exact words. Almost at once, the drafty air from the storeroom chilled me, and I hugged myself, leaning low over my knees.

Theros came around the corner, taking the steps two at a time. He stopped just below me and splayed his fingers through the hair on either side of my head. Tilting my face upward, he kissed me hard and deep on the lips.

"We go to San Rafael," he said. "To free Mother Jones at dawn. Others from Ludlow attack the Cardenas Hotel, to kill the Baldwins. And the jail and Columbian—"

"Oh, no, don't! General Chase keeps sharpshooters on the roof."

"No matter." His thumbs traced circles on my cheeks. "This is war. We are beaten too long, treated like animals too much, and now, our women and children have been hurt. Even Louis, who works for peace always, every day, says this is war."

"Don't go—"

"No, no," he said. "I have to go, I can't stay—"

He kissed me again, a warrior's farewell, then bounded down the steps.

※ ※ ※ ※ ※

I did not sleep again, but sat on the bed, smoothing my hand over the coverlets and barely breathing, waiting for the sounds of battle from the street below. Surely it would be a bloodbath—even the fiercest Greeks could not outgun General Chase's expert marksmen. Just after sunrise, Pearl came into the room where Theros and I had slept. She walked steadily and slowly, the cut on her forehead knotted into a purple ball. She kept one hand on her stomach, caressing it gently.

"We been here all night?" She squinted out the window at the sunlit street. "Whatever he gave me sure knocked me out."

I could not bear to tell her of the attacks on Trinidad. "How are you?"

"My head feels like a brick, but the baby's fine. She's fluttering away down there. I look terrible, don't I?"

"Like you'd survived a battle."

She laughed. "I guess I did. Where are we?"

"It's a Greek bakery." I cut the cheese and pastry breads left over from the night before. "Are you hungry?"

"Starving. You ain't heard nothing from Alex, have you?"

"I watched for him last night. I never saw him."

"He'll be crazy sick with worry," she said. "Oh, Christian, Theo Sky's a good man, coming along just when he did. But Alex sure will be uncorked to hear this. Rescued by a Greek."

I sawed so fiercely at the bread that it crumbled into bits. "Don't tell him, Pearl. Please."

"What are we going to tell him, then? We have to have been somewheres last night."

"I don't know. I'll think of something."

I reached for her hand, torn by a sudden desire to tell her about my night with Theros. We were equals now, Pearl and I, neither of us innocent, and neither of us repentant. Surely she understood the happiness I felt—*kefi*, as Theros had called it. But my courage failed me.

She knew anyway. Looking toward the bed, she said, "Did the two of you stay in here last night? What did you . . . oh, you did, didn't you?"

I nodded, laughed, then brought my hand to my mouth, hiding my flushing face.

She laughed, too. "What'd you think of it?"

"It was . . . oh, Pearl, I don't have words for it—"

"That's what it should be, then. Tell me all about it."

Hours later, a Greek man knocked on the door. His neat, clean clothing bespoke a man who lived in town. Wadding his hat in his hand, he said in clear, slow English, "I have got a wagon outside, Mrs. I can take you to Ludlow now."

"Is it safe to go?" I asked. "What about the fighting?"

"That never happens," he said. "The men put their guns away."

"Why? What made them give up?"

"Someone tells them, no more fight. They are done."

What he meant by that, I didn't know, but it didn't matter. "Where is Theros?" I asked breathlessly. "Is he safe?"

The Greek eyed me curiously, and Pearl took my hand. Afraid that my eyes would stray to the bed and I'd reveal the secret of Theros' and my time together, I looked out the window.

"He is with the others," the Greek said at last. "They are safe."

As the wagon rattled along toward Ludlow, the Greek offered rides to the weary men and women traveling northward. Outrage rumbled through them at Mother Jones' captivity, General Chase's arrogance, at the hapless women arrested or beaten, but I took no part in it. Instead, I kept an arm around Pearl's waist, her cheek nestled against my shoulder, and my thoughts on a patchwork quilt on a bed, and the whispering of a kerosene lamp, and hands and eyes and kisses.

PART IV

I have strain'd the spider's thread
'Gainst the promise of a maid;
I have weigh'd a grain of sand
'Gainst her plight of heart and hand;
I told my true love of the token,
How her faith proved light, and her word was broken:
Again her word and truth she plight,
And I believed them again ere night.
Sir Walter Scott

Chapter 23

The war in Trinidad had been halted by a telegram. Humming over the wires from Washington, D.C. to Denver, and from Denver to the union office in Ludlow, it called for a congressional investigation into the labor strife in southern Colorado. After he received it, John Lawson sent messengers to Trinidad to call off the attacks on San Rafael, the Cardenas and the Columbian.

The news changed our fortunes. With the same stealth as they'd been brought in, hundreds of strikebreakers were shipped from Berwind and the other coal camps and dumped on Larimer Street in Denver. The jailers in Trinidad unlocked the cells and flushed out the prisoners, including Mary Thomas and her toddler daughters, who had been locked up after the women's parade. Mother Jones was freed from San Rafael Hospital and escorted to Denver with a warning to stay away from Trinidad. Strikers freely boarded trains, and the Yellow Bands of Company B quit trolling the roads, looking to prey on lone women and drunken men. Even the weather turned warmer, the wind blowing in a mild thaw.

Alex grumbled. "And what will happen when all this ends, and Senator Montana and Congressman South Carolina go home?"

He had taken to reading every article he could about the

investigation in the newspaper, and every day, he went to the commissary to pick up bits of news from the men gathered there.

"John D. Rockefeller has refused to testify," he fumed. "He says he hasn't any knowledge of the situation in Colorado and will leave the testifying to the men who oversee his Colorado operations." He grew more incensed. "President Wilson had to extend a special invitation to Mr. Rockefeller to come to Washington and testify before the committee. The arrogance of that man!"

"Surely Johnny D won't ignore the president," I said.

"Don't bet on it."

"How'd they choose who's going to testify?" Pearl wondered. "The newspapers say it's them folks with grievances against the company, but there ain't a one of us who don't have a story or two to tell. They ask you, Alex?"

"What's ever happened to me that hasn't happened fourfold over?"

Pearl had no answer to that.

They didn't ask the Greeks, either. When the witness lists were posted at the public square, the names contained enough vowels, but not too many, for the American congressmen to pronounce. Most of the names sounded suspiciously American, most likely belonging to those who spoke clear, native English.

On a cold February day, Alex, Pearl and I journeyed to Trinidad to attend the hearings at the Opera House. There, we found Main Street in a state of uproar, as strikers, company men, militia and Baldwin-Felts spilled from the cobblestone pavement into the paths of automobiles, horse-drawn wagons, and electric trolleys. Only the balcony of the Opera House was open to the public, for the seating on the floor was given to union officials, lawyers, militia officers and newspapermen. In no time at all, the balcony steps were jammed with a shoving, quarrelsome throng.

We pushed our way inside and wedged into three seats overlooking the theater below. Around us, spectators posted themselves along the walls, sometimes two and three deep. The smell of damp wool and mud-caked boots wafted through the stifling air in the balcony, and scraps of newspaper were coveted as flimsy fans.

On the stage, the five congressmen sat at a long table, accompanied by several younger men in high-starched collars and thin, striped ties who tidied up piles of paper and poured glasses of water.

Witnesses, questioned by both CF&I's and the UMWA's lawyers, told stories that floated through the balcony like the refrain of a song we had sung for eternity. Strikers recalled years of being short-weighted, sometimes by thousands of tons, on the coal they dug from the ground, and of being cheated on blasting powder at the company store. They spoke of being forced to buy equipment that was rusted and faulty, of being beaten by mine guards if they complained of the dust and poor air in the tunnels. Women took the stand as well, speaking of insults and brutality from the mine guards and militia.

Mid-morning, James Fyler, the paymaster at Ludlow who handed out our dollars each week, took the witness stand. Moving as if his bones had seized up, he raised a swollen, bruised face to the gallery. Anguish swept through the balcony as he told his story.

"I was asked to testify before this committee by John Lawson," he said. "But a couple of days ago, a bunch of us was caught by some Yellow Bands—the soldiers from Company B in Berwind Canyon—as we was passing Water Tank Hill. They took a gang of us strikers up the canyon to Tabasco, lined us up against this wall and then made a firing squad. They had them Springfields all pointed and aimed. They told us they was going to kill us for agreeing to testify."

In the gallery around me, papers fans halted in mid-air and bodies stilled, as if no one dared breathe. All eyes rested on Fyler.

"Who told you that?"

"Lieutenant Karl Linderfelt. He's in charge of the Yellow Bands—of Company B, that is."

An angry outcry burst from the spectators. Congressman Evans beat his gavel on the table and shouted for silence.

"Obviously, you were not executed by a firing squad," he said.

"No," Fyler answered. "But they did this." He touched his raw face. "It ain't no way to treat an old man, no way at all."

"You don't seem old to me at all," another congressmen offered. "How old are you?"

"Forty-four. But I been in the mines for thirty-five years now. That makes a man old."

Protest rippled through the gallery, as the congressmen pondered Fyler's response. Alex whispered in my ear, "They care more about his age than about what happened to him."

Beside me, Pearl dabbed at her forehead. "It's plenty hot," she whispered. "I ain't feeling so good."

"Do you want to leave?"

She nodded. Alex stayed in the balcony, intent on seeing the morning's hearing to a close. Pearl and I elbowed our way through the crowd and clattered down the outdoor steps to the street. There, we strolled along the cobblestones.

"It feels good out here," Pearl said, raising her face to the sun. A brisk wind blew from the west. "As cold as we been this winter out in Ludlow, you'd think I'd never want to be outside again."

We dawdled past storefronts, searching for a café. Most of the places banned one group or another—strikers, or militia, or Greeks, or Irish, or "persons of foreign birth." Near the end of the block, the Greek bakery came into view. No signs forbade entrance to anyone, but the hand-written names of exotic foods painted in egg white on the windows served just as well. As we passed, I strained to see inside. Beyond the glass was a shadowy gathering of men, straddling chairs and shouldering up against counters and walls.

Suddenly, Pearl grabbed my arm. At first, I thought she had recognized the Greek bakery, but her eyes were set on a slow, mournful procession up the street. In a rolling chair of wicker, Russell Ruddy rode along Main Street.

"Oh, God, Christian!" Pearl breathed. "It's true."

He was no longer a man who could work or walk or laugh. His head tipped to his left, his mouth lolling open, his eyes watery and pale. His mother walked beside him, one hand on his shoulder to steady him. Jake pushed the chair. The three younger Ruddy boys—all full-grown men now—lagged behind.

I glanced back at the bakery, thinking we might hide there. But Pearl had already started to move, slowly, steadily, as if drawn by a net, into that pathetic picture.

Mrs. Ruddy looked Pearl up and down, taking in the bulging stomach, the sunstruck silver-black hair, the rosy cheeks. The younger boys stared, as if they'd never seen her before. Jake lit a cigarette. I could nearly hear him counting the months.

Everyone spoke at once.

Mrs. Ruddy's lips parted in an ugly sneer. "I've been hoping to see you, to give you a piece of my mind."

"I'm so sorry for you," Pearl offered at the same time. "Poor Russ—"

"You connivin' little bitch!" Jake exploded, his voice overpowering the others. "What the hell do you think you're doing? God damn you! I knew the day you left Berwind that you was hiding something!"

"Carrying my poor son's baby!" Mrs. Ruddy lashed the accusation. "And here you are, living in Ludlow like a whore with that Scott character. May every last fire of hell rain down on your head!"

The younger boys snickered, but Mrs. Ruddy wasn't finished. "That baby is my grandchild, and I mean to claim it. I would never let a slut like you raise my son's child!"

Pearl gripped my arm as if she were drowning.

"That's enough!" I said.

"That isn't even the half of it," Mrs. Ruddy screeched. "You are the most faithless, false—"

Her voice wilted under a strange, high-pitched racket. Everyone looked at Russell, whose hands flipped around on his lap, grasping his knees or catching his coat, unable to settle anywhere. Coughing and humming, he rocked in his chair. He had seen Pearl.

"Russell, oh, Russ," Mrs. Ruddy croaked. "Quiet, boy, quiet! Oh, look how you've upset him."

Lifting one twisted hand, Russell reached for Pearl. Without even a breath, she went to him. Dropping to her knees on the cobblestones, she put her hands on either side of his face. His hand fell on her shoulder. "Oh, Russ," she whispered. "Oh, Russ. I wish you was better."

Garbled words arose him his hacking and humming. "Puhl," he said. "Come 'ome, come 'ome."

Mrs. Ruddy dabbed at her lips with a handkerchief, humbled by such a sad spectacle, and Jake spun away, as if he could not stand to witness it.

"I'm so sorry, Russ," Pearl said. "I'm so sorry I said what I did the last time I seen you. I shouldn't never have said it. I'm sorry."

Tears trailed down Russell's face. With her fingertips, Pearl wiped them away. "Quiet, Russ," she breathed. "Don't be so sad, oh, don't be so upset—"

Mrs. Ruddy stepped forward. "You left him, so don't be all teary-eyed now. You have no right to sorrow."

Jake started toward Pearl, and as if a whip had cracked behind my head, I rushed forward and hooked her under the arm. "We have to go," I said. "Quick, get up."

She didn't move. Her sorrow was so great that it spilled out on the street, a wave that would wash away everything before it. She held Russell's hands as if her own had melded to them, and she kept searching his face, to see what she must have once known there.

"Get up, Pearl." Jake swayed impatiently. "Get the hell away from him."

I helped Pearl up, a firm hand on her elbow. She seemed unsteady, as if she couldn't place herself, and Jake took full advantage of it. He grabbed her by the shoulders and jerked her out of my hands. Her face paled, her lips withering with fear, a weak cry escaping from them.

"That baby ain't gonna be raised down in Ludlow," he declared.

"I'm gonna see it has a proper home."

"She has a proper home," I protested. "With us, with me—!"

"You're coming home with us! Now!"

His threats seemed to wake her up, and Pearl pushed him as hard as she could. He stumbled backward, and then, a wave of agony crossed his face as he realized he was about to crash into Russell behind him. Mrs. Ruddy shrieked, and the three boys ran toward the chair, desperate to move Russell to safety. Jerking his shoulders forward, Jake veered sideways, his feet tangling. Only the brick wall stopped him, and he stood there a moment, shoulders hunched against it, panting for breath.

Mrs. Ruddy turned on Pearl. "Look at the trouble you cause!" she screamed. "I will see that you pay for what you've done to my boy! To all of us! You have no right to keep that baby from Russell, and by God, I'm going to see to it that it comes to live with us!"

Jake righted himself. For a moment, I feared he would come toward Pearl, to throttle her or grab an arm and wrench it out of its socket. But he quietly took his stance behind Russell's chair. Gripping the handles, he rolled the chair around us, with Russell tilting to one side, his hand thrown out toward Pearl. His lips moved, as if he was calling to her, but only a monotonous drone echoed against the brick wall. I held Pearl back, both of her hands in mine. The Ruddys moved slowly down the street, the wheels of Russell's chair rattling against the cobblestones.

We walked in the opposite direction, but we had only gone a few steps when Pearl collapsed against the brick wall of a nearby grocery and sank to the ground. I knelt beside her, my hand on her arm. People brushed by us, skirting us with barely a glance of concern in our direction.

"Russ was so good," she mourned. "So sweet. There ain't a mean bone in his body."

But something was tearing at me. "Why is Mrs. Ruddy so determined that the baby is Russell's? You told me you never—"

She said nothing, her hands at her temples.

"You told me Russell and you were never husband and wife," I said, my voice rising. "But every time you see Russell, you act like you love him. And it's obvious that he loves you."

She crossed her arms over her knees and laid her head on it. "One night, when Russ came home from work, well, I was all unhappy. Jake had been picking at me again, making me all het up, and I was bound and determined that I was going to end it. So when Russ come in, I took him upstairs and fixed him a bath, and"—she lowered her voice—"we started kissing and it all just happened."

"When was this?" I asked.

"We'd been married near to two years by then. Two years! And somehow, well, the whole family knew about it. I don't know if they heard—them walls in that house is pretty thin—or just guessed."

I said nothing for a moment, thinking over her words. "So the baby could be Russell's? Oh, Pearl, you have to tell Alex!"

"That's the only time it happened, Christian. I swear, I would swear it on my baby's life. After that, Russ went back to what he had been doing, staying far away from me, but everybody in that house thought that he'd changed, that he liked me, and it was just so much easier for both of us to live with them thinking that—"

"Still, the baby could be—"

"You think it's so easy, don't you?" she said bitterly. "You think every girl has a father who reads poems and tell her she's some kind of princess, and you think love is just sitting under the train trestle with Theo Sky and cuddling and kissing all day. Well, it ain't like that at all, so clean and sweet."

Her words slammed into me, as if I'd been forced back against the brick wall. "I'm just looking out for Alex."

"Alex!" she snapped. "Don't you dare think that I'd do anything bad to him! I love him! I always have! But I've always had to fight for every little thing that come along to me, and now it looks like I got to fight for my baby! Mrs. Ruddy is just like you and Alex. It don't matter what's right, only what's proper!"

I stood. "You can't tell lies, Pearl. You can't just use whatever story that comes to mind."

"That's what they're doing!" She nearly shouted. "Old Mrs. Ruddy's saying that baby is Russell's because not one of them can just leave him be! He don't want no baby. He don't want no family. All he ever wanted was to be left alone and to be what he was. But the rest of them would poke out their eyes if they had to, just so's they wouldn't have to see what's right in front of them!"

I said nothing, too angry to speak.

"I ain't the only one here telling stories and keeping secrets," Pearl said. "Maybe Alex'd like to know what you get up to when you ain't being watched!"

Just then, the grocery owner barreled through the door of his store, broom in hand. "Move on, you two!" he shouted. "No begging here!" He jabbed the broom toward me, as if he could simply sweep us away.

"Give us a minute," I begged. "She's sick."

"Get away! You tent folks with your tuberculosis and typhoid!

Go away!"

I hauled Pearl up by the arm, swallowing to keep the rage inside me from bursting forth. I wanted to slap the grocer with his own broom, I wanted to shake Pearl, to fight it out with her. I wanted to chase after the Ruddy family and scream at them to stay away, to leave us alone. I wanted to run to Theros and beg him to take me away from it all.

"We have to find Alex," I said. "He'll be worried about us."

We plodded through the tangled, fast-flowing streets to the Opera House, our shoulders no longer touching, our hands no longer locked together. My face burned and my chest hurt, as if I'd been sobbing. At last, we found Alex, newly emerged from the hearings. He was so riled up about the travesty being played out inside the Opera House that he did not even notice Pearl's distress. On the train ride to Ludlow, he talked without stopping.

I watched the dried brown earth and hills of crusted snow rush by the window. I could not decide whether to tell Alex, or how much I should tell him. Surely he should know about Ava Ruddy's threats. But more so, he had a right to know that the baby might not be his. After all, it would be his to rear and support. I wondered if Pearl's threat to tell Alex about Theros was serious. I glanced toward where she sat in the corner, her face in profile, watching the same empty landscape outside the train window. Her dark lashes hid her eyes.

"—and with Company B moving down from Berwind Canyon to take over the patrols around Ludlow—"

I looked toward Alex. "What?"

"Haven't you been listening?" he demanded irately. "The little college boys of Company K are sick and tired of missing school. They're going home."

"And the Yellow Bands will be stationed at Ludlow?" My heart pounded. "When did this come about?"

"The state's run out of money. It can't pay the militia anymore." Alex flipped his hands. "So Colorado Fuel & Iron's talked Governor Ammons into letting it set up a 'clearinghouse' to hire replacements for the brave boys of the Colorado National Guard. Even General Chase is leaving and going back to his dentist business."

"That means the militia will be nothing but mine guards and Baldwin-Felts—"

"It's been that way for months now. This just makes it legal."

"God help us."

"Och, Christian, we'll need somebody bigger than Him."

That evening, I walked to the west, to the very edge of the tent colony, just before the railroad tracks. Beyond, in a small swale, were the two large tents of the Greeks. A path of dirty snow and mud led toward it. I don't know if someone told Theros I was there, or if his timing was simply right, but he appeared a few minutes later.

"Something is wrong?" he asked.

I did not answer. We walked down the banks of the arroyo and climbed up below the steel bridge. In the shadow of the girders and tracks, it was almost entirely dark.

"Tell me what's wrong," he said. "Are you mad—?"

I laid my fingers on his lips to stop him.

It was not words I wanted. I had no faith in them. They did not heal, they did not soothe. They only revealed, and cut, and left me empty and dazed. That night, the only comfort I could glean was from the solid press of flesh, and weight, and the gravity that held us to the earth.

The congressional investigation in Trinidad ended, and we waited for justice to be served by the United States government. We would be proved right, we were certain, our cause recognized for the noble and soaring truth that it was. We would prevail.

A week later, the soldiers of the Colorado National Guard were called in from the field. The harmless boys of Company K bade farewell to Ludlow and went home. Only two troops remained in the strike zone. Company A was stationed at the mines and tent colonies near the New Mexico border. Company B, the Yellow Bands from Berwind Canyon, remained under the command of Lieutenant Karl Linderfelt.

Within days, Company B looted and burned the Forbes tent colony while the residents attended a funeral for the stillborn twins of an Austrian striker and his wife. Sixteen men from Forbes were hauled to the jail in Trinidad, and their desperate wives and children were shooed away from the ruined tents. They straggled into Ludlow, without food, clothing or possessions.

A militia camp was built on the spot where the Forbes tent colony had stood, on land that had been leased by the UMWA.

Chapter 24

Pearl and I kept a sullen silence.

We lived too near one another to keep from speaking at all—we bumped into each other at the stove, or followed one another to the latrines in the mornings, or washed our clothes at the same community sink. We sat at the same table to eat and slept only a few feet from one another.

Still, everything felt broken, as blistered and windblown as the tents of Ludlow.

I spent most of my time away from the tent. Now that it was no longer a secret that Pearl was expecting, the women who had always loved her showered her with care, prayers, spells and songs to keep the baby from harm. They soaked her feet in Epsom salts and offered her strips of fabric to expand her ever-shrinking skirts and dresses. At their urging, she drank goat's milk and shielded her stomach with a tin dishpan during the full moon.

"The Mexicans say this will keep my baby safe from evil spirits," Pearl offered, when Alex questioned her about it. "It can't hurt nothing."

"Except your pride." He laughed, then swept into, *"I'll ne'er blame my partial fancy; Naething could resist my Nancy; But to see her was to love her, Love but her and love for ever."*

"I ain't heard you do your old Scotch poems in ages," Pearl said, her eyes glistening.

He was happy, transported back into the Alex who had once been my closest friend, with his quick wit and smiles and curiosity. He seemed a new man—or maybe, just a grown man—who walked without the numbing weight of the childhood promises he had been unable to keep. I wondered if he had put aside the past for a new life—a child, a beloved, a vision beyond the next day.

On a blustery morning in early February, a young Italian girl sought me out as I was on my way to the cook tent. She stuffed a wadded scrap of paper into my hand. "This for you," she said.

"Who gave it to you?"

"The union man has give it me."

"Which union man?"

"The Greco man."

I sought the shadow of a nearby tent and unfolded the note. In perfectly even block letters, Theros asked me to meet him in the attic room of the Greek bakery the next afternoon.

For an entire morning, I pampered and fussed over myself with shameless vanity. I washed my hair, shook out my best wool skirt, doused myself in lavender water, and donned my last pair of lisle stockings. Aboard the train to Trinidad, I re-pinned my hair, picked lint from my skirt, and knotted a ribbon on my felt hat over and over again, my hands veined purplish not from cold, but from excitement. I looked beautiful, I felt beautiful. Skipping up the steep slope of Commercial Street, my feet were light and sure, and I caught the eye of more than one man before dashing down the alley and through the screened back door of the bakery.

Theros waited for me on the landing, wearing traditional Cretan dress. "You have come," he said, as if surprised. He passed his hat from one hand to the other.

"Didn't you know I would?" I stood on tiptoe to kiss him, eager to go into that private room, where we would talk and laugh at our good fortune.

He stood aside while I passed, then opened the door of the small bedroom for me with gentlemanly grace.

Oh, what a surprise awaited me.

Seated at the table, on the bed, and along the walls, was a host of Greek men. I wheeled around, my heart clamoring at my ribs, and slammed squarely into Theros' chest. He clasped my elbows in his iron-grip hands. "Don't be scared," he murmured. "You are safe. Nothing will happen." With a backward step, he leaned against the door. It closed behind him with a click.

"Miss Scott, please," someone called. I turned and saw Louis Tikas seated at the table. He beckoned me to sit in the chair opposite him. I obeyed, gathering my coat about me and lowering my face, so that the men could not see the pains I'd taken with my appearance. How I hated Theros just then—how I hated myself. Pearl was right. I was a child, a stupid romantic, thinking love was as simple and lovely as a Burns poem.

I shot a look toward Theros. He had squatted with his back against the door, his elbows on his knees. His fingers were locked together, his hands drained of blood by his own merciless grip.

"Miss Scott, you must not be afraid," Louis said, his voice so low that I barely heard him over my own breathing. "We mean you no harm. We have only to ask for a favor."

"What is it?" I croaked.

"Do you want tea? Coffee?" He waved at two pots before us. A plate of sumptuous breads and pastries sat squarely on the table before me. "Please, have something to drink and eat. Please, take off your coat."

I accepted a cup of tea. Louis helped me off with my coat. Casting quick glances around the room, I counted eight Greeks. Theros' brother-in-law, Dimitrius, sat on the bed, next to an older man that I guessed was his uncle Spero. The other four were strangers, all about Theros' age, none older than twenty-five.

Seated once again, Louis spoke, his English tinged by a heavy accent. "You have been safe in Ludlow? Your tent is near the middle, I think?"

"Yes," I said tightly.

"Good," Louis said. "But you know what it is like in Ludlow. We fight off the mine guards and Baldwin-Felts, we fight off the militia, and now guards and Baldwins and militia are all the same men. No one lives without fear." Bitterness crept into his words. "Did the investigation bring us peace? No, it is the same now as it ever was. They are shooting at us again and keeping us from traveling the roads and trains. Our supplies are stolen or ruined, so that we have no good food or water in Ludlow."

I said nothing, sipping from the cup, for I had heard enough rumors in Ludlow to know that he spoke the truth. Once the congressmen and reporters had returned east, conditions in the strike zone had soured again.

Louis's eyes, nearly black, did not flicker from my face. "You went to the hearings?"

"Yes."

"Then you know that the congressmen decided that this strike is a matter of interest for Colorado, not for the United States. They decided to do nothing for us."

Terrible disappointment overcame me. A favorable ruling by the congress had offered our only hope of justice. "No, I hadn't heard that."

"It is true. The great government of the United States of America will do nothing for us. The men we vote for say, oh, no, your problems aren't important enough for us." Louis stirred his coffee. "Some say that Ludlow will be destroyed, that the militia will come to wipe us out, as it has Forbes. I think that is a true story."

His words unnerved me. My teacup clattered against the saucer as I clumsily set it down, unable to control the trembling in my hands.

"What do you want from me?" I asked.

He poured himself more coffee, then studied the street below. At last, he looked me in the eyes. "Theros tells me you are a woman of *time*, a woman of courage and strength. Is that true?"

My mouth opened, but words fled. I looked toward Theros, whose face had paled to the color of his bloodless hands. He gave no sign that he thought of me at all. His eyes, usually so warm, were blank and rigid.

Louis waved away an answer. "Things are bad in Ludlow. The Death Special drives around, scaring our children. Our men are hauled to jail. Not just Greeks, but Italians and Slavs, too—all of Ludlow's men. We are so bothered by militia that we must crawl in and out of Ludlow at night like thieves."

One of the other men offered a word that sounded much like my brother's "nae."

Louis glanced at the man. "Yes, he says, yes. You see, Miss Scott, our men can't buy rifles. We can't buy ammunition. So, what do we do?"

"You have guns—"

"A few." He shrugged. "But not enough for every man. Not enough to protect Ludlow against the soldiers. We can't get more, neither." The words tumbled from his mouth, gaining in speed and volume. "But a woman—the soldiers would never suspect her. She could bring in guns to the colony and never be caught."

For a moment, his message floated in my mind, without meaning. From the street below came the hum of the streetcars, the clip-clop of horses, the call of a newspaper boy. Then, understanding dawned. "You're asking me to bring guns to Ludlow?"

He nodded, cagey and cool. "What do you think of that?"

"How could a woman—?" I stopped, stumbling over the possibilities. "Women aren't allowed to ride the trains any more often than strikers. It's only luck that we're let on at all."

"Did you come by train this morning?"

"Yes, but—"

One of his fingers circled the rim of his coffee cup. "Then, you are lucky." His eyes flickered over my face and fastened on my hair. "Those who are pretty, Miss Scott, are often lucky."

Fear gripped me again. The others' eyes were on me, sizing up my features as Louis had. Even Theros watched me, as if assessing me anew.

"It is like this," Louis said. "Women wear heavy, full skirts and big, long coats. You are small—dainty, yes?—but you wear lots of clothes, so you look fat." His hands floated, wider and wider. "So you sew pockets inside your skirts—see, like a man's?" He stood and pulled the pockets from inside his trousers. "But your pockets are big, long and reach from the top of skirt to the, the bottom, the—"

"Hem."

"Yes. We can break the guns into pieces, so they can slip right into these pockets. You ride the train back to Ludlow—you must stand, not sit—and walk past the militia, no problem."

His words seemed unreal, impossible. Who would devise such a scheme? Who would believe it would succeed? I looked to Theros, but his head was bent, his attention on the floor beneath him. My heart, which had barely regained its normal beat, pounded again in my chest.

"The Italian girls are doing this for their men," Louis said. "There is pay, if you like, a little money—"

"That doesn't matter."

"Miss Scott, the union, it grows tired and weak. No one knows how it will end in Ludlow and the other tent cities. What will happen to all these people"—the phrase caught in his throat—"all these people who thought they would win their freedom? Even John Lawson knows there is no more hope, no more chance. Who, then, is left to save us?"

Every word rang fatally true. I made an attempt to pick up my teacup, but it tipped, and the little liquid in it spilled in a thin, copper-colored stream on the tablecloth.

Louis calmly blotted up the spilled tea with his handkerchief. "We Greeks do not kill for fun, no matter what is said of us. But we have seen enough of our enemies here in America to know that they do." His next words were soft, gentle. "You would never be alone. Greeks would be at the depot in Trinidad to watch you go, and in Ludlow to see you home. Two, maybe three men, waiting just for you. If the soldiers bother you, they would offer a, what is it, a mess, a—?"

"A distraction?"

"Goose chase," he said at the same time. "One of these men here would cause so much trouble that the soldiers would not even see you. Look around you. These are not bad fellows, no? But they will make the soldiers think so."

The eyes around the room, except Theros', fastened onto me. Dimitrius rocked back and forth on the bed, raising a rhythmic squeak from the bedsprings. Another man struck a match against the sole of his shoe, then lit a thin, brown cigarette. My gaze faltered under theirs.

"You'd be taken to jail," I breathed.

"No matter. We have all been there before. We aren't afraid." Louis drew something from atop the bureau behind him. "I have some fabric here. It's very pretty. You could make the pockets from it. Or you could make a new skirt and tear up an old one for pockets."

He pushed a length of cloth onto the table, a green flannel sprinkled with tiny pink rosebuds and yellow bows. Without thinking, I reached out to brush it, to feel its quality and weight, its softness. It was finer than any cloth I'd seen in years.

"Please, Miss Scott. Think about this. Take your time."

He spoke in Greek, then stood, and gave me a half-bow. The others rose, too, and gave me the same strange, courtly bow. They filed through the door that Theros opened for them, but when his turn came, he murmured something to Louis, and then closed the door.

He turned toward me, his face knotted. "I am sorry to trick you so—"

All the harsh words I'd held inside boiled out. "Why?" I demanded. "Why did you do this? Why did you ask me to come here, here where—?" My words failed, and I put my face in my hands.

"I am sorry." Kneeling beside me, he said, "But if I asked you myself and you said no, then I would be a fool to Louis and them." He touched my arms, trying to coax my hands away from my face. "Maybe I would be a fool to you, too. Who knows?"

A sudden unbearable shame came over me. "What did you tell him about me?"

"Don't be angry." His fingers closed around my wrists. "He knows you. He saw you on the day of steel train, bandaging men with Mrs. Jolly. He heard you speak to me at jail that day, he comes here after the parade for Mother Jones. I don't tell him. Louis knows."

"And does he know about . . . ?" My words withered, as if I might cry, weakly and stupidly, like a child. "What did you tell the rest of them about you and me?"

"I did not tell them." He shifted his weight from one knee to the other. "But men, they think bad thoughts. They joke and laugh. I can't do nothing for it."

"Oh, God, I'm so stupid!"

"Please, Christian," he pleaded. "You are American girl. They know how wild American girls are. They don't think nothing wrong of it. Don't be ashamed."

"I thought you wanted me, that you wanted to—!"

Another wave of shame overtook me—was I so weak that I had to beg a man for his affections? Just across the room was the bed where we had made love—and where the men had been sitting only minutes before.

This time he pulled my hands away from my face. "Look at me," he commanded. "Look, no, look here."

I struggled to raise my hands again, but he held them tightly in his. I was forced to look into his eyes.

"I am proud that you come here to see me. I tell Louis, you are good enough, brave enough to do anything. You are never scared, never nasty or silly like other girls."

I closed my eyes, resisting the urge to deny his words.

"Louis is a great man," he said. "He does not ask you to do this because he is almost killed so much. No, he asks you because union cannot go on, and we can't go back to Berwind without it. Louis knows this. He will tell you."

"Leave me alone."

He started to speak, then stopped. Rising, he moved uneasily across the room, as if he was afraid I would charge the door and escape. He had just reached the door when I said, "Louis said that none of you were afraid to go back to jail. That's not true."

He did not speak at once. "We will do what we must for Ludlow, for our freedom."

I turned away, watching the street below. There were women out there who would think of the green flannel cloth as nothing more than a trifle, and men who had no use for guns. They shopped in the fashionable stores along Main, ate at tables set with damask and china, slept in beds warmed by their own peaceful dreams. They had money, houses, beautiful furniture and things they could call their own. They did not tally their grievances in the number of dead, or the number of bullet holes in canvas, or the smoldering piles that had once been homes. And all the speeches in Denver and meetings with the governor and negotiations between company lawyers and union officials and congressional hearings had not given us a single victory.

"Tell him I'll do it," I said.

His eyes shone, warm once more. "You will not be sorry," he said, his voice eager, young. "I promise."

But regret assailed me long before I returned to Ludlow that afternoon, and it followed me far into the night. Huddled behind the blanket curtain in our tent, with only a dim lamp for light, I furtively cut strips of green flannel. Across the room, Pearl slept on Alex's cot. Again and again, I questioned myself. Why had I agreed? Was it for Theros, or for Louis, or truly for Ludlow?

Wielding the scissors, I remembered Louis' suggestion that I sew a new skirt and use a worn one to create pockets. Yet I could never explain new fabric to Pearl and Alex. Petulant as a child, I cuddled the flannel against my face, tearful and disappointed, outraged at the waste of this soft, fresh fabric.

Still, I kept my promise. On my first trip, I crept down the alley and into the bakery without notice. Upstairs, on the bed where Theros and I had slept, lay a shining new rifle, broken down, as Louis had said, into stock and barrel. All at once, nausea swept over me, and I sat on the bed, my whole body riddled with fear.

When I rose, I could barely stand to touch the cold metal and wood of the rifle. I fumbled around, trying to fit the parts inside the pockets, tearing my petticoat and staining the flannel with gun oil. Angered by my own clumsiness, I packed a weighty leather pouch of bullets into a third pocket that circled around my hips, which dragged so much at my skirt until I thought it might rip and slip to the ground. I tucked a loaf of freshly baked bread wrapped in brown paper—a gift or, perhaps, payment—into my bag.

Walking through the streets of Trinidad, I cowered every time my eyes caught those of a Baldwin-Felts agent or a militiaman. My instincts were to hide away beneath heavy scarves and veils, but Louis had urged me to flaunt my looks, my hair shining in the sun, neatly combed, saucy and jaunty. Yet surely everyone near me could see the outline of the rifle as I moved, surely they could detect the anxiety in my eyes, and feel the sweat on my palms as I offered train fare. Once on the train, dizziness overcame me, for my breathing had been so shallow on the downhill jaunt from the bakery that I now gasped for air. But barely had I swallowed down the last of the bile that rose in my throat, it seemed, than the train arrived in Ludlow.

"Good afternoon, Miss." A Yellow Band hailed me on the platform at the depot. "You've been in Trinidad?"

"Yes."

He peered inside the brown paper at the bread. All the while, to my right, stood my shadow—a man named Anton—his face buried in a newspaper, a cigarette burning between two fingers. I dared not look directly toward him, afraid of betraying our acquaintance. A Greek named Evangelo stalked behind the militiaman. I looked away as the soldier pawed through my bag, then handed it back to me.

I hurried away from the depot and into Ludlow, but both Anton and Evangelo followed me. My resolve crumbled. Were they still bent on protecting me, or were they to escort me all the way to the delivery spot, where I would be alone with a number of them? The fears I had carried with me since the meeting in the bakery crashed down upon me. Surely they respected Louis enough to let me arrive and leave unmolested, surely they liked Theros enough not to harm me. My chest tightened so that I heaved for breath, and my legs felt as if they would give way beneath me. Walking straight through the tent colony, I scurried down the path into the arroyo and headed east. To my relief, Anton and Evangelo remained in Ludlow.

An abandoned barn stood just inside the barbed wire fence of a neighboring ranch. No glass remained in the barn's windows, broken either by time or by gunshots, and a loft door banged ceaselessly in the wind. I shoved open the rickety door and went inside. To my right, the hinged doors of empty stalls and bins rattled and creaked. To my left, straw mounded halfway to the ceiling, its golden hue faded to the color of dust.

"Hello?" I called. "Theros?"

No one answered.

I stepped into one of the stalls and latched the door behind me. With the same awkward and trembling haste as I'd slotted the gun into my skirt, I pulled it out, tangling it again in fabric and petticoat. While I was wrestling with the pouch of bullets, the outside door opened and closed. Frantic, I ripped the bullets out of the pocket and banged open the stall door.

The noise scared the Greek—whose name I could not remember—as much as it startled me. We stared at one another, and then I said weakly, "I have your gun."

He held out his hands. I handed him the goods—the stock, the barrel, the bullets—and he slipped them beneath his greatcoat.

Silent yet, he tipped his hat and left. I was alone.

Chapter 25

"You're not spending money on baubles and such, are you?" Alex asked me.

I snapped back. "You don't see me wearing silks and furs, do you?"

He slapped down another round of Solitaire on the table. "So why are you going to Trinidad so often? What requires so much traveling?"

I cracked an egg in a bowl, watching the watery white swirl around the yoke. "It's fun. To get out of Ludlow, to see what's laid out in the store windows, to watch the people. Some of the women wear such beautiful clothes, those who have cattle money or fortunes in land—"

Pearl glanced up at me from where she sat on his bed, sewing clothes for the baby. Her mouth opened, as if to challenge when I'd taken a fancy to finery or frivolity. I jiggled the skillet, shifted the kettle, and pretended that the preparation of dinner was the most important feat of my life.

"You're using quite a bit of your union pay for train fare," Alex commented.

"I give you everything I don't spend," I said. "And most of the time, I ride the union trucks, anyway."

He seemed appeased, but I knew it was fragile, temporary.

Six times in two weeks, now, I had traveled to Trinidad, with fear my constant companion. Every part of my body quaked, leaving me sore and achy the next day. My heart pounded as I stole through the alley to the bakery or swayed heavy-skirted past the Baldwin-Felts agents who lounged in front of the Cardenas Hotel. My head felt likely to burst as I lied to the militia boys at the depot in Ludlow.

One day, I stepped off the train and onto the platform at Ludlow and found myself facing two militiamen, who'd rushed forward at seeing me. Someone must have caught onto the ruse, I thought, and telephoned ahead to arrange my arrest. Panicking, I half-turned, intent on escaping back into the train, but found the aisle behind me jammed with passengers.

"Please, Miss," said one of the soldiers. He whipped off his hat and offered a hand to me.

"Here, Miss." The other mimicked his friend's actions.

Quickly, I searched the platform for my Greek escorts. Evangelo stood near the door of the depot, his eyes wide and startled. His mouth rolled as if he might shout, then snapped shut.

Stunned, I put a hand in each of the soldiers', careful to keep my body centered and my skirts from swaying outward. With gentlemanly grace, they helped me from the train. "Thank you," I breathed.

"Our pleasure. I'm Sergeant Dailey, and this is Private Coleman. We're pleased to meet you."

The other boy winked. "Don't forget our names."

"In case you ever need company—"

The two moved to another car, where another lone woman was disembarking. Hats doffed, they proffered her their hands and aided her down the steps to the platform.

It was a game for them—bored and ill-paid as they were—a way to put some ordinary fun back in their lives. Shaken, I followed the other passengers to Ludlow, trailing a family whose children picked and pushed at each other as they walked. Yet, as I reached the gates of Ludlow, laughter rose up in my throat. It might have been relief at my escape, or amusement at the tomfoolery of the soldiers, or wicked delight at playing the world for a fool. Try as I might, I could not stifle my giggles.

Little by little, I came to know the Greek men. Dimitrius spoke almost no English, Anton smiled widely and thanked me again and again as he bowed his way out the door, and the youngest of them, George, did tricks or sang to entertain me.

One day, he juggled a set of three silvery balls. Seeing my smile, he asked, "You like this?"

"You're very good," I said, my hand on the door of the stall.

"You think I am good at this?" He laughed. "You should see me with gun. I can shoot"—he held up two fingers in a pinch—"tiny bird in sky or mouse in grass. Other day, I shoot the hat off tin willie from so far away that he cannot figure out where his hat go. He does not even know it is shot."

"Tin willie? What's that?"

"A soldier." He laughed. "Sorry, I should not say that to you. It is dirty word and you are pretty lady."

I sought safer ground. "You go out shooting often?"

"All the time, all the time," he said. "That is why we like you. You bring us guns."

On a blustery day, when snow fell in grand, lacy flakes, I found Theros waiting for me at the barn. He sat on a three-legged, metal milking stool in front of the stall where I usually unloaded the guns.

I stopped abruptly, my overburdened skirt slapping against my legs. It had been so long since the last time, and the thought of it still made my throat pulse with a soft, tender ache.

He jumped to his feet. "I am so glad you are safe," he said. "I worry."

He did not rush to me with kisses and sweet words, but simply stood there, his weight on one leg, his hands at his side, as if he didn't know what to do. At last, I breathed, "I need to unpack my pockets."

"Go ahead."

"Not with you watching."

He scooped up the stool and moved across the barn. I closed the stall door behind me and pulled out the rifle parts. I'd learned not to tangle them in my skirt, learned to slip them quickly and easily from my clothes. When I left the stall, Theros stood right outside the door.

"I could not wait," he said simply.

My entire body leapt upward—every muscle, every vein, every inch of flesh. His mouth covered mine, and his hands sifted through my clothes, releasing layer after layer. I lifted myself up to meet his body, wrapping around it, my lips on his, and my back pressed against the stall door. He entered me, his arms and legs both support and motion, and I felt again that same wild joy. The stall door battered against its catch, the echo resounding through the high, empty rafters of the barn.

"Oh, Christian, you are sweet."

Theros sank to his knees, and I pooled against him, half-sitting, half lying on the floor. My head nestled in the hollow of his neck, and I ran my hands over his shoulders. I'd missed the firm, even flesh of his chest, the weight of his legs on mine, the power of his body. "Always meet me here," I murmured, my lips against his hot, damp skin. "I'd bring a thousand guns into Ludlow just to see you."

"A thousand?" He combed straw from my hair with his fingers. "What about two thousand, and we do this every time?"

"Five," I said, and he countered with, "Ten thousand million."

We laughed, giddy and silly. He kissed me again, drawing me against him until we lay side by side on the loose straw, our coats pulled around us for warmth. I stroked his face, my fingers reading the dip of his temple, the curve of his cheek and jaw, and the sharp solid jut of his chin. "Oh, why have you stayed away from me for so long?" I asked. "I want to see you every day, every minute."

"Too dangerous," he said. "If I am always at the depot, soldiers may start to think. If I always come here, one may follow."

"I never dreamed I'd see Anton and George and Dimitrius more often than I see you."

"But you like them?"

"Not as much as I like you."

"Good." He laughed again. "They like you, too."

"Why can't you meet me at the bakery? If we arrived and left at different times, no one would ever put it together."

"They don't let me," he said. "They think it is good thing to not let me."

For a moment, his meaning was unclear. When understanding dawned, I sat up straight. "You mean, they're testing me?"

"Testing," he pondered. "Yes, like in school. You, me—they test us both."

"But I agreed! I told them I would—"

"It had to be," he said firmly. "They said, she has a brother who hates Greeks. She will take guns to him, she will not be brave enough to take them so far to the barn. But, Christian, you do good." He lifted himself onto one elbow, his coat around his waist, and ran his fingers down my arm. "Come back."

"What about you? Were you testing me?"

"I am watching to see who is right."

I lay down, feeling duped all over again.

Theros shifted so he could see my face. "Oh, come on, now you are mad—"

"I don't like being doubted."

He shrugged. "But you don't trust all Greeks? You must be testing us, too."

I had to admit the truth. "There's one—I can't remember his name—who scares me to death. He doesn't talk."

"Ah, him. He speaks no English, not one word. But no matter. He don't speak in Greek, neither. We don't know his name, so we call him Silent Mike."

"But you trust him, and you don't even know his name?"

"He is Greek."

As if it were that simple. But maybe the Greek men had been through enough heartbreak in America that the only solace was in finding another countryman. Still, it rankled that I had had to prove myself.

"But you are all right?" he asked. "You are not bothered by anyone when you do this?"

"No. I don't know."

"You don't know?"

"Every day, I wake up and think that I'll tell Louis that I won't do this again. But by noon, I've changed my mind."

He brushed my hair from my eyes. "Every day, I think, I will tell her to stop. Then I think, she is American girl. In America, girls think as much as any man. They are as mean as any man."

"What a thing to say!"

"You don't think it is true? Women here want to vote, want to work, want to spend all the moneys, want to tell their man what to do."

"That doesn't make them mean, only strong."

"Strong?" He flexed his arm muscle beneath my head, then crooked his elbow behind my neck and drew me up into the hollow of his shoulder.

I laughed and pushed away from him. "Not like that. Independent, sure of themselves—"

"Mean," he concluded, trailing hot, damp kisses across my collarbone.

Running my hands over the firm flesh of his shoulders and back, I said, "Sometimes, when I bring in the guns, I feel wild."

He barked a laugh. "What?"

"As if the danger is fun." The words sounded unbelievable to my own ears. Hastily, I added, "Even though I know it's not. But it's exciting, and, oh, I don't know—"

"A wild woman! Ah, what surprises you are, Christian."

Late in the evening, I left the barn, while Theros waited for the cover of darkness to carry the rifle into Ludlow. For days after, I dreamed of him, of his touch and voice. The next week, I harbored high hopes as I rushed through Ludlow. But when I arrived at the barn to deliver the gun and ammunition, I found Anton waiting for me.

On a late February afternoon, I debarked from the train and stepped right into the path of Jake Ruddy. He grabbed my arm, forcing me to halt. Fear jolted me—were he to draw me close or brush against my leg or place his hand on my waist, he would discover what I carried. Roughly, I twisted away from him, searching beyond him for my Greek shadows. A few feet away, Dimitrius leaned against a light post, smoking.

"Whoa up there, Scottie," Jake said. He wore the uniform of the Yellow Bands of Company B. In his hands was a new Springfield rifle. "I been hoping to run into somebody from Tent No. 18."

"You're no militiaman, Jake."

"Oh, you better believe it, I am," he said. "Just about anybody who wants to join up and knock some sense into dago heads is invited into the militia. John D. Rockefeller himself sent me my invitation." He grinned at his joke. "Written in pure gold."

"I have to go."

"That ain't no way to treat an old friend."

He sidestepped, barring my way. Dimitrius dropped his cigarette and painstakingly ground it out with his boot. Jake said, "It was real nice seeing you and Pearl the other day. But Russ didn't take it so well. He's been worse since."

"I'm sorry."

"Well, if Pearl weren't no better than a ten-cent whore, she'd be there, seeing to him. So tell me, how is precious little Pearl and her baby?"

"That's not your concern."

His face darkened, and he jerked my arm, pulling me closer. "You think that, Scottie? You really think that? I told you, just like I told her, that brat belongs to us."

Dimitrius began to saunter toward us. I wondered how close the second man stood behind me, and if he was ready to act. "Let me go, Jake," I said. "For your own good."

A militia officer passed, casting a questioning look in our direction. Jake grabbed my bag and pretended to search it. He pulled out the Greek bread. "Pearl would've come with us the other day if you hadn't stopped her," he said. "She would have come back to Berwind—"

"No, she wouldn't."

"Yes, she would've." Jake tore off an end of the bread and stuffed it in his mouth. "And she will, too. Pretty damned soon. Because, you know what, Scottie? After Ma saw Pearl, she went to some fancy-pants CF&I lawyer in Trinidad. He says there's laws against keeping my dear brother's child away from his legal daddy."

My heart dropped to my stomach. I did not know whether he might be speaking the truth. Dimitrius stood nearly at Jake's shoulder, staring down the tracks as if expecting a ghost train to appear. I grasped for words, garbling, "Did your mother tell the lawyer that Russell isn't any more able to take care of himself and feed himself than that baby will be? Did she tell him that Russell doesn't have any interest in Pearl as a wife? Besides, what makes you so sure it's Russell's?"

At once, I knew I'd made a mistake. His eyes widened, and he thrust my bag at me, spraying breadcrumbs as he spoke. "Your goddamned brother thinks it's his, don't he? Don't he? He was having her up there in Berwind, wasn't he?"

Dimitrius' eyes fixed on someone behind me—his partner—evidently awaiting a signal of some sort.

"Let me go, Jake," I pleaded. "Please, just let me be."

"Pearl's a whore, Scottie. That baby probably ain't your brother's or my brother's, neither one. It's probably some long-gone dago's, who paid her well for what she done. But you tell her, Ma wants a grandbaby, and I want to do right by Russ." He seemed near tears. "And by God, I'll see to it I do."

He stormed away, the loaf of bread tucked under his arm, and slammed through the door of the depot. I tried to calm my breathing, digging through my bag as if searching for something. By the time I looked up, Dimitrius had melted away, disappearing from sight. But from behind, someone passed close by me, brushing his arm against my shoulder. Theros, his face obscured by a low-slung hat, had been the second shadow.

That night, lying alone in my bed, I stared up at the thin, sun-bleached canvas of our tent. The searchlights from Hastings danced across it every few seconds, pinning me beneath them. I had to stop, I had to quit. I had to tell Louis Tikas that I would not play this charade any longer. Theros or any one of them could be hurt, killed, and I—

And, oh God, why had I let it slip that Alex might be the father of Pearl's baby? It made Jake even more dangerous than he already was to Pearl.

All at once, I could not stand the sagging walls and close air of the tent. I slipped from bed and put on my shoes, then let myself out the door.

Outside, the night was quiet, but it had been a long time since such a night was a peaceful one. On Water Tank Hill, campfires burned near the remaining militia tents. Cars trundled along the dusty roads, acetylene lamps burning. The searchlights swept over Ludlow in deadly arcs. Night was just a waiting game, just another unknown.

I could do what the other women did, I knew. I could sing with the ragged choir that straggled, its ranks slain by winter, to the gates of Ludlow each morning. I could join the sewing committee, trying to make warm underwear out of rags. I could teach English to the foreign girls, or volunteer at the schoolhouse to grade math problems. Oh, Mother Jones was right—women had a place, an important one, in this strike. But I had set myself on another path, and it was my own, mine alone. I knew that if I gave it up, it would haunt me.

I rounded the corner of the tent, seeking shadow. Pearl stood by the meat rack, her shoulders huddled against the cold. She had grown so heavy that her clothes no longer fit her well, but pulled into tight wrinkles just under her breasts and tummy. Her hands on the baby, she glanced up, as if trying to see the stars. Her face was pale, grayish in the weird gleam of the searchlights.

"What are you doing?" I asked, surprised, breathless.

"This baby don't let me sleep. She's always twirling and turning now, getting ready for her big day."

"You should go inside," I said. "It's too cold out here."

She said nothing, and I knew she had taken my words as a scolding, a send-off. Finally, I said, "Pearl—"

"I just can't stop thinking about it." Her words rushed out, as if she'd rehearsed them. "She's a baby. She don't have nothing to do with all the nastiness and stupid stuff that goes on out here. And I don't want her to know none of it." She caressed her big belly. "Christian, you always had decent people around you. Your father and Alex. Theo Sky. I want her growing up knowing about people like that. I don't want her to have to find out about it when she runs away and falls half-dead on somebody's doorstep like I done."

I knew she was asking me to believe that the baby was Alex's, but before I could speak, she said, "You wouldn't want your baby to be no Ruddy, neither."

Immediately, I knew my answer. Touching her shoulder, I said, "So you still think it's a girl?"

She grasped my hand in relief, pressing it against her cheek. "I know it. Every time she kicks, I know it."

"It's not long now."

"If I don't bust first. Oh, it'll be such a happy day."

"For all of us."

"But what's wrong with you?" she asked. "Why ain't you asleep?"

All my fears hurdled through my mind—Jake, the guns, Theros, the baby. But all I admitted to Pearl was that I was sick and tired of being in Ludlow.

Chapter 26

Early in April, I stepped off the train onto a platform that shook, rumbling with a deep thunder. From the far end, a dozen or so riders spurred their horses over the wooden planks. "Get out of the way!" a militiamen called. "Move!"

People scattered, screaming and cursing. Women dragged their children into their arms, and the men dropped bags and knapsacks to flee. The soldiers spread across the platform, sealing off the ends, trapping us in the middle. We cleaved together, clutching, trembling. Terrified, I gathered my coat about me, then let it loose, afraid of revealing what I carried under my skirt.

"Get off the train!" Lieutenant Karl Linderfelt, the leader of Company B, sat astride a sorrel horse. "Come on!"

After a wary moment, the pale, strained faces of passengers appeared at the doors of the cars. One by one, they stepped down onto the platform, clustering into frightened knots at the foot of the steps.

"Get out of here!" Linderfelt bellowed. "No trains! No travel! You hear me? You try it and you'll be arrested. Now get back to Ludlow!"

The soldiers began herding the people forward, flicking their quirts to ferret out the folks who'd taken refuge next to the building. We dragged along, afraid to move too quickly, but equally fearful of being too slow or last in line. Spilling out on the dirt road, we walked a narrow path back to Ludlow, flanked on both sides by horsemen.

Ludlow itself was surrounded, cordoned off. Everywhere, the khaki brown of militia uniforms stood out against the greening grass of the prairie. The Death Special idled at the gates.

As I moved, every eye seemed to follow me. Soldiers tilted their heads to watch me, officers raised their binoculars to focus on my progress. They knew, I thought. They'd already rounded up the Greeks, and now, they had only to spring the trap on me. Inside my skirt, catching against my thighs, was a new rifle, with smooth stock and virgin barrel. I had two pouches of bullets cached near my waist, weighing down the skirt toward the ground.

As we reached the gates of Ludlow, everyone scattered, running here and there, seeking shelter in the closest tent. But I went on, forging my way through the colony, past our tent to the arroyo. There, soldiers whipped their horses in frenzied gallops along the sandy bottom. I stood on the bank for only an instant. There was no passage to the barn.

I went to the west edge of Ludlow, where the Greek tents stood. There, too, the soldiers swarmed. I waited, shifting from one foot to the other, my hips and back aching with the weight of my burden, wishing that one of the Greeks—any one of them—would come and relieve me. Only the wind moved at the tent, making the sides billow, as if it were taking in breath, holding all its secrets inside.

At home, Pearl was fixing dinner, standing sideways at the stove, shielding her belly from the heat. "What's going on out there?" she asked, wiping a bead of sweat from her forehead. "There's been hollering and banging around all afternoon."

"I don't know."

I said nothing more, simply tending my chores. But my entire body felt as if it was being jerked here and there by puppeteer's wires. As I set the table, the gun in my skirt slapped against my legs, and I had to take pains to avoid clanking against the stove, or Alex's bed, or the barrels in the corner. When I dropped a fork beneath the table, I could no more bend and retrieve it than Pearl could. Quickly, I glanced toward her before I fetched another.

And then, she provided my salvation.

"Crawl down in the pit and bring up the milk, will you?"

Climbing in, I tried to pull the gun from my pockets. My elbows banged up against the walls of the pit, and I could not catch my breath in the musty dirt-filled air. Trying to hurry, I was as clumsy at the task as I'd been the first time. I tangled the barrel in my petticoat and nearly ripped off one of the pockets removing the stock. Stuffing the guns and bullets between two boxes, I slipped up the ladder, carrying the milk for Pearl.

She didn't notice my relief, but I no longer stumbled around like an overburdened mule. I did not talk, afraid that my voice would betray my fears, but my mind wheeled. By the time Alex came home, railing about how Lieutenant's Linderfelt's men had scattered the men on the picket lines, I was certain of my plan. The next day I would drop the gun down a latrine. Then I would tell the Greeks, no more. Never again.

But fate worked against me.

In the morning, a knock startled us all. We rolled from bed, grabbing for shawls and warm clothes and shoes. When, at last, Alex pulled open the door, he found two Yellow Bands.

"Privates Hollings and Pierce," one of the soldiers said. "We're here to search your tent."

"What's happened now?" Alex asked.

"Murder of a federal marshal up in Hastings."

"What?" I said. "Why are you searching here?"

"All of the tent colonies are to be searched," Hollings said. "Pierce, go ahead."

"No," I said. "No, please don't."

What a mistake that was. Wary and suspicious, the soldiers banged into the tent and tore through our goods—overturning mattresses, pulling open the drawers of the bureau, toppling pans and plates from the shelves. Pearl sat at the table, watching them in disbelief, and Alex lingered helplessly in the doorway. I stood next to my bed, my hands clutched in my hair, my mouth dry and opened in a silent cry.

When Hollings opened the trap door to the pit, I stepped forward. "All I keep down there are some old things that we don't use," I said hastily. "Some old clothes that don't fit any more—"

Pearl looked at me, wary. Alex stared, too, confused.

"I have to check," Hollings said.

"It's so dirty down there. And damp. It's so dark—"

Hollings' head disappeared down into the pit.

Suddenly, my knees gave way and I fell. Pearl pulled herself up from the table, and Alex lurched forward, but Private Pierce forbade them to move. "What's wrong?" he asked, coming to me. "Stand up." He fanned my face with his hat, then ordered Alex to open the door of the tent for fresh air.

A moment later, Private Hollings came from the pit, carrying the weapon I'd stashed there the night before.

"You've got a gun," he accused Alex. "Look at this. Ain't never been shot." He studied the barrel. "Jesus, this is top quality stock."

"That's not mine," Alex said. "I've never seen it before."

"That's one of ours," Pierce said excitedly. "A Springfield. There was a shipment coming in from Denver that was stolen off the trains just last week." He honed in on Alex. "Where'd you get this? Who'd you steal it from?"

"I don't know anything about it," Alex said. "You carried it in with you and planted it there, didn't you?"

"Come on, Mister, you're going with us to Trinidad." Hollings stepped out into the street and shouted an alarm. "Over here! We have arms!"

"Leave me alone, damn you!" Alex writhed as Hollings took hold of him. "You sons of bitches don't know what you're about!"

"Stand still or I'll bust you upside the head!"

Both Pierce and Hollings tackled Alex, grappling with him until they could pin his arms behind his back. For good measure, Hollings slammed his fist into Alex's stomach. Pearl and I screamed, and I rushed forward, trying to pull the militiamen away from Alex.

"Stop it," Hollings growled, twisting the skin of my wrist in one hand. "Or I'll take you in, too."

"Arrest me," I pleaded. "He didn't know anything about it. I put it there."

"Right, sister. You're a regular sharpshooter, I bet. Killed that federal marshal all by yourself." He thrust me back, and I grabbed the table to steady myself.

Alex collapsed, sinking toward the floor. Sobbing, Pearl fell to her knees beside him, but Pierce pulled him to his feet.

"Come on," Hollings said, shoving Alex out the door.

I ran out behind them. "Please listen to me!"

Dragging Alex along between them, the two soldiers marched toward the gates of Ludlow. I followed, begging them for mercy. A crowd gathered—pale, silent faces so still they seemed to be painted. As we passed their tent, Mrs. McCormick screamed, "Holy mother of God, it's Alex! John, they're takin' Alex!" She stepped out, James and Mary close behind them.

"Christian!" James stepped along with me. "What's happened?"

But just then, a lieutenant joined Pierce and Hollings. Pierce handed the rifle to him, and the lieutenant studied the two parts, one in each hand. I tried to reach Alex, but Uncle John grabbed my arm.

"Let me go!" I wrenched at his fingers, trying to break his hold.

"Ye gods," James said. "That's a brand new rifle."

"Kirstie!" Alex called to me. "Kirstie!"

I burst from Uncle John's grasp and ran to him.

"I'm sorry, Alex," I cried. "I'm so sorry."

"Here." He pressed something crumpled toward me. I caught his union card in my hand. Edged by grime, the words had smeared with handling. "You and Pearl will still be able to collect—"

"No, Alex," I cried. "Tell them you didn't do it! Tell them to take me! Please!"

They pulled him away toward the southbound train boarding for Trinidad. Thrusting him roughly up the steps, the soldiers clamored onto the car behind him.

Someone laughed behind me. "They don't want you, Scottie." Jake stepped up beside me. "Seems like just about nobody does."

"Jake," I begged. "Alex didn't know about the gun. It isn't his—"

"Just like that baby."

"Jake, please—"

"I'll make you a deal, Scottie." He nodded toward the train. "I'll go on that train and make sure your brother gets turned free"—he let the words hang in the air—"if you'll send Pearl back to Berwind with Russell's baby."

My head whirled. If I could stop Alex from being taken to jail, if I could just make someone listen to me, if I only had the time to stop this, to turn it in my favor, to fool Jake into believing—

"It don't look like she's got a man to take care of her no more," he said. "But I can do it just fine."

Rage whipped through my body. I started to pound on him with my fists. His flesh thudded beneath my knuckles, the buttons of his shirt bruising my finger bones. "Stop it! Leave us alone! You did this, didn't you? You sent them to our tent—!"

A sergeant rushed forward and grabbed me. "For God's sake, what is going on?" Beckoning to another militiaman, he barked, "Private, take this woman back to her tent and make sure she stays there."

The private grasped my arm, pulling me backward. Angrily, I strained against him until he yanked so hard that the joint of my shoulder popped. Still, I screamed. "You leave her alone! You hear? You leave us all alone! Alex didn't do it! He's innocent—"

Jake rubbed where I'd pounded on his chest. "Too bad, Scottie," he scowled, moving to board the train. "That's just too damned bad."

The Yellow Bands destroyed everything, senselessly, brutally. By the time I was delivered home by the private, our tent was in shambles. They had dumped all our food, shredded our clothing, split the mattresses, hacked the water barrel and coal bin to splinters, and pried up every plank of the floor. Holes gaped in the tent, where they'd slashed with knives or bayonets. And in the middle of it all, her hair white with feathers from the pillows and flour dust, Pearl sat on the ground, the chairs broken around her.

She rocked back and forth, hunched over the baby, her arms looped around her knees. "I thought they was going to kill me," she sobbed. "They kept throwing things around, and stuff flying everywhere—"

"Oh, my God," I wept, putting my arms around her. "Oh, God, oh, God!"

"Where's Alex? What did they do to him?"

"They took him to Trinidad," I said. "To the jail." I thought of the windowless, freezing cell where Theros had been held. "If only they'd listened to me!"

"This is because of me!" Pearl shrieked. "If I'd never left Russ and just kept pretending—"

"Don't think that way! Don't say that!"

"Then who put that gun down there? Jake must have come sneaking in when we was all gone—!"

"I did," I said. "I put it down there."

"What?"

"I had it! Last night. I was bringing it into Ludlow—"

"Why?"

"To give it to Theros. I've been running guns for the Greeks—"

She shook her head as if she couldn't understand my words. "My God, Christian, you really done that?"

I nodded, too ashamed to speak.

"All them trips to Trinidad, all them times you was nowhere to be found! I thought you was just seeing Theo Sky. That's what you was doing? Putting Alex in so much danger? Putting us all in danger?"

"I didn't keep the guns here! Not until last night, when I couldn't—"

"You stupid, lying little fool!"

I buried my head in my hands. This was all my doing, all my fault. How stupid I'd been, how careless, a traitor to my own kind. I inched away from Pearl, crawling over splintered wood and broken glass, through spilled coffee and spoiled food. On my own side of the tent—the bullhide curtain had been pulled down—I lay my head against the bent iron springs of the bed and sobbed.

Uncle John and Mrs. McCormick arrived. "Good Lord," Mrs. McCormick breathed as she surveyed the mess.

"We've come to see what we can do," Uncle John said, his face ashen, his voice gravelly with anguish. "I promised your father years ago that I'd stand by you—"

At the mention of my father, I started to cry again. Uncle John set about nailing down the planks of the floor. Already, the chilly wind swept through the severed sides of the tent. Mrs. McCormick tried to patch them with needle and thread, yet each stitch she took sliced a hole in the rotten, tinder-dry canvas. I wiped up broken eggs, shattered jugs, trampled meat, then set about sorting through our clothes, searching for what could be saved, stuffing what couldn't into the empty mattress tickings with the straw that hadn't been kicked aside or muddied. Pearl sat on the floor and wept.

James came to the door, scouting the place with narrowed eyes. "Where was the gun?" he asked.

I pointed to the pit, which had been pillaged as badly as the tent. Our belongings heaped at the foot of the ladder.

James crawled inside, rustling and clanking about. A few minutes later, he climbed out, dusting his hands on his pants' legs.

"It was the only one," I said bitterly. "There are no more."

"Where'd he get it?"

I did not answer, but silently refolded my stockings.

"I wouldn't have kept a beauty such as that from him," James announced angrily. "We were in this together. At least, I thought we were."

Uncle John and Mrs. McCormick spoke at the same time.

"That's enough, James. Let her be."

"Leave it alone and get to it, man."

"If it weren't for her, Alex wouldn't have done this." James pointed his chin at Pearl. "Ever since he took up with her, he's been playing us foul."

Distraught, Pearl ran from the tent.

I threw down the clothes I was folding. "Get out."

"I'm only trying to stand up for Alex. He's my mate."

"He's mine, too," Uncle John said sternly.

"Hush, James," Mrs. McCormick said. Then, to me, she comforted, "Don't listen to him. He's off his head. We're all shakin' in our boots over this."

James set to work, grumbling no more.

I went outside to find Pearl. She crouched on the far side of the tent, her face in her hands, her body quaking with sobs.

"I'm sorry, Pearl," I said. "I'm so sorry."

She shook her head, refusing to look at me. "All this time," she said. "I been thinking, if we just get through this strike, then we'll go back up to Berwind, and Alex will make enough money from the union mines to take us all to Scotland. You, me, the baby. I thought, we're safe down here. The Ruddys can't get into Ludlow and—"

"It's all my fault!"

"What if Alex dies in jail?" she fretted. Then, more horrified, "What if Jake's his jailer?"

"Come inside. There's no good in doing this. Think of the baby."

"They're so hateful in there. If they was gone—"

"I need their help. We both do."

"No," she said bitterly. "No, I didn't do none of this. They think I'm the one who's always bad, but this is all your doing—"

"I'll make it right," I promised. "I'll go to Trinidad tomorrow and turn myself in."

She rose to her feet, tottering as she went inside the tent.

We toiled steadily through the night—no one asked more questions, no one's eyes met, no one dared to speak again. The sole sound stemmed from Pearl, who sat on Alex's bed, her hands on the baby. Tears streamed from her eyes and dripped from her chin. I wondered if the baby could feel them fall, like rain, on her belly, or could taste the tears through the thin, tight skin. If so, she already had a deep knowledge of woe.

Beneath a pile of broken crockery, I found the book of Scott's verse that had served Alex and me so well for so long. The spine was broken, and the leathery binding trampled flat. When I picked it up, the pages fluttered out, like moths startled by light. Near the book lay Alex's kilt, torn and filthy. The handkerchief that had swaddled Pearl's hair—which I'd kept since that day in the Berwind schoolhouse—was wadded in a tattered ball. I spread it flat, hoping something might be saved.

Not a single strand of hair remained.

Chapter 27

The next morning, I climbed up the streets of Trinidad to the Las Animas County courthouse. It seemed deserted. Gone were the women rallying for their husbands' release. Gone, too, were the gangs of children who had chased behind the militiamen, hurling insults. No patrols stalked outside the walls, no militia horses were hitched at the watering trough. My head reeling, I walked up the steps and went inside.

The clerks had abandoned the office, their desks heaped with stacks of papers, as if they'd left at a moment's notice. The air in the room was bluish with the haze of tobacco smoke, and the rankling heat had not diminished since winter. I'd worn my tartan wrap, which had survived with only a single tear in the weave. In my skirt pocket was Alex's union card.

Alone, Colonel Drake lounged behind his heavy oak desk. He stared at me for a moment, then his eyes swept down my tartan to my hand, which suddenly throbbed as if it had been broken open yet again. A look of surly remembrance came into his eyes. "You're a fearless one, Miss . . . what was it?"

"Scott. Christian Scott."

"What do you want now?"

"I'm here to see my brother, Alexander Gordon Scott." My voice trembled on the words, and I cleared my throat. "He was brought in from Ludlow yesterday."

"You seem to have an outlaw family, Miss Scott," Colonel Drake said. "Wasn't it your father you came to find last time?"

Clasping my hands together, I pressed my fingers against the aching scar. My tongue felt enormous in my mouth, as if I hadn't tasted water for weeks. "No, it was"—I stopped myself from stumbling—"It was a Greek man."

Colonel Drake laughed heartily. "You do come up with some pips, Miss Scott." Pushing back in his chair, he offered, "I'll give you ten minutes with your brother—if this one really is your brother."

He led me up a wide, wooden staircase to a high-ceilinged room. Even here, on the second floor of the building, the windows were smashed into jagged peaks. The wallpaper had been peeled away from the walls in ragged strips, the plaster punched full of holes, and the furniture battered.

"Some of your women friends from Ludlow did all this," Colonel Drake remarked dryly. "After the women's parade. A man wouldn't have done half this much damage." He returned to the door. "Wait here."

I went to the window and looked below at the alley where I had fallen and gashed my hand. Although it was cleared of ice, the stench of rot thickened in the warm air. The smell turned my stomach, and I clapped my hand to my mouth.

Alex limped into the room, one foot dragging behind the other. His face was mottled with black and green bruises, barely recognizable through the swelling. Above one eye, a gash seeped brownish blood, and other cuts had gone equally unattended. He stumbled into the only chair in the room, which groaned under his weight. The effort winded him, and he hacked violently, his lungs already clogged with phlegm.

"Oh, my God!" I knelt beside him. "Alex, what did they do?"

His lips were so swollen that he seemed to be talking through a wad of cotton. "Jake told them that I'd taken his brother's wife. They laid into me with a vengeance."

"Have they let you see a doctor?"

"No." He laid his hands on the table before him. "I swear to God, Kirstie, that gun was not mine. I know nothing of it!"

"I know." I grabbed his hands to steady him. "I put it in the pit."

"You?"

"Yes." Guilt burned within me. Every bruise on my brother's body, every cut on his lips or cheeks, should have been mine. "I tried to tell them! I wanted to tell them—"

"How in God's name did you come by it?"

Haltingly, I told him of my business with the Greeks. My heart seized up so tightly in my breast that I could no longer breathe, and my hands turned icy and purplish from fright. My voice was no louder than a whisper.

"Good God, why?" Alex demanded. "You've made a deal with the devil himself!"

"I'm in love with a Greek man."

"A Greek!" He coughed. "What's this about? How did you even come to know him?"

"I've known him since we were in Berwind. We were in school together, and then—" I stopped, uncertain how I could explain it, make him see it as I did. "He's the one who fought up in Berwind—remember him? I started taking care of him, dressing his wounds and helping him heal. And then I found out he was organizing for the union, and—"

"What have you done with him?" he demanded. "How far has this gone?"

"I'm so sorry, Alex," I said. "I'm sorry it's not what you wanted for me."

Alex looked away from me, his body tense with anger or disappointment, or both, and I readied myself for the scalding torrent of his words.

Nothing came. He sat silently, his thoughts inward and hidden. His body sagged as the strength ebbed from him. "Dad would be so ashamed," he whispered. "Of both of us."

Kirstie, the girl of the Highlands, the Scottish princess. And Alex, the fine knight—

"Theros is a good man," I countered. "You'd like him—"

His face twisted in disdain. "And what will this Theros do with you once Tikas and his lot have no more use for you? Once the strike is over, and they decide to seek their fortunes elsewhere?"

"He is dedicated to the union—"

"How many?" he asked.

I had no idea what he meant. "What?"

"How many guns did you bring in?"

"I don't know. Twelve, fifteen. Sometimes a pistol, but mostly rifles or shotguns. And bullets, too—hundreds, probably."

"My God! Why not for us? Why not bring in the guns to us?"

I had imagined a hundred different replies, but this was not among them.

"I lie awake at nights," he said. "Thinking I don't have any way to protect you or Pearl. I wonder what kind of man I am to have brought you both to this terrible place—"

"I'm going downstairs now, Alex," I said. "To tell Colonel Drake the truth. I'll make him release you. You'll be all right once you're out of here. I'll take care of you until you're well, and then you can take Pearl away—somewhere, anywhere!—before the baby comes, and—"

"No!" Alex cried. "Good God, Christian! No!"

He struggled to stand, catching the flimsy chair beneath one hand. Miserably, he bent at the waist. "It won't do any good! They won't release me—"

"Pearl needs you," I said. "The baby—your baby—my God, Alex, it will be here any day. You could die here—I know what it's like down there. All of this, everything you've suffered, it's because of me!"

"No!" Wheezing, he lowered himself into the chair. When he spoke again, his voice was a gritty whisper. "They won't let Ludlow alone much longer. I hear them talk. They want this to end, they want to see it finished. If anything, bring in more guns. And give them to John and James, Rory—"

"Alex—"

"For God's sake!" His cough clattered in his throat. "This strike is going to end in bloodshed, and it might as well be theirs, as well as ours—"

"If everyone keeps saying it, then it will be true!"

"Kirstie, listen to me. You have to take care of Pearl. You have to make sure she—"

A uniformed soldier stepped into the room. "Time's up," he called.

I helped Alex to stand. Together we walked toward the door, where I let go his arm, praying he would have the strength to carry himself back down to the cell. "Don't worry about me, Christian," he breathed as I released him. "Do what you have to."

The door closed in my face.

Outside, I wandered blindly through the crowd, from storefront to storefront and across the cobblestone streets. At last, I slipped down the alley that I'd traveled so often in the past months and through the back door of the bakery, climbing the stairs.

Seated on the bed, I watched the bustle of Trinidad through the arched window. The silence in the attic soothed me, a refuge from the jar of human voices, the clatter of horses and bark of dogs, the smells of food and smoke. The light from the windows deepened and yellowed. Too tired to move, I lay down, my hands pillowing my cheeks. If I were forced from here, I would take shelter beneath a bridge. Anything but return to Ludlow.

The sound of footsteps woke me, great, reckless thuds up the steps, the sound of someone bounding up two at a time. The bakery below me echoed with chairs scraping against wooden floor and men gathering to eat and drink. Voices echoed up the stairs, calling out in syllables I could not imitate. The door swung open, and Theros joined me, a flickering lamp in his hand.

"Christian," he breathed. "They told me you are here." The bedsprings creaked as he sat beside me. "Are you sick? Are you hurt?"

"I didn't know anyone had seen me come up."

"What has happened?"

His face was shadowed, and I realized that darkness had fallen while I lay on the bed, feeling sorry for myself. Frantic, I croaked, "I need to go. Pearl shouldn't be alone—"

He laid a hand on my shoulder. "There are no more trains to Ludlow tonight."

No more union trucks would be running either. "I need to get back," I said. "She's so close to having the baby—"

"Someone else must help," he said. "But you—tell me what is wrong. Why are you here?"

"Did you know my brother was arrested? Did you know he's in jail?"

"What?"

I sat up. "Why weren't you there the other day? Why didn't you come by our tent and get your precious gun? Why didn't you meet me somewhere in Ludlow and take it? It's your fault Alex is in jail! You should have helped me, you should have been there—"

My rage ended in a helpless sob.

"It was just a mistake," he said flatly. "Terrible mistake. We heard about some scabs up in Walsenburg. We went up there to talk to them. We talked of the old country, of home and war. Drank ouzo—you know—and ate some food. We made them see they must not work for the company, that it is like fighting for Turks. When we were done, we went to the depot, but the soldiers said no. No train for you today. We looked for union truck, but no. We tried to walk, but no one gives us a ride. We can't get back to Ludlow."

"Fighting for the Turks?" I cried. "My God, Theros, how could you do this to me?"

"What could we do? We tried—"

"I begged the soldiers to take me instead, but they didn't even listen to me. And then Jake just laughed at me—!"

"Jake Ruddy? He was there?"

"He was on the train with Alex. Oh God, Jake took out all his hatred out on him. His foot is broken, and he can't even see, his eyes are so swollen! This is all my fault, it's all my doing, and now I can't—!"

He shook me gently by the shoulders. "Christian, stop. Don't do this. It's no good."

"I was going to tell Colonel Drake the truth today, so they would release him, so that he wouldn't suffer anymore, but Alex—!"

He swung away from me. "Did you?" he demanded. "Did you tell them about it?"

"No, I didn't, but I should—"

"You should? Then what happens to Greeks? What happens to

Ludlow? What happens to you and Miss Pearl, and anybody in those tents? What happens when they decide to come shooting at us, and we have no one to shoot back?"

His anger silenced me. In the bakery below, someone had begun to play a lively song on a guitar. The clatter of plates and glasses echoed in the stairwell outside, and the voices grew louder. Theros shouldered the door closed and locked it, then moved to the window, as far from me as he could be in the little room.

"I don't care! I have to do what's right! I have to fix this—"

His words slipped out of the shadowy darkness. "And if you tell the soldiers what you have done, do you think they will put you in jail? No, they will want the men who have the guns. Then your brother will be in jail, but I will be there, too. All of us will be."

The words dropped into the room. I covered my face with my hands. He was right. Colonel Drake would never jail me. He already thought of me as a silly girl with too much imagination. But all the same, he wouldn't hesitate to arrest every Greek in the strike zone.

"Did you tell your brother about the guns?" he asked.

"Yes."

His body jerked. "And what will your brother say when the guards beat him? What will he tell them?"

"He told me to keep on!" I cried. "He told me to bring in as many guns as—"

"He is playing games."

"What!"

"He wants Greeks to be caught. Maybe he will tell the guards, oh, just follow my sister, and she will lead you to them."

Fury scorched through me, followed by a wave of dread so strong, I nearly vomited. "He wouldn't do that," I cried. "He wouldn't betray me, he wouldn't do that!"

"But he will betray us." He flipped his hand to encompass himself, the bakery, and every Greek who sat at a table below and played cards or sang along with the guitar. "He will tell everything he knows about us."

"Why do you think that?"

"Because I know! You lie in that jail, on that stinking, wet floor, in the dark, and you think, I would do anything to be gone from here. Anything—kill my brother, hang my sister. As long as I am free."

"No—"

"They will tell him, we will let you go, we will take you to the doctor, get you medicine. Maybe they will give him money, if he only gives them names."

A deep terror overcame me. "I gave him your name!"

"You did what!"

"Your name," I rasped. "I told him about—"

"Who else? What other names? Spero, Dimitrius—?"

"No, no one else. Only yours—"

"Why didn't you just bring the soldiers here? Say, take this Greek? He is bad!"

My God, what had I done? To try to help my brother, I'd betrayed my lover.

Theros jabbed a finger toward the bed. "Did you tell him about what goes on here?"

"Yes."

"And what did he say?"

I did not reply.

"So, he still hates Greeks. So little he changes."

"Just like you."

"I change," he lashed. "I think I don't trust no more. I think I don't be nice no more. What we did—I think, it is her, it is me. Only that. I don't tell no one!"

I gestured toward the door. "They all know! You told me so yourself. Louis, Anton—"

"They guessed. I don't tell. They ask me every day, they tease me. Oh, American girl so ready to do what a man wants, so easy to take. But I say nothing to them. They say, what you get from her that you can't get from West Main Street? And still, I say nothing to them."

I flinched. "Alex has a right to know the truth."

"The truth, Christian," he said. "Here is the truth. You choose your brother. You choose him over me."

"And you always choose the others over me! You wouldn't have asked me to do this if it wasn't for them—!"

"They don't trust me no more, because of you! They laugh at me, they think I am weak. They think I will choose you over them, that I will become afraid, a fool—"

His voice caught, and he stopped. I sagged against the bed, grabbing onto the brass frame to keep myself from falling. Fear came over me—first to lose Alex, and now, Theros.

"I told Alex I was in love with you."

My words came out, unwished for. My head spun, and my stomach heaved again. The laughter and conversation from the bakery below rose, as if the gathering were just beyond the door, and the jeering was aimed at me. I knew that Theros would mock my words, laugh at them, make me feel as foolish as I was. I hid my face in my hands.

His voice sounded from the shadowy corner. "How true is that?"

"It's true. I love you."

"It don't matter now," he growled. "Tomorrow I will be in jail."

I began to weep in long, sorrowful bursts. The sign above the drug store across the street sputtered on, illuminating the room. Theros' face was tinged blue by the light, his raven hair silver. His eyes gleamed bluish gray, and his skin was veined with blue.

"Don't," he said, coming to sit on the bed beside me. "Don't cry."

"Leave me alone."

"No, listen, Christian." His voice was agitated. "Always, always, since this strike starts, I do not want it to end. If nothing changes, I will go back to Berwind into the mine. I will dig coal all day forever. I would never talk to no one, I would never think, I would never talk to you. You remember how it was?"

He did not wait for a reply.

"I could never have you in Berwind. We never could have did what we do here if we stayed in Berwind. I would be a goat-herder again, dago, stupid nothing. I would rather die than go back to what I was."

"If you go back to jail, it's my fault—"

"I will not go back to jail."

"What will you do, then?" My voice shrilled. "Leave? Oh, God, Theros, take me with you—"

"I am not a coward. I will not leave—"

"What else is there?"

He said nothing, looking out the window at the street below.

"Marry me," I said.

The words escaped from me, independent of thought. But in the same instant, a lifetime spread before me—dreams of eloping, of catching a northbound express and escaping from the coal fields, of living in a sun-filled, pleasant town, all our worries and fears and regrets left behind us in Ludlow. I saw a white Victorian house, like those in Trinidad, and a yard filled with children and dogs. No one fretted there, no one feared.

His hands fell away from me. "What?"

My mouth felt dry, my head leaden. I struggled to explain. "My brother thinks you are only using me to get weapons. He thinks you will . . . he thinks you'll leave, and I'll be left behind, without—"

The words sounded ridiculous and shabby. Again, I was trying to fix what couldn't be fixed.

"If we were married, we would show them all how wrong they are. Alex would understand that you aren't without honor, and the others would see that, well, that I'm not like the girls on West Main—"

"You would do that?" he asked. "Marry a Greek? Even though your brother hates me? Even though he would never look at me and think of me as a man just like him?"

"Yes."

"Even though the soldiers may come tomorrow, take me to jail, keep me there until I am dead? Even though I could be shot dead tonight?"

His words touched off a painful ache. "Don't talk that way—"

"Why not?" He laughed bitterly. "It is true."

I said nothing, ashamed of my impulsive proposal. Yet, now that I had made the offer, I understood how much I loved him, how much I wanted to keep him from harm.

"Surely Alex wouldn't betray his own brother-in-law," I said. "He would never hurt me like that."

He said nothing, letting the silence fester in the room. When he spoke, his voice was quiet. "Since we left Berwind," he said. "I know I am happier than ever I've been in America. I think, I want to be with this woman—with you—always. I can see in my head, have picture in my head—what is the word—?"

"Imagine?"

"I can imagine leaving Ludlow, and going to a city, where there are houses and cars for every man. I think, maybe I will go to New York City. Or Chicago. I will live like John D. Rockefeller and you like Mrs. Rockefeller. Why not?"

I waited, my whole body rigid and still.

"I will marry you," he said. "We can show them all."

Laughter rose up in me—tears, too—filling my throat and making my head sing. Catching his face between my hands, I kissed him. My shoulders shook as I tried to keep back my feelings, but my joy and fear burst forth. Theros put his fingers over my mouth.

"Shh, they will come up to see what we are doing."

"Let them."

His eyes shone. "Okay."

"No!"

He laughed. "So you don't want them?"

My face burned. "I'd rather . . . well, just the two of us—"

He kissed me again. "Good," he said. "Me neither."

The next morning, in a dress borrowed from the baker's wife, I became Mrs. Theros Skyrapoulos.

Chapter 28

In the afternoon, I visited the jail again. Colonel Drake would not let me see Alex, but he let me leave a note. I gave no names, only that I was married. I hoped that was enough to warn Alex not to mention Theros' name.

Colonel Drake read the note over, taking his time. "You should write dime novels," he snorted.

"Will you please give it to him?" I asked.

He folded it meticulously along the creases, then laid it aside. "Anything else, Miss, or should I say, Mrs.—?"

I thanked him and left the office. It was the best I could do.

After we returned to Ludlow, Theros and I parted at the public square. He went off to his duties as union deputy. I went back to the tent.

A mess greeted me. The floorboards were uneven and splintery, the trap door over the pit missing entirely. Sun sparkled through the rips in the canvas walls, and shards of smashed crockery littered the corners. The fire had long since gone out, chilling the air.

Yet someone had restrung the bullhide curtain between our beds, and a couple of chairs that I had never seen sat in place of the ones that had been dashed to splinters. Fresh but ratty blankets piled on the end of my bed, and Pearl lay on her bed with a blue quilt around her shoulders.

"You're back!" she cried. "I was so afraid you'd been put in jail, too. But they let you go! So it ain't so bad after all. Where's Alex?"

When I told her of his condition, her hands wrapped over the baby, as if it were the only thing tethering her to this earth. I sat beside her, stroking her hair. "Don't," I pleaded. "Don't do this."

"But you told them the truth, didn't you?" she asked. "You told them he didn't do it, that it was you all along?"

"I tried. Alex wouldn't let me. He wants me to bring in more guns."

"What!" She hefted herself up so quickly into a sitting position that I feared she might topple off the bed. "But he has to come home! Our baby! Why on earth would he want you to keep on?"

"He thinks something bad is coming to Ludlow."

"Oh, that!" she scoffed. "Something bad has always been coming for Ludlow! Since the day we walked out of them coal camps, something bad has been coming! All them soldiers, all the shooting and fighting and us just starving and freezing and dying off like sick dogs. I'm so tired of it! Just let it come! It don't matter to me one bit what happens to Ludlow!"

I went to the stove, kneeling beside it to stoke the fire. My hands shook with anger, my eyes pricked with tears. It did matter, I wanted to say, because we had fought for so long now, and so hard, and it had cost us so much. It did matter, because my whole life and heart was now wrapped up in what happened to Ludlow. I wanted to tell her about my own reason—my good, selfish reason—for not telling Colonel Drake the truth.

Instead, I jammed the kindling and wood into the stove. Outside, the sounds of Ludlow were the same—the frolic of children playing, the singsong of women who were hanging the wash, the bullhorn blasting in the public square—and yet every word sounded to me like some sort of warning.

Pearl spoke from across the room, repeating in dull disbelief, "He has to come home. Our baby's going to be here any day—"

"I'll be here with you," I promised. "I'll never leave you. I'll keep you safe."

"He don't care that he's the one they took to jail, when he ain't done nothing at all?"

"He wants me to bring in guns to James and Uncle John."

"He ain't hiding from me there, is he? He ain't ashamed, or wanting me to be gone—"

"No, of course not! Why would you think that?"

"Why do you think?" She held out her hands, turning them palms up, then back. "Sometimes I just think that he'd rather us not have this baby—"

"When he sees the baby, he won't think of anything but how much he loves her. And you."

"So will you keep on smuggling guns?"

I brushed the splinters of wood from my knees. I was a married woman now. Around my finger was a band of brass so thin that it looked as if it might snap—all Theros could afford, all I wanted. "I don't know."

She considered. "Maybe I should do it. I bet I could fit a whole Gatling gun under my skirt right now." Standing, she pulled her skirt tight over her belly. Amazed at the bulge, she added, "Maybe even two."

I started to laugh, despite myself. "I'm so sorry," I said, my laugh changing to tears. "You were right. I was so stupid to put us in danger—"

She drew in a sharp breath. "Hush, Christian, it don't matter. The way this baby's been tumbling around, I know she's winding up to come out. I'm scared, you know. I don't know what she'll be like, whether she'll have all her parts or what. I don't know if I can stand all that pain. You'll help me, won't you? You'll stay here with me?"

I reached out with both hands to touch her belly. The baby wrestled and rolled in big, looping movements, as if a snake was traveling beneath Pearl's skin. Leaning forward, I pressed my ear against it, hoping to hear that lively, curious heartbeat or a sigh or coo. Pearl laid her hand on my hair, smoothing it until I could bear to lift my face and look up into her eyes again.

"It ain't so bad," she said. "We'll see it through."

And still, I did not tell her that I was married.

That evening, I waited for my husband. My husband. The words sent a spike of delight through my body, as if it were humming, dancing, flying. Our wedding had been so simple—boring, I supposed, for the justice of the peace, who neither asked nor cared about anything other than his fee. Theros had worn traditional Greek clothing, all white, a kilt and embroidered shirt and a sash around his waist. The baker and his wife had stood up with us, and she had sung a song in heavy, thick Greek before we were pronounced man and wife. A wedding song, Theros had told me later, asking for God's blessing on the new couple.

When Theros knocked—ever so lightly—on our door, I danced over to him, running my hands up his shoulders to his hair. He wrapped his arms around me and kissed me.

Holding my finger to my lips to keep him from waking Pearl, I led him behind the bullhide sheeting. Once there, we could not help it. He laughed aloud, and so did I.

"You are still my wife?" he asked, cradling me in his arms.

"For nine hours now."

"I have been away too long."

We laughed again. Settling back on the bed, he pulled me close with one arm, and I laid my head in the hollow of his shoulder. With his other arm crooked behind his head, he surveyed the room. He nodded toward the shattered bureau, which had only one drawer left.

"You have so little," he said.

"What the militia didn't take, they broke."

At once, my mind clamored with the same thoughts I'd had the day before. Let's leave. Let's catch the last train to Denver, tonight, this minute. Let's steal if we have to, lie if we have to, but let's go.

As if I'd spoken aloud, he said, "I cannot leave. Louis, he has said to me, he has asked me—if something happens to him, if he is killed, I am to take his place."

The words came as no surprise. Louis Tikas, the great *strategos* of the Greeks, the famous organizer for the UMWA, and my husband, his lieutenant. I'd known it in Berwind, when Theros had told me the reason he was fighting in the ring. I'd known it the night we'd spent in the bakery, when he had to leave me alone to join the battle.

"I can't leave Pearl," I said. "I promised my brother—"

He cut me short. "So we will live in this hole and eat cheese like mice."

"I'll be happy enough."

"Did you tell Miss Pearl about us?"

"No."

He cocked his head, looking down at me. "Why not? She will be happy, won't she?"

"I couldn't. I can't. Not as long as Alex—"

So Alex's name had come up again between us. Alex—the reason why we had married, the reason why we worried still. Here I lay beside the man who should rightfully be in jail, while Alex should be free. I nestled into his shoulder, hiding my face. He stroked my hair with one hand.

After a long pause, he said, "Before my father died, back in Crete, we went to see great cathedral. It was beautiful, gold and light and so big. I wanted to touch it. So I jumped, as high as I could, up and up and up. I thought, if only I could touch this dome, I will be happy. Papi got so mad, said, what are you doing? When I told him, he said, you cannot touch God."

I breathed in his warmth, the smell of strong, lye soap and leather.

"You cannot touch God," he said. "Only He can touch you. Sometimes I think—why did I come here, to this ugly place? I hate myself, because there must be some place in America where it is better, there must be. It is a big place, huge. But I can't change it now. I can't say to God, this is a mistake, put me to some other place. I cannot say to Him, make me a different man, better fighter, make me what I am not. Make me be where I was supposed to be yesterday so that what happens yesterday does not happen."

"It's our wedding night," I whispered, my throat closed and tender.

"I am just saying that I am sorry—"

"I know that, I understand."

I took his face between my hands and kissed him, all the roiling feeling in me making me fierce, demanding. He pulled me closer, spoke words that I don't even remember now—were they Greek? were they English?—against my skin as he loved me.

The next few days, I suppose, were our honeymoon. April had ripened into spring on the prairie around Ludlow. In the arroyo, the snowmelt carved a sparkling path through the sandy soil. The brittle, bone-dry grasses greened, and the cholla and prickly pear sprouted wrinkled pods that would burst into violet and yellow blossoms by summer. The sage furred out, and the sky arced overhead in turquoise splendor.

We walked in the arroyo together, our heads tilted together. We sat side by side in the public square, our faces angled upward to the warm sun. We laughed at the shapes we pointed out to one another in the towering white clouds above our heads, and we concocted crazy translations of the foreign words we heard shouted through the ever-squawking bullhorn. In the afternoons, I watched Theros play baseball on the diamond across the road from the tent colony. He had once told me he was not good at the game, and he wasn't—his shoulders were too wide, his arms too long, and the legs that gave him so much height were too ungainly to give him much speed. I clapped all the harder, cheered all the louder because of it.

Maybe everyone in Ludlow had grown tired of pointing out differences, or maybe they were all too tired to care, because no one seemed to notice us. No one stared at the Scottish girl and the Greek-American man who walked shoulder to shoulder, or held hands, or kissed goodbye every morning at the door of her tent. No one whispered or pointed.

For those few days, even the heavily-armed soldiers who prowled the outskirts of the tent colony, leering and taunting, preying on the lost or careless, and always, always threatening, seemed already a part of the past.

Lily was born just after dawn on Easter Sunday. I had given Pearl my bed behind the bullhide sheeting, but when her friends crowded into our tent, they tied the curtain back to give themselves a better view of the birth. Jamming around the table, crouching by the stove, sitting three deep on Alex's bed, they waited, their rosaries rapt and ready for blessings. An old Italian midwife attended the birth, urging Pearl along in words that had to be translated by a young, dark-eyed girl named

Maria, childless yet herself and clearly agog at the spectacle.

I mopped Pearl's forehead with a damp cloth and let her twist and pinch my hands in hers. When Lily slipped from her, the Italian midwife spread her knees and caught the baby in the taunt hollow of her apron. She cut the cord and tied it with string, then rolled the ample apron around Lily, swaddling her so swiftly that the cool air of the tent barely touched her damp, sticky skin. She then jounced Lily until a resentful howl resounded from the bundle. With that, the old woman grinned—her mouth as toothless as the baby's—and laid Lily at Pearl's breast.

Maria turned to me. "Mama says, baby is born so easy. Mother Mary has blessed her."

I said my own prayer of thanks. Lily had eyes as dark as Pearl's and a shock of black hair sticking straight out like a crow's wing. Her skin carried the glow of a deep red rose before it wilts and fades to black.

"Do you think she'll be pretty?" Pearl whispered.

"She's beautiful now. Alex'll be so proud."

"I wish he was here to see her."

I dabbed at her forehead. "He will be soon."

"Do you think you could help me to see him, Christian? You were able to see him."

"We'll go when you're stronger."

But Pearl fared poorly that night. She lay in bed, barely able to lift her head to drink or eat. As she slept, perspiration formed on her pale, waxen features and her eyes darted madly under her shell-like lids. The midwife kept a constant vigil, spooning broth into Pearl's lips and wiping her forehead with a cool rag dipped in lavender. Occasionally, she paused to pray, crouching into a wizened ball, her knees on the rough floor planking.

"Should I call for Doctor Beshoar?" I asked Maria. "She's running a fever."

She conferred with her grandmother. "No," she said airily. "Mama says doctor—hah! She knows more than any doctor. She will take care of her."

It was not until the following afternoon, after the Italian women had left for their own homes, and the Mexican women had gone off for siestas, that Theros was able to creep into our tent and see me.

"Everything is okay?" he whispered.

"She's a little girl, just as Pearl wanted." I cuddled the baby in my arms. "She's fine. Pearl will be better soon, I'm sure."

I showed him how to hold her, and he gathered her to him and sat at the table. At first, he held her awkwardly, his back unnaturally braced, his wide shoulders hunched. Lily rested in his hands, so tiny she could nearly fit in just one palm. I patted his shoulder, smiling at his clumsiness.

"I have not held a baby, ever. You must not laugh."

"You'd better get in practice. Someday we'll have one of our own."

He laughed, and I peeked at Lily's face. Her eyes were wide open, a tiny furrow between her brows as she studied Theros' face. Her mouth puckered, as if she was mulling over whether to screech or settle peacefully into slumber. "She's wondering who you are," I said.

"Who is this big, dumb Greek?" he asked her. "Who is this big, stupid man?"

I stood behind him and wrapped my arms around his neck, smiling at Lily over his shoulder. "Her uncle," I whispered in his ear.

He chuckled, surprised and—I think—pleased. Shifting Lily into the deep pocket of his elbow, he said, "For Greeks, it is good to be born during the time of resurrection. It is good to die, then, too."

"Don't say that!"

He shrugged. "You are closer to God, then. Your soul can reach Him more fast. It is bright days, shining time. Everyone is singing, so much singing, and praising to Jesus, that the soul flies to heaven."

"That's right," I said. "The souls are accompanied to heaven by song."

"*Mirologhia,* yes. I'm happy you remember." He let Lily's fingers wrap around one of his. "She's pretty, yes?"

Pearl called to me from behind the curtain. Propping herself up on one elbow, she clutched the bedclothes to her breast. "Who's here? It ain't Jake, is it? Or Miz Ruddy?"

"No." I smoothed her hair from her forehead. "It's Theo Sky. Go back to sleep."

"Nothing's wrong with Lily?"

"Nothing at all. Theros—Theo Sky's—holding her."

The desire to tell her the truth swept over me, but she rolled over in her bed. "I'm so cold. Put more wood on the fire, would you?"

"Go back to sleep." I waited until her eyes closed, then pulled the coverlets close around her. As I piled wood on the fire, my forehead beaded with sweat. The tent was already sweltering in the early spring sun.

Theros still sat at the table, cuddling Lily just under his chin. I thought at first he was whispering to her, but then I realized he had just kissed her tiny face. Lily's eyelids drooped, and she sucked happily on one fist.

"She's fallen asleep for you," I assured him. "You're warm and gentle. She likes that."

I took Lily from him and laid her in the cradle. For a moment, we both stood next to her, watching her drift down into a deep sleep. Then he turned to me and said, "I missed you last night."

I stood on my tiptoes to kiss him.

The days that followed passed in a sleepless, dreamless blur. With Pearl unable to do little more than to feed Lily, the baby's care fell to me. I cooed to Lily, sang to her, walked her back and forth across the uneven wooden planking so often that my feet learned instinctively to avoid the boards that creaked under my step. Melodies flowed from my lips, lullabies that my mother had sung to me in my nearly forgotten childhood, but that now seemed to spring fully alive and ready in my head. I even went so far as to dance the Turkey Trot with Lily to a tune played on a cranked-up gramophone in a nearby tent. From her bed, Pearl smiled at my thin, reedy voice, at my clumsy dancing, yet her eyes closed long before the music slowed and then, with one long, sliding growl, stopped.

Plenty of eager hands helped me—the women who adored Pearl. They flocked to the tent to bless the baby. With them, they brought gifts of blankets and cloths for diapers and clothes, oils and soaps. For a few minutes, Pearl opened her eyes and spoke with them.

"One of them is bound to bring frankincense or myrrh," I remarked.

Pearl laughed weakly, a tattered madonna. "Look outside and see if there's a star shining above the tent."

"Just the Hastings searchlights."

She laughed again, a little stronger this time. It was a welcome sound.

Even Mrs. McCormick came to visit Pearl. With Jane and Mary by her side, she brought booties she had knitted. Mary offered some clothes outgrown by her own babies. Thanking them, Pearl put the booties on Lily's feet and smoothed her fingers over the soft yarn. I boiled water for tea.

"How are you, Mrs. Ruddy?" Mrs. McCormick asked, making a brave effort to be polite.

"I'll get better," Pearl said. "I've had quite a time with fever."

"Childbed fever." Jane nodded her head. "Better get up and get to walkin' right away. Christian, you give 'er lots of tea to chase it away. It can turn into something fierce if you don't take care."

"I will," I said.

"Is your husband coming to take you and the baby to Berwind?" Mrs. McCormick asked.

Pearl's body shifted, ready for a fight. "No, he ain't well enough yet."

Mrs. McCormick looked around the tent, her gaze falling on the open pit. "Pity we couldn't find enough wood to fix this floor. The union supplies have run out."

"James and Uncle John did a fine job," I said, pouring the tea.

"What do you hear from Alex?" she asked. "Does he know about the baby?"

"We sent word by messenger on a union truck," I said. "As soon as we can, we'll get down to Trinidad to see him."

"John's still grievin' over what happened here. Alex just doesn't seem the type to be mixed up with those hothead Greeks who carry guns. It's them, you know, who stir up all the trouble."

If Alex was to suffer for what I'd done, the least I could do was to save his reputation. "It wasn't Alex," I said. "It was me."

"What?" Mrs. McCormick asked.

Jane's teacup tipped in midair, amber drops falling from its lip. Mary absently wadded the baby gowns that lay in her lap, her wide-eyed gaze on me.

Pearl shifted Lily closer to her breast. "Christian thought Alex could protect us better if he had a gun," she said. "She was thinking of us."

I glanced up at Pearl, and she nodded at me. And I saw at once that spreading the tale about the Greeks and their guns would only cause more bad feeling and jeopardize us all—Alex, Theros, Pearl and Lily, even Ludlow itself. Lowering my gaze, I mumbled, "That's what I thought."

"Why would you do such a thing?" Mrs. McCormick roared. "And Alex takin' the blame! Why, you need to march yourself right over to the union office and tell John Lawson that you want Alex released from jail today! Tell him to call the jail himself and set things right! Your own brother!"

The agony of it rose up in me, and I closed my mouth to keep from blurting out the whole story. Pearl spoke for me.

"Alex says it's all right," she said smoothly. "He says he'd rather be in jail than have her there. It's a miserable place."

"Is that true, Christian?"

"Yes," I said.

"Where did you find that gun?" Jane wondered.

"Oh, if she told you that," Pearl said. "Everybody in Ludlow would be standing in line, waiting to get one. It'd look like the Catholic Ladies' soup kitchen at the commissary on Thursdays."

Jane's mouth opened, a dark, silent hole. Mary's eyes narrowed, disbelieving. But Mrs. McCormick laughed. "Well," she said bitterly. "You sure pulled one over on us all, Christian. Maybe you think you're awful smart, but it's Alex who's paying the price."

As if commanded, both Jane and Mary set down their teacups and scurried to leave. Mrs. McCormick stood, haughty and cold, and wished Pearl luck with the baby. I received a sharp look of dislike.

After they left, I leaned against the table, my palms flat upon it, swallowing back the urge to vomit.

"Old biddies," Pearl said.

"No," I breathed. "No. She only spoke the truth."

"Maybe, but I wasn't about to let you spill the beans about . . . what's his name—?"

"Theros."

"I like Theo Sky better. Don't you tell them nothing about him."

"He's my husband, Pearl."

She started so violently that Lily protested. "What!"

I smiled at her surprise. "I married him last Tuesday."

"Well, if you ain't something else! So tell me all about it!"

All at once, we were talking as we had long ago, when we were girls in Berwind, playing hero and heroine in the sand wash, a lunch hidden in the shade of the piñon scrub. This time, I truly was the heroine, swept off her feet by the romantic, brave knight, and carried away to a happy ending.

"I knew it," Pearl said. "I knew it from the first day I met him in school. You remember, I used to sit right next to him, and all day long he'd just lollygag in his seat, just watching you like you was some princess or something. He never did a bit of schoolwork."

My face reddened, just as it had all those years before, and I covered it with my hands to hide it. My joy bubbled out through my fingers.

"What about Alex?" Pearl's face puckered. "What do you think he'll say about this?"

"I don't know," I said. "But he knows. I sent him a note."

"Well, ain't you a little sneak!" Pearl laughed. "When Theo Sky gets here, you let him talk to me. He needs to know all about who he married."

But long before Theros arrived, Pearl's fever had risen so high that she could not keep her eyes open. Yet her sleep was far from easy.

Her damp hair stuck to her forehead, and her skin was icy cold. I wiped away the perspiration with a rag soaked in rose water. "What's wrong?" I whispered.

"A dream," she said. "Terrible, stupid things."

My skin felt chilled, prickly. "What things?"

"I spilled my tea, and then I ripped a button from my coat—and I cried and cried in the dream. I wouldn't never cry over nothing like that if I was awake."

"No, much worse happens when we're awake."

"But that ain't all." She clutched at my wrist. "Oh, Christian, I was holding Lily and she turned right into this huge man, and then I was holding him, and his arms and legs was all soft and loose, like he's dead in my arms. I think it was Russ, in the dream. He ain't dead, is he? You ain't heard nothing, have you?"

"No, I haven't. Don't work yourself up so much."

"I'm just so sure something bad's happened to him. I keep dreaming of walking back to Berwind, of going back up the canyon, but I don't find no town or house or mine. When I call out for Russ, it just echoes off the ugly rock walls. But then I'm holding Lily again, and I'm all mixed up about who's who."

I smoothed her hair. "It was just a bad dream. You're safe here with me. Lily's safe."

After Pearl had drifted off into her dream-scarred sleep, I sat near the stove and pulled the blankets from around Lily. I undressed her, letting her suck on a rag soaked in sugar milk to keep her quiet in the chilly air. Then, I searched for my brother's blood—for a familiar mark, for a freckle or mole, for a stray red hair in that bottlebrush of black, for a glint of green in those dark eyes. No sign was visible. But just as I could see nothing of Alex in her, I found nothing of Russell Ruddy, either.

I heard the whistle of the late night freight, destined for Denver, as it chugged slowly into the Ludlow station. For days now, the arrival of every train in Ludlow had made my heart strain against my ribs. If Alex had been released, he might be on one of those trains, at any time of the day or night.

I had started to count the minutes, clocking how long it would take him to climb from the train and cross the platform, how long it would take for him to follow the road from the town to the crossroads, and to come to the front gate of the tent colony. From there, he would come to the door of the tent, step inside, greet Pearl, marvel over his newborn daughter, and finally, turn to me and—I prayed—forgive me.

And every night as I slept in Theros' arms, I was afraid that it might be my last. I worried that Alex's resolve would crumble, that he would grow ill or desperate enough to tell the truth to Colonel Drake. Every morning I expected to wake to a knock on the tent door and to the sneers of soldiers, who would take from me my *kefi*, the great happiness that I had just found.

Chapter 29

"Sunday is Greek Easter," Theros told me.

We sat at the table in the tent. I washed potatoes, scrubbing the sprouting eyes from them and cutting away the black and spoiled spots. They were the best the union could provide. Theros held Lily, something he had taken to doing each time he came to visit. One of his fingers hovered over her, her tiny hand hooked around it.

"The Greek Easter?" I asked. "It isn't the same as the Catholic Easter?"

"No, nothing is the same," he said. "In Crete, we clean—houses, sheds and fields, our clothes. We wash them until they are fresh and dry them in the sun. When everything is clean, we go to church."

"What's that like?"

"Oh, the churches are big," he said. "Beautiful paintings, colored glass. Lots of statues, and gold cups and things. There is wine and bread, the body of Christ. Everywhere has so many flowers of all kinds. Lilies, too." Lily mewled, as if she had heard her name, and he clicked his tongue at her. "Beautiful words are said about Christ rising from the dead. But here, there is no church for Greeks. So we have prayers in meeting tent at sunrise."

"Will you have a minister there?"

"You mean a priest. No. No priest." He shrugged. "But, Christian, I must tell you. Before Easter, Greeks fast. They don't eat nothing but bread and water. They don't smoke or drink. They can't have . . . no pleasures."

"What?"

He nodded toward the bed. "No—"

"I'm your wife!"

He laughed. "You are Greek wife. I am supposed to fast and not do nothing for a week"—he shrugged—"so I am already late to start. But I am a just married man, and I am the only Greek in Ludlow who has a wife. So, next Easter I will fast more days to make it right. But not this Easter."

"What will change by next Easter?"

His eyes shone. "Maybe nothing. Maybe new baby?"

I looked down, a smile on my lips. "So you won't come by—?"

"I will come by, but I won't stay. I will come by every night, every day to see you."

"And what will we do with our time? Play cards?"

"No gambling." He laughed again at my dismay. "I am afraid to tell you this before now, because I think, you will say, What do I want with a worthless husband like him? Why do I want Greek who has stupid church that won't let him be a man?"

"No, I'd never . . . Can I kiss you?"

"All you want, as long as you do not do more."

My indignation exploded. "Do more!"

He reached over and ran a finger across my lips. I licked them to quell the tingle of his touch, but I could not keep from laughing. "On Easter day," he said. "We will dance, we will drink and be happy. We will be together, and let everybody see we are husband and wife. You will come?"

"After so long without you, of course I'll come."

But the days passed so slowly. I lived a solitary life, rarely leaving the tent, rarely seeing anyone but Maria and the girls who came to visit Pearl. They crowded into the tent, vying to hold Lily, to change her or dress her, or to carry her to Pearl.

"We all want baby," Maria told me, and I said, "Yes, I know."

Later, alone and lonely, I made up my mind. I could run guns for the Greeks, or for John and James, as Alex wanted me to, but I wanted what Maria and the other girls wanted. I wanted to laugh, I wanted to think of nothing more than what would happen that day, that morning, that minute. A new life awaited me, as a wife, as a mother.

I stripped the flannel from my skirt, carefully cutting away the stitches to save as much as I could. Sitting on the edge of my bed, I sewed the strips into a square of pink roses and yellow bows and quilted it with tiny, even stitches. Lovingly, I tasseled each square with yarn.

When Theros stopped by, he saw the green flannel lying on the table. "What have you been doing?" he asked.

"Making a blanket for the baby."

He said nothing. I studied the blanket, too, as if I'd never seen it before. "So," he said at last. "You will not run guns no more?"

"No."

"It is okay," he said. "You cannot. They are watching you." He paused, then added, "They are watching us all. The bakery, too. Baldwins stand outside every morning."

His voice carried a wistful tone, one of loss and regret. "Have you had any trouble?" I asked.

"No." His face twisted. "But, Christian, stay in Ludlow. Don't leave this tent. Don't go to Trinidad, don't go to train station."

"I'm hoping to take Pearl to the doctor soon."

"Wait until after Sunday. I will go with you so you are safe."

I ran a finger from his temple to his jaw. "What about you? Will you stay in Ludlow?"

He smiled and kissed my finger. I knew better than to expect an answer.

At last, the morning of the Greek Easter dawned, windless and warm.

Leaving Pearl in the care of Maria, I nearly danced through Ludlow's paths, eager to reach the celebration, to hear the chatter of others, to smell the fresh air. Days had passed since I'd left the tent for anything other than a trip to the well or the privies.

The festivities were already in full swing under a cloudless sky. On the baseball diamond, women played women, dressed in silly-looking red gym bloomers that stirred the Greeks'—and all the men's—blood. The men catcalled and teased, whistling and bawling with laughter at missed catches, plentiful strikes, graceless gallops to the bases.

Most of Ludlow's residents had collected on the wooden grandstands near the baseball field, dressed in Sunday finery. Around me, women flirted, and men pressed them for waltzes that evening at the dance to be held in the public square. Children scrambled in and out of the grandstands, playing in the sun. Nearby, lambs roasted over an open pit fire, the smoke sweet with the smell of mesquite, and men helped themselves to beer from barrels on a wagon bed.

The women's baseball game ended, and the Greek and Italian men took the field. Theros claimed third base. I could not take my eyes from him. My palms grew hot, my wrists tingly, as I watched him move, the familiar excitement building in the pit of my stomach. I swallowed against the tenderness and love welling in my throat.

He shaded his eyes to search the grandstands. I waved wildly, and he grinned before turning back to the game.

But the carefree mood did not last. Halfway through the seventh inning, four uniformed horsemen arrived, rifles swinging from their saddles.

"Here comes trouble," a woman in the grandstands squalled.

Almost at once, she began taunting the soldiers, threatening to chase them off with BB guns. Other women joined in, haranguing them about their dirty uniforms and slovenly ways. The baseball game faltered. The players kicked at the bases and slapped fists into mitts, as if sorry to give up the sport. At last, they moved toward the riflemen, Louis Tikas leading the way.

Words passed between the soldiers and the strikers, with Louis gesturing fiercely. The soldiers' horses pawed the ground, restless, whipping their heads. In the grandstands, panic rose in the murmurs. Women shielded their mouths from view with their hands and spoke in hushed voices, and the men sat on the edge of the stands, their bodies tense.

At last, the horsemen wheeled away.

"Have your fun today," one of them called. "We'll have ours tomorrow."

They galloped south toward the town of Ludlow. With determination, the men took up the baseball game, but some of the Greeks slipped away. A few of the Italians broke off and marched staunchly toward the tent colony. I searched the settling dust for Theros, but he had abandoned the base that he'd manned only a few minutes before.

I ran through the tents, heading toward the Greek camp. As I passed by the public square, I saw a tight knot of men milling about near the tent that housed the union office. They were Greek.

Inside the office, everyone seemed to be shouting. Anton and Dimitrius loaded guns and tossed them to others standing at the door. Theros stood near the back, searching through a stack of papers. Louis talked on the field telephone, barking into it in his heavily accented English.

"Christian!" Theros called.

"What's happening? What's going on?"

He grabbed my arm, his grip a vise that made my flesh ache, and pulled me into a dark corner, where shelves were piled high with papers, books and crates. "Why are you here?" he rasped. "Go back to the game. Go back to Miss Pearl."

"What's going on?"

Speaking almost into my ear, he said, "They say there's a man down here in Ludlow that doesn't want to be. His wife's from Segundo, says she has not seen him in a week, so he's been kidnapped and taken to Ludlow. Louis tells the soldiers, no, this man is not here. Never heard of him. He is not union striker on union payroll. Never has been. We looked at the payroll books, every page. No man by that name is ever in Ludlow. But the soldiers say they will search every tent for him, if he does not come out by morning."

"What are they trying to do?"

He shoved the papers onto a shelf. "They want trouble, we will give it to them."

"Oh, be careful—"

He kissed my forehead. "Go back to the game now. Go back to the picnic and eat. Show them, we are not scared. Don't let them ruin it for us. I will meet you at the dance tonight."

"Where are you going?"

"To patrol," he said edgily. "Just to keep Ludlow safe."

I asked no more. Standing on tiptoe, I kissed his lips and whispered my love to him.

I went back to the baseball diamond and sat in the warm, afternoon sun. The women in red bloomers were now playing the men who had stayed behind. I tried to enjoy the game, but every flurry of dust on the horizon, or horseman loping across the prairie, or car that sped out of the town of Ludlow caught my eye and made me hold my breath, certain it was the onset of disaster.

Halfway through the afternoon, the meal was served—a smattering of lamb in a deep gravy, a few vegetables, a pint of beer. Louis Tikas himself filled the plates, dressed in the spotless white dress costume of the Cretans. As he handed me a plate, he nodded gravely.

The crowd began to drift away, headed toward siesta, mothers urging cranky children toward the tents, the men settling in to smoke and drink. I searched the lanes outside the barbed wire fences for Theros, but I did not see the patrol. Feeling queasy, I went to the tent. Inside, I sagged onto my bed, my stomach knotted and my head aching. Pearl sat in the rocking chair, nursing Lily.

"What's wrong?" she asked.

"Nothing."

"Did something happen to Theo Sky?"

"No," I said. "He's all right." Suddenly, a violent desperation overcame me. "Oh, Pearl, I have to get out of here! We have to leave!"

"Leave?" she asked faintly. "And go where?"

"I can't stand it here any longer. I can't listen to all this—"

She clutched Lily against her breast. A vision of Alex passed before my eyes. He should have been there. He should have been enjoying his new daughter and tending to the woman he loved.

"I'm sorry." I knelt before the rocking chair and clasped her hand. "I didn't mean to frighten you. People are talking, that's all."

"About me? About Lily? Don't they have nothing better to do?"

"No." I touched her cheek, which burned under my palm. "Believe me. It's not that at all. Here, let me put Lily down for you."

Gladly, she handed the baby to me. Stretching out on her bed, she was asleep in minutes. I rocked Lily to sleep, nodding off myself, Lily's sweet warmth in my arms.

A strain of a lively melody woke me, signaling the start of the evening dance. Leaving Pearl and Lily sleeping, I ran to the public square.

I knew what I would find. Although most of Ludlow's men and women and children had turned out to cap off the day's celebration, the Greeks were scarce. As the fiddle played, and the accordion breathed in and out, and the soft evening air twinkled with the joy of dancers and lovers, I walked through the crowd, taking long looks at the faces of the dark men gathered in tight, shadowy knots to drink. At last, I went home.

Inside the tent, Lily squeaked in her sleep, and Pearl spoke aloud, in a fit of night fears. I smoothed her hair, dark and wild in the light from the lamp.

Her eyes opened. "Lily's been sleeping since you left," she murmured groggily. "I expect it's about time for a feeding."

As if she'd heard, Lily woke with a full cry. I lifted her from the cradle and carried her to Pearl. As Pearl nursed her, I sat on the foot of the bed.

"Do you remember," I asked, "the first night you stayed at our house in Berwind? You talked of reading a book about a girl who had a house and a bed and a fancy-painted horse carriage to take her to town."

Smiling, she shook her head. "I sure was hare-brained back then. I wanted so much, I wanted everything." She shifted Lily to her other breast. "Then I grew up and found out how hard it is to hang on to any little thing at all. Why was you thinking of that?"

I reached out to stroke Lily's wiry black hair. "I don't know."

"Why ain't you with Theo Sky?" she asked. "You ain't had a fight already?"

"No, he's busy, that's all."

The music and laughter from the public square wafted to us through the silent pathways of Ludlow. The searchlights spilled over our tent. A pack of dogs barked wildly, then howled and yipped in frantic chorus.

It was our last night in Ludlow.

Chapter 30

Early the next morning, an explosion rocked Ludlow. I rolled from my bed, bedclothes tangled around my ankles, my hair in my eyes. Ludlow was at once awake. Shouts echoed through the tents, pots crashed from shelves and stoves, and dogs howled madly. In her cradle, Lily screamed.

"Christian!" Pearl called. "Christian! What's going on?"

I thrust Lily into Pearl's hands.

"I don't know," I said. "Maybe a mine went up in Berwind or Delagua."

Grabbing a shawl, I ran outside. People flooded the pathways, rushing for the arroyo, retreating to their tents, scattering toward the gates. Before me, a young mother grabbed her child roughly by the arm and cried, "Soldier, soldier!" The boy tripped and fell to his knees, only to be dragged through the dust.

Near the gates, a striker waved his arms madly at the throng. "Get back to your tents! Are you crazy? Look! Look over there!"

I whipped my head around. Directly south of Ludlow, on the slope of Water Tank Hill, the sage and piñon scrub seemed to writhe with life. The mouths of militia cannons gaped toward the tent colony, manned by soldiers with campaign hats cocked against the morning sun. Troopers swarmed around machine guns nested along sandy ridges and in ditches. To the west, soldiers crouched on the gravel embankment of the railroad tracks, the barrels of their Springfields glinting in the sun.

"My God," I whispered. "There are hundreds of them."

Swinging his arms, the man yelled, "Go back to your tents and get in your pits! You'll be shot!"

Another explosion rent the air. The ground buckled beneath my feet, and a woman near me screamed and fell to the ground. Clutching handfuls of dirt as if it were rope, she began to crawl forward. "Come on, come on," the striker yelled, yanking at her clothing. "Move!"

Bullets sprayed the dirt, as the machine guns unleashed their fire. I ran toward our tent, screaming Pearl's name. She sat on the floor, her nightgown bunched around her knees and the blankets caught beneath her. "I fell." Her arms tightened around Lily. "What's happening? Oh, God, is it the militia?"

"They're attacking Ludlow. We have to get to where it's safe!"

"Where? I can't walk far—"

I rubbed my hands over my eyes. Before me gaped the pit that Alex had dug beneath the tent. The door and hinges had been stripped off by the militia search, but the ladder was still in place. Swallowing back my fear, I said, "The pit. Go down there. Hurry! Give me Lily."

She inched down the ladder, and I followed, a screaming Lily bundled in my arms.

"There's no room down here," Pearl said.

"Just push everything aside."

In the pit was a heap of dented pans, splintered crates, smashed trunks and other junk, left over from the militia's search. Giving Lily to Pearl, I heaved what I could into the back corner until we found enough room to sit.

Exhausted, Pearl collapsed on the dirt floor. Lily howled.

"It's cold down here," she said.

Already, she shivered. Lily's diaper was sopped from a long night's sleep. Both Pearl and I wore thin nightdresses. We needed blankets, clothes, diapers, food, water. The gloom settled around us, so that I could barely see Pearl across the floor. "I have to go up and get some things," I said.

"No, you'll be killed!"

"I'll be quick."

I crept up the ladder, barely raising my head above the ground. The hum of gunfire was steady now, the screaming of women and children in the tents no less so. I climbed out and crawled on my elbows to Pearl's bed. The rough wood flooring chafed my skin, lacing my wrists with splinters. We would need every warm piece of clothing I could find. Opening the bureau drawer, I pulled out my mother's tartan, then reached up a single hand to pull down the blankets.

Without warning, I let the stuff drop inside the pit. Pearl screamed. "It's all right," I called. "It's blankets and clothes. Wrap up in them. Make sure Lily's warm."

I wallowed to the stove to find water and biscuits. Sloshing water from the barrel to the bucket with one hand, I dragged the heavy bucket along the floor behind me. Suddenly, a jug exploded on the shelf, spewing shards and the last of Alex's whiskey into my hair. I screamed and dropped to the floor. On my stomach again, I wrested the bucket toward the pit. The biscuits were left behind.

Below, Pearl huddled in the blankets, Lily clutched to her breast. "What's going on?" she asked. "Why did you scream?"

"Something broke, that's all," I said. "Let me help you get dressed. You'll be warmer."

I dressed Pearl in our warmest clothes—a heavy wool jacket and skirt. After I had dressed, I draped a blanket over both of us and leaned back against the wall of the pit. Pearl laid her head on my shoulder.

Around us, the darkness quivered, barely touched by the lamp's light. The timbered ceiling loomed over my head, and the walls that held the thickness of the earth behind them crumbled as I leaned against them. I could not escape the sense of crushing weight that pressed in on me there, stealing my breath. With all the clutter, the pit was more airless than ever before. The unsteady jumble of metal and wood rattled, in a ghostly echo of the machine gun fire above. A dusting of wood splinters from the bullet-torn wooden floor floated onto our heads.

"God, what's happening?" Pearl cried.

"Shh." I pulled the frayed blanket around us. "We'll be all right. Nothing can hurt us here."

I closed my eyes and willed truth to my words. Somewhere, crouched behind the scrubby piñon on the mesas or burrowed into the sandy bottom of the arroyo, Theros was undoubtedly swept up in the siege. Silently, I prayed to God to keep him safe.

Pearl shifted Lily in her arms and whispered in a shaky, weak voice, "Tom Ruddy said this strike wouldn't come to no good. Jake said the strikers would all die and the company'd dance on their dead bodies."

Bile rose in my throat. "Jake will burn in hell one of these days."

Her breath rasped in her throat. "Do you think we'll ever see Berwind again?"

"I don't know," I admitted. "Sometimes I think we can't go back, just like we can't stay here. There's nowhere we belong anymore."

"I still dream of Berwind," Pearl said. "There ain't never nothing there in my dream."

Slowly, the hours crept by. We leaned against one another, as if neither of us could stay upright without the other's help. We shifted to lie flat, to sit with our backs against the wall. We stretched our legs, then curled into balls for warmth. All the while, Pearl grew quieter. She did not sing with me as I lulled Lily to sleep, she did not speak. The heat that radiated from her skin should have been enough to keep us both warm, yet she shivered under the bedclothes piled on her.

At last, we lapsed into a queer, lonesome silence. Lulled by the rhythm of my own breathing, I fell into a cold, restless sleep. Dreams troubled me—ugly visions of men running here and there, of fighting and anger and strife. I woke to the sound of Lily's bellowing. The lamp had burned out and cast us into total darkness. "What's going on?" I asked Pearl. She scrabbled along the dirt floor like a rat.

"I can't find Lily! Why's it so dark? It ain't night yet, is it? Lily, oh, blessed baby, where are you?"

It was pitch black in the pit, the light from above as quenched as the lamp's flame. I dropped the blanket from my shoulders. My face and hands were pricked with heat, my back and armpits drenched in perspiration. My hair drooped heavy and damp over my face and shoulders. "Something's wrong," I said. "Something's happened. I can't breathe."

"I can't either. Where's Lily?"

On all fours, I groped in the darkness for Lily. My hands knocked against Pearl's, and our heads cracked together. The stuffy air lodged in our lungs and left us muddled and clumsy. At last, I found Lily amid a wet tangle of blankets. Handing her to Pearl, I said, "We have to get out of here."

But the mouth of the pit was blocked. "My God," I cried. "Somebody's put something over the hole!"

The weight was solid, and it scratched against my hands, making them itchy and raw. It gave as I slapped my hands against it, but remained firmly planted over the pit. Hand over hand, I tried to slide it from the hole. It would not budge.

Balanced on a narrow rung of the ladder, I pushed against the bundle with my shoulders, my chin against my breast. The air seemed even ranker up here, and my gasps grew louder and more desperate. At last, the weight gave and a small corner of light appeared. My arms aching, I punched my way through and into the tent. Scrambling up, I heaved myself out the mouth of the pit.

"It's the mattress," I cried, as I reached the fresh air above. It had slipped from Alex's cot and fallen over the trap door. Yet surely, a mattress filled with straw was not that heavy. Crawling forward, I found that the bureau had tipped and pinned the mattress solidly in place.

My arms burning with pain, I folded the mattress back, so that it cleared the mouth of the pit. "Come over by the steps," I yelled to Pearl. "Stand up and hold Lily up, too." Sinking down, I jammed the mattress against the bureau and tried to catch it somehow on a corner. At last, the ticking caught on a sharp edge of metal.

Dazed and exhausted, I sprawled on the tent floor, half-sitting, half-lying, my thoughts thick and slow. The light in the tent was brilliant and orange with sunset. Around me, things lay shattered by bullets. Pieces of the shaving mirror on the bureau spilled across the floor, and the chimney pipe hung disjointed above the stove. Alex's bed tilted toward me, two of its legs shot out from under it. The canvas of the tent seemed made of tatted lace.

But I heard no gunfire, no shouts or screams.

"Christian!" Pearl called. "Where'd you go?"

"I'm all right! I'll be back in a minute."

Yet I could not bear the thought of crawling back into the pit, of breathing air that reeked of dirt and damp and our own fear. What if the whole tent collapsed over our heads? We would be smothered under that bulk of canvas.

I willed myself to go back down into the pit, to check on Pearl and Lily, and yet I did not move. My arms and legs were petrified and could no longer obey my brain. The light faded to gray as the sun dropped over the mesas in the west. Minutes later, it was dark.

Something banged against the tent door. "Anyone home?" a voice called. I cringed and scurried toward the pit, fearing that the soldiers had come into Ludlow, to loot and gather prisoners. The door opened just as I latched onto the ladder.

A hand touched my shoulder. "Are you hurt?"

It was Mrs. Jolly, the nurse who I'd helped at the hospital tent so long ago. With her was Louis Tikas, his face shadowed in the half-light. He seemed as surprised to see me as I was to see him.

"Why are you here?" I cried. "Is it Theros?"

He squatted beside me. "We are going tent to tent." He squeezed my shoulder. "No, he's not here."

Clutching his arm to steady myself, still feeling as if my lungs were empty, I gasped for air, my head swirling.

"Miss Scott," Mrs. Jolly said. "Are you all right?"

I tried to calm myself. "The mattress fell over the hole, and we were having trouble breathing. I'm just dizzy."

"Who else is here?"

"My friend and her baby."

"You need to get out," Louis said. "You need to go to the arroyo, then to the Bayes Ranch. That's where the women are going."

"She's not well," I said. "She had a baby just a few days ago."

"It isn't safe here. The soldiers could come into the tents."

"Where are the men?"

"They have run out of ammunition." He looked at the ruptured canvas walls, the shards and splinters on the floor. "Come, help me with her."

He lowered himself into the pit and brought out Pearl, then lifted Lily up to Mrs. Jolly. Pearl had wrapped my mother's tartan around her. She clutched it to her breast and looked about wildly, as if she had never seen me before. Trembling, she sank to the floor.

"She got too chilled in the pit, I think," I said to Mrs. Jolly. Then confusion overtook me. "Or too warm. We had too little air, and we couldn't breathe. The mattress and bureau—"

Quickly, Mrs. Jolly looked over Pearl and Lily. "Neither one is injured," she said to Louis. To me, she added, "We can only take gunshot victims to the hospital tent right now. I'm sorry."

"You must go to the Bayes," Louis said. "Now. Leave now." In the distance, someone shouted, and shots pounded once more. "Come on, come on!"

With Lily in my arms, we followed them out the door. Louis and Mrs. Jolly bolted toward the next tent as Pearl and I turned north toward the arroyo. At once, she reeled backward toward the tent.

"I can't do this!" she cried. "Christian, I can't make it!"

"You have to." With a merciless grip on her wrist, I dragged her with me. She stumbled along beside me, her hand pressed to her belly.

"Christian," she moaned.

Rousted out of their tents, women and children crammed into the avenue. Near us, a mother grabbed a screaming child around the waist and ran. The child's shoes shook off and landed in the path before us.

"Get back in your tents," a man raged from a nearby tent. "Get back in your pits! My boy's been killed—shot in the head! Get down! Get down!"

His words caused panic. Some of the women sought the shelter of the tents, nearly trampling their children in their haste. At once, the marksmen on Water Tank Hill picked up the commotion and began to shoot.

"Behind here!" I cried, pushing Pearl down behind a water barrel. She bowed over, head in her hands. Lily wailed, and I put my hand on her mouth.

For a time, I could hear nothing but the pounding of my heart. Even the beating of the machine guns was drowned out by the sound of my ragged breathing, and Lily's whimpering, and Pearl's moaning. The searchlights swept over the colony, and shots shattered a nearby cart. Pearl buried her head in my lap as wood splinters sprayed over us.

The searchlights moved on, and we ran out again into the deepening night. As we rounded the next tent, we dropped to our knees behind a woodpile while the beam trailed over them again. But this time, the light lingered.

"Get down lower!" I breathed. "They see us!"

I crouched over Pearl and Lily to shield them from the bullets. Expecting the wood to burst apart behind me at any moment, I nestled my face against Lily's blanket. They were waiting for us, I knew, waiting for our fear to grow so great that we would rush out into the open, like spooked rabbits. Then they would unleash a full barrage of fire on us.

"Take Lily," I whispered to Pearl. She jostled the baby back into her arms.

Slowly, I crawled to the edge of the woodpile and peered around it. Not more than five feet away lay a dead man, spread-eagled on the ground. His face had been blown into a pulp of blood by the bullets. The ray of the searchlight rested on him. "Oh, my God," I breathed.

"What?" Pearl asked. "What is it? Soldiers?"

"No," I said. "Don't look." But my stomach heaved, and I vomited onto the dirt.

All at once, a low thunder rose above the gunfire, and I thought of the Death Special, come to take the living to a grim fate. But then, a familiar screech ripped through the air. It was the evening freight from Denver.

The locomotive rolled past, then squealed to a stop, squarely planted between Water Tank Hill and the tents. The engines pulsed lazily as the engineers took on water and coal. Shouting echoed through the night, the words lost but the sentiments clear—someone was ordering the conductor to move the train. "Come on!" I took Lily from Pearl. "It's our only chance."

We cut a jagged, haphazard path through the narrow, clotted alleys between tents. A meat rack gashed my face, and I stumbled, but kept running. At last, we slid down the slick path into the arroyo. Losing my footing, I rolled the last few feet, with Lily snug against me. On the sandy bottom, Pearl dropped to her knees, her strength gone.

"Over here!" someone grunted. "Come here!"

Blindly, I followed the sound, unable to see who was speaking. Someone grabbed me and pulled me into the shadows of the ravine, where several strikers had gathered, their dark coats buttoned tight to hide their light-colored clothing, their faces dabbed with charcoal and grease. Women and stunned children clung like rooted plants to the sandy walls of the cliff. A second striker lifted Pearl and brought her to safety. Her arms hung limp, and her head lolled against his shoulder. I reached for her hand and squeezed it in mine.

"We're out of Ludlow," I whispered. "We're safe."

More than a hundred women had taken refuge at the Bayes Ranch, a mile away. Barricaded in a towering, drafty barn, we waited, our clothes torn or caked by mud, our hands, elbows and foreheads scraped and bruised, our ankles and shins swelling from the jabs of yucca and cholla. Pearl sank into a limp heap on the thick straw in one corner, fully spent by the long journey down the arroyo. I sat beside her with Lily, my arms numbed from cradling the baby for so long. Almost at once, women assailed me, begging for news about friends, husbands and children.

"Did you see the Costas?" a woman pleaded. "None of them are here, not one. Not Cedi or the kids, not Charlie."

"I don't know them," I said. "I'm sorry."

There was no food in the barn, and no blankets or bedding. The only warmth rose from the breath and bodies of a herd of milk cows, penned in one corner, and a few horses, who whinnied wildly and kicked at the walls of the stalls, unnerved by the weeping, ragged mob outside. A single lamp flickered thinly in the back of the barn, its light veiled from the militia's scopes.

Two wide-eyed, weeping women rushed forward to embrace Pearl, rosaries clutched in their hands. Pearl's face shone ghastly pale and sweaty in the dim light of the barn. She lay motionless, her hands splayed beside her. Her forehead burned beneath my fingers.

"Your fever's up again," I whispered, alarmed. "Way up."

"I'm so cold, I can't have no fever."

She was still clad in a coat and my mother's tartan, but I shed my coat and laid it over her. "Go to sleep. You'll be better tomorrow."

She seemed to sleep deeply, almost at once. Her breathing was heavy, harsh, her brow and hairline washed over by perspiration.

Cuddling Lily, I went to a nearby window and tried to see beyond the gritty dust and bird droppings on the pane. What would happen, now that we'd been chased from our homes, now that our men had had to forfeit the fight? I thought of the speeches of Mother Jones and John Lawson that we'd heard in September—ages ago—and the hours we'd spent singing and picketing at the gates of the colony, the proud parades we'd held. And then, I thought of the guns I'd given the Greeks. My God, it wasn't enough, it would never have been enough. What a fool I was not to see that.

"Missus, please." Anton stood behind me, his face smeared with grease and dirt, lined by grim weariness. "Theros." He pointed toward a high hayloft.

"He's here?" I cried. "Take me to him!"

I settled Lily with one of the women, then followed Anton up a long, steep ladder. In the loft, loose hay drifted away from a wide path down the center. At the far end, the weak light of the moon shone through the open outer doors. Men sat in the hay, their hands idle in their laps. Some slept, arms thrown over their heads or hugged around their chests, their hands planted in their armpits for warmth. A dozen or so strikers clustered near the loft doors, their wary eyes set Ludlow.

Theros rested his right shoulder against a post, his eyes closed. The left shoulder of his shirt was blackened by blood, and his greatcoat lay over his legs. I ran to him and knelt beside him. His face was as hot and sticky as Pearl's.

He opened his eyes. "Your face is cut."

I'd forgotten about the slash from the meat rack. I touched it and felt the roughness of dried blood. "What happened?"

"A bullet catches my neck. It is not so bad."

But pain blanched his face. Long, deep hollows ran down his cheeks, as if his face were carved from some dark wood. The fingers of his right hand sought my hand, gripping it so violently that my wrist throbbed. I covered his hand with my own.

"Your hands are so cold," he whispered. "You have no coat?"

"I left it with Pearl," I said. "Let me see your neck."

Gingerly, I peeled away the ragged, stained collar of his shirt. Below his left ear, the skin at the base of his neck was flayed and bloody. He hunched forward, gasping in agony. My hands shook so badly that I was afraid of causing him more pain. When I took them away, my fingers were tinged with blood. Desperately I looked around the barn, hoping for help.

"I think it breaks my neck bone," he said. "My arm does not move."

In the dim light, I could not explore the wound. "Is the bullet still in it?"

"I don't know."

"Oh, God, Theros," I whispered.

"I am stupid to get shot. I know better! Keep my head down, don't lift my shoulders so high, but this bullet hits me—"

"Don't. Just rest—"

"And now, we can't fight no more. We have no bullets."

"You need a doctor. Has anyone cleaned this?"

He jerked away from me. "I need bullets. I need to fight. They slaughter us like Turks kill Greeks."

"Be quiet," I said. "Don't move around so much—"

"We must stop them!"

I sat back on my heels, tears slipping from my eyes. "Let me take care of you. Let me help you. I can wrap it, I can clean it."

"What good does that do? I will not be able to shoot, to stop them, to keep Ludlow—" He twisted away from me, overcome. I put a hand on his right arm to still the sorrowful quaking of his body. With another violent spasm, he pulled me to him, my head in the hollow beneath his neck.

Around us, men spoke in deadened voices. A few cleaned or fiddled with guns, and some smoked guardedly, shielding the cigarette's glow from sight, lest it attract a bullet. Here and there, wives clung to their husbands or tended mute, watery-eyed children.

The cry of a man at the open doorway suddenly split the night. "Holy Mother of God!"

Theros lurched, working to aright himself. I helped him to his feet, knocking the greatcoat aside and hoisting him upward with my arm around his waist. He staggered to the door, his left arm locked against his ribs. Together, we looked toward Ludlow.

Flames ripped through the darkness, and thick, black smoke curled into the night sky.

"They're burning the tents!" shouted a man who peered through field glasses. "Sweet Jesus, they're dousing them with oil! Bastards! Look, see for yourself!" He thrust the binoculars into the next man's hands, and they passed slowly from one to another.

I clutched Theros' arm. "There are women still in the tents," I whispered. "Someone told them to go back and they did. I saw them."

"We have no bullets," Theros mourned. "We cannot fight."

The flames leapt from tent to tent. The tinder-dry canvas crumbled like paper, and frames gave way and crashed to the ground.

"Oh, God," I said. "I can't watch."

I turned into Theros' shoulder and hid my face against his chest. He brought his right hand up and clutched the side of my head, his arm pressing me against him, but his body wavered, as unsteady and wracked by grief as my own. I could not see, but I could hear—the distant shouting of soldiers, the mad shrieks of dogs chained among the tents, and the faint, piercing whine of screaming.

After what seemed like hours, Theros spoke.

"It is done."

Chapter 31

I stayed in the loft, lying with Theros under his greatcoat. His skin felt clammy to the touch, and tremors ravaged his body. Pressing myself against him, I hoped to bring back warmth, to stop the raging cold in his body. He moaned in his sleep, words I did not know. Yet late in the night, he reached for me. I clasped his hand and kissed his knuckles, holding it against my cheek.

"I don't want to die," he whispered.

"You aren't going to die. We'll find a way to Trinidad, to Dr. Beshoar—"

"Who knows? No one knows when he dies."

I kissed his palm. "I'm here. Don't think this way."

"I am afraid I will be a coward," he said. "Because I don't want to die. Maybe I won't fight hard enough, maybe I won't be smart enough—"

Reaching for his face, I felt tears mingling with the dampness of fever. "You'll live and be a father. And a husband. You'll live to be with me."

Around us, men stirred restlessly through the loft, their voices at times sad and faltering, at others jagged with anger. After Theros had fallen into a broken sleep, I rose and went again to the loft door. The smoke of Ludlow still bruised the night sky. Climbing down the ladder, I sought to check on Pearl. She rested yet on the straw, her face nearly buried beneath my coat. A few feet from her, a young mother nursed Lily along with her own baby.

"Is she any better?" I whispered.

The girl shook her head. For a long time, I sat beside Pearl. A lock of her hair, grown nearly to her waist, had strayed from beneath the coat. I let the curl lace around my finger and settle in my palm.

Near dawn, a freezing rain fell and doused the embers on the prairie. Grimly, the men sloughed off sleep and gathered their coats, their packs, and their guns. Theros struggled to his feet, leaning heavily on me. Overnight, his neck muscles had tightened so that he could barely move his head. With Dimitrius' help, I fashioned a sling for Theros' left arm from a raggedy grain sack, then helped him to slide his right arm into his greatcoat. Buttoning it across his chest, Anton looped an empty bandolier over Theros' head, which followed the same path as the sling. Theros nearly toppled under the weight of the leather.

I tied his red bandana, stiffened by dried blood, around his neck and tucked it around his collar. Touching his haggard, blood-parched face, I kissed him goodbye.

"You will find me?" he asked, his voice harsh. "We will find each other when this is over. We will be together then?"

I did not answer, afraid I would cry or beg him to stay. At last, I bobbed my head a couple of times. His eyes misted, and then he blinked, and looked straight ahead, beyond me.

One-handed, he crawled down the loft ladder into the barn, slower and weaker than any other man. I climbed down after him, then watched as the army slipped through the door and out into the deep gray light, destined for the Black Hills east of Ludlow.

Downstairs, most of the women slumbered, their children tucked beside them like so many chicks under a mother hen. The spot where I had left Pearl was abandoned—Pearl, Lily, and the other women were gone. I supposed they had sought warmer quarters near the back of the barn, near the animals' stalls. Yet I hadn't the strength to seek them out. My limbs aching and my head clouded, I lay down and fell into a cold, numb sleep.

When I woke, the sun had risen, and the heavy-uddered milk cows were lowing in distress, awaiting a milking. Shaking off the drowsiness of so little sleep, I wandered through the barn, searching for Pearl. Around me, women grumbled into wakefulness, and their children awoke, famished. To stave off her baby's howling, a woman cornered a cow and milked it furiously, then let children scoop steaming milk from the bucket and into their mouths. Others did the same, until nearly the whole herd had given up its milk.

As more women woke, the news of the burning of the tents spread. Sorrow filled the barn—from those who crumpled into tears and wailed, to those who raged against the militia, to those who tried to sing union songs in brittle, weary voices. Still others seemed too befuddled by cold and hunger and lack of sleep to care. Like the men in the loft, they sat with shoulders drooped, eyes dull, hair matted by dirt and straw, scarcely able to greet another day or whip themselves into the acts of living.

I circled once more around the animal stalls. With every step, my heart pounded faster, my breath became more choked. I stared into every face, hoping that Pearl had tied a borrowed scarf over her head or traded my coat for a heavier one. Frantically, I searched the dull grays, blacks and browns of the women's clothing for the cheerful colors of my mother's tartan.

At last, I saw my coat on one of the women who'd sat with Pearl the night before. Rushing to her, I asked, "Where's my friend? The one with the baby?"

"*Si, bambino,*" she said, then spoke rapidly in Spanish.

"I'm sorry," I said. "I don't know—"

"She scare." She waved her hands. "*El fuego del infierno.*"

"Fire?"

"*Si, si.* She is . . . oh, no! Cry. Sad."

A voice sounded behind me. "She woke up halfway through the night and started in yelling about fire. God knows what she was on about, but she was sure the fire was coming for her."

I turned toward a dark haired woman who stood with hands on her hips.

She spoke again. "She said something about going to see her baby's father. Where is he?"

"Trinidad."

"Why ain't he here, fighting with the rest of them?"

"He's in jail."

"Well, I told her it wasn't no time to go traipsing back through the tents, with the soldiers rampaging around like mad dogs. I tried to get her to just lay down and go to sleep. But she was tearing on so about getting back to him—and pretty soon, she wasn't to be found. I guess she headed toward town."

"Oh, no! She was feverish and worn out—"

"She was more than feverish," the woman said sourly. "She was crazy. All that's been going on, and she's screaming her head off and scaring every living creature in this barn."

"What about Lily? The baby?"

"She must of taken her along, I guess."

Wildly, I ran toward the door. A host of women lingered near it, peering out in curiosity and fear. I shoved through them and fled down the path that led to the arroyo.

"Where are you going?" someone called. "Come back! You'll be shot!"

The gully walls were not nearly as steep at the Bayes Ranch as they were in Ludlow, and I rushed down them without tripping. Voices begged me to stop, but I tramped through the wet sand, heading toward the burned tents.

As I scrambled up the steep, well-trodden path to Ludlow, a terrible sight greeted me. Where once had stood one hundred and fifty tents, the earth lay scorched and black. A throat-stinging smoke rose from smoldering piles of clothing, bedding and coal and flooded my lungs at every breath. Charred tent frames, chimneys and bedsteads poked up through gray ash like broken bones. Cinders floated up to my face and pricked my skin and eyes with quick, sharp stabs. Wheezing, I trod a tortured path between bicycle frames and baby prams, tins of flour spilling white across black soot, singed washtubs, half-burned water barrels. On the stoves, pots still held sodden, ash-strewn oatmeal and barley, as if the families might return at any time.

The ashes crusted on my stockings and skirt, flecked my hands and face, and caught in my hair. I came to the flagpole that had once marked the public meeting square. The American flag dropped heavily, its red and white stripes seared black by flame, and half of the Ludlow flag had burned away. For some time, I could not think which way to go to find Tent No. 18, our tent. Wending along a southward path, I counted the pits dug into the ground. At last, I came upon a cot that bore some resemblance to Alex's, with two legs shot out from under it.

But I could not remember—could not even imagine—what had once stood in the place of that pile of rubbish. What had our tent looked like, where had its walls met ground to shield us from the wind, where had the door hung on its flimsy frame? We had lived in that tent—our bodies jammed together, our every movement pinched and strained, our words heard by others far beyond the canvas walls—for nearly nine months. I had celebrated my wedding night there, and Lily was born there. And yet, I could not see anything but the ashes, the charred lumber of the frame, the black marks of the fire's rage over the mouth of the pit. My memories had vanished along with the canvas.

I knelt down near the pit. With effort, I called, "Pearl! Pearl!" Nothing answered me but a dull echo. I swiped at my nose, so crusted now by ash that I could barely breathe, and rubbed gritty hands across my eyes, then started down the ladder.

"Hey!" someone shouted. "Hey, you aren't supposed to be out here. Come on! Get out! This is a military zone."

For a moment, I saw nothing in that bland expanse of dead earth. At last, the soldier—no more than ten feet from me—waved his arms.

"You could be shot dead—they're looking for strikers, you know," he said. "Doesn't matter if they're man, woman or child."

"I'm looking for my friend and her baby," I said. "She may have come back into Ludlow last night, I think, on her way to Trinidad. She was wearing a Scottish tartan—"

"Nobody's supposed to be here. Come on, you have to go to the depot."

He grabbed me by the arm and escorted me over the smoldering heaps of charcoal, moving forward even when my shoes sank in the soft ashes or I veered to avoid live embers. At the depot, a tattered band of strikers, women and children who'd been prodded out of Ludlow's pits huddled on the benches and floors, like lumped sacks of grain.

The soldier pushed me down onto one of the benches. "Stay here," he ordered. "You're a prisoner of the Colorado National Guard."

I settled against the hard wood, hugging myself for warmth. A fire blazed in the stove at the far end of the room, but soldiers lounged around it, drinking coffee and telling tales, their bodies soaking up the heat. Two other women slumped on the hard bench beside me. One sat with hands folded in her lap, as if awaiting a schoolmarm's arrival, but the other, a Mexican woman, had wound a rosary so tightly around her fingers that the blood was pinched away. She coughed into a red neckerchief until she gagged.

Somewhere, a telephone rang, but no one answered it. The railroad ticket window was tightly locked, as if trains would never run through Ludlow again. Soldiers tramped in and out of the building, bringing reports to officers. Outside each window loomed the shadowy silhouette of a militia sentry, and the doors opened only on the command of a pair of guardsmen, one inside and one outside the entryway.

In a nearby corner, a man sat on the floor, rocking a long-limbed, bruise-faced boy in his arm. Blood stained the shoulder and arm of his coat, and he shed tears without shame. His loud voice seemed familiar to me as he pled with an officer to give him transport to Trinidad. I realized that he was the one who had warned the women to go back to their pits, whose son had been shot.

The boy in his arms was dead.

"Please," he begged. "I just want a decent funeral for him. He's only twelve, and he didn't know nothing about this strike—"

"That's enough, Mr. Snyder," the officer snapped.

"He just went out to get some milk," Snyder moaned. "His sister, she's only two, she wanted a drink, and he crawled up out of the pit to get some, and a bullet caught the back of his head—"

"That's too bad." The officer eyed the rest of us. "But you people have been asking for this."

I stepped forward. "I need to find my friend and her baby. She has long, black hair, and—"

"My babies!" The Mexican woman cried out. "Please, señor, please—"

"Keep still, all of you," the officer commanded, then stalked away to the end of the building.

I closed my eyes, but tears slipped from them. When Pearl had come to live with Alex and me, it had been in the darkness and rage of a storm. When she'd walked down the canyon to Ludlow, it had been in a silver cloud. How had she traveled this time? By shadow? By smoke? And why hadn't I been there to meet her at the end of her journey? I always had been before.

Mr. Snyder's voice cut through my thoughts. "I saw your friend. The one with the black hair."

"Yes," I cried. "Yes, that's her!"

"She was here." He rocked his son. "Early this morning, just after the sun came up. Pretty sick little gal, too—they had to carry her into the station."

"Where is she? Is she—?"

"She said she was looking for her husband."

"Oh, God! They didn't take her back to Berwind!"

"I don't know."

"What about the baby?" I demanded. "She had a baby."

"She had a baby with her, all right."

"But you don't know where she went? Did she go back to the tent colony, or toward Trinidad, or—?"

"I'm just telling you what I saw. I don't know anything more."

I jumped up and ran to the door. One of the soldiers caught me immediately, grabbing my arm. "Slow down," he said. "You're not going anywhere."

He pushed me back. I crumpled down on the nearest bench, my head in my lap.

We waited, never offered food or drink, never told of our fates. The sun dropped low in the sky, sending a yellow glow through the arched windows of the depot. Every time the door opened and closed, I willed myself to see Pearl's glorious hair and face, the sweet bundle holding Lily. Every time, I turned away, more heartsick than before.

At last, Lieutenant Karl Linderfelt entered the depot. His stout body draped in a flapping greatcoat, he strode briskly up to me. "Are you one of the women whose kids are missing?" he asked.

"No," I said. "I'm looking for my friend. She was wearing a Scottish tartan—"

"A what?"

"A plaid shawl, with red and green—"

"Where are the women whose kids are missing?"

From the other end of the bench, the two women rose. One stood tall and straight, but the other leaned into her, her breathing ragged.

"Have you found them?" asked the tall woman. "Have you brought them to me?"

"Who are you again?" Linderfelt asked.

"I'm Mary Petrucci."

The Mexican woman spoke, "Alcarita Pedragon."

"And you say your kids are still in Ludlow? Now, tell me, they were in the pit of which tent?"

"Which tent?" Mrs. Petrucci asked, as if the question had been posed in a foreign tongue.

"The number of the tent. You people had painted numbers on all of 'em, hadn't you?"

At once, her proud bearing crumbled. "Oh, God, I don't know. I don't know. We were in Tent No. 1 and we ran, but the bullets were coming so strong that we just crawled into the nearest tent. I don't know which one! I don't know!"

"The tent," Señora Pedragon rasped, her voice raw. "In it is Señora Costa and all her little ones. That tent. It is her tent. And Señora Valdez is there, too, and her babies."

"Well, why didn't you just get out?" Linderfelt asked. "Why'd you leave your kids behind?"

"I don't know! I don't know!"

Overcome by tears and coughing, she dropped down onto the bench. Lieutenant Linderfelt peered at her for a moment, then moved on, without any news or words of comfort for either of them.

Blindly, I rose and went toward the window. The smoking ruin of Ludlow shone gold in the twilight. I wondered how many lay in the pits, having breathed a mouthful of smoke in their last moments. If Pearl was in Berwind, at least she was alive.

"Listen up!" Linderfelt stood at the front of the depot, his hands cupped around his mouth. "Your attention! All you women and you folks"—he looked toward the Snyders—"are to be taken south of here and met by a union escort, somewhere near Suffield. The men remain military prisoners. Now, you need to go get yourselves on to that truck outside."

"But my babies," Mrs. Petrucci cried. "What about them?"

"What about my friend and her baby?" I demanded at the same instant.

"We'll arrange for prisoner releases as soon as we find the rest."

Haltingly, we shuffled toward the doors of the depot. Outside, a flatbed military truck had parked close to the platform. A soldier scurried around it, tying white flags on every loose bolt, wire or grill. Two troopers hoisted the children, women and the members of the Snyder family onto the truck, then thrust the dead boy into Mr. Snyder's arms. Along with two more guards, they leaped onto the truck with us, their bayonet-laced Springfields in their hands.

The truck rolled slowly forward, but was halted by another militia officer, who charged up from the direction of the tent colony. Before he reached the platform, he shouted, "Hey, Lieutenant! We found some folks in a pit. A couple of women and a whole bunch of kids! Even a little baby. Probably a dozen altogether."

Linderfelt shrugged impatiently. "Bring them in. We'll take them to Trinidad with the rest."

"God, no, sir. They're dead, every last one of them."

Mrs. Petrucci screamed, and Señora Pedragon jumped up, only to be wrestled back by one of the soldiers. I leapt from the truck and fell onto my weak ankle, but was caught as I collapsed into a heap. Annoyed, Linderfelt yanked my arm. "What the hell are you doing?" Roughly, he picked me up and loaded me back on the truck, then yelled at the driver, "Get 'em out of here."

A soldier clamped his arm around my waist. The truck sped away from the depot, the soldiers with sure grips on both Mrs. Petrucci and Señora Pedragon. Mrs. Petrucci fainted, falling roughly against the soldier's shoulder, but Señora Pedragon struggled.

"Stop it!" the soldier commanded.

At last, she broke loose, but instead of leaping from the truck, she threw herself down and rolled around the bed as it slogged and jolted over the muddy roads. Mr. Snyder wept, his arms wrapped around his son, too waylaid by his own sorrow to help. The others cowered, too afraid of the soldiers to move. With a jerk, I pulled away from the guard. Unsteadily, I crawled forward and put my hand on Señora Pedragon's back to keep her from slipping off the bed of the truck like a loose potato. "Shh," I whispered, holding her head in my lap. She sobbed without relief.

As Linderfelt had promised, a union truck waited for us at Suffield, bedecked in white flags. "Stay inside," one of the soldiers yelled at the union drivers. "Don't get out or we'll shoot." Two militiamen raised their Springfields, one sighting the women and the other aiming his gun at the drivers.

The soldiers hefted Mrs. Petrucci and Señora Pedragon, carrying them to the union truck and dumping them onto the empty bed. My guard pulled me along by my arm, then pushed me upward onto the bed. Herded by the soldiers, the others marched in a sorry, straggling line to the union truck and climbed aboard. The two strikers in the cab watched with angry eyes, but did not move.

"Go!" shouted the soldier.

White flags waving, the union truck raced toward Trinidad.

With every passing mile, I saw strikers crouched in ditches, gathered at road crossings, standing guard along the railroad tracks. I whipped my head around more than once, thinking I had caught a glimpse of a familiar dark face, or a greatcoat the same color as Theros'. The town of Trinidad was securely in the hands of the strikers, and the streets teemed with armed men in red bandanas. Castle Hall overflowed with souls from Ludlow and from the other tent colonies, who had come to town to share food, weapons and ammunition. At the door, a union secretary frantically wrote lists of the missing, the found and the dead. I gave my name, then told him of Pearl's and Lily's disappearance.

"They say there's a dead baby in one of the pits in Ludlow," I said. "Please, please, you must let me know if it's my friend's."

Mrs. Petrucci spoke after me, sobbing, "My babies—Frank, Lucy and Joe—they died in the pit under one of the tents." She gestured toward Señora Pedragon. "Her two little ones, too."

The union secretary winced. "I'm sorry," he said hopelessly. "I'm so sorry."

The meeting hall had been cleared to make room for the distraught and homeless. I sat on the floor, my hands idle, my thoughts vacant.

"Christian!" Mrs. McCormick bore down on me. "Oh, God, where have you been? Oh, isn't it awful, what's happened?" She wiped her eyes. "We were caught in the well all night. About seventy of us, just standin' on the ledges in there, waitin' for God to lift us out of harm's way."

I grabbed her arm. "Have you seen Pearl? She wandered away in the night, with Lily. I couldn't find either of them."

Her lip twitched, but her face softened in pity. "I haven't seen her. Listen, why don't you get yourself cleaned up. There's a box of clothes that the ladies of Trinidad brought in earlier—they've been right generous. See what you can find. You're so dirty, honey."

In the bathroom, I looked over the pitiful state of my clothes and skin. My hair was matted with hay and gray ash, my eyes ringed by soot, my hands mottled by dirt, dried blood and charcoal. The gash across my cheek was red, inflamed. I scrubbed at myself with the harsh soap I found, then splashed water on my hair, trying to root out the filth and tangles with my fingers. I dressed in a brown wool dress trimmed with white piping around the collar and cuffs. Too tight for me, the fabric scratched around my arms and neck.

Mrs. McCormick waited for me in the hall, holding a plate of cold meat, cheese and bread. A pitcher of milk stood on a nearby table. "There you go," she soothed. "Make yourself a sandwich."

My hands trembled as I tried to fold the meat into the bread and to sip the milk. I had not truly eaten since the Greek Easter, two days before.

As I forced the food into my mouth, she talked in a low, mournful voice. "Oh, it's a sad situation. No one knows where anyone else is, and the things they're sayin'! About soldiers bayonetin' the women and kids they found in the pits, and about the burned bodies out there on that plain—more than fifty of them, I heard. If all this is true, Christian, Lieutenant Linderfelt and that bunch of hooligans should be shot at daybreak. There's no other punishment good enough."

Her words sparked terror in me. "I didn't see any burned bodies," I choked. "And no one who had been bayoneted."

"You were in Ludlow?"

"Yes, I walked through. I was looking for Pearl."

"Good Lord, how did you survive? They say the militia guns are pickin' off anythin' that moves on that prairie." She lifted the pitcher and poured more milk for me. "Did you see any of the Costas? Everyone is talkin' about them. The whole family is missin'. The wife—her name's Cedi, I think—and kids were in one of the pits. They're still gone, and she's near to havin' another baby. Any day now, they're sayin'. And the father, Charlie—he organized for the Italians—was killed. Shot dead in the arroyo. They say he was singin' 'The Union Forever' when he died."

I started to speak, to reveal Cedi Costa's fate in the pit, but the food I'd eaten threatened to come up again, and my throat closed on a painful sob.

"And Louie the Greek is dead," Mrs. McCormick went on. "They say his body's all twisted up and torn apart by Linderfelt's men. He went to give himself up, thinkin' if he did, maybe the militia would lay off the tent colony. But they shot him in the back, just like that, even though he was carryin' two white flags. He's layin' out there on the prairie, too, guards all around him like he could still jump up and run off."

I burst into wrenching sobs, unable to speak, nearly unable to breathe. Mrs. McCormick patted my hair and tried to comfort me, but my cries grew louder, wilder, becoming the wails of a wounded animal. At last, one of the union officials came and took Mrs. McCormick and me to a small room, where sleeping rolls had been spread on the floor. He wrapped a blanket around my shoulders, then promised to bring hot tea. As he was leaving, he said, "I'll send the doctor, once he comes in."

I shook my head, knowing no doctor could heal me, but before I could speak, the room went dark and silent.

PART V

Well, I don't sing anymore. And my husband doesn't laugh as he used to. I'm twenty-four years old and I suppose I'll live a long time, but I don't see how I can ever be happy again. . . . But you're not to think that we could do any differently another time. We are working people—my husband and I—and we're stronger for the union than we were before the strike. . . . I can't have my babies back. But perhaps when everybody knows about them, something will be done to make the world a better place for all babies.
                 Mary Petrucci

Sound, sound the clarion, fill the fife!
To all the sensual world proclaim,
One crowded hour of glorious life
Is worth an age without a name.
                 Sir Walter Scott

Chapter 32

I woke to a vision, an angelic face smiling down at me, golden hair curling around her chin.

"Christian," she said. "It is you! Christian Scott!"

I closed my eyes. I wanted darkness, stillness, the silence of eternity. Dim, half-formed thoughts nagged at me—where was? what was? Voices arced into my ears, and my head banged as if an army was drilling on my forehead.

"Remember me?" the golden-haired girl said. "Ethel May Farrington? We were in school together in Berwind. Remember?"

"Where am I?" I asked, unsure that I spoke aloud.

She did not answer. "Remember how good we both were at math and elocution and writing? But you were smarter. You were always better than I was at everything."

"Where am I?" I asked again.

"You're in San Rafael," she said. "The hospital in Trinidad. They brought you here because you wouldn't wake up. You've been asleep for three whole days!"

Three days. Three days lost. Where was Pearl? Where was Theros? I tried to raise up on my elbows, but a dark slash of pain seared my head. I did not feel like I'd slept for three days. My bones and joints ached.

"Why are you here?" I asked Ethel May.

"I'm your volunteer nurse. The nuns are too busy to take care of everybody, so the ladies from town offered to help."

"Where's—?" But I could not recall any names, except Pearl, Theros, Alex, and I knew none of them were there.

"Dr. Beshoar has been here every day to see you," Ethel May said. "He's treating all the folks brought in from Ludlow. Some of them are pretty badly burnt or even shot. What happened out there was terrible. I feel so sorry for you all."

"I need to go," I said. "I need to go back to Ludlow."

"You can't. It's a war out there. There's all sorts of killing—"

I struggled upward. Ethel May helped me to stand, but my head whirled so badly that I grabbed the windowsill to hold myself up. I looked down the long corridor of the ward, at the shapeless lumps under the white bed sheets. Their faces seemed featureless, missing eyes, noses and mouths. I wanted to run along, ripping off the protective sheets, until I found someone—anyone—I knew. "All these people are from Ludlow?"

"I think so. Here, look out the window."

On the prairie beyond the hospital, people strolled, rushed along, gathered in knots. Horse-drawn wagons pulled heavy loads, and an automobile or two crept through the throng. Ethel May nodded toward the feverish activity. "That's where all the people who've come to fight are staying," she said. "It's where the militia camped last fall."

"Who's come to fight?"

"Oh, I don't know! They say men from all over America."

I squinted against the bright sunlight, trying to make out a familiar face or two in the men carrying lumber or the women walking with their children.

"Come back to bed," Ethel May said. "Oh, Christian, I'm so glad to see you! I wish you could have come to high school with me. The teachers in Trinidad are so much better than the ones in Berwind were. You'd be graduating with me next month and going on to teachers' college."

Her words jarred me. The order and routine of the schoolroom was so far from me, so foreign, now. Sitting at a desk, opening a book, reading a passage and writing on clean, perfect slate. Did I remember how to parse sentences, or to neatly copy sums, or to recite in a crisp and clear voice?

"Do you remember Theo Sky?" I asked.

"The Greek boy?"

I nodded, the words tender in my throat. "He's my husband."

"Oh," Ethel May mouthed. "You're so young!"

"And Pearl? The girl who came to school with me?"

She looked as if she wanted to escape.

"She just had a baby. It's my brother's."

"He's been here."

I clutched at the bedclothes. "What? Theros?"

Confusion flitted across her face. "Your brother. He was here last night."

"He's in jail."

"Maybe he escaped," she said with relish. "Now that the Colorado National Guard has been called back, the jails are so full with all the men they're bringing in from the battlefields that they've had to send some of them to the stables south of Trinidad."

So Alex was alive and well enough to visit me in the hospital. My eyes filled with grateful tears, and I closed them. "The militia's been called back?"

"General Chase arrived from Denver yesterday. But only a few of his soldiers came back with him. Most of them refused. They were too scared!"

A tent colony, General Chase, men hauled into jail in flocks—it was all too familiar. Had it all started over?

"Christian," Ethel May said. "Let me wash your hair. It's so dirty."

"All right," I said. "Please."

While she was gone, I stood and edged my way to the end of the bed, holding to the mattress for support. My brown dress and underthings were folded in a nice, clean bundle at the foot of the bed. I dressed as quickly as I could.

In the corner of the ward, a small, streaky mirror hung on the wall. I had not looked at myself in a mirror in weeks. In the colorless reflection cast by the dim metal, my face looked starved and hollowed out. Dark bands circled my eyes, and my hair hung in a shapeless, greasy tangle. I brought one hand up to caress the cheek that Theros had kissed so tenderly, but my fingertips were cold, the skin roughened by neglect.

The sun burned into my eyes as I left the hospital. Moving as if every muscle was bruised, I set out onto the streets of Trinidad, which were more crowded than ever. People wandered without purpose, clustering on street corners or before storefronts, oddly hushed, as if afraid to speak to one another, but equally afraid to be alone. No one took note of me, and I followed along, flowing listlessly toward nowhere.

From a second-story window at Castle Hall hung a wide, hand-painted banner that read UNION HALL. Below it fluttered the American flag, and beneath that, the blue and white flag of Greece. An unbearable fear bent my bones. Why had they displayed the Greek flag? For Louis Tikas, or for other Greeks who had met their deaths in the past few days? My God, how I wanted Theros, to feel his hand on my breast, to lie next to him, his legs heavy and hot on mine. I wanted to hear his voice, to see his smile, to watch his bear-like, clumsy hands as he lifted Lily from her cradle or untied a ribbon on my chemise.

I turned abruptly, jostling a woman behind me, and ran toward San Rafael.

The new tent colony straggled across the prairie east of Trinidad, pegged lopsidedly against the earth. Some of the tents were the brown, conical tents of the militia, the spoils of war. Many were just pieces of canvas tied to stakes. Water barrels, trash heaps, clothing lines tied to saplings or sagging poles—all the mess of living festered in the open alleys between tents.

Gone were the neat, exact rows of Ludlow, the orderly white tents with flaps tied back for the photographers, the proud, public square and baseball diamond and exercise bars, the defiant flagpoles with the flags of every nation. This ramshackle colony stretched for nearly a mile, winding itself around the creek and trees and patches of unwieldy scrub. Brutally, the sun beat down on the field.

Men ate from tins of beans and soup they'd opened with knives. Others shaved, played cards, or cleaned guns. In nearly every shaded spot, a man slept, his pack under his head and his gun firmly in hand. Women moved among them—wives with children, nurses with red crosses on their sleeves, church ladies in saucer-brimmed hats who read from the Bible, and social workers. Reporters and politicians from Denver lolled importantly near a white tent that was almost identical to the union office in Ludlow. It seemed the strikers of southern Colorado were suddenly worthy of notice.

Near the far edge of the encampment, a striker loaded a truck with water barrels and crates of ammunition. He hefted a barrel onto the bed, then let it roll forward into the care of another man. His red bandana fluttered at his neck.

"Please, sir!" I blurted. "Please, I need to go to Ludlow. Or

Berwind."

"Berwind!" He pushed back his hat and wiped his sleeve across his sweaty mouth. "Why in the world would you go there?"

"My friend might be there. She's ill, and I need—"

He squatted down. "Listen, honey," he said. "You can't get to Berwind. You can't go to any one of the camps. They're all under attack."

"But this truck—"

"Goes as far as the Black Hills. Any closer to Ludlow and we'd be dead." He wrestled another barrel across the bed. "Hasn't anybody told you? General Chase and his gang are back in town, and now no strikers are allowed north of Suffield. You can't get within a mile of Ludlow."

"So the militia has taken over the colony?"

"To investigate, they say." He laughed bitterly. "More like to hide whatever they can. But, take heart. We've dug trenches up on the mesas, so we can pick off those sons of bitches. And six mines are burning up in the canyons, and the smoke is enough to choke the devil himself."

"Is Berwind burning?"

He did not hear me. "And in Aguilar, you know where that is? North of Ludlow? Well, a bunch of our boys have chased the superintendent and his wife and kids and a few other company men inside the mine. They've been holding them down there by dropping dynamite down the air vents every so often. And in Walsenburg, our boys are just sitting on the ridges around the town, just waiting for anyone in a Colorado National Guard uniform to be foolish enough to walk down the street. So, you see, it's a hell of a fight. And it ain't no place for a woman."

"Please," I implored again.

He heaved the barrel onto the truck and rolled it to his partner. "Load up and let's go!"

"Where are the Greeks?"

He waved a hand to the east. "Camped over there, close to that cottonwood tree. They've taken up the whole place. A couple hundred of them came in from Raton last night."

"Raton?" My head ached. "No, I'm looking for the Ludlow Greeks." I searched my mind for their names, but Theros was the only one I could find.

"Yeah, and a gang of them are up from Texas, too. There's more than three hundred of them camped over there. They're here to revenge old Louie the Greek—"

"Louis Tikas."

"There's a hundred Italians from Denver here, too," he went on. "To fight for that Italian, Charlie Costa, whose wife and kids died in that pit. And a couple of hundred of all sorts from the northern coalfields. John Lawson published the Call to Arms, and they've come from every crick and corner in America. Don't you worry, honey. We'll get even. Every time there's a battle, we're yelling, 'Remember Ludlow.'"

He opened the door of the truck and stepped in. "Now you need to get somewhere safe. Just like anywhere there's men, there's some characters here you don't want to get mixed up with. But if you want to help, they sure do need someone to cook over at Union Hall—you know where that is? Find the Red Cross ladies. They'll tell you what to do."

The truck roared away and left me in a cloud of exhaust. Hot wind blasted sharp bits of dust around my ankles. My woolen dress rubbed against my skin, making it sweaty and itchy. So much had happened, so much had changed. How did so many men come to be here? Where had they been before?

I limped along a jagged path toward the cottonwood tree. Soon the skin of the faces I passed grew swarthy, the black hair coarse and thick, and I heard the rolling rhythm of Theros' language. Too desperate to be afraid, I looked directly into their eyes. How I wished I'd learned Greek. I knew only a few useless words—honor, leader, great happiness. I could not ask where he was, could not beg anyone to help me find him.

The flap of a tent blew up in front of me and slapped at the sky. Inside lay a bedroll, a tin cup and rifle. Behind me, the Greeks had gone back to playing cards, their interest in me waning. I slipped into the tent.

When I came out, my hair was stuffed under an old hat, my hands were hidden in the long sleeves of a shirt and coat, and my clothes were wrapped in a tight bundle with the mug and a packet of bullets. Gripping the rifle in one hand, I strode to the spot where the union trucks were loading. Keeping my gaze on the ground, I hoisted myself up on to the bed of a truck jammed with men and water barrels and crates just as it roared out of Trinidad.

The driver did not follow the roads, but cut across open ground and bounced through ditches, the truck's chassis shrieking as it raked the scrubby brush of the prairie. Every bump thrust my body against the splintery wood siding of the truck. Barrels tipped and threatened to roll over my feet. The crates shifted and were shoved back by the men crammed into the tiny nooks between. I kept the brim of the hat pulled low, one hand on it so that the wind did not whisk it away. No one bothered me. No one even spoke to me.

The truck stopped in the shadow of the Black Hills, on the eastern side of Ludlow, far from the canyons of Berwind and Delagua. The place was a makeshift supply depot, with barrels and crates and trash heaps scattered through the scrub and sage. Probably fifty men waited there for food, water and ammunition. Once the truck stopped, they rushed forward, wrestling the supplies from the bed as quickly as they could. I slid off the bed and worked my way over to a jumble of empty crates.

Suddenly, someone ripped off my hat. My hair fell heavy onto my shoulders. I cried out, afraid.

"Christian! Good God!"

Alex stood before me, his face pale and gaunt, his rust-colored hair matted with dirt. "What are you doing?" he demanded. "Why are you here?"

He grabbed my arm, wrenching my shoulder, pulling me back toward the truck. I struggled against him, trying to unlatch his vise-like fingers. His words raked over me. "How did you get here? Why aren't you in Trinidad? My God—!"

"Listen to me," I pleaded.

"Take her back to Trinidad!" he shouted at the driver.

Every eye fell on me, every hand that had been moving a box or barrel fell still, every grunted word died in the air. The driver stared at me, motionless, disdain spreading over his face.

"Please," I begged. "Pearl's missing. Lily, too. The baby."

His grasp on my arm tightened. "I know that!" he roared. "Why do you think I'm here? I'm not good for anything else!"

"We have to find her, Alex. We have to get to Berwind."

"Come on!" The driver of the truck shouted. "They'll start shootin' if we don't get out of here quick!"

"If you send me back, I'll just find another way," I threatened. "I'll get there somehow."

His face twisted, caught in indecision.

"Please," I whispered.

"Go!" he barked at the truck driver. The man climbed into the cab, gunned the motor, and backed away. The smell of exhaust trailed into the wind as the truck sped away over the prairie.

"Sit over there," Alex said roughly.

I sat on a pile of crates, my head aching with fatigue. After a few minutes, Alex came to sit beside me, anger snarling in his eyes. He shot edgy looks around him, as if daring someone to try to harm me or even to mention me. I wanted to tell him I wasn't afraid, that he didn't need to be afraid for me, but my throat closed up, parched and tense.

Around us, men loaded empty bandoliers with bullets, filled canteens, and jammed flour sacks loaded with food into their pockets and packs. Almost every man carried a gun, and boxes of ammunition were tipped over, spilling bullets into the sandy soil. I thought of the few guns I'd brought into the tent colony, of how prized and precious they were, how coveted by the Greeks. How jealous Alex had been of them.

"How did you get out of jail?" I asked.

"They dumped us out." He held the rifle up to his eye. "The morning after Ludlow burned, they unlocked the doors, told those who could still walk on their own to get out. Carried out the rest, left us on Main Street in Trinidad. Some of them headed direct for Ludlow. I couldn't—"

I picked at the buttons on my shirt, sweat pricking around my neck. "I'm so sorry, Alex. I never meant for you—"

"It doesn't matter."

"Where did you get a gun?"

"All you do is show up willing to fight for the UMWA and they give you one." Bitterly, he added, "We've plenty of friends, now. Supplies are coming in every day, from as far away as West Virginia. Food, ammunition, guns—you name it."

He listed away to fill his pockets with bullets, his left foot splaying. His weight was heavy on his heel, as if he were trying to grind a cigarette butt into the ground. When he came back to sit beside me, he stretched out his leg, letting the foot fall inward. He rubbed his knee, a gesture that seemed to be automatic.

"No one ever saw to your foot?" I asked.

"It's healing as it is."

I said no more. Was this what was left of him, this bitter, hard husk? He had not offered one word of gratitude or relief that I was safe, that we had both, somehow, survived. He had not mentioned that he had visited me in the hospital, or expressed any surprise that I was awake again, and whole.

He had not asked about Pearl or Lily.

"Kirstie girl!" Uncle John stood to my right, James at his side. "Holy Mother of God, lass, what are you doing here? Why, the last time we heard of you, you were in hospital, near to death. Edith said they feared you might never come out of it."

"I woke up just this morning."

"What was it, then? Fever or the shock of it all?"

"I don't know."

"Aye, well, praise be to God that you've come back to us," Uncle John said. "Are you comin' with us, Alex?"

"I'll stay," Alex said gruffly. "You go on. I'll see her back to town tomorrow, and then come and find you."

James eyed me with distaste. "We're headed toward Forbes."

"I'll find you."

They strode away, swinging their packs onto their shoulders. Alex watched them go with a cold, empty envy. He whipped a greasy rag from his pocket to polish his rifle, his movements jerky and rough. The sun had started to set, burning orange in the sky before it slipped behind the mesas in the west and disappeared.

"What happened to Pearl?" he demanded. "Why weren't you with her that night?"

"Theros—my husband—had been shot. I went to tend to him—"

His next question cascaded from his mouth before I'd finished speaking. "Why did you marry him? Are you in a family way? Who is he, anyway? What would he want with you?"

"He loves me! I love—"

"You turned us into a laughingstock. Oh, I heard stories when I was in jail. The redhead in Ludlow, they said. Si, they said, or Ja, or whatever gibberish they spoke. We know that one. The one who walks with the Greek, and talks to him, and doesn't even bother to hide it that they're sneaking out of Ludlow to—"

"No one would have thought anything of it if he wasn't Greek."

He ignored me, too angry to argue. "You made a fool of me, you and your secrets."

"Alex," I pleaded. "We're alive." I swallowed back the bile that rose in my throat. "When Pearl and I left Ludlow, we didn't know if we'd even reach the arroyo. There was a man lying on the ground who'd been shot—it was so awful. And at the station the next day, there was a father holding his little boy, who'd been shot in the head—"

"And where was I? In jail, where I couldn't do a thing about any of it."

"I would have confessed, Alex," I said hotly. "I would have told them—"

"Stop." He leaned forward, his elbows on his knees. Looking out at the men who still loitered around the depot, smoking or eating, or just lounging against the heaps of rubbish, he said, "I was in that jail for so long. I know it was only—what?—three weeks, but every second in that place became an hour, every instant a year—"

He faltered, and I laid my hand on his shoulder.

"Every question I'd ever asked myself, everything I'd ever wondered, I asked it and answered it again and again and again, in a thousand different ways, until I didn't know what was true and what was my own folly anymore." He coughed, cleared his throat, and spat. "And I think I talked myself into believing that when I got out, it would all have straightened itself out. It would have ended, and Ludlow would be just a bad dream."

The evening wind blew through the camp, swirling cigarette papers and tin can labels around our feet. I pulled my jacket closer around me. The air nipped, growing colder with night, but no one moved to build a fire.

Alex drew in a wheezing breath. "And you and Pearl—I don't know. I think I convinced myself that all the problems would go away. There'd be no baby. There'd be no Russell Ruddy, or Jake, or any of them to peck away at Pearl's heart. There'd be no Greek, and you'd be just my sister again."

"But Lily is beautiful, Alex," I said. "She's so sweet. And Theros"—I stopped, then pressed on, deciding not to spare his pride—"he loves her so much. He would hold her for hours, just like you will, Alex, when we find them."

He looked at his hands, his brow wrinkled and tender. I could tell that he wanted to give in, to let himself feel again, to hope again.

"We will find them," I said again.

"How?"

"If we can find Theros and . . . and the other Greeks, we can get to Berwind."

"Greeks again—"

My annoyance overflowed. "They've spent months now on the mesas, learning every twist and turn in those canyons. They know how to move without being seen or caught."

"Why do you think she's in Berwind?"

I told him that Mr. Snyder had seen her in the train station. "She was confused and sick. She said she wanted to see her husband, but I'm sure she meant you. She may not have known where they were taking her."

"She better not have gone back to Russell—"

"Oh, for God's sake, Alex," I said. "Stop, just stop. Don't you see? Nothing matters anymore. Nothing! Except that we find each and hold onto each other—"

My words ended in a sob. Alex hung his head, staring at his hands. "I feel so helpless," he said. "I've not been in any place that I was needed for so long. Jesus God, how I have failed both you and Pearl—"

"It makes no difference now. All that matters is what happens today."

He looked defeated. "Aye," he said. "I'm afraid you're right."

"Let me tell you about Lily," I offered. "Your daughter."

He said nothing, but his hands were calm on his knees.

We talked until late in the night, sheltering next to a rocking jumble of crates. We ate from the flour sacks that had been sent out from Union Hall, and drank stale water dipped from a barrel. No fire was built for warmth or to cook, and the men who smoked crouched behind rocks and barrels to keep from being spotted. When I fell asleep, it was only with the wad of my dress for a pillow against the hard ground. I brought my knees to my chest, hoping to harbor some warmth in the curl of my arms and legs.

I woke in the morning when a warm hand covered the entire socket of my shoulder. For a moment, I could not remember where I was, or why I felt so stiff and bruised. The smell of the earth clung to me, dust and sage and the cold of the wind. When I rolled onto my back, I saw that the sky was the liquid gray of dawn.

Theros squatted beside me. In the near darkness, he looked hungry, worn, his eyes hollow and dark, as if he had gone for weeks without sleep. A dark beard clung to his cheeks. The left arm of his coat hung limp, empty.

"Someone says there is a woman in this place," he whispered. "I asked, is she dressed as a man? Because if she is, she is my wife."

I sat up, clasping his face between my hands. "Oh, you're here, you're all right—!"

"Ssh, you will wake them all."

I kissed him. "I don't think I could have lived another day without knowing you were alive."

"But why are you here?"

"Pearl and Lily are missing."

The sorrow of the long, bitter days washed over his face, and his eyes registered a deep, dire anguish. He glanced toward the east, where the sun had colored the horizon a milky yellow.

"Come on, then," he whispered. "We have to get back to the hills before it is light."

We climbed upward into the Black Hills. They were only scrubby, loaf-shaped mounds of earth, but rising as they did from the flatness of the prairie, they grew tall and solid. Nothing about them was soft or easy. Scrub, cactus and piñon snagged at our shoes, and the rock formations we shinnied up were grainy enough to scrape skin from my knuckles and wrists.

There were eleven in our group, all fully loaded with supplies from the depot below, all of them Greek, except for Alex and me. Alex trailed behind us, every step painful and difficult. I helped him through the roughest terrain, my heart aching as I remembered how as children we had scrambled up and down the mesas of Berwind.

He kept his head down, his thoughts to himself. He had shaken hands with Theros and the others, yet his eyes darted toward Theros again and again, trying to take the measure of the man.

The sun shone brightly by the time we came to a basin carved into the hillside by wind and water. A shelf of stone overhung a sandy spot that was fronted by massive boulders. Here was the Greek camp, a few bedrolls and broken crates that served as seats, and a circle of stones meant for fire, but cold and empty of ashes. About forty men waited there, Anton, Dimitrius and the others that I had known among them.

The men dropped their bandoliers and rifles, their sacks of food and canteens of water. Some of them crouched under the overhang, seeking shelter from the wind and lighting cigarettes. Others split flour sacks open with knives and dug ravenously into the dry, cold food packed by the women at Union Hall. A few stretched out on the ground, exhausted by the prowling patrol of the night before. With his good arm, Theros unpacked the supplies he'd brought. He had carried up as much as any other man in the camp.

Alex slid down with a rock behind his back, as far from the others as he could, and stretched out his left leg.

"Do you want me to take off your boot?" I asked.

"I won't be able to get it on again."

Theros brought us both breakfast—sausage wrapped in a biscuit and a cup of cold, brown liquid that was supposed to be, or had once been, coffee. We ate in silence, too tired to talk. After we ate, Theros beckoned me. "Come over here."

I glanced at Alex, as if I needed his permission, but he simply looked away. Theros and I rounded the boulders to a nook that was sheltered from the wind and hidden from the prairie below by an overhanging slab of sandstone. Theros crouched low, then sat with his good shoulder against the rocks behind him. I followed.

We both looked out toward Ludlow, our eyes reflexively, achingly, drawn to it. The blackened wreck of the tent colony sprawled in the bright morning sun, an open sore on the greening prairie. Chimney pipes and the hulks of furniture rose up like ancient ruins. Beyond the burned tents, locomotives stood idle, one after another, stalled by the fighting along the tracks or by lack of water or coal to fuel the journey.

The high mesas of Berwind and Delagua rose just to the west of Ludlow, the canyons hidden from view.

Theros pointed. "If you have field glasses, you can see Louis's body lying there. Along with dogs and horses." His voice ratcheted. "To do that to him—he is Greek, and to not honor his body, it is a sin in our country, terrible sin. They know that. But they shoot whenever the dead wagon comes to take him."

The memories of that night clattered in my head, and I hunched forward, my knees against my chest, my head laid on them. The morning sun had not yet breached the spot where we sat, and it was chilled and damp. I shivered, from cold, sorrow, loss. Theros laid his hand on my hair, gently stroking, his thumb tracing a path over my temple, and down my cheek to my jaw.

"Why aren't you in Trinidad?" he asked, all the tight, pent-up feeling rushing out in his words. "I have been thinking, she is safe, she can't be hurt. I can keep shooting and fighting because I know that. Then, this morning, when I saw you laying there, I was so angry. So crazy. I think, why does she do such a stupid thing? Why is she so bad? She wants me to look like a fool, so the men will laugh at me. Don't talk"—he silenced my protests—"So I stand around, and I think, what do I do with this woman who makes so much trouble for me?"

I held my breath.

"And then I think, I am the fool. Because I don't care. I don't care that she's here, I don't care that she's dressed like a man. I don't care that she doesn't act like proper wife. The others want me to punish her as Greek husband would. Send her away, back to her family, make her feel shame. But this is America. Where else would I find a woman so brave as this one?"

I choked, torn between laughter and tears.

"I think, this is what makes me love her like a man should love his wife. I am ready to fight for her, ready to die for her. Ready to do anything because of her."

I kissed his jaw, tears rolling freely from my eyes. He gathered me closer with his good arm.

"Where did you get these clothes?" he asked. "They are ugly."

Now, I laughed. I told him of San Rafael, of the hundreds of men camped there. "They've come to join in the fight," I said. "I walked through the entire colony without seeing a single soul I knew."

He snorted. "And they are there, drinking and playing cards, and we are here." He motioned for me to help him with his coat. "Help me. I am like a baby, I cannot dress myself."

As I slid it from his left shoulder, he groaned. His shirt was only partially buttoned, one sleeve hanging useless. A clean, white bandage wrapped around his shoulder, swooped down around his ribs and pinned his arm to his chest. He could not move it more than a couple of inches.

I fingered the soft cloth. "Who did this?"

"Doctor Beshoar," he said. "He came out one day from Trinidad. I said to him, how can I load a gun with one hand? He said, you do not. You stop fighting. I said, when this war is won, I will stop. So I learn to load my gun anyways—see how my fingers can move?"

His brow knotted in pain as he wiggled the fingers of his left hand.

"For God's sake, don't do that."

"No matter."

"Was the bullet in your shoulder?"

"No, the bullet goes through. Doctor says I was just nicked"—he pronounced it "neekt"—"How do you like that word? Nicked. He says, don't move your arm, it is too weak."

"You need to go back to Trinidad and—"

"Christian," he said.

I stopped. No matter what I said, it would change nothing. He would stay and fight.

Clumsily, he spread the coat over both of us. "Why is Miss Pearl missing?"

"She wandered away from the Bayes ranch while I was—"

"With me."

"With my husband," I said fiercely. "That's why I need to go to Berwind."

"You cannot get to Berwind." He swept his hand toward the empty, open prairie below. "Look out there. There is nothing to hide behind for all those miles. Nothing to keep you from being killed. And how would you get into Berwind? They are dynamiting it, blowing it to pieces."

I leaned into him, my lips close to his throat. "I'm a woman," I said softly. "Men don't fear me, sometimes they don't even see me, and if they do, they just treat me like I'm silly or a child. You know that—that's how I brought the guns in to Ludlow."

He said nothing. The wind caught at his greatcoat, lifting it from us. I grabbed a sleeve, and he pulled it closer, so that we were wrapped tightly in it. As I kissed him, I felt his heart beating, edgy and quick.

Chapter 33

  We traveled to Berwind that night, crawling in and out of ditches and gullies, crouching behind piles of scrub, and flattening down on the ground as searchlights swept back and forth across the prairie. We had blackened our clothes and faces with gun grease. Theros led the way, and Anton, Dimitrius and George followed. Alex came, too, struggling along in silence behind us, his jaw clenching with every step.
  By midnight, we had reached the southern side of the mesa, where we climbed upward through scrub and rock. By dawn, we had crested the mesa and started down the other side toward Berwind. We sheltered behind a sandstone formation on the side of a ravine. Carved by snowmelt, the ravine was probably fifteen feet deep, yet it was so narrow at its beginning that a full-grown man would not be able to walk facing forward in it, but would have to slink along, one shoulder thrust before the other.
  Theros passed around biscuits, and we all drank from a canteen that George carried with him. No one spoke. Alex sat a little distance from the group, his leg extended and his lame foot flopping inward. Anton, Dimitrius and George kept their gazes on the ground or peered off into the distance. They had come willingly, I knew, but they made it clear that they balked at the task—risk their lives to save a woman, a baby. They spoke only in Greek, and Theros answered them the same way. Not knowing the language, I could not gauge his thoughts, but his voice sounded sharp and tense.
  As the sun rose, we could look down on Berwind. Never pretty, it was now a mess of broken structures, ramshackle buildings. Windows were shot out of houses and tipples, and holes gaped where bullets had torn away the wooden siding of the meeting hall and stables. The great machinery of the mines was stalled. The massive cables and pulleys hung slack, and the railroad tracks were barren and empty, except for a few half-loaded cars. A single train engine sat on the turntable, which had been pivoted, but never fully rotated, so that the locomotive looked as if it might steam off onto bare ground.
  A putrid smell rose from the valley. "What is that?" I asked.

"The dead," Theros said.

Alex surveyed the sight below through binoculars. "Mules," he said. "They've shot them."

Stacked at the mouth of the mine were bloated carcasses, stiff legs spearing the air. Crows perched on the heap, pecking at the loose skin and eyes. I turned away, sickened at the needless cruelty and waste.

"Look at our house," Alex said.

The house where we had lived had no windows, and part of the porch had collapsed into a heap of weathered boards. It looked as if no one had lived there for a long time, but then, the whole town seemed deserted. No women washed clothes at the creek, no dogs or chickens roamed between houses picking at cast-off food. No children played on the playground near the trash dump. No men hurried toward the mine, or crawled up from underground, their faces dusted black by coal. What had once been home to more than a thousand people was now a silent hole.

"Which one is the Ruddy house?" Theros whispered in my ear.

I pointed. Russell's prize for being a company stooge sat high on the slope, where it would not flood or be shrouded by the smoke of the smoldering slag heap. The house was an easy walk, only a few hundred feet into Berwind.

Theros touched my hand, and I swallowed against the sour taste in my mouth. My hair was hidden beneath a plaid scarf, and I carried a stack of kindling wood we'd gathered on the mesa. My hands trembled, my lips fluttered with anxious, unspoken words. Trying not to show my fear, I busied myself with straightening my skirt, smoothing down my sleeves.

"Are you sure?" Alex asked, his eyes narrowed with worry. "I could go with you, Christian—"

"No. I'll be all right. Just wait here."

Theros' gaze flicked to Alex in shared sentiment. "We will wait here," he said to me. "We will be watching."

I put my hands on either side of his face and kissed him. Then, I walked down through the ravine and into the stink and ruin of Berwind.

Every step, I was certain I would be gunned down. Every breath, I prayed that the strikers on the hills would see the scarf, the dress, the wood, and know they were the trappings of a woman on her way to care for her family. I stayed close to the buildings, creeping across porches, hugging posts, slipping behind barrels. When I came to the Ruddy house, I did not knock, but opened the door and darted inside.

The house was as dark and shadowy as ever, the curtains pulled and the lamps shaded. An awful smell rose from the room, a mix of soiled clothes and overflowing slop jars and the filthy hair of humans and dogs. No one had bothered to clean up food scraps from the table, or wash the dishes, and the smell of greasy, rotted meat swelled into the air. I put my hand up over my nose, my stomach churning, and blinked until I could see into the room.

Mrs. Ruddy sat almost directly before me in a rocking chair. A blanket spread over her legs, and a heavy knit shawl wrapped around her shoulders. In her lap, she cradled a tiny bundle wrapped in green flannel.

A breath of relief escaped from me, and I had to stop myself from rushing forward to Lily, from taking her in my arms and kissing her tiny cheeks.

Mrs. Ruddy's eyes honed in on me. "Why are you here? Where did you come from? Good God. Jake!"

Her call whipped me into action. If Jake was there, I had no hope of saving Pearl or Lily. "I want to see Pearl," I demanded.

She did not answer me, but settled back into the rocking chair. Her lips were clamped together in a smug grimace, and her eyes glinted even in the dim light. Folding her arms over her chest, she began to rock slowly back and forth, Lily shifting perilously in her lap. The floor creaked beneath the rockers.

I tried to peer into the darkened corners of the room. "Pearl! Pearl!"

From the back of the room came a sad cry, an utterance that was not quite a word, but not just a meaningless moan, either. I went forward, feeling my way around the table and chairs. A hand snaked out and grabbed my wrist. The touch was clammy against my skin, the fingers bony. The smell of menthol and sweat wafted up to me.

I jumped sideways, knocking against a small table and nearly spilling the kerosene lamp onto the floor. Looking down, I saw Russell, lying on a daybed. He looked weak, yellowish, as if his skin had melted away and left only a skeleton. One side of his face did not move, but the other was desperate. His eye rolled, his nostril flared, and he tried to speak from the right side of his mouth. "Puhl," he said. "Puhl."

"Where is Pearl?" I asked him. "Where is she, Russell?"

"Puhl," he moaned again, his hands flailing.

"I'm sorry," I breathed.

I backed away, inching toward Mrs. Ruddy. Kneeling beside the rocking chair, I pleaded, "Please, Mrs. Ruddy. Where's Pearl? I've come all this way to see her, up from Ludlow—"

She hissed. "I hear Ludlow's a stinking mess. Half the people there are dead, and the other half chased off to die in the hills."

"Did Pearl come up here? Where is she now?"

She rocked back and forth, more stubborn with every creak of the floorboards.

"Oh, you folks finally got what was coming for you. Jake was down in Ludlow that morning, and he saw it all. He said the Greeks started it. Got drunked-up at their heathen celebration and started shooting at the militia tents. Then the mighty UMWA set the tent colony on fire just to get you people to clear out and go. And too bad, some poor Mexicans and Eye-talians are too stupid to get out alive!"

I shook my head. "Did Pearl come up that day?"

"She came up here, all right. Jake brought her up, and here she came, walking through that door as if she'd just been gone to the store. Said she needed to see Russell—"

"Where is she now?"

"Did you know she was sick? Out of her head with fever? What a farce! Russell got all happy again, seeing her here, thinking she'd come back to him, and what did she do but die?"

"Die? Oh, my God, my God, no!" I sagged back onto my heels. Losing my balance, I fell to the floor. The room went dark, as the lamp near Russell flared out. I could hear him weeping and speaking Pearl's name. I crouched over, trying to stop the wrench of my stomach and heart.

"And now I'm stuck with this useless brat," Mrs. Ruddy said. "She's not Russell's. He's not her father. She has your eyes. Your brother's eyes. I should have known that she was playing Russell false."

I lifted my head, drew my hand over my eyes to clear away the tears, desperate to see Lily. Was she breathing? Was she still healthy, with her rosy, chubby cheeks and her tiny, beautiful hands that flailed in the air when she cried? Were her eyes truly Alex's and mine?

"Please, Mrs. Ruddy," I begged. "May I hold her?"

She kept rocking, back and forth.

"Where's Pearl now?" I asked.

"We sent her down to Trinidad. What else could we do? She is Russell's wife. But we won't be going down to claim her, unless we want to join her in the ground. You strikers have turned into murderers, shooting if we even step out of these houses. I guess she'll be buried in a pauper's grave, and wouldn't that be too bad."

I pulled myself up on my knees, just in front of her, so close that she could kick me if she chose. I did not bother to wipe away my tears. Folding my hands as if in prayer, I said, "I'll take the baby, Mrs. Ruddy.

You don't want a baby that's not Russell's. You aren't well, and you need to take care of yourself and of Russell—"

"She did that. To my boy. She's the reason he's like he is. She broke his heart, running off to Ludlow. Look at him!" She began to weep. "I just wanted him to be like every other man, and not have to be so ashamed and sorry—"

Russell moaned again, one hand flopping in the air, trying to coax me over to him.

Mrs. Ruddy motioned toward Lily. "I can't stand the sight of this thing. She looks so much like her. She's going to have the same wild hair and dark skin, like the devil himself. I have half a mind to let it starve to death."

"No, Mrs. Ruddy! She's a baby. She's doesn't know anything—"

"She knows plenty. Conceived in sin, born in sin. She'll die in sin, and all the better if she dies now. She's going to have that same way of making men pant over her until they can't think for themselves. Just like her whore of a mother."

"I'll take her," I begged again. "You'll never have to see her again. I'll take her, and you can forget about both her and her mother and the sorrow they've caused you. Please, Mrs. Ruddy, please."

She said nothing, just rocking back and forth. I pressed forward, my feet beneath me, ready to snatch Lily and run for the door.

"Please, Mrs. Ruddy," I said. "You wouldn't want to do that to a little baby. You couldn't—"

"Get out of here!"

She whipped upright, straightening so quickly that Lily rolled from her lap. I tilted forward, grabbing at the bundle and catching Lily as she gave a terrified scream. My heart leapt, thankful. She was alive.

Jumping up, I inched backward, afraid to turn away from Mrs. Ruddy. She might pick up a pistol or poker, for all I knew. Jake might be hiding in the shadows after all, just waiting for me to try to leave. "Thank you," I said. "Thank you."

She disappeared into the darkness at the back of the house.

Outside, I ran, dodging in and out of sight, stumbling up the slope with my head bent, my arms wrapped tightly around Lily. She howled in fear, and I clasped her against me to muffle her screeches. My own breath came in sobs. As I ran into the ravine, my shoes skated in the bright, pinkish sand.

The ground shook beneath me as an explosion wrenched through Berwind Canyon. I slipped and fell, landing hard on my knees to protect Lily. Pressing her to my breast, I grabbed at the piñon brush growing from the ravine wall to lift myself up. When I looked up, Jake stood before me.

He was wearing civilian clothes, and he squinted as the sun hit him fully in the face. Pockets of sweat stained his shirt under his arms. All at once, I felt the damp stick of my dress against my back and arms, and the soggy softness of the bundle that was Lily.

I panted, from the heat of the sun, from running, from fear.

"Jesus Christ, Scottie," he said. "You are stupid. Don't you know they're dynamiting the hell out of the mines back there?"

"Why aren't you down in Ludlow with the militia?" I cried. "Why are you here?"

"What're you doing back here? Begging to come back home?"

"Let me go, Jake. Please let me go!"

His gaze fell to the bundle in my arms. "That's Russell's daughter."

"No! No, she's not! She's Pearl's—!"

"How'd you get your hands on her?" He started for me. "Give her back."

I backed up, my shoes sinking into the soft, damp sand. My heels caught on rocks and scrub, and I teetered, making Lily cry even louder. "You can't take care of her," I said. "Your mother can't. She won't. She told me so."

"That baby don't seem to like you none too well. Listen to it bawl."

"Don't do this, please," I pleaded. "Please don't stop me."

"You think you're so smart, coming to steal my brother's child."

"She's not his. Alex is her father."

"Shut up!" he roared, his voice echoing against the walls of the ravine. I cringed, afraid that he would attract gunfire from Berwind. "That baby is Russell's. It proves them all wrong. He's a man, as good as any other."

"He's a better man than you," I said. "He never treated Pearl with anything but respect, and you had your hands all over her—"

"That's because I wanted her!" he shouted. "Not Russ, not Ma's little favorite. You are stupid. How do you think Russ got hurt? It wasn't no accident."

"What?"

"After Pearl left, he just went back to doing what he'd always done. He didn't even bother to pretend anymore. Ma, she was beside herself, and Pa was so ashamed, and I thought, what if he's hurt some, what if he has a broken arm or leg? We can get her to come back and he'll stop—"

"What are you saying?"

"I caused that collapse. To try to get him to stop taking up with every man who'd have him—"

"You nearly killed him! And look at what he is now!"

"And to make her come home," he finished. "And it would have worked if it wasn't for you and your god-damned brother down in Ludlow."

"You may as well have killed both of them with your bare hands!" I cried. "How could you—?"

He stepped forward, so close that his shoulder nearly touched mine. I took another step back, but I had reached the narrow part of the ravine. I would have to twist sideways to move farther.

Jake laughed at my dilemma. "Don't try to fool me. You ain't alone up here today. He's with you, ain't he? Why don't he show himself? I bet you he's too cowardly to do his own dirty business. Has to send his little sister in to do it for him."

"No, I'm alone. I'm—"

He lifted his rifle and sighted the rim of the ravine, turning in a slow circle. "Hey, Scott!" he yelled. "Come on down here! Come on! Show yourself, you son of a bitch!"

His voice echoed, twisting up, into the air above our heads. I cringed against the ravine wall, stooping over Lily, expecting a barrage of gunfire from Berwind, or from the ridge above our heads. Nothing happened. Straightening, I said, "Please, let me take Lily and—"

"Lily? That its name?"

"Didn't Pearl tell you?"

"Pearl didn't say nothing. She was too sick by the time she got here. Sick and crying all the time. Shivering even though she was burning up, wanting water and then puking it back up in our faces. Don't make much sense, does it?"

Pain pierced me, so strong that my chest ached as if I'd been punched. My voice came out in a sharp shriek. "Why didn't you send her to Trinidad to the doctor? Why did you bring her up here? You could have saved her, if you'd only let her go! You had a chance to—!"

"Stop it!" He swung his gun down, pointing it at me. I jerked backward, my shoulders against the packed sand wall. Where was Theros? Where were the others?

"Listen here, Scottie. We won. We won it all. Your stupid tents ain't there no more, and nobody who spent even one night down there on that prairie will work in any mine in Colorado ever again. Believe me, all you people did was damn yourself to starve to death." Suddenly, he shouted, "You hear that, Scott? You hear me? It's finished, it's through! You ain't got nothing! Nothing!"

Again, his voice echoed, and I shrank back, crushing my face and shoulders into the sandy wall, squeezing Lily into a tiny ball to protect her. She cried out and squirmed against me.

"I'm right here, Ruddy."

Alex stood high above our heads, on the lip of the ravine. When I looked up at him, the sun flashed in my eyes. Jake took a step backward, craning his neck to see Alex. He shaded his eyes with one hand.

He laughed. "Well, well, come to save your precious little sister, huh? Too bad you couldn't save old Pearl. But what's one or two more dead women and babies from Ludlow? I'll just throw Scottie here in the pit with the rest."

He grabbed at me, but fell sideways, his shoulder slamming into the ravine wall. A broken expression came over his face, and his eyes crossed, as if he was trying to see inside himself. He looked up at me again, puzzled, his lips pushing outward. Blood trickled from his mouth. Slowly, he slid down the wall into a heap at my feet.

A scream rose in my throat. "God, oh, God!"

"Jesus," Jake moaned. He groped blindly, trying to find the ravine wall. I skittered backward a few inches, just out of reach of his hand.

Behind him, Anton raised the butt of his rifle again, and brought it down between his shoulder blades with a muted crack. Jake's hands and knees went out from under him, and he sprawled facedown on the sand. Someone grabbed my arm, and I heard Theros' voice.

"Come on, come on!"

He dragged me out of the ravine, thrusting me with one arm over the rim. From above, Alex pulled me by the shoulders until I rolled onto the hard ground, Lily in my arms. Theros shoved me behind the rocks and forced me to squat down with a hard hand on my shoulder.

"You are all right?" Theros asked. "Where is Miss Pearl?"

I shook my head, my breath coming in shallow wheezes. Lily squawked, and Theros put two fingers over her mouth.

"Where's Pearl, Christian?" Alex demanded. "Where is she? Is she there?"

"No," I cried. "No, she's gone! She's dead!"

"That god-damned bastard!" Alex lurched away, and I followed, crying, "No, don't!"

He stopped, staring down into the ravine. Below, Anton, George and Dimitrius brought the butts of their rifles down again and again on Jake's face and chest and shoulders. Jake's legs angled away from his body, his boots digging convulsively into the sand, and one arm was thrown up and out, as if wrenched from his shoulder. His other hand covered his face, his mashed fingers drenched in blood.

Alex turned away and vomited.

"Theros!" I cried. "Oh, God, you've got to stop them. Make them stop!"

Theros looked down into the ravine, his face twisted as the desire for revenge warred with his better judgment. "He knows," he said quietly. "If he lives, he will come after you and your brother. He will come after the baby—"

"I don't care," I said. "You have to stop them! This isn't right—!"

He took a step forward. With his right hand, he steadied his rifle against his hip, cocking it with his bandaged left hand and sending four quick shots into the air. The sound echoed down into Berwind Canyon, raising a volley of gunfire from below.

Dimitrius squinted upward, and Theros shouted in Greek. Dimitrius shouted back, angry. With one last kick, he jerked away from Jake. Jake rolled onto his side, limp and bloody.

With George and Anton behind him, Dimitrius clambered up the side of the ravine and struck out across the rugged ground, running. Theros' lips twitched as he watched them go.

"Come on, hurry," he said, taking my arm. "Somebody will come to see what the shooting is about."

Chapter 34

In Trinidad, the funerals began.

Five days after Ludlow burned, more than two thousand people gathered in the chilly April wind outside of Holy Trinity Catholic Church—townspeople, strikers with bandanas defiantly tied around their necks, reporters, politicians, and women and children dressed in the clothes they had worn at the Greek Easter celebration. On the steps of the church, a priest said mass for the two women and eleven children who had died in the pit under the tent at Ludlow.

Their coffins lay on two hay wagons, pulled by dark, dappled horses. An American flag waved above the driver's head. The two full-length caskets were of dark wood. The smaller ones, arranged from the largest to those no longer than breadboxes, were of whitewashed pine.

Tossing flowers and paper poseys on the wagons as they passed, we honored Patria Valdez and her four children, the three Petrucci and two Pedragon children, and the two young Costas. Cedelina Costa's unborn child went to the grave with her.

We marched a solemn path behind the wagons to the Catholic Cemetery north of Trinidad. There, the thirteen were laid to rest on a prairie that was as open and sweeping as the one on which they'd died.

Lily cried.

For hours, she wailed, inconsolable. I walked her back and forth in the bedroom above the Greek bakery, where Theros had arranged for me to stay. I recited Burns: *Tho' mountains rise, and deserts howl, And oceans roar between; Yet, dearer than my deathless soul, I still would love—* But the words troubled me, left me without comfort.

"What do you know?" I whispered into Lily's soft warmth. "What do you remember? Do you know your mother was the most beautiful woman in the world? Oh, let me tell you about her—"

I fed her from bottles filled with goats' milk, but she spat up most of it and cried more. I searched her little body carefully. She had lost the chubbiness in her cheeks and the fleshy roundness of her arms and legs, but the stubborn lock of black hair still stood straight out from her forehead. An angry rash spread over her bottom and back from lying in filthy diapers at the Ruddy house, and bruises dotted her arms and forehead from rough handling. I knew I might have caused some of them when I'd carried her out of Berwind.

I took Lily to Doctor Beshoar, waiting in a long line of the poor and ailing at his office in Trinidad. Looking tired and gaunt, he saw nothing in Lily's condition that would cause her such distress.

He was more concerned with me. He gave me laudanum so that I could sleep.

During the day, I sought out the company of others at Union Hall. The meeting room overflowed with women and children who were living there yet, camped out on sleeping rolls, their worldly belongings in a solitary heap beside them. Alex was usually there, too, no longer able or willing, maybe, to traipse through the rough, rugged land beyond Trinidad to fight. Doctor Beshoar had seen to his foot and predicted that it would heal, although not entirely properly, and had told Alex that he would have the full use of it one day. In the meantime, he was to keep it propped up on a milk crate.

"Hold Lily," I said to him. "She needs to know her father."

He cupped Lily awkwardly, upset by her tears. He did not nestle her against his body to keep her warm or rock her in his arms, as Theros loved to do.

"What's wrong with her?" he asked. "Is she sick?"

"I don't know."

He studied her, as if looking for a sign or message. I had not seen the resemblance to Alex and myself that Mrs. Ruddy had mentioned. Evidently, Alex did not, either.

"Here, take her, Christian."

He settled back in his chair, brooding. The time he'd spent in jail had made him more inward, more reserved. Coupled with his grief for Pearl, the hardships of the last few months had cast him into a well of darkness and silence which I could not breach. He barely spoke unless he was compelled to speak.

Nights were not easy for Lily. She exhausted herself into sleep, but even that was anxious. She twitched and shuddered and seemed already to have memories that haunted her. I sat beside her most of the night, my hand resting gently on her stomach, trying to let her know that she was not alone.

It did not matter that I did not sleep. For me, nights were broken by voices and fears and anger. Again and again, I relived every moment from the day that Ludlow burned. Every time my eyes closed, I saw what

I did not want to—the striker's body lying on the path in Ludlow, the fire, the dead boy in his father's arms, Jake's battered body.

But I saw Pearl's face, too. It beckoned me, hovering just beyond the windowpane, or in a dark corner. I felt her whenever I touched Lily, as if her hand lay atop mine, and sometimes, when I turned, I glimpsed her in the changing light. Was she a ghost? Was she a memory? Was she nothing more than the breath of my own sorrow? I did not care, as long as she stayed with me.

One week after Ludlow burned, Louis Tikas was buried.

The crowd outside the funeral parlor already blocked the street by the time I arrived. Around me, men scuffed at the ground with worn, dirty boots, fidgeted with the hats they carried in their hands, fingered the coins in their pockets. So many days of fighting, so many hours of vengeful anger had left them impatient with waiting, and they recounted again the story of Louis' death, mumbling in voices fraught with emotion.

"There is heel print on his face," a striker whispered. "Where they step on him. Yes, right here, on cheek."

Another man spat. "Linderfelt broke a rifle over his head. It shattered the gunstock, it came down so hard. Dropped Tikas to his knees, and while he was trying to stand, they shot him. Three times in the back. The militia's been passing that broken Springfield around and bragging about it."

"He went to the depot alone," the striker said. "No gun, no bullet."

"The Greeks have vowed revenge," a third man uttered. "At the wake, they touched old Louie's forehead, then crossed themselves and pounded their rifle butts on the floor four times. They're goin' for death to every last one of them militia son-of-a-bitches."

"God grant them success," someone whispered.

When the doors of the parlor opened, everyone surged forward, and I elbowed my way to the front of the crowd. A Greek in worn denim overalls, corduroy coat and red neckerchief led the way, a burning censer in his hands. Behind him tottered an ancient priest in flowing white robes, his white beard trailing nearly to his waist and his jewel-studded headdress buffeted by the wind. He crossed himself before the flower-bedecked hearse and prayed again. Theros walked at the foot of the coffin, his face gaunt, his left arm hidden beneath his shabby coat. He kept his gaze on the ground, ashamed of being too weak to carry Louis' body to his resting place.

The driver flicked the reins, and the two black horses stepped forward. In two silent, single-file columns, hundreds of Greek men followed the hearse through Trinidad's streets and up the steep slope to the Knights of Pythias Cemetery. I marched near the end of the procession, more than a thousand people and a mile behind the hearse.

At the cemetery, most of the mourners gathered outside the gates, unable to squeeze inside. I stood with them, my hands clutching the wrought-iron stakes of the fence to steady myself. From there, I could see the Greek men gathered near the casket, clad in coats so old that the fabric shone greasy blue-black.

I waited through the afternoon, as the sun dropped behind the towering height of Simpson's Rest and cast the cemetery in shadow. Slowly, the mourners scattered, until only a few remained. Theros had planted himself beside the grave. Stubbornly, he shook off the concern of others, who spoke with him before they shrugged and went on their way. At last, he kept an unyielding, solitary vigil.

Near dark, at the limits of my own endurance, I entered the cemetery and went to him.

He wrapped his right arm around me, pressing me against him, his body raked by sorrow.

That night, he came to stay with me.

As I walked Lily to sleep, he sat at the table, looking at the deserted street below and drinking ouzo that he had brought up from the kitchen downstairs. We did not try to talk over Lily's cries, but waited until she fell asleep.

Downstairs, the Greeks had gathered to mourn their fallen leader. Low, dark voices drifted up the stairwell, and someone played a mournful guitar. A few voices rolled into song, and glass after glass clinked as it was lifted in honor of Louis Tikas. After I had laid Lily into the drawer I was using for a crib, I sat at the table across from Theros.

"Should you be downstairs with the others?" I asked.

He said nothing, only staring out the window. The light from the drugstore across the street streaked his hair with silvery blue. At last, he drummed up words, speaking in a voice that was hard with grief. "I want to be alone."

"Do you want me to leave? If you'll watch Lily—"

"No, no, I mean, without them, without . . ." His voice trailed away.

Below, it sounded as if someone was giving a speech or telling a long, complicated story. As the heavy, Greek words floated up the stairwell to us, Theros shifted, as if wishing he were somewhere else.

"Down there," he said, "they are saying, oh, Louis is such a great hero. All of Crete is proud, all of Greece." He poured another glass of ouzo. "But he is not Greek hero. He dies here, in Colorado, in America. They are wrong."

"Come to bed," I said. "Don't think about it."

His response was slow. "I am no good to you right now."

"I just want you here, with me. That's all."

I knelt to take off his boots, and he reached out one hand to brush back my hair. When his palm touched my cheek, I kissed it. Slowly, tenderly, I unbuttoned his shirt and slid it from his shoulders.

"Take off the bandage," he whispered.

"So soon? Shouldn't you wait—?"

"Take it off."

I unwrapped the thick white cloth that pinioned his arm to his ribcage, and he tested it, moving it gingerly, like a tin doll whose arm only went forward and backward, its elbow bent. His muscles looked shriveled, weakened by idleness. A second bandage looped over his shoulder and around his armpit, protecting the flesh that had been torn by the bullet. Carefully, I pulled it away, revealing the tattered wound.

"Let me wash that." I went to the pitcher to get a clean cloth and fresh water.

When I came back, he caught my hand in his. "Christian," he whispered. "I think all day, all night. I think, if only I was a man, not a striker or fighter. I think, why has God given me this, not a wife or child or home?"

"We'll have those things." I knelt before him again and looked up into his face. "I'll be with you from now on. Wherever we go, whatever happens, we'll be together."

"I think of buying a coffeehouse, like this one, and spending all my days playing cards and sitting around doing nothing, nothing at all, not even thinking, only joking and talking, and we can have so many babies. But now, I can't do nothing else." He laid his hand on his heart. "I can't, because it is here forever and I will have to fight forever."

I leaned forward and kissed the hand that lay on his heart. "We both will."

"Some of the things we did, I know they are wrong. In Greece, in America—anywhere. But we didn't have no choice—"

I thought of the guns I'd brought to Ludlow. They had never been, would never be, the answer.

"They don't let us choose nothing else," Theros said. "Never can we live in peace, like men should, with homes and laws and families. Never did they say, no, these people are not bad, not wrong. They just brought in more soldiers and more guns. No one, nobody—I could not choose nothing else."

I offered no argument, no comfort. As powerful as we had believed the UMWA to be, it had given us so little, protected us so poorly. Our every move had been thwarted by powers so much greater than any we could harness. I spoke softly, "It's all right, it will be all right."

"I cannot stay," he whispered. "I have to go back."

"I know."

He rose and went to the bed. He lay on his back, tilting toward the right so that his wounded shoulder did not touch the mattress. Lying down beside him, I kissed him, and he stroked my hair.

My fingers played through his hair and on his skin, tender and eager. My lips roamed over his chest and neck. I could feel the warmth passing between us, the heat, the growing desire.

He rolled toward me, careless and needy, and I wrapped myself around him, throwing one leg over his waist. I wanted only to feel him inside me, so strong, so powerful, so certain of himself.

Words ran through my mind. We are alive, we are here, we can never lose this. We will heal, we will be together. But I whispered only the sweet syllables of love-making, because it was enough.

Lying beside him, I slept through the night, for the first time since I'd come to Trinidad from the Bayes Ranch. When I woke, weak sunlight shone through the window and the bustling noise in the street below was that of mid-morning. Rested and warm, I reached for Theros.

But he had vanished, returned to war.

Alex and I claimed Pearl's body at the mortuary. We were shown into a poorly-lit back room, behind the rooms where the bodies of strikers killed in battle were laid out—heroes, now, visited and viewed by hundreds, their death photos snapped by newspaper reporters from across the nation.

Pearl lay on a wooden slab. Whether from the fever that had claimed her life, or simply because Pearl had never been as tied to this world as the rest of us, she seemed untouched by death. Her cheeks were the dark rose color that had always made her so beautiful, and her hair was as silver-black as it had ever been in full sunlight.

Wrapped around her was the tartan that had been my mother's, the one I had draped over her shoulders to keep her warm as we sat in the pit beneath our tent. Spattered by mud and torn in spots, it lay heavy and soft on her shoulders. Sobbing, I wadded one corner in my hands and held it to my face. The tartan was my last token of Scotland, the last of the treasures that I'd carried with me from Berwind, the lone remnant of mine that had survived Ludlow. Pearl was taking all I'd known, all I'd been, to the grave with her.

Alex sat beside her, her hand clutched tightly in his, as if he were willing her to live. Laying his forehead against her breast, he wept.

We buried her at the Knights of Pythias cemetery. Alex's friends gathered—the McCormicks, the McKennas, Rory Capstan, even James and Mary O'Keegan. Others came, too. A bevy of foreign women climbed up the steep slope to wail into the black scarves clutched in their hands. Theros arrived, a murmured blessing on his tongue. With him were Anton and Dimitrius and George and some of the others, their heads respectfully bent.

As the roughhewn casket was lowered into the ground, the wind picked up, blowing in a storm from the west. And with the wind came a thin wail, a wavering thread in the restless afternoon. For a moment, I could not place the sound. I lowered my face to Lily's.

The noise came from her tiny lips.

"What's wrong with her?" Alex whispered.

Lily breathed in and began again, keening on a high, sharp note. With tears seeping from the corners of her eyes, she sang a long, mournful strain. The minister stammered to silence, and Theros brought his hand beneath her, supporting her as she lay in my arms.

Alex leaned toward me. "You better get her in out of the wind. She could be coming down with pneumonia—"

"No, she's all right," I said, my heart flooding with love and wonder.

I looked up at Theros. In his eyes was the light of release and hope, and I thought, this is what she has been moving toward all along, through so many hours of crying, through so much misery. This is what she has been trying to do. The faintest smile touched Theros' lips, and I felt mine curve upward as well.

Lily was singing her mother's soul to heaven.

Chapter 35

On the first day of May, federal troops arrived in Trinidad, ordered by President Wilson to restore peace in the strike zone. Professional and free of partiality, the soldiers quickly routed the last of the Colorado National Guard and calmed the strikers. The civil war in Colorado ended.

Stillness fell over Trinidad. The crowds disappeared, and the town grew sad and quiet, a place of broken hearts. The UMWA rebuilt the tent colony near San Rafael, but it was nearly twenty miles from the nearest Colorado Fuel & Iron mine. Men straggled in, their red scarves stuffed in pockets or crammed in packs, their arms surrendered to the federal military force, their faces haggard and their bodies worn and spent by the turmoil. They settled into the tents without hope or conviction.

Then the arrests began. More than four hundred charges would be brought against the men who had lived and fought in the strike zone. Even the president of UMWA District 15, John Lawson, was accused of first-degree murder for a death that had occurred on a day he was in Denver. He would serve two years in jail for it.

Charges were brought against members of the Colorado National Guard, too. Of the sixty-seven counts, all were eventually dismissed.

The Greeks disappeared from the strike zone, fleeing in the night to places where their countrymen would hide and protect them. I waited for news of Theros' whereabouts in the room above the Greek bakery.

Alex came to visit me. We sat at a table downstairs, served coffee and pastries by the owner, who had stood up with Theros at our wedding, and who brought in fresh milk for Lily every morning.

I thanked him, while Alex looked on uneasily. Lily wiggled in my arms, barely waking from her nap. "Do you want to hold her?" I asked Alex.

He made no move to take her from me. "She's not crying so much, now?"

"She's beyond that, I think."

He looked at her as he would a curiosity, a small animal. "James and Mary are going to Pennsylvania," he said, his gaze on the baby. "James hopes to hire into the mines there."

"They are?" I started at the news, and Lily squeaked. "What about Mrs. McCormick and Uncle John?"

"John wants to wait out the strike. He thinks that surely something good must come from all this sorrow. Edith's heart is breaking over the little ones leaving, and with Mary expecting again."

At once, I realized why Alex had come to visit. "And you?"

He played with his coffee cup, turning it in a slow circle on the table. "I'm going home, Christian. I'm going back to Scotland."

His words struck at me, making the blood race to my head. Alex—who had been my one constant, my companion and caretaker—gone. I would be, as I'd always feared, the last of my family in America.

"Jake was right," he said. "We lost everything."

"Jake is a fool," I argued. "The fight has become ours forever now."

His eyes darted around the bakery, then he leaned forward so I could hear. "Your Greek," he whispered. "You saw what they did to Jake, you saw what they are. They're brutal and lawless, they have no sense of right and wrong—"

"Jake let Pearl die—"

"Are you so cold-blooded then?" he asked. "That you would live with him and his pack of vicious friends?"

"You know he stopped them." I leaned back, resettling Lily in my lap. "You saw him—"

"Not in time."

I inhaled sharply. "What do you mean?"

"Jake died," he said. "It was in the newspaper two days ago."

"I didn't know that," I said, afraid once more.

"Where is your husband now?" Alex asked "He's a wanted man. They all are."

"He's in Denver. I'm to meet him when he's settled."

"Come home with me," he pleaded. "Scotland's a different place. I know you don't remember it—but it's not so new, not so dangerous and violent as this state. It's already seen all that, and now it's a place at peace. I can't go off and leave you here in this mess—"

"Alex, this is home."

He glanced around, as if I were talking about the bakery. "No," he said. "It never has been. We've never belonged here, never felt right in our skins. We've never found the place where we could be who we are supposed to be. Remember what Dad told us—"

"He told us stories, Alex," I said. "About Mary Queen of Scots and dark lakes and forests. They were true only when he told them. They were never true for us."

My words silenced him, and I regretted them. Looking into his coffee cup, he said, "I won't go into the mines again, Kirstie. I was never meant for that."

I looked down at Lily, who sucked on her fist, remembering the light in Alex's eyes as he trotted along the mesa, gathering his scientific samples. "No, you weren't," I said. "Dad knew that."

Alex said nothing, his eyes tearing.

"How will you get to Scotland?" I asked.

"I'll work my way back to the east, traveling with James and Mary." He paused. "I promise, once I'm home, I'll send for you."

"Going home to Scotland has always been your dream, Alex. Not mine. If you can make it come true, do it."

"I need to know that you're safe and happy. I owe Dad that much."

"I am safe and happy. I will be." I reached for his hand. "You don't owe Dad anything. This is my home, Alex. I don't remember Scotland. I don't have any ties to it. I'm an American. So is my husband."

"An American!"

"What happened to us here couldn't have happened in any other place or time in this world. It's made it ours, it's made it home. We have to stay, we have to see if we can't find some justice or make it better—" My words faded, and the thoughts that had been creeping into my throat spilled out, shaking and fraught. "What about Lily?"

He said nothing, only looking at Lily as she lay in my arms. I had packed away the green flannel blanket and wrapped her in a white blanket that the baker's wife had given me. When Alex spoke, his face pinched with shame or fear or distaste. "Whenever I look at her, I see the reason why Pearl died."

"How can you say that!" I reached down and touched Lily's face, drawing my finger around her soft jaw and chin, and love for her poured into my heart. "Surely you can see—she has Pearl's lips and hair and skin. She has Pearl's orneriness and her sweetness. She is Pearl, she's what we have left on this earth of Pearl—"

"And that is what I can't bear," he said. "I don't know how I'll go on without Pearl. I don't know how I will survive. I was such a fool—she could have been mine all along, and I lost her, I lost her because I was so weak and wrong—"

He put his hand over his brow, hiding his eyes.

"Alex, don't. In the end, you loved her, and she loved you. Don't forget that."

"In the end. Only in the end." He shook his head. "I have to put it behind me. I have to move on, or I will—"

"Let me raise Lily," I said impulsively. "I'll take care of her—no, we will. Theros loves her, Alex. I can see that in the way he handles her. We'll raise her the way Pearl wanted her to be raised—with two parents who love her."

He mulled it over, looking at Lily, his eyes teary and weak. "Would your husband agree?"

"Yes," I said with certainty.

"To raise another man's child? Why would he?"

I wanted to explain, but I could not. Somehow, Lily had become our child—Theros' and mine. Maybe it was because her care had fallen to us so soon after she was born, or so soon after we were married. Maybe it was because we had saved her from Mrs. Ruddy's venom. At last, I said, "She survived Ludlow, Alex."

It was all I needed to say. He nodded, pain etching his face.

"If we quit, Alex, they win," I said. "Just as Jake said. The company, the militia, everyone who fought against us." I looked up at him. "America's supposed to be the land of freedom for all. We have to keep on, to make it that way."

Alex nodded. "You are your father's daughter."

My eyes clouded with tears, and I looked down at Lily.

"I'll send money," he offered. "I'll give you anything you need to take care of her. Do you understand, Kirstie? Don't think me weak or—"

"I understand," I said. "You don't need to worry."

He stood. Coming to me, he embraced me for the first and last time in our lives. "I'll be leaving tomorrow, then," he said. "I only want the best for you and for the baby, you know, Kirstie."

I held Lily out to him, but he shrank back. "Tell her goodbye, Alex," I said. "She is your daughter."

Pain flicked over his face again, but he leaned forward and kissed her cheek.

It was the last time I would ever see him.

We had lived. We would live on.

In the fall, I would receive a letter from Alex telling me that he had reached Scotland. He settled in Arbroath, a town on the North Sea, but he did not stay there long. Within months of his homecoming, he was a soldier in the War to End All Wars. He wrote long, thoughtful letters from the front, reworking the stories of his life in Colorado and quoting Burns—*When Death's dark stream I ferry o'er (A time that surely shall come), In Heaven itself I'll ask no more, Than just a Highland welcome*— to remind me of what we had once shared.

After the trenches in France, he came home with his lungs, already weakened by his days in the mines, burned raw by mustard gas. In a convalescent hospital, he met the daughter of a Presbyterian minister, who either did not know about his daughter in Colorado or who forgave him. They married and raised five sons, all of whom found their way to the university in Edinburgh.

Theros and I moved north, to a town in the northern fields called Lafayette, but he would never enter the mines again. Instead, he was an active organizer for the United Mine Workers of America, setting up an office in the coalfields and taking the wrath of company men and mine guards alike. We worked for the union side by side, reliving the heartbreaks of Ludlow again and again. I would clean and bandage wounds for him and the other organizers, for anyone who took up the union cause. I taught their wives to speak English, fed their hungry children from our stores of food, brought them into our home to live when they were poor and cold.

Twelve years after Ludlow burned, we would see another strike, where once again, strikers and organizers were gunned down in the streets and the union was lost.

And Lily, the baby born during the bright and shining time of Easter, would grow up to be what we all had hoped she would be—an American girl. She spoke the language of the country of her birth, free of any accent or bur. She sang "The Star Spangled Banner" at baseball games and teased her equally American brothers about their smelly feet. She wore pigtails and patent leather shoes, and she donned a gown and high-heeled sandals for her high school graduation. Although she always knew that she had been born in a tent on a prairie, it was easier to let her believe that her dark skin came from her father and her eyes from me. When she was old enough, I told her of her mother and father, of Ludlow, and the dark days after. It was no surprise to me that she already knew, that she had intuited it, somehow.

But all that was far in the future on the day I left Trinidad, on a train bound for Denver.

That day, Lily lay in my lap, wrapped snugly in her blanket. At my feet was a cheap valise with a few dresses and baby clothes, and in my bag was a telegram from Theros and a few dollars given to me by the owner of the Greek bakery.

When the train slowed to take on passengers at Ludlow, people craned their necks, whispering, pointing. There, there is the Death Pit. There is the spot where Louie the Greek lay for five days, dead and dishonored. I looked, too, to where the metal remains of stoves, beds and chimneys marked the tent colony like tombstones in a dark, haunted churchyard. No one walked through the mess now—the do-gooders and gawkers had packed up and left. The militia investigation had been concluded. Only the wind tugged at the half-burned flags, still aloft, in the center of the colony.

It was then that I remembered how my father had gazed beyond the solid rock mesas of Berwind, beyond the width of the sky, toward another place. Oh, Scotland, he had said, my heart lies there. Now I understood, now I knew. My heart beat in the wind that would scatter the ashes of Ludlow, in the sand that would bury the ruin. It harbored in the cholla that would grow—the prickly pear, too—from roots that had been hacked away, but never vanquished, and the grass that would sprout year after year, green and sweet. No matter where I went, or where I lived, my heart would lie on that prairie.

I swallowed back tears. In my arms, Lily gave a sharp cry, then shuddered and pressed her trembling lips together, and I sensed that she knew my loss and sorrow, that she understood it, for it was hers, too. I gathered her to me, afraid that if either of us shed a single tear, we might both weep forever.

Oh, Ludlow.

Such heroes to heaven, such martyrs to earth.
Sir Walter Scott

Died in Tent No. 58 at Ludlow
April 20, 1914

Cedelina Costa
Patria Valdez
Elvira Valdez (age 3 months)
Mary Valdez (age 7 years)
Eulala Valdez (age 8 years)
Rudolph Valdez (age 9 years)
Frank Petrucci (age 6 months)
Joe Petrucci (age 4 years)
Lucy Petrucci (age 3 years)
Cloriva Pedragon (age 4 years)
Rogerlo Pedragon (age 6 years)
Lucy Costa (age 4 years)
Onafrio Costa (age 6 years)

Also Killed April 20, 1914

Louis Tikas
Frank W. Snyder
James Fyler
John Bartolotti
Carlo Costa
Frank Rubino

Author's Note

The main characters in this novel are fictional. The major incidents, however, comprise a cruel chapter in Colorado's labor history. Although some of the details are products of my imagination, I tried to depict the events of 1913-1914 in the spirit in which they are described by participants and eyewitnesses. Any real-life characters depicted in the book are also represented according to the historical record.

My research for the novel included a perusal of newspaper accounts, the congressional records of the trials held in Trinidad in February of 1914, and the oral histories collected in the 1970s. In addition, there are four books that proved especially enlightening. *Buried Unsung: Louis Tikas and the Ludlow Massacre* by Zeese Papanikolas provided invaluable information on the Greek immigrant experience in Colorado and the American West. Mary Thomas O'Neal's *Those Damn Foreigners* addressed the dynamics of the immigrant workers and families in the coal camp of Berwind and at the tent colony of Ludlow. *The Great Coalfield War* by George McGovern and Leonard F. Guttridge offered a scholarly, objective approach to the labor struggles in Colorado. Lastly, Barron Beshoar's heartbreaking *Out of the Depths* is the classic source for any student of the Ludlow Massacre.

I am also grateful to the late, great photographer and gentleman, Glenn Aultman, who not only shared with me his photographic treasures, but took me on my first tour of the coal canyons. I must also give credit to the Colorado Endowment for the Humanities workshop on the Ludlow Massacre. Under the leadership of Dean Saitta of the University of Denver and Randy McGuire of Binghamton University, participants were immersed in a week-long discussion of the massacre at the site where it occurred. It was during this seminar that I heard the true-life stories of Joe Bonacquista, a coal miner and the son of an Italian miner who fought at Ludlow, and his wife, Martha. Their tales appear in the novel in slightly altered forms.

So many wise and knowledgeable individuals contributed to the creation of this novel that it is impossible to name them all. My thanks to Bob Lowenberg, whose offhand comment set me to researching the

Ludlow Massacre. I also appreciate the practical advice of Kenn Amdahl, who set me on the road to publication. Joanne McLain lent not only her fine artistic talents to the novel, but her invaluable support and wisdom. My thanks to the intrepid writers at the National Writers' Club, who edited an early draft. Tom Reeves, Constell Steinhaus, Gayle Weinstein and the late Lana Hayward were all instrumental in the editing process. I also wish to thank C.J. Prince and Karen Steinberg for their years of enthusiastic, holistic support of my writing. A special thanks goes to Mark Putch, who read and critiqued the entire novel for me.

  I must, of course, thank the members of my family who have encouraged my writing. My mother, Wilma Marr, is the world's best editor. Were it not for her guiding hand in my writing when I was a girl, I would not have gained the proficiency that I have. My sister, Carol Bryant, is a wonderful sounding board, as is my daughter, Julie Newlin. My most heartfelt thanks belong to my husband, Bill, who has supported and loved me and my writing for more than three decades now.

Made in the USA
Charleston, SC
28 September 2012